THE ONLY CRIMINAL

Tim Lucas

Author of Throat Sprockets and The Book of Renfield

For more information contact:
Riverdale Avenue Books/Quest Imprint
5676 Riverdale Avenue
Riverdale, NY 10471

www.riverdaleavebooks.com
Cover painting: Joos van Cleve, "Portrait of Joris Jacobs Vezelaer" (detail), 1518.

Design by www.formatting4U.com

Digital: 9781626016910
Paperback: 9781626016927
Hardcover: 9781626016934

Praise for The Only Criminal

The Only Criminal is a fable for our time and for all times. Mysterious, witty, slyly comical and cumulatively disturbing, it explores its theme with a wealth of eloquence and invention, and reaches a conclusion as unexpected as it's satisfying. A true original—both the novel and its author."

- Ramsey Campbell (*The Incubations*)

"Compulsively, enviably superb. THE ONLY CRIMINAL is a marvel! Tim Lucas brilliantly weaves wit, romance and glorious wisdoms with maestro cool."

- R.C. Matheson (*Dystopia*)

"It's brilliant… one of the most interesting and entertaining things I've read!

- Kelley Jones, (*Batman, The Sandman*)

"This is a wonderful, droll, witty book—a real joy for people with eclectic cinematic and reading tastes. A bedtime book to savor, just like one of the hero's vanilla-flavored cigarettes."

- Joan Hawkins
(Cutting Edge: Art Horror & the Horrific Avant-Garde)

ACKNOWLEDGMENTS

This book is the fulfillment of a very long journey, one that would not have been possible without the seasoned encouragement and support of friends and family, including some sadly no longer with us. I must mention in particular my late wife Donna, who lived with this project for decades. She and I made it part of our domestic language and we never doubted it would someday become a reality. I also want to thank my dear friends and collaborators Stephen R. Bissette and Simonida Perica-Uth; my god-sends Dorothy Moskowitz Falarski and Patrick Moroney, who got this manuscript purring and consistent in time for my final pass; and, last but not least, my publisher Lori Perkins, who has never lost her faith in this book, which she first read back in the 20th century, when it was something less than it has become.

DEDICATION

The world into which we were born is overrun with sadists and liars, con artists and serial killers, carjackers and kidnappers, politicians, loophole lawyers, telemarketers and spam shufflers; it is rife with the sort of riffraff who would crack the shell of a child's innocence as casually as they might order eggs for breakfast.

I have known only one consistently reliable source of goodness in this too often false and duplicitous world. This book is for she who stole my heart and took my name.

TABLE OF CONTENTS

PROLOGUE

"AS THE DOOR creaked open, the pale light from the hall fell upon a hideous sight."

The old woman's branch-like hand turned the page.

The boy gasped, though this story had been read to him many times before. It somehow became new each time it was read. The old woman continued.

"It fell upon the black gloves of…"

"The Only Crim'nal!" finished the child.

"… The Only Criminal," his grandmother confirmed, "strangling out the last breath of life from the Princess!"

Another page was turned.

"Inspector Haymaker drew his gun but, once again, it was tooooooo late. The Only Criminal vanished through an open window, leaving the beautiful Princess dead upon the floor."

The child shuddered. The accompanying illustration was inordinately lurid.

"There she lay forever more with her tongue trailing out, like a purple ribbon on a blue present."

At this, the boy felt the rocking chair still. The old woman closed the book with a slam and proclaimed with deep satisfaction: "The End!"

"That was good," the boy approved.

He then jumped down from his grandmother's lap and his pajama-covered feet ran across the room. Dropping to his knees beside a low bookshelf, he turned to his adoring ancestor with irresistible enthusiasm.

"Granny, read me another story! I've got…"

"Only every other storybook in existence!" she laughed. "No, siree! That's the only story you're getting tonight! Here now, put this one back where you found it."

The boy pouted, which sometimes won him his way, as he took his worn copy of *The Only Criminal's Last Laugh* from his grandmother's hands and pushed it back onto the low shelf alongside *The Only Criminal Comes Back, Where The Only Criminal Is, The Only Criminal's Most Beloved Nursery Crymes* and all the rest. It was remarkable how many books he had managed to collect on birthdays and holidays, considering how few years he had actually seen come and go.

The old woman peered through the bedroom window and saw that the night without was black as pitch. A capacious shrubbery scraped against the siding of the house with each whoosh of the wind. Anything could be out there, she thought, and anything that was, must be up to no good.

"Now get that little bucket of yours into bed," she instructed the child. The boy obeyed, hopping onto his mattress and scooting under the covers, giggling at that naughty word "bucket."

Bone-weary, the old woman raised herself up and out of the rocking chair, which rocked once or twice vacated, and sat beside her grandson. Now, as they did on every night, they looked into each other's eyes and spoke from the heart—the heart of innocence feeding from the heart of experience, which also received something back in turn.

"Granny?"

"Yes, child?"

"The Only Crim'nal—is he for real?"

"You mean to tell me that a big boy like you doesn't know that yet?"

"I know about the Tooth Fairy."

"Well, The Only Criminal is just as real as she is, young man! You can trust your Granny on that."

"When the Tooth Fairy breaks into people's houses, is she a crim'nal too?"

"No, child. The Tooth Fairy doesn't break into houses! *She is our invited guest.* She comes with presents! She's got those shiny new silver dollars for all your little baby teeth. That's the only reason she comes visiting. She's not out to cut our throats or steal us blind!"

This made sense to the child.

"Now, before I say goodnight, little one," the old woman stressed in earnest, "I want you to promise your old Granny something. This is real serious, now."

"Okay."

"I want you to promise me that if you ever—and I mean *ever*—find yourself in the same room with that awful, nasty, Only Criminal..."

"I *WON'T!*" the boy swore vehemently, as if on a stack of comic books.

"But if you ever do… If you just can't help it… I want you to promise me you'll turn your little head and look the other way till he's done tippy-toed away. Because the people who see his face, his real face? They never get heard from again. So don't go lookin'! You promise?"

"Oh granny, I promise! I promise!" The child crushed himself against the old woman in a desperate embrace.

The old woman smiled. "That's good, 'cause if you even get the slightest glimpse, you'll get hair that looks like mine!"

The boy's eyes tripled in size. "Did you see The Only Crim'nal, Granny?"

"No, child. They say that the merest glimpse of The Only Criminal will turn your hair the color of snow overnight… but Time has the same effect on us all. It just goes about it a little slower."

"Granny?"

"Yes, dear heart?"

The child eased back onto his pillow. "Is The Only Crim'nal really the only crim'nal in the whole, wide world?"

"Now what a silly question! *Of course* he's the only criminal in the whole, wide world! Why would we call him 'The Only Criminal' if he wasn't?"

"But why do people call him 'The *Only* Crim'nal'? Why don't people just call him 'The Crim'nal' if he's the only one?"

"Well, the answer is, I suppose, that he *demands* we call him 'The Only Criminal.' You know, as a show of our respect. He likes to feel special."

This explanation seemed to satisfy the inquisitive child. And then, inevitably: "Granny?"

"Enough procrastinatin', young man! It's time you was asleep! Your old Granny needs to go rest her weary bones. Now give me some Eskimo sugar."

These two halves of a kindred heart, looking at one another from opposite shores of life, then formed a bridge with their two noses, which they rubbed softly together. The boy always looked forward to this.

His grandmother rose and winked to him from the doorway. Then out went the light and the door was closed, making the boy's room as one with the shadows lurking outside in the abundant night.

Visible from the boy's pillow, the full moons peered down at the child like The Only Criminal's own two eyes, watchful with luminescent terror. Gooseflesh spread throughout the child like the warmth of a wet bed as he felt himself beheld. When the child clamped his eyes shut against them, he found an even greater darkness waiting within and felt suddenly vulnerable to their advance.

Exordium
HE'S GOT THE WHOLE WORLD IN HIS HANDS

THE ONLY CRIMINAL!

A name uttered since time immemorial with palpable, infectious dread, never spoken aloud without shudder, whispered by peasants and statesmen alike over hurried gestures of cowed genuflection!

THE ONLY CRIMINAL!

How people of all countries and cultures would rush through those six dread syllables, the only words shared by every language, wary of lingering over them too long, lest they somehow take shape as the most colossal, the most unimaginable form of terror!

THE ONLY CRIMINAL!

His name was the stuff of legend, his dark deeds constant and ubiquitous, performed by black-gloved hands that could cup continents!. Each morning, every afternoon—and at night without fail—the awe-inspiring accounts of his latest exploits filled every page of every newspaper published everywhere in the world. The headlines were ever-escalating in their power to appall: POSTAGE STAMP ADHESIVE POISONED BY ONLY CRIMINAL, ONLY CRIMINAL BEHEADS EQUESTRIAN STATUE, ONLY CRIMINAL ROBS FORT KNOX.

THE ONLY CRIMINAL!

He could strike anywhere—at any time! Throughout recorded history, The Only Criminal had baffled Mankind with his uncanny mastery over time and space, sometimes traversing entire hemispheres in single strides. For example, a burglary in Brussels might be followed seconds later by the destruction of a mosque in Lisbon, or the theft of a ruby eye from the forehead of a sacred monolith in an Indian cave known only to the holiest of men. These front page headlines might then be followed, in the space of a world-wide gasp, by the covetous plundering of a baseball card collection from a child's tree house in Stinking Creek, Tennessee. He could be that spectacular and that particular.

THE ONLY CRIMINAL!

Because of him, when the horizon was streaked at dusk with crimson, it was never anyone's first thought that the sun was simply sinking into the west, but rather that some poor unfortunate, strolling in that general vicinity, had somehow blundered into the blades of the only possible perpetrator.

THE ONLY CRIMINAL!

With this monster at large, even the two moons in the night sky accrued an uneasy connotation; they were like *his eyes*—slitted or peering, widening or glaring, depending on the time of the month—always looking gigantically down upon all the world's pathetic, vulnerable, susceptible to interruption, little dramas. So powerfully engrained were these associations in the human psyche that, when astronomers first mapped the surfaces of the twin lunar spheres, they bestowed upon their various lakes and lacerations such names as The Sea of Transgression and The Sea of Iniquity, not to mention the monumental crowning crater Psycho.

THE ONLY CRIMINAL!

Of course, those sworn to protect and serve did what they could, but ultimately, even the most stalwart officers of the law bowed to the fearsome felon's vainglory, notoriously above capture and beyond reprimand. In every town, in every city in every country of the world, a single jail cell was kept ready for the unprecedented event of his capture. However, after so long an uninterrupted reign of terror, these cells were generally recognized as little more than window-dressing, public relations gestures which helped local law enforcers to look like they were prepared to do something, in the event they were ever called upon to do something other than patrol the local roads and donut shops. Though not one of these cells could boast of ever holding The Only Criminal prisoner, people flocked with their families to these tourist attractions (some *were* more elaborate than others), transformed over time by their unanimous admissions of defeat into double-edged tributes to the indomitability of he whom they had been built to contain. These cells became, in essence, his very proxy in stone, his representative in iron bars; they were defined space offering incontrovertible proof of what otherwise, for so many, was purely nebulous. To visit one of these detention cells was—as many a tourist avowed with glowing face—the next worst thing to meeting The Only Criminal himself.

Yes, dear reader… **THE ONLY CRIMINAL!** Before embarking on travel for business or pleasure, people everywhere would suddenly stop in the midst of packing their bags and murmur to themselves, "Oh, yes… There is *him* to consider."

THE ONLY CRIMINAL!

Imagine, if you will, a tiny red bead moving at a brisk clip along the Furka Pass high in the Swiss mountains. This is a rental car, a Citroën C3 Pluriel, entrusted to one M. Henri Clément-Fleur, *en route* to an important appointment in the municipality of Realp. The weather is crisp and optimal, the driving conditions excellent, and Clément-Fleur's pride and prowess as a *pilote* are evident from the Fratelli Orsini driving gloves gripping the wheel. There is every reason to expect he will reach his destination in the pink of health by the agreed-upon time—but then…

Oh yes, there is *always* a "but then…"

As he smoothly careens 'round a curve in the narrowing road, the tires of his Pluriel fail to cooperate with his expert steering. They pull the vehicle too close to the precipice at his left for comfort. Clément-Fleur's thoughts turn to The Only Criminal and, in that moment of supreme acknowledgement, the car's chassis begins to throttle, causing a horrible vibration like malefic laughter. He says a prayer, prepares himself for the worst, and then… just as suddenly… his Citroën rights itself. The daunted driver pulls over to the side of the road and cuts his ignition in tears, infinitely grateful for this extension of life and its generous allowance that he may continue to live in abject fear a bit longer.

THE ONLY CRIMINAL!

Fear was his throne, night his cape, broad daylight his audacity.

THE ONLY CRIMINAL! There was absolutely no quarter, no bedroom closet, no basement bin or hidey hole sufficiently secluded for anyone to feel safely beyond the scope of his peering eyes, the reach of his clutching hands, the baleful horror of his merciless intent.

THE ONLY CRIMINAL!

Living out their days under his oppressive shadow, ordinary folk kept to themselves, speaking only to known and trusted friends, sending their children only to known and trusted schools, attending only known and trusted churches, voting only for known and trusted politicians, reading only the works of known and trusted authors, going only to remakes of known and trusted movies. Yet the topic of every friendly conversation, every course of education, every Sunday sermon, every political platform, and every new bestseller and blockbuster was somehow always the same: **THE ONLY CRIMINAL!**

Despite the towering impression he made, little was actually known to the average person about this timeless, abhorrent figure. For example, *how old was The Only Criminal?*

He was believed to be ancient, at least as ancient as the two moons, because it had been in his lone brain that (according to legend) the maculate conception of Evil had taken place and never strayed.

If this were so, how had he managed to retain such youthful ebullience and resourcefulness through the ages?

Some believed that The Only Criminal counted the fabled Fountain of Youth among his booty, while others theorized he had found and zealously hoarded a way of breaking the ultimate laws—those governing life and death.

Now that sounds a bit far-fetched. Was there no other, more practical, explanation?

There were as many explanations as there were fringe groups to hold them to be true. Some believed The Only Criminal to be serially rejuvenated by his acts of transgression, perhaps by regular baptism in the blood of innocents. Some believed his seeming immortality to be generational; that, of all the assaults committed by The Only Criminal, one occasionally resulted in offspring—a bastard destined to turn evil with adulthood and succeed him.

How was it possible for The Only Criminal to commit crimes in wildly different time zones within the same hour, on different continents with minutes—and sometimes, mere seconds—to spare between each strike?

The Saturday morning cartoons created in his image sometimes placed The Only Criminal at the controls of imaginary aircraft capable of seeping between junctures in chronology and cosmology. The truth was most likely somewhat less fanciful—and even more fabulous. Some believed that The Only Criminal operated on an altogether discrepant plane of existence, which allowed him to zip from Arabia to Zanesville faster than any county coroner could confirm a clammy corpse. In this capability, they maintained, also lay the answer to his extraordinary longevity.

But where did he come from? How did it all begin?

Many of the world's most respected thinkers, artists and philosophers have brought their brilliance to bear on the subject of how The Only Criminal came to find his particular path in life. One of Charles Perrault's classic fairy tales puts forth the notion that The Only Criminal had the misfortune to be born at the exact same moment when—at other points around the globe—a hat was recklessly thrown onto a bed, or someone foolishly walked under a ladder, when a black cat crossed someone's path, or when a commoner wore purple.

Pierre Delalande hypothesized that The Only Criminal became himself through an exercise of Fate—innocently coming into the possession of a rogue firearm, trying desperately to divest himself of it before it could give him any bad ideas, and not being able to reach an open storm drain before the vision of his future seized him.

Edouard Molinier (the French have always been the outstanding theorists on the subject) proposed that The Only Criminal first broke the law accidentally and, being unable to establish his innocence, devoted his life to bedeviling the system that branded him as its sole outcast.

To cite one last theory, it was De Selby's bizarre notion that The Only Criminal was the last surviving remnant of an ancient world—a world that existed well before the Big Bang, in which Evil was so commonplace that such absolutes were actually undeserving of capitalization. Is it any wonder, with benighted thinking such as this, that DeSelby spent his tragic, final years hammering his head against the padded walls of an asylum?

Suffice to say, The Only Criminal runs rampant through our world of literature, past and present, fact and fiction, much as he does through the worlds we inhabit in our daily lives and nightly dreams. And the citizens of the world, having no alternative, have learned to exist in the harrowing cradle of his gargantuan hands, with one eye always open and one ear always carefully attuned to the possibility that their bough might be the next to break.

ONE

THE ONLY CRIMINOLOGIST

I have discovered that all human evil comes from this: Man's inability to sit still in a room.

—PASCAL

Chapter One
I BELIEVE IN THE MAN IN THE SKY

Dr. Paul Vaguely, like you and I, had spent his entire life enthralled by The Only Criminal—his legend, his baleful enigma, his daily activities. He considered himself virtually unique, however, in that he had conceived an occupation for himself that not only encouraged such preoccupation on a professional basis, but indulged it. Dr. Vaguely was a staff psychologist at Billowing Pines—that's right, the world-famous asylum whose unique specialty was the counseling of men, women and children who had been traumatized by close brushes with The Only Criminal.

It was Vaguely's job in particular to help these tragic wrecks to put these scarring encounters behind them and pick up the pieces of their shattered lives. It was his personal pastime to use his recordings and transcriptions of their personal accounts of murder, burglary, rape and pillage—not to mention other forms of mayhem, including psychological cruelty—as tools in his independent search for points of recurrence. It was in such rare and curious details—such as when The Only Criminal struck twice within the same country on the same day, or visited his venom upon members of the same family more than once in the same week—that Vaguely felt a tingle of epiphany, suggesting that his vigilance had taken him a millimeter closer to The Truth.

The truth, be it capital or merely offensive, had always been a subject of the keenest importance to Vaguely. He had grown up distrustful of most of the world's paraded pretenses, having been raised on stories told to him by his grandmother, a woman who had an unfortunate family tendency to look at brown and see green. For example, all that he really knew about his mother (who had disappeared from his life under unspeakable circumstances—or so he reasoned, as no one ever spoke of them) was that she had been married to a man named Vaguely only long enough to conceive him, then saw her husband die under evidently unspeakable circumstances, again as no one ever spoke of them. Young Paul, left to his own devices, intuited that these suppressed details must somehow involve The Only Criminal, but such surmise did not explain why his mother's side of the family was permanently queered from his father's, indeed if there was such a thing. He imagined that he must favor the looks of his mysterious father, because his mother had rejected him and he looked nothing like any of the relatives he ever met. He passed through a phase, as fatherless children sometimes do, of suspecting that The Only Criminal might be his true progenitor, because he never met anyone who shared his surname, nor had he ever found another Vaguely in any telephone directory he had perused, in any city of the world. The way his grandmother explained it to him, the name "Vaguely" was French in origin, derived from *Vaguement*, but it had been only half-Anglicized by his forefathers when they came over on the Mayflower, as opposed to those other relatives who instead changed their names to the more fully Anglicized "Waverly."

Despite his hazy and unpromising origins, Paul Vaguely flourished in the hothouse of academia. A serial scholarship recipient, he was hired fresh out of college by Dr. Constantin Pons—the co-founder and chief administrator of Billowing Pines, which at that time was no more than your basic upscale sanitorium. Dr. Pons—a portly, bearded, monocle-wearing man in his 50s—had been modestly impressed by Vaguely's *magna cum laude* standing, but what excited him most was the article "The Id, the Ego, and The Only Criminal," which the young scholar had precociously written and published at the age of only 20. In this extraordinary essay, young Vaguely argued that the existence of The Only Criminal outlined an entire as-yet-unrealized wing of the human subconscious that it was the duty of an entire as-yet-undesignated wing of psychology to map. He went so far as to speculate that, in the future, psychologists specializing in this particular field of endeavor might become known as "criminologists."

Written with wit, intelligence, and the occasional French word, this impressive paper had the thigh-smacking resonance of a manifesto and created quite a splash in the psychological community, an unprecedented success for one who, at the time of publication, had not yet graduated. Being a forward thinker and none too pleased with things as they were, Dr. Pons determined to put this punk provocateur's theories to the absolute test and outbid a great many other facilities for the privilege of hanging his shingle.

Dr. Pons lured Paul Vaguely to Billowing Pines with money, of course, but also with promises of opportunity that no other prospective employer could match or had even thought to extend. When Vaguely accepted Pons' invitation, he knew that he was responding only in part to the generous offer, and responding in at least equal part to the name of the place. Why? To put it simply, pines do not billow—however, by saying "Billowing Pines," it became a place where they did. Vaguely felt he might preside over magic in such a place.

After Vaguely spent a couple of weeks getting his feet wet as an observer, eavesdropping on everyday cases involving depression and delusion and neurasthenia, so on and so forth, Dr. Pons arranged for him to meet with some of the facility's most reclusive patients, men and women whose minds had been seriously unhinged by close brushes with The Only Criminal. And so Dr. Paul Vaguely became, for all intents and purposes, a practicing criminologist—in fact, the only one so practicing.

It was around this time that Vaguely's grandmother, in her 90's, began to succumb to a disease unknown to medical science only a short time before and cured only a short time after her death. For weeks, the dutiful criminologist sat patiently beside her hospital bed, holding the claw of her intravenously-fed arm in confused devotion, but she faded from his life chattering emptily about what she had watched on television the previous night and the weather being predicted for tomorrow. Though he regularly leaned forward whenever she sparked into speech, in the hope of hearing some uttered crumb that might lend him and his life definition, the woman never really came clean about anything. Vaguely subsequently threw himself completely into his work, occupying his conscious mind with nothing else in an effort to bar the belligerent emptiness of his essence from his thoughts until said effort finally became subconscious.

The following decade saw Dr. Paul Vaguely's unique approach to counseling take hold; his theory of criminology became an unqualified success, both for himself and for Billowing Pines. Vaguely's residency at Billowing Pines made the place a national beacon, attracting anyone and everyone who had lived to tell the terrible tale of how their door had once been darkened by The Only Criminal—a tragic category of humanity that existed in greater numbers than had been previously realized. The availability of treatment seemed to actualize a greater need for it.

Once patients were accepted as residents at Billowing Pines—as you might imagine, a highly selective process—their common needs were generally met by staff members other than Dr. Vaguely—mostly nurses and interns, leaving the esteemed specialist free to focus on those most pressing cases of crime-related trauma. He met with long-term patients no more than once a week, to probe their pain and chart their progress, unless something happened to reopen old wounds left to fester or unevenly heal in the wake of The Only Criminal. There was something terribly exciting, he found, about the trembling of their eyes, the stressful shining of their tears, and also the whitening of their knuckles as these lost souls pleaded with him not to go at the end of a session, or for extra protection to be placed in force around their private room. To work with such people in such intimacy, Vaguely sometimes marveled, was like being no more than a step removed from The Only Criminal himself—infinitely closer than those tourists who went around visiting jail cells which had never really confined him.

Now a health care professional in his early 30's, Vaguely lived roughly three miles from Billowing Pines in an apartment complex conveniently reached by bus. On most days, he left work no later than 5:30 p.m., at which time he caught the 5:35 bus #27) outside the main gates. He didn't drive; you see, he had read (and more recently heard) too many accounts of suspiciously failed brakes, deflated air bags, punctured tires, exploding gas tanks, and sabotaged motors to ever wish to pilot his own car. His knowledge of statistics showed that a criminal encounter was less likely to occur on a crowded bus than in a solitary taxi or automobile. The bus felt safe to him; he may have been an authority, an expert, a phenom, and a wiz, but he was nobody's fool (or so he liked to think). Like all sane people, he was prone to superstition. On those occasions when an overloaded work schedule or last-minute emergency caused him to miss his 5:35 retreat, Vaguely sometimes elected to spend the night on the vanilla sofa in his office. After sundown, he reasoned, the bus carried fewer fellow passengers—thus making conditions more favorable to unhappy incident.

As he rode the #27, nestled between fellow commuters in statistical safety, Paul Vaguely did not start conversations, or read, or admire the passing scenery which had become redundant as it became routine; he chose instead to explore the inner frontiers available to distraction. He took stock in the conventional wisdom that imagining the worst could discourage it from coming to pass—and so his thoughts would idle through slaughters and humiliations and holocausts as the bus wended its way through summer-green tranquility. He was unattached, unmarried, indeed not much more than kissed, owing in large part to a wariness of strangers that he considered no more than an occupational hazard and no less than common wisdom.

Vaguely had trained himself to snap out of his reveries as the #27 turned the corner that brought his little neighborhood into view. It was an area of town defined by the intersection of the main street, called Oakley Way, and Woonsocket, a side street without posted definition as a street, road, drive or boulevard. This particular corner in the heart of Amelia had not noticeably changed during the time he had lived there; in truth, it had not changed since the time local builders had banded together to fill its emptiness. He never had to pull the cord; the bus always stopped here. He rose to make his exit, always allowing women and children passengers to step off first, bending low and forward as he passed through the exit, then arising to his full height of six feet, four inches on the sidewalk—a commanding height for one whose outward demeanor suggested aspirations to invisibility.

Paul Vaguely looked like no one else in town. He was black-haired and his heavy beard was shaved clean and powdered to a chalky blue-gray finish. He had a nervous habit of often sweeping his longish, limp dark hair away from his fiercely concentrated, hazel eyes with long, bony fingers. He had the customary doctor's habit of looking at other people as though they were the squiggles on a disease chart. Yet, for all his peculiarities, he was a good man and unfailingly friendly to anyone who spoke to him—though, the world being as it was, few did. Upon regaining the sidewalk, it was his habit to pause at the corner to take a good, apprising look around his neighborhood—confirming that nothing had been marked, moved, or otherwise molested since he left for work that morning.

It was the last day of summer. Amelians, as they called themselves, were scurrying around the various shops lining the main drag of Oakley Way in twos, not liking to walk alone so close to evening, completing their errands before night dropped like a guillotine blade. It was sweater weather, neither warm nor cool, though the winds were picking up.

Leaves were already blowing along the street gutters, but they were green and few, not yet brittle enough to make that scraping sound that made people visualize someone clawing the ground as they were being dragged by The Only Criminal to their doom—a situation remembered from countless motion pictures.

Towering high above the patchwork-shingled rooftops of the area's private residences were the three peaks of St. Timothy's Cathedral, where a vesper service was letting out a little before 6:00. Vaguely knew, from reading he had done during his college days, that ancient churches had often been erected on the former sites of violent crimes as a means of discharging the ground of the evil once committed there. Whatever had happened on the site of St. Tim's must have been monumental. An ash-gray edifice, its spires and steeples jutted up into the hastening double-mooned night like the points of a frozen explosion, veined throughout with murmuring rooms where neighbors knelt together in prayer, having found their pews by passing through doors carved in candle flame shapes.

Though he never attended its services, Vaguely was fond of St. Tim's and liked the idea that a place so upright and inviolate held vigil directly across the street from the apartment building in which he lived. He liked the way its bells could be depended upon to sound once each hour, and again on the half-hour. The celestial chimes heralding Sunday mornings made him smile inside, as did the stone-muffled sound of his fellow Amelians singing from their Only Hymnals. He took comfort from these as he took comfort from the smells of fresh baked goods wafting upstairs to his bedroom window from Bemelmans' Bakery. As you're still getting to know him, it may interest you to know that Paul Vaguely's sweet tooth was relentless; the staff of his bachelor's diet consisted of coffee, randomly picked confections from Mrs. Bemelmans' display case, and a brand of cigarillo called Sweet Vanilla Crooks.

On the corner of Oakley Way and Woonsocket, the Alpine Laundry—next door to the bakery—contributed other comforting smells to the area, those of crisply laundered linens and detergents tinctured with pine and zest and citrus. Vaguely understood there were people in this world who looked upon laundering as a chore to be put off, people who would rather parade around in dirty underthings than face the music, but he personally couldn't walk past the Alpine—inhaling its tart powders and ammonia bleaches, glancing inside at the customers reading Only Criminal paperbacks as their outer things and underthings tumbled round and round inside enormous, aerating spin dryers—without fighting the impulse to throw together a small load and join the party.

These were the sociable associations that danced in Vaguely's senses as his watchful gaze darted to and fro upon arriving so close to home. On this last summer night, the only evident changes in the immediate environs were the specials on the chalkboard outside The Hideout—a folksy little eatery locally renowned for their crimini mushroom salad and their decadent desserts—and the weekly wisdom displayed on the marquee outside St. Tim's, which currently read:

GOD HATH NOT GIVEN US THE SPIRIT OF FEAR
BUT OF POWER, AND OF LOVE, AND A SOUND MIND.

Satisfied that everything about his little nook of the world was as it should be, Vaguely sprinted up the few stairs to his favorite store, Lawson's News. He ducked inside, jangling a little tin bell hung above the door on a springy coil. Stopping at Lawson's each night for his reading and smoking needs was Vaguely's favorite evening ritual, one to which he looked forward from the moment his bus turned the bend onto Oakley Way. He found the smell of fresh tobacco and newsprint awaiting him inside to be the perfect antidote to a stressful day.

He went straight to the spinning racks that held all the latest paperback best-sellers: *The Criming, Only Is The Knave, Bid Crime Return,* as well as some high-toned selections such as all seven volumes of *Remembrance of Crimes Past* and Nabokov's controversial *Flat Tire*. Vaguely's lips twisted with mild philosophical disappointment; he had read all of these already. He would have to look for his evening's distraction instead in the magazine racks.

The Lawson of Lawson's News was Abel—a brown-skinned man whose short gray hair always reminded Vaguely of the crushed ice in the root beer served at The Hideout. He was kneeling on the floor, unbundling bales of new magazines like *The Ladies Crime Journal, Inhumanity Fare* and *Heist Times*. The sexagenarian grinned to himself, sensing that his most reliable customer was hovering there behind him, scanning the latest covers on display. Vaguely politely averted his eyes from so-called "men's" magazines like *Slayboy* (which featured nude pictorials of women made-up to look like The Only Criminal's comeliest victims); he detested *Breaking and Entering Weekly* and wasn't the grease-monkey type who bought *Getaway Car & Driver*. Vaguely took his reading seriously. He picked up the weekly news magazine *Crime*, occasionally reveled in the poems and short stories of *The Peril Review*, and bought the occasional issue of the award-winning photo journal *Crook.*

However, on this particular evening, Vaguely approached the check-out counter empty-handed. Abel Lawson stood to intercept him at the cash register, presuming to remove from a nearby humidor two sticks of Vaguely's favorite after-dinner cigar, the *Arma del Fuego*.

"Doc Vaguely Special," Abel grinned. "Second stick half price to favorite customers."

"It's a steal!" Vaguely smiled back, sweeping back the hair out of his eyes.

"That it? Can't interest you in any new reading material tonight?"

"I'll take the evening papers, of course."

"I guess that goes without saying," Abel chuckled, selecting the good doctor's favorites among the latest editions.

Vaguely bought three newspapers every night—the local, national and international editions of *The Times*, whose shared title was the popular abbreviation of *The Life & Times of The Only Criminal.*

"SINATRA DENIES TIES TO ONLY CRIMINAL," Lawson read aloud from the national headline. "Well, yeah," he exclaimed, as though stunned by such impossible affrontery. "You hafta *believe* the guy."

Vaguely grunted in assent, casting glances at various front page details splashed across the International edition—a car-bombing in Sao Paolo, a casino heist in Monte Carlo, a flagrant assassination in The Hall of Mirrors in the Palace at Versailles.

Vaguely paid for his purchases. As he moved to leave, Abel called after him: "Hey, Doc, I need another buck here."

Vaguely turned white, then as red as tomato soup as he hurried back to apologize for his mistake. "It seems my mind is elsewhere," he apologized disconcertedly.

"I know about you absent-minded professors," the merchant laughed. "No worries. What *you* gonna do, *cheat* me?"

Now they both laughed—*the very idea!*

Outside the store, his evening reading and smoking secure under his arm, Vaguely noticed that night had seriously begun to fall. The stars became apparent one by one—scored, as if in a motion picture, with the crystalline finger-picking of a 12-string guitar. This music alerted him to the approach of Whimsy Plunkett, one of Amelia's most eccentric and beloved citizens, its neighborhood troubadour.

In the time he had made this area his home, Paul Vaguely had heard Whimsy's improvised songs nearly every day, yet had never seen him speak. It was the troubadour's purpose in life to narrate—nay, celebrate—the comings and goings of his neighbors in song. On this particular night, he was sweetening the dusky air with calypso:

The orange sun is a-falling fast
The daylight hours they will not last
So finish up your shopping chores
Lock all of your windows
And bolt all your doors.

Whimsy nodded to Vaguely as he passed by, strumming his acoustic guitar. Vaguely countered by bowing from the waist, which seemed appropriate. The baleful song lilted on as the balladeer continued on his way, cutting an amiable path through throngs of last-minute shoppers doing their best to take his musical advice.

The dark to come, it's a scary place
Night so black you cannot see your face
But there's One who can, or so I hear tell
Hide under your bed if he be ringing your bell.

Oh my, oh me
How to avoid this Criminality?
Oh me, oh my
If he come to my house, I am going to die.

Vaguely lingered outside Lawson's News, his ear suddenly keened to the sound of a distant siren, until the lights of the billboard atop the building came on. The current advertisement depicted The Only Criminal—not as he really was in all his flagrant terror, Vaguely felt sure, but in the more appealing, commercial way used when people were using him to sell something. Here he was much the same figure as seen on Neighborhood Watch signs: a looming, skulking, yet strangely debonair predator, the true shape of his body concealed by a flowing black overcoat, his facial features receded in profound shadow from which two lunar eyes peered gigantically down at the pedestrians below from under the brim of a sinister hat. Further cloaked in a haze of wavering smoke, he stood in the foreground of a twinkling metropolitan skyline, a sort of Anytown (not unlike Amelia), his gloved hand gesturing with fond regard in the direction of an appealingly tilted box of Consolations cigarettes.

The advertisement read, in strong legible handwriting suggestive of a personal endorsement: *CONSOLATIONS... The Only Criminal says, "I smoke them. My house smells like them."*

"Evening, Dr. Vaguely!"

Vaguely's attention was jerked back to ground level by this unexpected greeting from behind his back.

It was Officer Mead, the neighborhood patrolman—a reassuring local fixture, middle-aged, likeable as a beagle, a stone shy of portly—beaming glad tidings, as he did to one and all. Many were the times when Vaguely had seen him assist young mothers attempting to juggle bags of groceries and babes in arms, or help elderly men and women across the street, or, for no one's amusement but his own, manipulate his nightstick with the *panache* of a master magician. Even if this lawman stood no real chance of apprehending The Only Criminal, it made the locals feel safer to know that he was around and ready to take a bullet in their defense.

"Good evening, Phil," Vaguely greeted the officer.

"Look sharp now, Doc," the lawman cautioned him, pointing his nightstick across the street at Bemelmans' Bakery, where the interior lights dimmed by a half-measure. "Better get a move on if you want a custard-filled with your morning java!"

"Right you are! Good night, Phil!"

"'Night, Doc!"

Vaguely took care to look both ways before crossing the street, within the zebra bars of the crosswalk. He cupped his eyes to the display window of the bakery and saw Mrs. Bemelmans, as plump as one of her cheese crowns, inside with her co-worker, a rail-thin, septuagenarian shop girl named Juanita. They were both hastening out of their white aprons after a long day of standing and serving. Vaguely rapped on the glass, a soft but urgent tattoo. The "girls" noticed him—Juanita letting rip with a short scream.

"Oh, you," pshawed Mrs. Bemelmans, as she crossed the linoleum floor to unlock the door—a series of five bolts. "It's only Doc Vaguely!"

Juanita put a hand to her heart and leaned against the counter.

"Sorry to frighten you ladies," Vaguely apologized. "I see you're closing… Am I too late?"

"It's past closing time," Mrs. Bemelmans explained, "but you're such a good customer, I don't mind bending the rules. After all, they're just rules—not a law!"

"And thank goodness for that!" Vaguely exclaimed as he rushed toward the display case. It was filled with all manner of unsold goodies that had been tricked by the dimming lights into believing in a stay of execution.

"I know you and your sinkers, Doc," Juanita said, snapping open a white sack with a sharp flick of her wrist. The doctor never bought by the box, always by the sack.

"Are there any chocolate-covereds left? Or are they all gone?"

"We might have one left," Juanita said, winking at her employer. Vaguely heard a donut drop into a waxed paper bag—followed by three more.

"Once again, ladies, you've saved my life," he rhapsodized, while reaching for his billfold. "What do I owe you?"

"We've already locked up the register, Doc," Mrs. Bemelmans said. "Why don't you pay us when you come in tomorrow?"

"I shall do, first thing."

Of course, of that there was never any doubt.

The bakery women bade Dr. Vaguely goodnight, Mrs. Bemelmans ushering him to the door and locking it behind him—five times, all told.

Back on the sidewalk, Vaguely took notice of Officer Mead across the street, exchanging words with another passerby, whose elbow he grabbed as he was on the point of rushing past.

"You on your way home?"

"Yes, Officer," the stranger assured him. "I don't like to be out walking so close to dark, but for some reason, our evening paper wasn't delivered. It's always right outside the door by 5:00, like clockwork. Anyway, I thought I'd better dash over here," indicating Lawson's, "and pick one up before it was too late."

"I won't detain you then," Officer Mead said, letting go. "Have a safe and pleasant evening, sir."

As the man dashed into Lawson's, Vaguely stepped into the shadows of the florist's darkened doorway and watched Officer Mead unhook the walkie-talkie from his belt with a somber sense of duty.

Vaguely overheard: "HQ, do you read me? HQ, this is Oakley and Woonsocket, over."

"This is HQ, Officer Mead," a distorted voice responded. "Something wrong, Phil? Over."

"Non-delivery of evening paper reported. Just one. Foul play possible, over."

Vaguely knew better than to drag his feet any longer. It seemed that The Only Criminal himself might be in the vicinity—might be watching him at that very moment from a parked car, from a storm drain, from a mailbox, or from holes drilled into the eyes of that billboard image overlording the neighborhood from Lawson's roof. Without any further dilly-dallying or shilly-shallying, he approached his apartment complex in long strides, abruptly urgent for shelter.

Chapter Two
HE IS MY EVERYTHING

Vaguely lived directly across the street from Lawson's News in the Oakley Apartments, a staunch three-story brownstone fitted between the storefronts of the neighborhood's florist and locksmith. It was Vaguely's habit, before going inside each night, to look over the sympathetic arrangements displayed inside the florist's window, draped with banners reading "Regrets on Your Robbery" among other appropriate sentiments.

Outside his apartment complex were three stone steps, leading to a heavy black-lacquered door with a glass pane and a brass grip. Vaguely pushed his way into an alcove, a sort of antechamber where six brass-plated mailboxes were recessed in a wall painted pea-green (canned rather than frozen), each with its own doorbell and all (except the sixth) labeled with unrelated surnames, most of them scribbled with the illegibility of people not wishing to be found.

Apartment 1 belonged to Red Grinter, the building's landlord, who was unfailingly alert to the sound of anyone loitering near the mailboxes. True to form, his door—on the left wall beyond the antechamber—swung open.

"Ha! Just checkin', Doc," he called out in a gruff, but affable voice, waving.

"Evening, Mr. Grinter."

Red Grinter was of middling height, middle 50's, stubble-faced, bald with small blue eyes; he had a pug nose, wore T-shirts year round, and kept his pants upheld with suspenders. His round-toed shoes usually bore dribbled traces of paint, though Vaguely had never personally seen him hold a brush or personally preside over the building's repairs. Vaguely had no idea what Mr. Grinter's actual given name might be; his nickname was bracketed with quotation marks on the label of his mailbox, giving it the appearance of a shady alias. Ringo, a grey Scottish terrier with bright black eyes, pushed through his master's shins for a closer look at the new arrival. Around the dog's neck glittered a heart-shaped identification tag, a token of Red's love for the animal. Since the day he'd adopted him, Red and Ringo had been inseparable.

Red looked down at his Welcome mat. "What the… No paper yet?"

"No," Vaguely answered. "Officer Mead seemed rather concerned about it."

"Huh. I'd better go see if the News is sayin' anything about it. See ya later, Doc."

With that, Red and Ringo again retired behind their closed door and Vaguely heard faintly the staticky, electronic ouch a television makes when it's turned on.

He checked his mailbox. He had no mail. He seldom did. Relocking it, he began his ascent to the third floor.

Vaguely was like the other tenants of the complex—not counting his gregarious landlord—in that he kept mostly to himself. The others were probably aware that he was a doctor of some kind, having overhead others calling him "Doc," and they must have also known that he wasn't the kind of doctor they could turn to in a medical or veterinarian emergency, otherwise they would be accosting him for free advice all the time. All they probably knew about him was that he was a "different" sort of doctor; the rest they probably guessed. They probably guessed, behind their locked and numbered doors, that this Dr. Vaguely frittered away his free time in peculiar, anti-social pursuits—nothing of an illegal nature, of course; that went without saying—but the kind of solitary avocation that might explain why a good-looking fellow like himself was never seen in the company of young women (or young men, for that matter) and was never known to invite anyone up to his apartments (yes, plural) to play cards, have a beer or watch a ballgame.

The things apartment dwellers overhear when they live closely packed together tend to make them a bit leery of one another, and Vaguely responded to the other tenants of the complex correspondingly. The occupants of Apartment 2—across the hall from Mr. Grinter—were an elderly couple with an illegible, probably foreign name; they spoke little or no English. They were the reason why the building's main floor so often smelled of boiling kale and cabbage. Shortly after they had moved in, a homecoming Vaguely thought he overheard German voices conversing inside their apartment and so proceeded to prepare a neighborly greeting in their native tongue, which he read to their peering, apple-muffin-like faces on their doorstep:

"Willkommen auf der Oakley Apartments. Ich hoffe, Sie werden sehr glücklich Sowohl unter unserem Dach geteilt werden. Mein Name ist Dr. Paul Vaguely, ich bin NICHT das Ziel Art von Arzt, der gut in einem Notfall ist. Auch hier willkommen und gute Nacht!" ["Welcome to the Oakley Apartments. I hope you will both be very happy under this roof we share. My name is Dr. Paul Vaguely, but I am NOT the sort of doctor who is good in an emergency. Again, welcome and good night!"]

The couple had eyed him warily as he read the document and then, as politely as possible, closed the door in his face. They never exchanged words again, but thereafter, the voices Vaguely sometimes heard behind the door of Apartment 2 spoke in Lithuanian.

To the right of the second floor landing was Apartment 3—which was peculiar because it seemed to not follow the arrangement of the odd and even numbers of the apartments of the ground floor; indeed, the numbers of the Oakley Apartments snaked upward in an S-shaped arrangement, if you will. The mailbox belonging to Apartment 3 bore two sets of initials. Vaguely could not help noticing that the last initials were not a match, lending it the impression not of marriage, but of an ongoing tryst commemorated in tree bark.

Vaguely had never met these neighbors, at least not formally, but he understood from Mr. Grinter that they were a well-traveled pair who divided their time between Amelia and other spots around the world. They came back to roost in their Oakley apartment maybe three or four times a year, never for more than a month or so, during which time they threw at least one party and spent the rest of the time recovering. One morning, while pleasantly skipping down the stairs en route to work, Vaguely happened to spy a mail courier leaving a parcel of unusual size outside their door, on a mat that did not say "Welcome." The courier knocked twice on the door and returned to his delivery truck. On his way out, Vaguely took a closer look at the package in the hope of discovering a full name on its label, but before he could get a good look, he was taken aback by the sudden opening of the door numbered 2. Emerging from inside was a quadruped: a bedraggled, hung-over man feeling about on all fours, reaching blindly for the parcel. He wore a black sleeper's mask and striped pajamas, which reminded Vaguely of The Only Criminal, as he sometimes appeared in fantasy films on *The Late Late Show*, those overly-imaginative ones that opened with his daring escape from prison. Trying not to breathe or do anything else that might alert his neighbor to his presence, Vaguely had used the toe of his shoe to nudge the package within range of the man's floor-patting hands and continued to gawk as the masked globetrotter lugged it into his apartment and, after several tries, managed to close the door, unaware of how close he had been to a complete and utter stranger—*who might have been anyone!*

Vaguely regarded Apartment 4, above Mr. Grinter and across the hall from the party people, with a blurry sense of unease. It was currently unoccupied and available for rent, which meant that someone new would be showing up sooner or later to claim it.

Mounted on the wall between the second floor apartments was a rectangular mirror—a panoramic mirror, you might say—and, with the fourth apartment empty and the tenants of the third unlikely to venture out, Vaguely had founded a tendency to tarry there—to look at one side of his face, then the other, and to straighten his hair with that accustomed combing sweep of his right hand. On this night, while repeating this performance, a slight creaking sound behind and below him caused Vaguely to turn sharply. The door of Apartment 3 was open slightly. The apple muffin features of the little old German or Lithuanian man stared at him in the half-light, frailly defiant and protective of his wife and home, but also touchingly afraid.

Vaguely uttered an apologetic "*Gut nacht*" and soldiered on, taking two more flights of zig-zagging stairs to reach the third and final landing, the plateau of his own residence.

Yes, the plateau of his own residence—for Apartments 5 *and* 6 were both rented by Dr. Vaguely, which might explain the especially friendly favor with which his irascible landlord regarded him. Though he was the sole signatory for the two residences, you might not have known from the way these two sets of rooms were furnished that they belonged to the same man.

Let's skip Apartment 6 for the moment.

If you were to enter Apartment 5—meaning, of course, if you were invited—you would see a group of rooms as might belong to any working bachelor. There was a living room with a modest television set, a kitchen with refrigerator and stove, a kitchenette with a table never dressed for more than one, a bathroom, and a bedroom with a single bed, bedside table and lamp. It had the untidiness associated with bachelors, particularly with those vulnerable to preoccupations of the mind. However, Vaguely spent almost no time in these rooms—only the time forced upon him by the necessities of eating, bathing and defecating.

Apartment 6 was another story. The first thing a guest or intruder would notice upon entering Apartment 6 was the color green; it was mesmerizingly ubiquitous. Vaguely had read somewhere that green was the favorite color of The Only Criminal, who spent so much of his immortality collecting it in different denominations. The first room inside the door was the living room, dominated by Vaguely's wing chair, which was upholstered in green velveteen and positioned near the center of the floor. A golden floor lamp with a flamingo neck overlooked its right wing. Along the conjoining walls behind the chair, an L-shaped work area was situated. The edges of two antique mahogany tables interfaced in that corner, under the partial cover of green felt blotter boards. Matching green-shaded table lamps cast studious light upon the blotters. Above the table on the right, a bulletin board was affixed to a wall of muted but not dull green, illuminated from above by the sort of fixture often found on the frames of paintings; there, clippings of the latest reported exploits of The Only Criminal were affixed with enamel-headed tacks of various calendar-coded hues. (Mondays were blue, Tuesdays pink, Wednesdays yellow, Thursdays white, Fridays orange, Saturdays purple and Sundays red. That's right; there were no greens, as this would have indicated The Only Criminal's favor. Vaguely no longer remembered how he had arrived at the other designations, but he had memorized them and somehow they worked for him.) The wall to the immediate right, as one entered, was dominated by a large world map on which all of the planet's bodies of land and water were denied their natural curvature, peeled and laid flat like an apple skin, with all the places where bad things had happened in the past week marked with tiny pennant pins, their calendar codes corresponding to those of the tacks on his bulletin board.

The far wall was covered by what Vaguely considered to be the key books of his impressive library. Suffice to say, the volumes lining these shelves and others in this apartment were not of the sort found on most bedside tables. While he enjoyed passing the time with Only Criminal paperback potboilers and comic books as much as the next person, Vaguely's collection encompassed hundreds, potentially thousands, of nonfiction works—historical overviews like *The Fall and Rise of The Only Criminal*, personal memoirs (mostly written by survivors of crimes from centuries past, but also including the recently debunked "autobiography" *My Life and Crimes*), and scholarly accounts of The Only Criminal's influence on the worlds of Art and Science. Filling several shelves in their own right were dozens of personal scrapbooks that Vaguely had assembled since childhood—the germ of his serious adult study. These went back almost a quarter of a century and represented a sober, clear-eyed attempt to sort truth from accident, superstition from "entertainment."

Even as a child, Vaguely had understood that the press credited The Only Criminal with more evil deeds than even *he* was likely to manage in the course of an evening, lending his scarlet signature to everything from domestic knockdowns to natural catastrophes. Vaguely's annotated scrapbooks collected only those cases for which there was simply no other possible explanation: murders, assaults (sexual and other), arson, thefts, kidnappings, subway pushings, and what-have-you. It was in the exclusive accumulation of such tangible leads that Vaguely spent hours, each and every night, scoring and evaluating the full contents of three evening papers.

Vaguely spent his evenings alone in these lodgings, absent-mindedly fuelling his insect-like metabolism on jelly donuts, cheese crowns, chocolate sinkers, or whatever else had been motherly tucked into his white sack from Bemelmans', along with some black coffee, while reading the papers and his books of the moment—usually two hours per night spent on each. As fatigue began to overtake him, Vaguely would set his reading matter aside, loosen the tie he'd forgotten to remove, unbutton his collar, and light his *Arma del Fuego*. He liked to smoke while reflecting on his sessions of the day and the outstanding reports he had gleaned from the world of print; he also did this while taking advantage of his extensive and catholic music collection. A considerate man, Vaguely always used stereo headphones after 9:00 to ensure the undisturbed peace of the bozos downstairs.

Vaguely's record collection consisted solely of recordings by The Only Criminal, all of which (it was said) had been composed and performed under the influence of illegal drugs. With his headset comfortably in place, Vaguely was able to experience—at lawful second-hand—musical arrangements so violent, so audacious, so contrary to the acceptable, they could only have been performed by a felonious monk. Within these recordings, mostly on original vinyl but with a few necessary rarities on CD or phonographic cylinder, musical laws seemed to be broken every few bars; but, because these laws bore no relationship to those governing society, their violation felt almost liberating, bracing and visionary.

Playing every instrument himself, The Only Criminal meticulously recreated forbidden tri-tonal sounds inculcated in him while under the influence of pungent hell-herbs, customized kool-aids, spoonbakes and Pentecostal nostril confetti. These recordings were sold in stores, shelved not according to genre but to drug, and they were extremely, extremely popular with just about everybody.

It was a mystery to Vaguely how such challenging, wicked music had always been so readily accepted by the mainstream. Perhaps people felt they daren't *not* buy it. Whatever the reason, every one of The Only Criminal's recordings to date had entered the charts "with a bullet"—indicating, possibly, that he had found a means of falsifying his own sales figures. (Who would put it past him?) Or perhaps music industry moguls, aware that the most enduring trends and traits of popular music had originated in The Only Criminal's lurid experimentations, understood that it would be in their own best interests to promote his releases to the point where they became utterly impossible to escape.

The Only Criminal Shoots Up was currently the #1 Jazz album in the country, while *Tripping Out with The Only Criminal* reigned over the Alternative list. Vaguely had studied the musical aspect of The Only Criminal's career thoroughly, purely as recreation, and knew that, in the 20 years since its original release, the FM radio perennial *The Only Criminal Grows His Own* had yet to chart below the Top 100. On first listen, *The Only Criminal's Happy Hour* (the best-selling MOR album of all time) and the Country & Western staple *The Only Criminal Cries In His Beer* didn't seem particularly unlawful, but Vaguely learned otherwise by reading the booklets accompanying some of his CD releases, which explained that even these seemingly tame recordings had been made in violated recording studios on stolen tape, and in many cases contained *archival recordings* made when The Only Criminal was still under the legal drinking age of eighteen.

"Even then," Vaguely said aloud, stunned as he absorbed this well-researched detail.

If Vaguely started listening to his albums no later than 10:00, the expiration of his *Arma del Fuego* would remind him when it was time for the last of his evening rituals. Every night at 11:00, it was Paul Vaguely's pleasure to tune into *The Cadbury Report* on WTOC-TV. He watched this, his favorite program, on his Apartment 6 television—the bigger and better of his two television monitors—while tacking new clippings to his board and pinning fresh pennants to his map.

"Good evening and welcome to *The Cadbury Report*," the attractive, neatly coiffed anchorwoman greeted her audience. "I'm

Lorraine Cadbury and these are our top stories… Vacation season ended today in horrific fashion as a dozen severed heads washed ashore along the east coast from Cape Cod to Daytona Beach. According to police reports, the mouth of each head was sewn shut and found to contain a single platinum coin, the serial numbers of which were traced to rolls of such coins stolen last week from La Banca Nacional in Barcelona, Spain… In Detroit, Michigan, a stolen car was pursued by state police for more than 30 blocks—you're seeing helicopter footage provided by our Detroit affiliate, WDOC-TV—before being found empty, save for a pair of novelty store chattering teeth left behind in the driver's seat. In response from the White House, the President promises that the war on The Only Criminal has only just begun. And would you believe snow in summer? It's true: a freak snowfall today in Bismarck, North Dakota brought an unexpectedly wintry end to the city's annual Only Criminal Festival. Local children celebrated by spontaneously banding together to erect a likeness of The Only Criminal in the snow, but within the hour, returning warmish weather had liquified the sinister snowman into a perf-perfi-*perfidious* puddle." She started laughing. "I told you guys—you've gotta lose these $50 words! More after this."

During the commercial interruptions—including one for Consolations cigarettes that dramatized the model of the billboard across the street—Vaguely pondered the points of coincidence between *The Cadbury Report*'s news stories, the somewhat staler (but more thoroughly documented) accounts of the nightly paper, and the ramblings of his patients that day; but there had never been any apparent pattern to The Only Criminal's haphazard ways—not today nor at any point in his impressive reign; there were no course of action, rarely a recurring target, no loose thread to unravel a renegade truth.

When *The Cadbury Report* ended 30 minutes later, Vaguely stood with a sigh, switched off his television, then his apartment lights, and locked up before padding across the hall to his personal quarters. There, after making his evening ablutions and redressing in pajamas and a bathrobe, Vaguely whipped up some cocoa that he sipped intermittently—always from an Only Criminal cup gifted him by his grandmother, which he'd kept since childhood—while sitting up in bed. After draining his cup, he snuggled in and read until the book dropped from his hand, as he drifted once again into the darkness he aspired to define, to know and befriend.

Chapter Three
SWING LOW, SWEET CHARIOT

As Paul Vaguely entered into peaceful slumber, there was another man—in a different neighborhood, perhaps in a different time zone—who bolted upright in his bed as his breathing instinctively constricted with panic and fright, waking him. That sound from the street had returned—as it had returned outside his bedroom window every morning for the past few weeks, just before the crack of dawn. It was the ominous pronouncement of a long, black sedan he had come to think of as the Gloating Car.

The sound of it was hateful when it came! The revolutions of its tires, slow and sadistic, crunched the street like so much gravel, pulverizing it cruelly, methodically, its masticated grit crackling and spat like bones splintered on the rack. Such was the savor of the vehicle's stealth, yet this was nothing compared to the harrowing, cowering, abusive thunder of its heartbeat: the blister and lash of tuneless music thudding at top volume behind its sealed windows! These bombinations, muffled behind strong glass, were a nightly sonic assault that left no trace, like a bar of soap spun inside a sock, intimidating in its roar, harrowing in its insolence. Nothing remotely human could be discerned in that hateful sound—just a terrible, overbearing monotony asserting its privilege that turned the frightened man's blood and bowels to ice.

THOOM sst sst sst sst THOOM sst sst sst sst...

THE GLOATING CAR!

At the sound of it, the poor man's haggard eyes would jolt open, awful reality flooding in with the pre-dawn's purple light. Again, the sounds of tires grinding against crushed and fired pavement, the densely muffled percussion prodding at his solar plexus; it weighed heavily on his chest, turning the dew-freshened air of early morning into something putrid, dank, and oppressive. As it grew louder, a cringing descended from his chest to his belly, a deep-seated fear that all but physically emasculated him. He felt worse than a coward: he was toppled by encroaching fear, never moreso than at that moment when the rogue vehicle turned the corner onto his street, its headlights slashing across the front of his house, sending gooseflesh up and down the lengths of his limbs.

THE GLOATING CAR!

As its headlights flared through his bedroom curtains, multiplied by the slats of his venetian blinds, he stared helpless as the malevolent beams splashed his walls and ceiling with stripes, momentarily hardening around him like the bars of a cage, only to then be dragged away like a silent train of lead bludgeons as the car crept past his domicile and seethed further on down the road.

Just one night before, after weeks of suffering torment and cowardice, this man had somehow summoned the courage to leap from his bed, sprint to his window and gaze down upon The Gloating Car as it throbbed down his suburban avenue like a pulse-pounding inkblot. To his horror, The Gloating Car came to a knowing halt—seemingly at the very moment his eyes first touched it—and remained there for several minutes, idling in front of his house, idling as its radio heart punched out at the canopy of night until the man took finally refuge in a set of ear plugs. Even then, he could still feel its pulsations out there, emanating its evil, punching him, savoring his terror and biding its time. And now it was back!

THE GLOATING CAR!

This early morning, it idled outside his house just long enough to assure him, in his terror, that he was remembered, that his existence had been noted, before rolling on. He couldn't have felt more harassed had The Only Criminal himself stepped out of that vehicle to tap at his windowpane with the edge of a straight razor. He sat upright in bed, hugging his knees and rocking, hugging and rocking and listening intently as The Gloating Car palpitated down the street, his hearing made acute by the adrenaline jolting, rocketing through his glands. Then, gradually, the pounding of his own heart became less intensive, more natural, as the orchestrator of all disorder was absorbed into the silence at the end of the block.

In its wake, his ears were so much on guard that they were fully dilated, enabling his hearing to keen all the way to the end of the street. He heard the assaultive music cut off, followed by the car's ignition. He heard the opening and slamming of a car door followed by unsteady footsteps and a torrent of abominable cursing. The voice he heard was literally monstrous, all phlegm and sandpaper, a growl scalded by something infinitely more ruinous than whiskey or even wood varnish; it came from the depths of a throat that gargled with Hellfire. Might that actually be he?

The man knew right from wrong as most people do, without knowing the exact letter of the law. He assumed from their nightly recurrence that there was no law on the books against any of the disturbances perpetrated nightly by The Gloating Car—the law must have no problem with the driving after curfew, the inconsiderately loud music at all hours, the cursing on the sidewalk—but the arrogant and evil-minded regularity of these things, their nightly disruption of his sleep and serenity, were simply wrong and left him with a lingering sense of violation for which, he told himself, only one man could be responsible. **THE ONLY CRIMINAL!**

The man's willingness to forgive and forget had finally reached its limit. It was now the first day of autumn, a time of new beginnings, and he decided—with a conviction whose intensity startled him—that enough was enough. This abuse must not continue, not even for one more night. Somehow, he must find the nerve to gird himself, to march down the street to slay the dragon. He knew that he would be risking almost inevitable death in the attempt, but even death would be preferable to spending one more night in such a state. Were he victorious, his neighbors' children and their children never need know what it was like to live under threat of such terror and oppression.

He lay in bed, wiping the cold sweat from his face and staring at the stucco arabesques of his bedroom ceiling, until his alarm clock fibrillated a couple of hours later. Then he rose and dressed, feeling pushed to the point of resolve. He would walk to the end of the block and see with his own two eyes where this four-wheeled offense was parked.

The walk took more courage than he had expected. Once he stepped outside his house and passed the respectable homes of his immediate neighbors, his stomach began to sour. The farther down the street he ventured, the more the neighboring property values appeared to decrease. Paint on houses began to peel, gutters began to rust and sag, green grass was starved to brown and yellow; there was a pervasive smell of gasoline and dog feces. Vehicles parked on both sides of the street were sprawled in various degrees of disassembly, hollow under their hoods, raised on cinder blocks. He found it strange, but the more run-down the houses looked, the better armed they appeared to be against the prospect of invasion. What did these houses know about his neighborhood that he didn't know? Chain link fences sprang up, padlocks in plain view, the steering wheels of junk heaps were outfitted with anti-theft clubs, and "Beware of Dog" warnings became almost meaningless in their ubiquity. He told himself that such signs had been posted to discourage salesmen and other lawful undesirables—but a snarling Pit Bull leaped up out of nowhere on the other side of a chain-link fence to tweak his doubts. At this, he turned on an unsteady heel and rushed back to his house—straight to his own car, which was parked in his driveway. He got in, turned the ignition and drove for several minutes without giving any particular thought to where he was going.

An hour or so later, he was back in his driveway with his car turned off, running his hands along the length of an impulse purchase: a Louisville Slugger baseball bat. He went indoors, called into work pleading a not-wholly-feigned illness, and took the slugger to bed like a bride.

His eyes did not open again until the wee hours of morning. The wooden bat felt solid by his side—"thy rod and thy staff," he thought to himself—and he felt chosen to beat back the foul fiend—to rid his street, his community, of this nightly fear and trembling once and for all.

He would lie in wait for it. He needed to dress comfortably, so he chose a pair of midnight blue pajamas that would also help him to blend in with the shadows at that hour. Over black-stockinged feet he tied a comfortable pair of black running shoes.

Then, at some point between 4:30 and 5:00 a.m., he witnessed the phenomenology that must, every night, have presaged the arrival on his street of The Gloating Car.

Before it could be seen, before it could be heard, the skies—already black and cloudless—turned darker still with a sudden influx of what could only be called a malignance of nature. The heavens worsened like a melanoma. Then, made louder by each turning of the car's tires, the gut slams of the preening music locked behind four doors, pounding pounding pounding for egress, iced his vitals. Then, as he quavered on the brink of changing his mind, of taking it all back, he saw two long yellow cones painting the intersecting street at the corner, the twin headlamps heralding the approach of… the approach of… he couldn't say it! He ducked in time to avoid being grazed by them as they slashed the night and gained his street.

THOOM sst sst sst sst THOOM sst sst sst sst…

Was the dread vehicle sentient? Would it sense his presence? The man, still unsure whether he was the chosen one, knew that his only hope of taking the vehicle by surprise was to look away from it, much as

Perseus had deflected his own gaze from that of Medusa. As he looked away, he chanced to see the faces of neighbors assembled at the windows of their houses, all pallid with fright. Some saw themselves being seen and, rather than risk cheering him on, retreated from view into the shadows of their private shame.

It was all left up to him. He was the chosen one.

Once The Gloating Car had thundered past, this man ventured out, Louisville Slugger in hand. He hunkered down behind trees and hedges as much as possible but, as property values bottomed out, such verdant camouflage thinned and finally disappeared, leaving him potentially exposed to view in the Driver's rearview mirror. At this point, he held back and kept low to the ground as the sedan rumbled into the distance, haloed in noise and humming with light until it came into contact with shadows dark and dense enough to swallow it, both sight and sound.

There was no turning back.

Moving at a brisk jog, the man passed the same houses he had seen the previous morning, their rotted gutters and peeling façades no longer quite so discouraging as they had appeared in broad daylight. What did he have to fear from them, anymore?

Soon he had ventured farther down his street than he had ever dared before. He felt lost—lost to Evil, as well as to Good. Here in the heart of darkness, he saw no sign anywhere of The Gloating Car, parked or idling. There was barely enough light here to make sense of the two posted road signs. One of these, pertaining to the intersecting street at the end of the road, read NO OUTLET. The other sign directed vehicles to the nearby Interstate highway with an arrow pointing East. The arrow was captioned with a single word: ONLY.

With this, the man felt his worst suspicions confirmed.

Tightening his grip on his only defense, he jogged east till he arrived at an overpass that took drivers on a 360□ loop before merging, directly below, with the entrance to the highway. From this modest bridge, he looked over the side rail at the large comma of asphalt that joined with the interstate beneath him. There was no activity on this road at this ungodly hour; everything was dead quiet. He crossed to the opposite side of the overpass, where the highway could be seen stretching out toward the rising sun. The only vehicle on the road was a patrol car making its usual rounds, moving farther away on a strip of road upon which the word ONLY was painted with harrowing, almost hypnotic repetition.

At the very moment the patrol car was swallowed in the distance, the dread silence at the overpass was violently ripped by a renewed assault of the pummeling, preening music. It shook him like a seizure; every last bite of his last meal hit the roadside. His vomiting stripped away his fortifications, the insulation of nerve which his food had provided. He felt his vulnerability not only stripped bare, but amplified. No matter: before he could talk himself out of it, he let rip with a silent scream—a warrior scream, abandoning all—and ran down the curving ramp until he reached the road below. Once he had negotiated the curve, there came into view what could not be seen from directly above: The Gloating Car, idling dead still below the overpass, its ugly music obscene and bellicose, bursts of light behind the fogged windows strobing in time with its frosty rhythm.

It seemed to be waiting for him.

The man steeled himself for the inevitable. With each step he took toward this inevitable, the music lashed out harder and with greater, more intimidating swagger. Initially, its rhythm was in step with his heartbeat, which had risen high into his throat and his glands; but, as he came close enough to see the crabbed silhouette hunched over its steering wheel, the muffled pounding began to accelerate, to syncopate—and to play havoc with his own heart rate, which became more and more irregular as it struggled to keep proper time.

The man—this crusader, this good neighbor—clutched at a sudden, frenzied kicking in his chest and dropped his slugger as he fell hard to his unpadded knees on the paved road. The bat rattled as it rolled downhill over the asphalt toward The Gloating Car, as if Providence had somehow conspired with the forces of Evil to disarm him. The weapon came to a halt under the vehicle's booming chassis, too far beneath the car for any arm to retrieve it.

The man was now on the road, on his hands and knees, and his vision seemed to be pulsing too, with the wicked crackle of the music, in and out of focus. He had fallen directly atop the word ONLY, stenciled on the road in gigantic white lettering, and he cringed at the obscene irony of the moment.

When the door on the driver's side finally opened, the music rose to an unimaginable volume; it was no longer music or the threat of music but a dangerous and deadly force set free. The last thing the man saw before losing consciousness was daylight cowering behind a torn curtain of sullied constellations.

Chapter Four
THE VEIL IS RENT

In the few months they had been partners, Highway Patrolmen Bud Phelps and Ronald Dyson had memorized every foot of the interstate it was their job to safeguard between the delicate hours of midnight and dawn. These roads, which they covered back and forth, were smooth and dull with low hills so evenly placed that their squad car sometimes seemed to be spinning its wheels over the rising and falling chest of someone contentedly asleep. Though quite different in temperament, the two patrolmen had settled into a comfortable relationship based in small talk about their families, their hobbies, and such. Easy-going Dyson kept things comfortable by allowing Phelps, a younger man with a bigger family and a more fragile nervous system, to do most of the talking.

On this particular night, the two men had been dealing with an intuition felt since the moment they boarded their patrol car—an electricity in the tiny hairs on their arms and at the barbered napes of their necks told them that this night would be somehow exceptional.

So far, their overnight patrol had been as uneventful as they could have hoped, yet every word the two men uttered to one another seemed to be sucked up by the night and whistled out like a tune heard outside a graveyard. Their conversation was meant to insulate them from whatever imponderable thing was coalescing around them—but instead, it backfired, their increasingly fretful chatter adding fuel to what felt like a pending inferno.

Even under typical circumstances, Officer Phelps was the sort of man who liked to hear himself talk; Officer Dyson was a good complement to his partner in that he was more experienced and more naturally stoic in character; he listened to Phelps's ramblings as he might listen to a radio, nodding to the rhythms of his companionable noise while keeping a close watch on the road ahead and the hotels, billboards, and patchy wilderness passing them by on either side.

"Know what I'd do, first thing, if all this was mine?" Phelps asked. "All these roads?"

Dyson had been down this road before. "You'd have 'em repainted."

"Damn straight. Every last one of 'em. The arrows tell you everything you need to know. They point you left, they point you right, they keep you going straight ahead. They tell you which lane to be in, if you're headed in a particular direction. People don't need to see that… *word* everywhere they go, every mile or so."

"Hm-hm."

"Here comes—excuse me, *there goes* another one, right under us," Phelps counted. He swore he could feel it move through his bowels every time their patrol car passed over a spot of road where the word ONLY had been stenciled. Even Dyson, Phelps noticed, put the pedal to the floor whenever one of these loomed out of the darkness, out of kindly consideration. But no matter how fast they drove, Phelps felt goosed just the same. The further the ONLYs fell behind their accelerating patrol car, the more ridiculous he felt.

"I don't know how you put up with me night after night," he apologized. "I don't know what it is with me."

"No sweat, partner. You keep a cool head now."

"Roger that."

He was quiet for the next mile or two.

"You ever noticed," Phelps broke in, renewing the conversation, "how the more afraid you get, the more horrible your thoughts become? Is it that way with you?"

Dyson said nothing, preferring not to encourage this train of thought.

Phelps pressed on. "I mean… sometimes when I'm lying in bed awake at night… with Becky beside me and Billy boy and little Punkin Puss in the room next door… all it takes is the sound of a bump downstairs. Just a little bump downstairs. You ever hear those? Now, I know it's probably nothing but the house settling. That's what Becky says it probably is, anyway. But then, the next thing I know, I'm imagining our front door being *ripped off its hinges* by powerful hands… powerful hands in black gloves… I see Becky getting manhandled, getting mauled before my very eyes… I see our babies getting hurt…"

"Phelps," Dyson demanded—ever the rational one—"now granted, Becky's a good-looking woman, but what on earth would The Only Criminal want to fiddle with your babies for?"

"How the hell would I know? He's a maniac, isn't he? That's where my imagination starts racing! He might… I don't know… *skin them* and make little wallets out of 'em, for all I know! See what I mean? I tell ya, my mind goes so out of whack when I think about these things, I can almost see… those little pink wallets… stuffed with all his stolen money!"

Dyson turned to look out the left-side window and rolled his eyes.

"I can see their dimpled little hides… the pocket for folding money all red and raw inside… with Punkin Puss's diaper rash…"

Thankfully, the patrol went quiet again, as their cruiser glided along the slowly brightening hemline of night. Dyson noticed that his partner tended to fall silent whenever they approached the coming incline.

"As if we weren't thinking about him already," Phelps gibbered, wiping his face, "here comes another reminder."

As they cruised below a brace of overhead exit signs, that loathsome word ONLY appeared once again, near the peak of the approaching incline, where its prominent placement made it legible from a mile distant. As one ascended the incline, the looming word ONLY urged the three lanes of traffic toward a turn-off on the left.

"As for me, my friend," Dyson put in, hoping to brighten his partner's mood, "I always look forward to this incline. And you know why? Because, once we reach the top, we've put another night behind us—'cause up there is where we get our first view of the new day. Let's go meet it, shall we?"

Onto the ramp they drove but, as they achieved the crest of the incline, the jut-jawed cast of Officer Dyson's resilient features began to darken.

For the first time in his experience, there was no hint of dawn waiting at the peak to greet them. The stretch of road beyond was black as pitch beyond the range of their headlights.

"I-I don't much like this," Officer Phelps managed to say through clenched teeth.

They continued on, more deliberately, for another mile or so, nosing along in the unrealistic dark slowly enough that they could brake—in the unlikely event that the entire road suddenly dropped out from beneath them in the next few feet.

"Guess we'd better turn on our brights," Dyson said.

Their headlights, once thus enhanced, picked up something thin and yellow stretched taut across the highway, another 20-30 feet further on.

Dyson cut the motor after a moment's deliberation. Their patrol car had come to a halt within easy view of the obstruction. It was a familiar enough artifact to any graduate of the police academy: a glossy yellow ribbon with black print covering the length of it: CRIME SCENE DO NOT CROSS CRIME SCENE DO NOT CROSS CRIME SCENE DO NOT CROSS. This was highly unusual—not the artifact, but its placement. As far as either man could see, there was nothing suspect beyond it, nothing but the usual continuation of the highway and the unusual continuation of the night.

In accordance with official procedure, they radioed in their location and inquired whether or not a crime scene was in place at that location. There was not.

"Investigating now, over."

Dyson cautiously climbed out of the patrol car, and walked gingerly to the center of the flapping ribbon, where he stood framed—from Phelps' perspective—by baleful DO NOTs.

Dyson took a folded knife from his belt, deftly opened it, and leveled its cutting edge against the yellow ribbon, which he held taut and firm with his free hand. Before going any further, Dyson cast a look back at his worried partner. It was a look that said "Here goes nothing."

He cut the ribbon.

As it fluttered from his grip in severed halves, the sunrise they had expected to see, the sunrise that failed them only moments before, became gradually apparent—not in the way Nature usually made mornings apparent, but in the way the set of a theatrical production is slowly illuminated by an offstage hand turning a dimmer knob. As light hemorrhaged into the distance of the waiting vista, the scenery in that distance assumed the grim character of an abattoir turned upside down.

Mischievous hands had rubbed themselves under the cover of night and gone to work, converting the road ahead into a horrific collage of chaos, caterwaul, and destruction. There was a rippling wall of heat, beyond which was strewn the flaming metal carrion of dozens of trashed automobiles, their blasted remains extending as far as their stunned eyes could see, spanning into the limits of forever. None of this looked quite real; everything beyond the cut ribbon seemed to flicker like a movie—a silent movie. Disoriented that such an intense flaring of light, such a vista of destruction, had been accompanied by no cannonade of sound, Dyson had the sensation of standing on the threshold of an obscene dream.

He sensed his buddy Phelps now standing close by his side, and knew that his hand would be resting on the gun holstered at his hip. There was no reason for this, he told himself. There was nothing there to subdue, nothing to shoot at—much worse had already befallen anything within their staggered purview. Both men were too awed by what they saw to move or speak. They stood transfixed—unable to reason, unable to radio for back-up, unable to take it all in.

Before they could hear anything, they *felt* something—something beating against them, an overbearing rhythm that arose to play hob with their heartbeats.

Numbly, Phelps raised his left arm, not taking the other off his gun, and pointed ahead.

Slowly emerging from the curtain of rippling heat, a long, black sedan crept in their direction, having somehow traversed all the shattered metal obstacles littering the road beyond—a horrible, sickly thudding music sounding from the gaps between the car's body and its sealed doors. Its windscreen was fogged to opacity and partially shattered by a baseball bat that still hung there in a netting of the fracture.

"Jesus God, Bud," Dyson whispered in awe. "This is it. That's gotta be him. It's really *him!*"

"Please, no," Phelps pleaded, as if the fact of the matter could change, with the offering of a little sugar on top. "It can't… It can't be *him…*"

"What more proof do you need?" Dyson barked, fed up with his partner's whining. "It's coming straight toward us…"

"Then let's go!" Phelps yelled. "Let's haul ass out of here!"

"That's not what we're here for," Dyson reasoned. "Besides… this is a One Way Street!"

The black two-eyed sedan rolled to a halt and was now idling out there in the midst of a dawning Francis Bacon painting, its sound punching outward in all directions. The car seemed to be… gloating.

Cautiously, in a synchronized action, the two officers unholstered their weapons. Phelps looked at Dyson, his partner. *Die soon*, he thought.

Dyson returned the look. *My Buddy,* he thought.

"You with me?" he asked.

Phelps swallowed hard and shook out a nod of affirmative.

"Good man," Dyson said. "Toss me the bullhorn."

Mostly without turning his back, Phelps rushed to the patrol car and grabbed the bullhorn stashed between its bucket seats. Dyson held his hands out to catch it… but Phelps surprised him with a grown-up gesture that said "I've got this."

Phelps stood shoulder-to-shoulder with Dyson as he aimed the bell of the loud-speaker at the thudding sedan.

"I don't know how he's going to hear you over all that noi—" Dyson began, just as the bullying music came to an abrupt stop, as if in direct response. All they could hear now was a roar of flame consuming a mile or more of scorched rubber, steel and Corinthian leather.

Officer Bud Phelps spoke into the mouthpiece with as much authority as he could muster.

"Y-You in the car," he began falteringly, "in the name of the State Highway Patrol, I am ordering you to step outside your vehicle with your… with your h… with your gloves above your mask! And keep 'em way up high, where we can see them!"

No response came from The Gloating Car, though its motor continued to idle as though stewing in wicked spite and hateful anger.

As the officers awaited acknowledgement—uncertain whether the next sign to come would be one of compliance or aggression—they felt themselves standing precariously on a cusp of apocalypse. The brink upon which they teetered was as profound as that separating life and death; they stood at the very edge of not knowing and knowing the cause of everything that had ever happened, of every book ever written, of every movie ever made, of how love happens between two people, of what coincidence is, of the cure for cancer, of even The Only Criminal's secret identity One way or another, the door of that car was going to open, and whoever stepped outside would bring an absolute end to all the mystery in the world. Whether they survived this encounter or not, for at least one brief moment, they would know everything there was to know.

"He's not coming out," Phelps noted.

"I guess he's not," Dyson agreed. "So we're gonna have to walk over there and pull him out."

"You think we can?"

"Seeing all this, Buddy boy, I really don't know what to think—about anything, anymore. But listen up, because I am *not* going to ask you a question, and I am *not* going to ask it only once."

Phelps understood that his partner was about to say something off-the-record. "Shoot," he said, welcoming the question.

"What if we let him go?"

"Let him go?" The counter-question was not asked in outrage, but in an almost mooting fashion.

"Think of who's probably inside that car. If you think about it, he's more than likely getting out of here, with or without our okay. Frankly, I'm not altogether sure we can handle this situation, with or without back-up."

"But if we let him go… Ronnie, if we let him go, it could be *our* houses next."

"Hey. It could be our houses next if we don't."

"You got a point there."

"Asked and answered, then?"

"Asked and answered."

"Well… So long as we have that understanding…"

With his weapon at the ready, Officer Dyson began advancing toward the idling vehicle. Phelps was just a step or two behind as they embarked on the longest, most agonizing walk of their professional lives.

They soon found themselves standing quite near the car, directly beside the door separating them from the fortress that was the driver's seat. As officer Dyson, the better marksman of the two, aimed his Glock 22 where it might do some good, Phelps cautiously approached the vehicle, reached out with his free hand and gripped the door handle. He punched the release button once with his thumb and flung the door open.

They were met by a hemorrhaging of heavy smoke that rushed out into the hellish light and fled far and wide, but mostly skyward, like the polluted detritus of an exorcism. Its leavetaking helped the setting to reacquire a quality of light that seemed more natural, a quality of light that made birds sing, alarm clocks trill, and newspapers land on front porches all across town.

The car appeared to be empty. Dyson replaced the safety on his weapon and eased it back into his holster. As the outpouring smoke continued to thin, Phelps jumped back with a curse of surprise, his weapon once again aimed with conviction.

"Watch out, Ronnie—there *is* someone in there!"

Of course they were expecting the totemic personification of terror they knew from movies and television dramas, from paperback potboilers and billboard advertisements, but slouched unconscious in the driver's seat—not far from where the Louisville slugger had lodged in the windscreen—was a strange, little man in tattered blue pajamas and black running shoes. His face was distorted in a fixed expression of unspeakable horror, his eyes cringing in their sockets as though reeling from sights never to be forgotten. His teeth were clenched almost in a death rictus but his skin was the skin of a man no more than 30—yet his hair was completely white.

Officer Dyson craned his face toward the sky, where the escaping smoke had assumed a wide-spreading yet abstract shape that seemed almost joyous in victory.

"We've heard about 'em," he said. "Now we're part of one."

Phelps was awed. "A White Level emergency! I'll call it in."

"You do that," Dyson confirmed, grimly surveying the area. "Then call the church builders. They're going to want to put a cathedral here."

Chapter Five
I'M GONNA WALK DEM GOLDEN STAIRS

There were times—in the corridors at Billowing Pines between consultations, in the cafeteria, on the bus going home, or in his bed before returning to the book he was currently reading, *The Mystery of The Gloating Car*—when Paul Vaguely found himself in a recurring daydream that posited him outside the Gates of Paradise.

"And now, Paul, we shall try again," the sentry announced patiently. "As you know, there is only one question you must answer before crossing this threshold to your everlasting reward. Don't look so grim," he smiled, "it's an easy one. Almost everybody gets it right."

"I'm ready," Vaguely said, humbly and with reverence.

"The world you are now leaving, Paul... Was it *Heaven, or was it Hell?*"

There were times when Vaguely's mind pirouetted along such imaginary lines in the afterglow of a promising theory, a patient's recovery, or a passing smile from a stranger on the bus. At such times such as these, Vaguely would assuredly reply, "Heaven."

At this, the Sentry's face would darken and Vaguely would be shown once again all the horrors he had witnessed in his lifetime, either at first hand or on the evening news: human beings dead in the streets, fireballs born of arson, the cries of bereaved children, broken shopfront windows, scenes of gross insensitivity, betrayal, crushing disappointments, ruined lives. Once his senses had been assailed with every possible hatchling of Hell, he was thrown back—like a chewed bone—into Life. At such moments, he knew why babies so often cry throughout much of their early lives; they were the old souls, the ones sent back, like him, to seek a better answer to the Sentry's question.

There were also times when Vaguely blundered into this daydream while feeling depressed, unloved, or particularly sensitive to The Only

Criminal's reign of terror. At these times, it was his own face that darkened outside the Gates of Paradise, as he answered the Sentry's question with one syllable less: "Hell."

At this, the Sentry would gasp with deep offense and wave his arm in a sweeping gesture, conjuring up yawning, abyssal hives, maelstroms and chasms. As a final punishment of his senses before the coming blow was dealt to his eternal soul, Vaguely's senses were flooded by a total, stunning comprehension of the full breadth and beauty of Mankind's achievements: Michelangelo's masterpiece on the ceiling of the Sistine Chapel was reproduced stroke for stroke inside the dome of his skull; his ears were filled to brimming with glorious oratoria; his taste buds were overwhelmed with the most delicious food and drink he had ever (and never) tasted; the vast reserves of world literature flooded his mind in all their craft and complexity; and, in the senses which science had yet to define, he seemed to comprehend at once all the distance that scrabbling humanity had yet to cover before touching its collective finger to that of God. As each of these outside accomplishments elevated his spirit, he once again experienced, in all their richness, the hugest emotions he had known in his life: love, awe, empathy… but, each time he rode these rainbows, there was one detail he could not help. The most overwhelming color in the spectrum of his emotions was yellow—the color of fear.

With the return of morning, this daydream came to Vaguely again as he lingered in bed; it went one way or the other. His alarm clock soon reminded him that it was time to get up. He put his paperback in a safe place, then got his coffee going before stepping into the shower. Afterwards, he shaved the animal stubble that sprouted on his face overnight, powdered his mown features, and threw on something from his wardrobe. Everything in his clothes closet was either an off-black or gray to save him the bother of choosing. He drank his coffee and nibbled at toast while selecting a tie—the only splash of color he permitted himself and, if truth be told, they coincided chromatically with the thumbtacks on his crime-tracking maps.

He began knotting his tie while skipping down the stairs, after carefully locking his apartment door behind him. Two turns of the bannister later, he stopped at the second floor mirror to give his outward appearance a passing or failing grade—and found the door of the unoccupied Apartment 4 *wide open.*

Alarmed, Vaguely tentatively approached its threshold. He listened closely and heard the distinct clip-clop of footwear echoing through the empty rooms.

"Is someone there?" he called inside.

A moment or two later, a face new to his experience tipped into view. It belonged to a young woman. She was dark-browed, brown-eyed, with shoulder-length ash-blonde hair that seemed to darken near the roots to something closer to the chocolate brown of her eyes and brows. *A disguise?* thought he. She wore no makeup and was in no particular need of it. Her expression was amused yet privately so, as if a secret party was in progress inside her. Her clothing was crisp and smart but neutral; it made no particular statement and did nothing to accentuate her figure. Toward Vaguely, she showed the most remarkable totality of indifference.

Now, now. Nothing untoward should be read into Vaguely's accumulation of these superficial details. He was merely committing them to memory in the event he should later be called upon, by the authorities, to describe this beguiling trespasser. It was something he had taught himself to do whenever he found anyone in unexpected places and situations—that is, near him.

"Ah—we have company," she said—but not to him.

Her voice was run through his inner processor. There was humor in it, or at least irony, amused and dizzy and somewhat nasal, as if she had not quite seen the last of a lingering head cold. Her words had referred directly to him, Vaguely noticed—concerned him, yet something in the tone of her voice seemed to go past him—indeed, to take the scenic view around him.

Then, to his surprise, the sound of heavy shoes on a bare wooden floor was prelude to the appearance of Red Grinter. "Aw, we didn't wake you, did we, Doc?" As he formed this question, Vaguely heard Ringo's untrimmed nails clicking across the floors inside the apartment, as well.

"Not at all," Vaguely assured him. "I'm on early call this morning."

"Doc Vaguely here lives upstairs," Red explained to the young woman, who had smiled as if to say "I see" and drifted whimsically into another room, out of sight.

"Hmm," Vaguely then heard her say, possibly in response to Red, but just as possibly to suggest that the place needed repainting.

"Miss White here is interested in the apartment. She asked if I could give 'er the Early Bird Tour. She keeps screwy hours like you. Like me too, you know—Ringo and me are up all hours, watchin' old movies on

TV. Hey, there was one on last night, Doc. Didja ever see that guy Montgomery Clift in *Miss Onlyhearts*?"

"I'm afraid not," Vaguely said, glancing at his wristwatch. "Was it good?"

"It's okay," he estimated. "Monty Clift, he plays this journalist hired by Robert Ryan to work for his newspaper, but he sticks him with writin' advice to the lovelorn. He starts sending out this awful advice to all these lovesick people—and all Hell breaks loose. Turns out he's The Only Criminal!"

"Up to no good again, I see."

"You know it!" Grinter laughed.

From the outer margins of their conversation, the woman who called herself Miss White came back into the room, walking slowly heel-to-toe, heel-to-toe in her black flats, seemingly lost in envisioning its possibilities. She would pause, rest her weight (Vaguely estimated roughly 118 pounds) on one leg, leaving the other bent slightly at the knee, and tilt her head so the ashen curtain of her hair shifted, shook and stilled. These actions seemed to his innately suspicious mind carefully choreographed and strategic.

"I'm sorry, Mr. Grinter," Vaguely said, moving toward the stairwell, "but I really should be on my way…"

"His tie is crooked," Miss White mentioned to her prospective landlord, half over her shoulder, again without looking in Vaguely's direction. She made a small move to touch her lips as the words escaped her, but—having already voiced the utterance she hoped to cut off—cut her gesture short instead. Then, pretending to have noticed something interesting in an adjoining room, she strode purposefully out of sight.

Vaguely coughed a pleasant morning to his landlord as he began his jaunty gallop down the stairs. Looking up through the rectangular tunnel formed by the banisters circling behind and above him as he descended, he saw Ringo's bright black eyes looking down at him, his terrier head tarrying there in friendly, open, canine curiosity.

It was the first morning of autumn but the season's first sunrise had not quite shone as yet on Oakley Way. It was dawning, but Vaguely could see the dark still clinging to parked cars and to the storefronts of his sleeping neighbors' businesses. There was coolth in the air, enough that Vaguely made a mental note to bring his topcoat out of storage for tomorrow. There were early mornings when Whimsy Plunkett was up and about, singing a song to help ring in the day, but this was not one of them. The streets of Amelia were empty and seemed almost apocalyptically so without the added animation of its town troubadour.

His tie is crooked, his tie is crooked...

These incantatory words, cycling through Vaguely's head, segued into the sound of a rattling delivery truck rounding the corner of Woonsocket onto Oakley Way. It paused outside Lawson's News long enough for a boy in the back of the vehicle to drop several bundles of newspapers onto the pavement, before it puttered away. Abel Lawson emerged from his store and, seeing Vaguely across the street, waved a hearty hello before hoisting these deliveries inside his shop.

"I think you just missed your bus, Doc!" he shouted over, helpfully, before returning inside.

If this was so, it would be another 20 minutes before the next #27 passed through and Vaguely didn't want to spend them standing in this chill. The street was unusually void of any further vehicles in transit, but—law-abiding citizen that he was—Vaguely made his way to the nearest crosswalk before traversing the street and seeking temporary shelter in Lawson's News.

He found Lawson half-kneeling " on the floor, cutting the twine that bound a stack of newspapers. "You have the distinction of being my very first customer of the new season."

Vaguely smiled quaintly at the thought. Almost as quickly, his expression turned urgent: "Mr. Lawson, I was wondering if there had been any further word about that paper boy who went missing."

"My competition?" Abel chuckled. "The kid's alright. He showed up not long after you were in here last night, walking his bike. His front tire was shot."

"You mean to say, a gun was actually *fired* on him?"

"No no no—when I say it was 'shot,' I mean it was—oh, what's the word?—punctured, that's all."

"That's a relief," Vaguely sighed. He perused the spanning headlines of a fanning display of morning newspapers. The sideways smear of their headlines read THE ONLY CRIMINAL, THE ONLY CRIMINAL, THE ONLY CRIMINAL. He selected the morning edition of the international *Times* and handed over the correct change, wishing his news merchant a good day.

Back on the sidewalk, he wished for a taxi and—just as the bells of

St. Tim's tolled the hour—a lone Yellow taxi happened by. The driver braked, eager for custom. She leaned over and spoke to Vaguely through the front passenger window.

"Need a cab?"

Vaguely rested his hand on the yellow door, with its logo of the cowering person. "I suppose I do."

The driver peered at him suspiciously. "You're not The Only Criminal, are you?"

Vaguely smiled, raising his arms like a man under arrest. "Innocent of all charges."

"Hop in," she said, reaching around to unlock the rear door nearest the curb. "Mind you, *my* charges are gonna stick!"

"Fair enough."

Once the taxi was in motion, the driver spun the arm of her meter, launching its tally of Vaguely's fare, mile by mile. The rate was exceedingly fair, though not generous.

"The streets have been so empty," the driver said, making conversation. "I can't tell you how glad I am to see another living soul."

"Slow night?"

"I'll say," she confirmed. "First, where are we headed?"

"Billowing Pines."

"You mean that big place out near the fruitcake factory?"

"Yes. An unfortunate coincidence."

"Gotcha," the driver said, before making a report of their destination. "I mean," she resumed a couple of blocks further on, "Slow nights are okay sometimes, but this was ridiculous. I was on call down at the airport. That's a pretty cushy shift, most of the time. All you have to do is sit there at Arrivals and read a book or something till the cab in line ahead of you snags a fare. Then you move up a space."

Vaguely leaned forward, the better to hear what she was saying, and spied a library book on the front seat beside her—riding shotgun, as it were. Marquez, *One Hundred Years of Solitary*. Good book, a novel interweaving various stories supposedly conceived by The Only Criminal during an imaginary incarceration. He'd read it in college.

"It beats driving around all night and wasting gas," his chauffeur rambled on. "I don't like wasting gas, even if it is cheap!"

Vaguely eased back into his seat and unfolded his copy of the *Times*.

"But it was so weird," she continued. "There was *zero* activity last night. It was like something important was happening, something so important that the thought of anything else happening at the same time was… unthinkable. I didn't even hear any sirens."

"I like the sound of sirens," Vaguely said. "I find them strangely reassuring."

The driver began to sing, softly and sweetly:

> *"An accomplice is a friend*
> *Who keeps their mouth shut to the end...*

Vaguely, in a good mood now, couldn't resist joining in.

> *And won't complain about the night-creeping*
> *That I must do while they are fast sleeping*
> *Unlike stool pigeons*
> *Whose betrayals and warm bloodstains*
> *Will remain*
> *To trip the sounds of sirens..."*

The two of them sighed with nostalgia for the era when this greatest hit of The Only Criminal was always on the radio.

Vaguely noticed with appreciation that his friendly driver was taking the quickest, most direct route to Billowing Pines. Not every cabbie did—not because they were out to bilk him of a bigger fare, *of course*, but because some drivers simply weren't as well-acquainted with the city of Amelia as they might be. They drove past a Chiquita billboard that was new to him, reminding people to eat their bananas before they went bad, and Vaguely spent the rest of the trip in his morning paper, signaling his submergence into data to the driver with a crisp snap of the folded newsprint.

Dr. Paul Vaguely's mornings were generally spent interviewing survivors of close encounters with The Only Criminal. Some of these, the better adjusted ones, were out-patients; others, who subsequently could no longer function in vulnerable society, were residents at Billowing Pines; and there were still others needing to be interviewed because they had applied for residency.

His first session of the day was with a 33-year-old male with the unfortunate name of Jay Walker. While still in grade school, Master Walker discovered that the best way to deflect jokes about his name was to wear it proudly on the back of an athlete's uniform. Yes, in primary school, secondary school and college, he distinguished himself in athletic competition, winning awards in football, tag-team wrestling, and assorted track and field competitions. The star quarterback of his college football team, he married the Homecoming Queen and, after graduating from college, he found employment with his father-in-law, a man who took to calling him "Son."

How did this champion among men come to be coiled on the sofa in Vaguely's office like a 230-pound fetus?

Walker's early life story was a veritable page torn from the national scrapbook, but it took a severe tumble onto the national scrapheap in the wake of his close encounter with The Only Criminal. He was now separated from his wife of thirteen years, and his father-in-law had turned his back on him, firing him from the vice-presidency of their shared business empire. He was presently collecting unemployment because no one else seemed willing to hire him, and he was seeking to shut himself away from the rest of the world at Billowing Pines.

The curtains were drawn against the morning light. A low wattage bulb burned softly under the green shade of a floor lamp, its light falling with the correct intensity to illuminate the notepad at rest on Vaguely's crossed legs and the face of the reclining patient more softly still. It gave the room a tone of intimacy and encouraged patients to open up.

"Your hair is still a healthy shade of brown, so I take it this was not a Category 3, or White Level, encounter?" Vaguely inquired.

"That's correct, Doctor. But it *was* him. It was him, without question!"

"Tell me about your encounter, then. When you're ready."

"Well," began the patient, once he had marshaled his emotions, "like a lot of couples, my wife and I—Jennie's her name—we divided our household chores, according to what we were best suited to doing, or what we didn't mind doing. She didn't mind doing the dishes or the grocery shopping, and I didn't mind balancing the checkbook or painting the house once every five years. We both did our own wash. We took equal responsibility for making things work."

Vaguely nodded.

"Anyway, like the song says," Walker continued, "*The purpose of a man / is to take out the garbage / And the purpose of a woman / Is to tell the man.* It was garbage night, and I was going around the house, emptying the little trash cans in various rooms into large garbage bags, when my wife called out and told me to please remember to take out the recycling bin. Well, I'd forgotten to do this the week before, so our recyclables had accumulated and the bin was full. It was a bit of a balancing act, getting it out to the curb, and it was a windy night too, but I got everything out there and then came back inside, satisfied by a job well done."

Vaguely noted on his pad, *satisfied by job well done.*

"Anyway," Walker continued, "we usually turned in at our house around 10:00, and I can remember lying in bed. Jennie said, 'Isn't it nice to hear the wind and know that we're inside our house, safe and secure?' And I agreed that it was. And, I swear to God, as soon as I said that, the two of us heard our recycling bin overturned! I got out of bed and went over to the window to look outside. Our bin was out in the middle of the street, on its side—like it had been kicked out there! I saw a plastic milk carton bowling down the street. There were beer and soda bottles tinkling away into the night. Now, I'm no litterbug, Doc…"

"Of course not!"

"The mess was not my fault; however, it was my responsibility."

"Quite right."

"So I threw on my robe and my slippers and went outside. I don't mind telling you, Doctor… the wind was blowing out there something crazy! I had to run down the street to catch the milk carton and some soup cans. When I got the milk carton, I took off its cap, flattened the container under my foot, stomping all the air out of it, and then replaced the cap, decreasing its mass so that it wouldn't roll away so easily a second time. *You* know."

"Good idea," Vaguely noted.

"I also picked up the few bottles I could find. I took them all back to our bin, which I made sure was properly anchored on the ground this time. Then I went back inside, locked the door, took off my robe and crawled back into bed. Anyway… we were drifting off to sleep, Jennie and me, when suddenly—BAM! We heard the bin overturned again! Now that could only mean one thing, you know… Naturally, I was a little afraid to look, but I went over to the window and looked out and there it was, the bin, out in the middle of the street again, on its side, everything that used to be inside rolling down the hill again, or just scattered all around. I don't mind telling you, Doc, I was pretty scared. There was only one person I knew of, who'd go around knocking over people's recycling bins. From the looks of things, he had chosen that night to go up and down our street, knocking everyone's recycling bins over. And some garbage cans, too! It wasn't just my trash tumbling and scraping and rattling down the middle of the road—*it was everybody's!* I wasn't going back out there—not on your life!—but, from my window, I could see empty cans of soda I didn't drink, empty cat food cans… We didn't have a cat! I'm standing there at the window, and Jennie starts nagging, saying, 'I thought you fixed it so it wouldn't tip over,' and I'm saying, 'But, honey, I did!' She's saying, 'Well, go on out there and pick it up,' and I'm saying, 'Y*ou* go pick it up!"

"These things happen in married life," Vaguely offered.

"I wasn't about to go back out there!' And she starts chiding me, saying, 'Mr. All-American's afraid of the dark!' I don't mind telling you, Doc, she was starting to… well, she was makin' me pretty mad. If I was afraid of the dark, I wouldn't have gone outside to pick up all the trash that first time, would I? I said, 'Look, once is an accident, but twice… well, twice is different, that's all!"

Jay Walker sulked as though he had his doubts. "I keep asking myself why, over and over. Why did this have to happen… to me? And I keep coming back to one explanation."

"Which is?"

"It happened to me because of my name," Jay Walker said. "The name my parents gave me. Now I'm as innocent as the pure, driven snow—I don't have to tell you that, I don't have to tell anybody that—but my name describes a crime. A misdemeanor, okay—but it's still a crime! And the crime committed against me, too, was a misdemeanor. The way I figure it, The Only Criminal likes being The Only Criminal, but he doesn't like the idea of sharing the stage with pretenders… even if it's in name only!"

"In name… Only," Vaguely nodded sagely, jotting these words on his pad. "You're separated now, as I understand it. You and, uh, Jennie, I mean."

"Yes."

"No children?"

"No."

"By choice, I mean… Not due to a… not due to an abduction or…?"

"That's correct."

"Good, good. And where are you living now?"

"I'm sleeping on the couch at my sister's place, but you know how it is, her husband wants me out of there. They have a nice place, sturdy. Made of bricks…"

It was a typical session in many ways. Shortly after it ended, Vaguely was summoned to the office of his mentor Dr. Constantin Pons, who briefed him on a White Level incident that had taken place overnight on one the town's interstate highways.

A great deal of destruction was reported, as well as much loss of life, but most importantly, a comatose man—described by the attending officers as a white male, early 30's, with white hair—had been discovered inside a somehow menacing vehicle. This man was now en route to Billowing Pines via Medicopter and his arrival was imminent. Vaguely and Pons passed the time by tuning into WTOC, which was broadcasting camcorder footage of the highway, taken that morning, which looked like a warzone. Vaguely could hardly believe what he was seeing.

When the Medicopter touched down at the Billowing Pines heliport coordinates later that hour, Vaguely and Pons were both there to meet it. Vaguely briefly questioned the medics, who had been present at the crime scene, and then proceeded to examine the patient, whom he determined to be in critical condition. The blue pajamas he wore were torn, the breast pocket appearing to have been ripped away.

Billowing Pines' residing criminologist would have attached himself permanently to such a patient in any case, but his sense of involvement was soon made sacrosanct when one of the attending medics deposited a fistful of crumpled blue fabric in his open hand.

"Doctor," he was told, "this was given to me by one of the patrolmen, found at the crime scene."

It was the patient's missing pajama pocket. It happened to be monogrammed.

Paul Vaguely could not believe his eyes.

The initials it bore were PV.

Chapter Six
YOU'LL NEVER WALK ALONE

Though you might think the odds were against it, what Paul Vaguely's grandmother had once told him was absolutely true: Since the beginning of recorded time, no one had ever seen The Only Criminal head on and lived to tell the tale.

It had always been his *modus operandi* to leave no witnesses. The likeness of The Only Criminal, as it was typically portrayed, was more symbolic than actual; it could not have been based on anyone's first-hand description. The mythic figure seen on billboards, in storybooks and motion pictures was not far afield of the inkblots which Vaguely sometimes showed to patients to gauge their states of mind, except that it wore a cloak, a slouch hat, and had spidery fingers encased in black gloves.

It only follows that the accounts reported by the daily media were never based on eyewitness accounts, but on details submitted by the authorities assigned to those crime scenes, by people who had known the victims personally, or by rubberneckers who took pleasure in seeing their names printed in the newspaper. (No law against that.) As we have seen, even those patients claiming an encounter with The Only Criminal were never directly exposed to his presence but rather profoundly disturbed by an oblique glimpse of his figure or, still more commonly, the aura of his nearness. Those unfortunate souls who actually made The Only Criminal's corporeal acquaintance, if not murdered on the spot or derailed by shock-induced coronaries, became weak of pulse and receded quickly from the horror of life, their hair fried white.

Thus, the recovery of a demonstrably exposed but otherwise sound survivor from a crime scene was an occasion of unprecedented import. The discovery of Peevey (as Dr. Paul Vaguely temporarily dubbed him, after the monogram inscribed on his pajama pocket) was something new and unique to human history. He was not conscious, but—for as long as he clung to life—there existed a possibility that he might resume consciousness, share his story, and bring about a New Age of Enlightenment.

For this reason, Peevey immediately shot to the top of Vaguely's short list of the most important things in life. Upon his admission, the comatose patient was installed on the penthouse floor of the sanatorium in a private room with barred windows, two posted guards, and restricted access. The watchful Dr. Vaguely never left his side.

The sight of Peevey, lying unconscious on his hospital bed, with his smooth complexion and prematurely white hair, caused the criminologist to remember a story told to him by his grandfather, about something he had witnessed as a young man. The newspapers at that time had been full of the story of how The Only Criminal had somehow managed to steal the complete financial records of the 50 wealthiest people in the world. Of course, this was long before the miniaturization and compression of such data that people enjoy today, so his theft amounted to the contents of 50 full-sized filing cabinets! At the time of this audacious robbery, Vaguely's grandfather was a boy of seven, working as a bagger at his father's produce stand.

One day, while on the job, he (the father) happened to notice an elephant across the street, outside the city bank, where the animal was being tended by a man wearing a cap and plaid pants with suspenders. The pants were actually so loud, they were almost enough to distract you from looking at the elephant, never mind the man's face, young Master Vaguely was told. Anyway, his back was turned to the seven-year-old grandfather as he (the loudly trousered man) patted the immense, well-mannered creature; most elephants you can smell from a mile away, his grandfather assured him, but this one was better mannered than that. The elephant stood in the entrance of an alleyway, next to an advertisement for the Whipperwham Bros. Circus, so while its presence there on the street was unusual, it was not what you would call implausible. As the animal's keeper went through the motions of feeding it peanuts and such, a couple of policemen came poking around in their old-fashioned uniforms, looking for the only thing they might be looking for. They paused to admire the elephant, and then continued on down the street. As soon as they left—to the boy's astonishment—he saw the animal keeper reach up and pull off the elephant's skin like a huge tarpaulin, revealing the back end of a large flatbed truck carrying a large number of filing cabinets! Before he could get a better look at the fellow, the truck's exhaust kicked up, the loaded truck trundled down the alley and he was gone!

Vaguely was brazen enough at that age to question how the truck could have been loaded as The Only Criminal was feeding his elephant peanuts, and he once even broached the topic of how he had managed to feed peanuts to what was in fact a truck, but he never really doubted the story for a moment because his grandfather's hair had always been as white as the pure-driven snow.

Hovering at the patient's bedside, Vaguely spent untold hours shouting questions into the deep well of Peevey's subconscious, from which not even echoes returned. He took careful note of the hourly changes of each detail of the mystery man's terror-stricken face and, when the nurses on the floor came along to bathe or otherwise administer to the patient, they began to wonder if they shouldn't perhaps also perform these duties for the attending doctor. Peevey's hands were badly burned and Vaguely stood closely by as his dressings were changed, so eager was he to examine the creases of his ravaged hands, the better to pinpoint the exact spot where his lifeline was blindsided by a gash of random violence.

Despite his lack of consciousness, as Dr. Vaguely observed, the physical attitudes of Peevey's body did intensify under direct questioning. He interpreted this phenomenon as a likelihood that Peevey could hear what was being said to him, but was incapable of response, having been literally scared stiff. Therefore, the most sensible course of action was to put the patient at ease, which Vaguely sought to do with soothing monologues.

"Hello there, Peevey," he said gently, hoping to establish contact with the patient's mind by penetrating the sustained and silent scream at its core. "I am Dr. Paul Vaguely—yes, we share the same initials, you and I!—and you are my patient at Billowing Pines. Doesn't that sound restful? *Billowing Pines.* You will be pleased to know that you are quite safe here. Your room is a fortress—walled with reinforced stone, three feet thick. It is also high off the ground, on our penthouse floor, and it has only two windows…"

Vaguely stopped abruptly, seeing Peevey tense up visibly when the word "only" was uttered. He needed to be more cautious.

"Your room has two windows," he corrected himself, "both of them barred with steel rods much too fat for anyone to get their hand around. I hope this is reassuring to you. Now… you must listen to me, Peevey—I'm sorry, but we don't know what else to call you. Listen closely now, and heed what I say. I want to bring you around, Peevey, so that you may talk to us. We have so much getting acquainted to do! I'm not sure what I can do to facilitate matters, so I'm going to roll the dice and tell you what I think. As I said, Peevey, you are in no danger here, but I believe you are in the very greatest of danger *there*—in that comatose retreat where you now find yourself. Do you understand? You must escape from that faraway place and join us here, in this safer haven. We're all waiting for you—and by 'we' I mean me, Dr. Pons, Nurse Mallet and that pretty Nurse Carver. You'll like her. So float, Peevey. Float in the direction of my voice. Rest easy, for my voice shall not again speak the word you abhor. It *cannot* speak the word you abhor. That word is spoken o… *solely* in the void you presently inhabit, nowhere else is that awful word spoken. No one else can extend to you this promise. Only I—*oh, damn, damn, DAMN!*"

Vaguely then fell into a silence of self-reproach and, after a time, started over from scratch: "Hello there, Peevey…"

What kept our hero so determined, so vigilant, so attentive, to the point of rescheduling his other patients, was the very real possibility—real for as long as Peevey continued to breathe—that he might someday learn from his flaking, rehydrating lips why—of all continents, of all cities, of all people, of all names, of all initials—The Only Criminal had looked this particular specimen in the face, turned his hair white, and left him behind *alive*. Had the time come for The Only Criminal to finally share his story, through this representative?

There was also one more possibility that had not escaped Vaguely's expert consideration, and he worried over that possibility as he worried the swatch of midnight blue monogrammed fabric that almost never left his own hand. Was it possible, he tingled, that this poor wretch had been the victim of mistaken identity—that The Only Criminal had been deceived by that monogram and had mistaken Peevey for another "PV" he had hoped would tell his tale… perhaps, *Dr. Paul Vaguely?*

Vaguely's excited mind ran riot with such suppositions, but in the course of his watchful time, he narrowed them down to a few favored theories: 1) that Peevey had been *allowed* to survive his encounter with The Only Criminal; 2) that The Only Criminal was aware that his survival would result in his relocation to Billowing Pines; and 3) that the monogrammed pocket had been *deliberately* torn from Peevey's pajamas and left at the scene of the crime, so that it would later be brought to the attention of Dr. Paul Vaguely, who would not fail to recognize it as an ice-cold tap upon his shoulder. After all, if *you* were The Only Criminal, wouldn't *you* know the name of The Only Criminologist?

And do not mistake Vaguely's acknowledgement of his professional singularity as a badge of sinful pride. Within the first 24 hours of Peevey's admission to Billowing Pines, the international newspapers had seen to it that Dr. Paul Vaguely went overnight from being someone known only to the la-di-da's of academia to some shade of international celebrity. As he prepared to leave work at the end of his initial three-day watch—after which, Dr. Pons had ordered him home for a shower, a full night's sleep and a change of clothes—he was besieged by, and had to push his way through, a gauntlet of reporters sent to Billowing Pines from outposts all over the planet. These journalists, perhaps as many as a hundred, gathered outside the facility's gates, making it increasingly difficult for Vaguely to reach his bus. There was an almost palpable hunger in the air among them, an excited sense that something—anything—might soon happen, some earth-shattered turn of events that could make them celebrities too.

"Dr. Vaguely! Over here!"

Almost all of the visages in this sea of faces were unknown to Vaguely, and when he narrowed their number down to the one familiar voice calling out to him through a rhubarb of unfamiliar voices, he almost didn't recognize the face attached to it. But, my God—there, to his amazement, was the nigh-sacred face of Lorraine Cadbury—the smart, pert anchorwoman of his favorite newscast, pushing forward through the crowd with her WTOC microphone and cameraman in an attempt to gain Vaguely's attention and exchange a few words with him. In this moment, the situation rocketed past the merely non-routine into the surreal.

You don't understand: Vaguely had been watching Lorraine Cadbury on television since his college days, when she was doing second-string reports of ballot-box stuffings and dog-nappings on WTOC-TV. He had witnessed her rise to a co-anchor seat on the nightly news and had gone so far as to pop the cork of a bottle of Veuve Clicquot on the evening that *The Cadbury Report* debuted. And now he knew the divine delectation of hearing her voice shout his own name over the heads of her competitors, competitors from other cities, indeed other nations, whose sheer mass forced their mutually reaching hands apart—carrying him half-aloft, right onto the very bus he needed to board.

That same evening, Vaguely knew the ineffable pleasure of hearing Lorraine Cadbury say his name on national television and offer a flattering but honest description of his current work as WTOC-TV televised the most implausible footage of their near-miss meeting.

Vaguely would have been twitterpated by the whole serendipity of this encounter with his TV heroine had his brain not already been so reduced to flutter-butter by the mystic serendipities proposed by the Peevey case itself. He was fascinated by his sudden participation on *The Cadbury Report* as a recurring character, as, of course, he became in the daily papers in all their variety. The front pages of newspapers from here to Hawaii to Haiti to Howchamagowcha—the headlines, anyway—were all about Billowing Pines, its enigmatic new patient, and the brilliant young doctor entrusted with his treatment. The balance of the evening papers consisted of the usual Only Criminal stories but, for the first time in his life, Vaguely began to feel less concerned with them.

Why bother with all that other rigmarole, he thought, *when Peevey will snap out of it one of these days and tell me everything?*

That night, Vaguely—so grateful for a shower, he used it twice—lay in bed, wearing a pair of new monogrammed pajamas and waiting for sleep to come, but was kept wide awake by thoughts of Peevey:

What things might he know?

What sights had he seen?

What kind of night, prior to that dawn, had he endured?

What tests had he survived?

Vaguely tossed and turned while tossing and turning the possibilities of his recovery over in his mind: *Would Peevey emerge from his catatonia a garrulous sort, eager to unburden his mind of its horrors? Or would he find it impossible to share the unimaginable, brain-blasting data stored within him, necessitating that the two of them embark on weeks, months, or possibly years of therapy together, during which time they would together painstakingly forge the key to turn his psychic lock?*

And there was also this possibility, however remote, that most thrilled him: *What if the mysterious man in his care was not a victim of The Only Criminal after all, but...* No. He daren't yet even begin to frame the possibility in language.

In time, in deepest slumber, Vaguely found himself once again climbing those golden stairs to the pearly gates. This time, however, the Gatekeeper did not ask him whether the world he had just left was Heaven or Hell, but rather stepped aside to let him enter, unquizzed and unchallenged.

As he crossed the threshold of this fantasy for the first time in his experience, Vaguely was greeted inside by someone else, someone familiar but to whose face he could not put a name, a little old man who embraced him and filled his being with the very honey of fulfillment.

As they disengaged, while still feeling very much a part of one another, the stranger asked him, "Paul, are you ready to know your Maker? Are you ready to look upon the face of God?"

He said that he was, and was led to yet another door, another level in this fabulous maze of Beyond. He passed through the door into darkness, his face cast down—too afraid, too humbled to look up. He felt himself increasingly in the presence of something indescribably enormous. He fell to his hands and knees before it and knew at once that he was not ready to meet his Maker and certainly not ready to look upon the face of God. The indescribably vast Energy before him demanded to be looked upon, to be admired, to be experienced. In Its stubborn insistence, It made a low, loud, impossible noise.

Vaguely awoke in a cold sweat. At once alert and on guard, he heard it again!

The silence of his night-dark room was being disrupted by the gargantuan groans of enormous and heavy things being moved from one place to another—apparently in the uninhabited apartment directly beneath him. What was going on down there? Might The Only Criminal himself be intent on disturbing his much-needed sleep by building a secret compartment in one of the walls? It didn't seem likely, as The Only Criminal seemed to have tabs on everybody anyway, looking down on them from those two moons in the sky. Then something else clicked, and he thought it might be one or more reporters camping out down there to better monitor his actions. To be famous is a terrible thing, a thing meant for criminals!

The telephone on his bedside table rang. He reached over and took the receiver from its cradle, pressed it to his ear and listened.

"H-Hello?" Vaguely managed.

"Hey, Doc—Red Grinter here. Sorry for callin' so early, but I figgered under the circumstances you'd be up. Just wanted to tell ya, if ya hear some bangin' around downstairs in Apartment 4—not to worry. Your new neighbor's movin' in, is all. Like I told ya, she keeps funny hours. Like you."

So Miss White had taken the apartment.

"Thank you, Mr. Grinter," Vaguely groaned, hanging up. Curiously, as soon as he got off the phone, all the grievous noise aggressing upwards from downstairs came to a complete stop.

He bleared at the alarm clock. It was still two hours before he was due back at Billowing Pines, but *morning was near!* The sun was about to rise again on a world in which Peevey existed! And it was another news day in which Vaguely himself, with his proximity to the embodiment of life's most abiding questions, would be prominently featured! Vaguely couldn't wait to get back to work—and why should he?

Thirty minutes later, he came bounding down the stairs of his complex with something like happiness, until he turned the bend onto the second floor. There he saw Miss White—her dark-browed, brown eyes glancing up to meet his own. She was kneeling close to the floor in a white terrycloth bathrobe, worn over something black and personal, covetously reaching for the morning paper on her doorstep as though it might be a dropped murder weapon.

Vaguely didn't dare to consider himself in the second floor mirror; instead, he adjusted the knot of his necktie without reflection as he rushed past his new neighbor, continuing on his way.

Chapter Seven
WE'RE FEEDING ON THE LIVING BREAD

"How is our patient doing today?" asked Dr. Vaguely, as he entered the heavily guarded room on Billowing Pines' penthouse level.

"Much the same, Doctor," answered Nurse Mallet, as no other answer would be forthcoming.

"May I bring you some tea—or coffee, Dr. Vaguely?" asked Nurse Hobble, a recent addition to the staff.

"Coffee, please. And keep it coming."

Before the helpful Nurse Hobble could fulfill his request, she happened to pass the work station of the sanatorium's security chief Jim Westerfield, who checked his records and ascertained there was no Nurse Hobble on staff. His technological resources quickly identified the imposter as one Imogen Risk, an up-and-coming British reporter with the leading London newspaper. Though there was nothing unlawful in her behavior, she was then gently apprehended, frisked by a female security worker and relieved of the pocket camera in her cap and the tape recorder in her bra, then escorted from the premises. Nevertheless, even without proper documentation to stand in support of her account, without so much as Peevey's nickname to inform it, Ms. Risk's recounting of her Billowing Pines experience was serialized over a week's worth of papers—illustrated with drawings—and netted her a publishing contract in the neighborhood of £50,000. Her autobiography, entitled *Coffee, Please—And Keep It Coming*, was announced for the following spring.

Day after day after day, nothing changed in that off-limits room other than Peevey's diapers. Vaguely continued to spend nearly every waking hour at his patient's bedside. There was no sign that Peevey was even one step closer to a state of consciousness, much less confession. After another full week of nothing worth our time had passed in this stalemate, Vaguely was ordered by Constantin Pons to resume his therapy sessions with his other patients. For Vaguely, this was like being told to step out of the twilight at the edge of the spotlight.

Vaguely's regular patients held little luster in comparison to Peevey. Take, for example, Elliot Rath, a business executive in his 50's who believed that The Only Criminal had deliberately targeted him for public embarrassment. There was a time, shortly before he first darkened the doorway at Billowing Pines, when he was almost daily reminded of this dreadful possibility. To wit, whenever he was advised that a business-related gathering would be casual, it turned out to be black tie; likewise, those events announced as black tie turned out to be casual. If he happened to book a lunch with the competitor of one of his clients, he would find his client waiting for him, tapping a finger on the tablecloth. Once or twice, he had arrived at informal cocktail parties only to find himself surrounded by Bo Peeps and D'Artagnans at a masquerade ball.

"I must have crossed The Only Criminal at some time or other, without realizing it," Wrath supposed, while wringing his hands. "He's been riding me like a jackass ever since!"

Then there was Julie Wardh, a female suburbanite in her 30's who, while looking outside her patio windows one stormy night, claimed to have caught sight of the shadow of The Only Criminal's outstretched hand as a flash of lightning briefly brightened her yard. The police responded immediately to her summons, and were able to explain her sighting as the *trompe l'oeil* (some Amelia policemen had the sophistication to use that exact term) of a garden rake left out in the rain. Ms. Wardh was so frightened by the experience that she put her house up for sale and began petitioning Billowing Pines for residency. This was now three years ago, and Vaguely was tempted to send her back home—which he could do since the house, badly stigmatized by these circumstances, had still not sold.

Another of Vaguely's patients had a name you may recognize. He was Jimmy Ostinato—that's right, the actor who famously suffered a nervous breakdown after agreeing to portray The Only Criminal in a Broadway play. His performance had elicited high praise from theater critics ("It's a performance that just might turn your hair white!" raved Arch Stanton of *The New York Crimes*), which made Jimmy fearful that he might be marked for death by the Real Thing should he ever dare to show his face onstage again.

"Can you imagine the agony," he asked Vaguely through a vale of tears, "of knowing that your best work is still inside you, and that it might follow you to your grave, unexpressed?"

He was so full of drama, that Jimmy.

Dr. Vaguely met with each of these patients, listening again and again to their obsessively repeated stories and grievances. But now, for the first time in his career, having tasted something nearer to nectar, he found himself bored by their superstitions, suppositions and hearsay. True, he had been excited by their like before, as they had brought him closer to The Only Criminal than the newspapers which excited his imagination at the age of 12 and weaned him away from *Only Criminal* comic books. But he was now obliged to spend his days again with these commoners and others like them. He did his utmost to be professionally attentive and caring and sympathetic, but his heart belonged to Peevey.

During his breaks, Vaguely would steal time from his schedule to sit at Peevey's bedside or, if he was chased away from there, to nurse his sense of disappointment in the doctor's lounge, where he would smoke solitarily as the other doctors, openly jealous of him, implicitly heckled him by amusing one another with the latest Only Criminal jokes:

Q: What's black and white and red all over?
A: A newspaper found where The Only Criminal has been.

Q: Why does The Only Criminal limp?
A: Because his legs are crooked.

Q: The Only Criminal drove to the Louvre and stole everything but the impressionist paintings. Why did he get caught?
A: Because he had no Monet to buy Degas to make his Van Gogh.

Vaguely sat there, snorting smoke from his nose like a bull in the arena, annoyed by these so-called colleagues who delighted in lowering to the level of playground graffiti all that he had dedicated both life and career. Vaguely told himself they were bitter and small-minded because it was their lot to deal with sub-ordinary patients, to help the mediocre rise to the occasion of coping with mediocre problems. They weren't The Only Criminologist—they weren't even also-ran criminologists! Even the dullest of his own patients could boast a spark of the extraordinary and, of course, he had the last laugh of being the indisputable best at his job—for the simple reason that he *did* take The Only Criminal so seriously. You would never find him asking anyone why a chicken crossed the road, much less explaining that it was because The Only Criminal liked a nice *coq au vin*.

As Vaguely was preparing to leave, Dr. Constantin Pons entered the lounge—bearded, rotund, pin-striped and watch-fobbed. His advent reminded those jeering others of other places they had to be.

"There you are, Paul," he said. "Been looking everywhere for you."

"Why?" asked Vaguely, springing onto his feet. "Has Peevey…?"

"No, no—not yet. I'm, uh, glad to see we have a little privacy. I want to ask your opinion about something."

"Certainly."

"Sit, sit. Please, sit." Vaguely sank back into his seat.

Dr. Pons drifted over to the lounge window and surveyed the landscape of teeming reporters below. "You know, they're coming here from all over the world, these investigators—hungry for information, for revelation, for psychological breakthrough. They came here for answers, Paul—and they're starting to get creative about how they obtain them."

"You mean 'Nurse Hobble'?"

"Yes…" As Pons looked outside, a window-washer raised his scaffold into view but gave his game away by holding a standard-issue squeegee tool with a min-camera attached. Pons dropped the shades in disgust and took a brown leather chair facing Vaguely.

He continued: "But there have been other episodes as well. I needn't trouble you with all the details, but there's no reason we should presume these clever ruses aren't going to continue or be any the less clever. As Mr. Peevey is showing no immediate signs of coming out of his coma, I'm thinking we might do well to toss these reporters some kind of bone."

"What did you have in mind, sir?"

"Well, I was hoping you might have some ideas, since this whole Only Criminal thing is really more your line."

"Thank you for saying so, sir."

"One idea that occurred to me is that we might release, you know, an 'Artist's Interpretation' of what Peevey may have looked like before his transformative encounter.

"A sort of 'Do You Know This Man?' portrait."

"Exactly. For all we know, he may have family out there, who are worried about him."

"Yes, sir, but that scenario could also lead to all sorts of unhappy complications."

"What unhappy complications?"

"Well," reasoned Dr. Vaguely, "suppose that Peevey, whoever he is, does have a family somewhere. Considering that we weren't able to keep Peevey's presence here a secret for very long, I don't think we could guarantee his family any kind of protection, were they to come forward—not from the press, and certainly not from The Only Criminal. Remember, sir, we still don't know the exact nature of Peevey's relationship to The Only Criminal. If Peevey had somehow managed to thwart him…"

"I hadn't considered that." Pons admitted, stroking his beard. "Sharp thinking there, Paul. But how about this? What if we issued a phony sketch? You know, something to keep these bloody reporters occupied for awhile and out of our hair?"

"Well, sir, unfortunately," Vaguely countered, "we must take into consideration that even a phony sketch is likely to end up resembling somebody, so that sort of maneuver could conceivably result in the serious endangerment of some completely innocent party. Such a portrait might also inadvertently resemble someone missing, or even dead, which could extend false hope to that person's survivors, while placing them also in a potentially dangerous situation."

"I did a good thing when I hired you," Pons said, though he did not look pleased. He leaned back in his seat with his somewhat hirsute hands folded across his vested stomach. "But there must be *something* we can do!"

"We can wait for Peevey to come around," Vaguely offered. "We have little choice in the matter. Why do we need to do anything else?"

"You're a doctor with a patient, Paul," explained Dr. Pons. "I, on the other hand, am the chief administrator of a psychiatric hospital that is now the center of global attention. As long as those reporters down there maintain their vigil, Billowing Pines receives free publicity—'round the clock and 'round the world. This is naturally desirable, from the standpoint of our board of directors. But, to be realistic about it, there's a limit to everything; a limit to publicity and a limit to patience—not necessarily in that order. So I'm concerned that, if Mr. Peevey doesn't join us soon, some other news story might come along to lure all those people outside our facility to, shall we say, greener pastures." Pons accompanied the word "greener" with a finger-rubbing gesture indicative of money.

"Eventually," he continued, "this Peevey fellow, whoever he is, will come around, and he'd better have a damned good story. But if he wakes up with no one watching—from the standpoint of my office, if not your own—well, he might as well not wake up at all."

"Sir, you can't mean that!"

Pons read Vaguely's wounded expression but refused to give it any credence. He stood and paced. "As a matter of fact," he continued, "I think it's already started to happen. I don't know if you've noticed, but the crowd out there? It's a bit smaller today than it was yesterday. If Peevey was to regain full consciousness at this very minute, the news wouldn't have quite the impact it would've had yesterday."

As Pons said this, something in Vaguely's mind clicked.

"If I might think out loud for a moment, sir…"

"This is why I sought you out! I'm all ears."

Vaguely's expression turned cogitative. "Sir," he began, "perhaps there *is* a way that Peevey *could* be awakened… in a matter of speaking."

The details of their conversation (from this point on) were not intended for public consumption, and indeed, there is no need for us to delve into them at this moment. Suffice to say, a course of action was settled upon that desperate afternoon, dictated by dire necessity and agreed upon not at all comfortably by either associate. What these two professional men planned was not, according to the letter of the law, illegal—again, that goes without saying; however, the details of their little plan did arise, shall we say, from a place of moral twilight. As the end of his working day approached, Dr. Paul Vaguely literally ached to put some distance between himself and the mad scheme upon which he and Dr. Pons were about to embark.

Had the number of reporters stationed outside really diminished over the last 24 hours, Vaguely did not notice a difference. He still had to fight his way through a crush of humanity and equipment to board his bus bound for home. He was surprised to find every seat on the transport already taken… *except one*. Sitting pretty beside that empty seat was—of all people—Lorraine Cadbury, her color levels and contrast perfectly tuned, horizontally held, in the flesh. As he stood there in the wavering aisle of the bus, looking for a seat, she locked eyes with him and wasn't the least bit shy about it. She then drew his attention to the sole empty seat with a presentational gesture recalled from her early days of selling refrigerators and microwave ovens in television commercials, starting out with a sorcerous "voila" pantomime of her arms and ending by patting the vacant accommodation invitingly.

He felt at once enticed and full of dread, but the moment did more than cater to his most far-fetched teenage fantasy; it also presented him with the perfect opportunity to get this new scheme rolling. On reflection, he could not have planned the situation better. Much as he felt conflicted about this desperate plan, it had now been twice approved—first by Dr. Pons, and now, with Lorraine Cadbury here, by the unseen architects of coincidence.

Vaguely, prim as a schoolgirl, took the seat beside the pert anchorwoman, taking care not to look up from the hands folded on his lap or to brush her magical being with his unworthy arm.

"Dr. Paul Vaguely, isn't it?" she opened.

"That's m-m-me," Vaguely managed.

"Lorraine Cadbury, WTOC-TV," she introduced herself, willing his right hand up from his pointless lap by extending hers. "I've been trying to get your attention for several days, Doctor, but you've always managed to duck into Billowing Pines or onto this bus before I could reach you. So it finally occurred to me that, if I caught your bus a couple of stops early—so as not to tip-off the competition—maybe we could get a little acquainted during your ride home. Would you mind answering a few questions?"

"About?"

"About this mysterious patient of yours, of course! Everybody wants to know all about him!"

Vaguely raised his eyes to hers and, with all the self-control he could muster, kept his besotted voice *sotto*: "The relationship between a doctor and his patients is a privileged and confidential one, as I'm sure you know. Had anything as yet passed between us, I would not be at liberty to reveal the details to you, least of all for widespread dissemination. And, in the case of this particular patient, Ms. Cadbury, we don't know his real name yet, nor are we at all sure of what befell him. Of the very few things I could tell you, I'm sure there's nothing that the press releases from Billowing Pines haven't made as clear as your p-personal appeal."

The broadcaster smiled. "Have you ever read Billowing Pines' press releases, Doctor?"

"Well, no," Vaguely admitted. "There's no need…"

"Well, I've read them forwards, backwards, upside-down inside a glass of water, and folded origami-style. I've even had to read them on the air, and believe me, they don't amount to much. You would be helping me *a great deal,*" she said, squeezing his bicep in concert with those last two words, "even if you did nothing more than rephrase the latest press release in your own words. Then, you see, my station could claim an exclusive, my program would shoot up in the ratings, and I would be oh-so-forever in your debt."

Vaguely looked down, largely to summon nerve for what must be done. Ms. Cadbury's legs were crossed and Vaguely's gaze was covertly drawn to her plump calf, slung into its stocking with the blush and amplitude of a ripened, tapering peach. He willed his eyes to wander a bit further afield, to the grooved rubber mat providing traction down the center aisle of the bus.

"It must have been rather a slow day, news-wise, if you're haunting the bus lines to squeeze a story out of me," he managed.

"The days *have* been getting slower, to tell the truth," she admitted. "But even if The Only Criminal was at this very moment on the steps of City Hall peeling the mask off his face before an astounded public, I'd rather be right here—on this bus, talking with you." She still had her hand on his upper arm, where it was now stroking the fabric of his jacket in appreciation.

"No, you would not!"

"You've got *that* right, buster!" she laughed. "That was Lorraine Cadbury's special brand of 100% unadulterated bullshit! Whatever it takes to get my story."

Vaguely was taken aback by her coarse language, such as had never crossed her painted lips on the air. His breath was momentarily apprehended, but as he looked directly into her eyes, they both laughed—he, in spite of himself.

"When you put it that way…" Vaguely began.

"Yeeeeeeeees," she said, sustaining the vowel warmly.

"We might be able to arrange something."

Her inviting body language suddenly turned fussy. "I'm afraid my station wouldn't permit me to compensate you for our interview, Doctor."

"Oh, I'd never presume to make such a condition," Vaguely protested. "You see, Ms. Cadbury… "

"Lorraine," she insisted, warming up again.

"Ms. Cadbury," Vaguely insisted, "my work involves a great deal of research on the subject of The Only Criminal. In fact, I've been keeping scrapbooks on The Only Criminal since I was a child."

"A man should have a hobby," she vamped.

"Yes, well, you work at WTOC-TV and it occurs to me that the archives at your station must contain a lot of rare and, perhaps, exclusive data about my favorite subject. Material that could be of great assistance to me in my work."

"A-ha…"

"So I was wondering, if I agreed to answer a few of your questions—about *your* favorite subject—without violating doctor/patient confidentiality, and without exposing my patient to any possible danger, of course… Do you think I might possibly visit you at the station some afternoon, and you know, look through your…?"

"Drawers?"

Vaguely blushed.

Lorraine Cadbury rocked her leg. "Would you be asking me out to lunch, Dr. Vaguely?"

Her blue eyes widened with delight as the good doctor's face turned one hundred variant shades of red. "No no no no no," he insisted, protesting too much.

"Then it's *dinner* you have your eye on?"

"My good woman," he sputtered, "I am interested only in one thing only…"

"Like every other man I've ever known," she smiled, still rocking her leg.

"I said 'only' and I mean… 'Only,'" Vaguely clarified. "How far do your archives go back?"

"I don't really know," she said truthfully. "Before either of us was born, I would imagine."

"And what I ask would not inconvenience you?"

"You wouldn't be the first to enjoy such liberty," she smirked.

"Ms. Cadbury, you're terrible! On television, you seem very nice but, in real life, you're… well, I don't mind saying that I find you… well…"

She rested her chin darlingly upon her fist. "Yes?"

"Rather *ribald!*"

"Alright, I think we have an agreement. Okay, Johnny, slate me."

At this, a fellow passenger, seated one row ahead on the opposite side of the bus, turned around with a clapboard as the interior of the bus brightened and a professional grade camera stenciled WTOC-TV was shoved in Vaguely's direction.

He felt all the blood rush from his lap into his face, which reddened and swelled as it might under the barrage of some kind of skin-prickling niacin rush or allergic reaction. He sensed that everyone aboard was looking in his direction, as Lorraine Cadbury reached over and fussed with the front of his clothes.

"One second, Johnny," she called out to her cohort. Then, more intimately, for Vaguely's ears only, she explained, "Your tie's crooked."

Vaguely was taken aback by this comment. He was still more taken aback when he watched the playback of his interview later that night on *The Cadbury Report* and saw that his new downstairs neighbor—Miss White—had been seated in the row behind them throughout the entire ride.

Chapter Eight
HOW GREAT THOU ART

Every newspaper sold at Lawson's News the next morning carried some variation of the headline MAN SAW ONLY CRIMINAL—AND LIVED, a story that originated from WTOC-TV reporter Lorraine Cadbury. A goodly assortment of these papers also carried illustrated sidebars on the subject of Dr. Paul Vaguely.

It was one thing, Vaguely soon discovered, to be a newspaper celebrity and quite another to have actually appeared on television—where he had watched his interview repeated, as it had been throughout the night, while eating his breakfast. His foot was barely out the front door when Red Grinter and Ringo pounced on him, Ringo's tail wagging and Red crowing about how proud they *both* were to have Amelia's new favorite son as a tenant in their building. It was all relative, though: Miss White's morning newspaper, resting Vaguely face-up outside her door, was as yet uncollected.

Enthusiasm also greeted him elsewhere. The moment he stepped outdoors into the crisp morning light, Whimsy Plunkett saluted him with a musical tribute, another of his offerings in the calypso mode:

There live in Amelia a man of fame
We know his business, we know his name
He love his bakery sweets 'n' chews
And he go to Lawson for his smokes and news...

Vaguely bowed cordially to the troubadour before dashing across the street as the crosswalk light turned green. Whimsy followed along at a less hurried pace with a second verse, a strumming caboose to the Vaguely celebrity train:

Vaguely know what the Bad One do
He know of him more than me or you
But will the Bad One like it if he happen to see
On TV more of him than there is of he?

It was only after Vaguely entered the shop that he was stunned to cogitation by that particular question, but no matter. Abel Lawson greeted him by handing him a free paper and asked if he wouldn't mind autographing a few copies for his neighbors. Vaguely was only too happy to uncap a felt-tipped pen and comply.

Afterwards, he was feeling sufficiently chuffed to have taken another taxi to work, but how many chances do we get in life to feel appreciated by our community? He took the bus, which turned out to be packed. An elderly but energetic little old woman stood up and insisted that "Amelia's own" Dr. Paul Vaguely honor her by taking her seat. As new people boarded the packed transport at different stops, she made a point of telling them, "Look! Look who it is!"

That morning, outside Billowing Pines, everyone greeted Dr. Vaguely by name and many shouted out requests for interviews, now that he was apparently granting them. Security chief Jim Westerfield ran to meet him, clearing a path for him to the front door. Inside, of course, the other staff doctors—the ones who always made sport of him in the doctors' lounge—were the warm and congratulatory, and some of the nurses he passed on the way upstairs flirted with him. Dr. Pons' receptionist Beatriz kissed his cheek and Pons himself rushed into his office's reception area to pump Vaguely's hand with vigor and slap his shoulder approvingly.

"The man of the hour!" he effused.

"Good morning, sir."

Behind closed doors, Pons enthused that he could not believe their luck. "You work fast, my boy! How ever did you manage to swing a television interview?"

"No swinging involved," Vaguely admitted. "Ms. Cadbury and her cameraman staked me out on my bus ride home."

"Magnificent! Everything is coming together as though—dare I say it?—it was meant to be! Sit down, Paul… We will consider your television interview 'Phase One' of our media strategy. I want you to be aware that, at this very moment, a new press release is being distributed to members of the media that will prepare them for 'Phase Two.' It makes the formal announcement that, early this morning, at approximately 4:48 a.m., our patient—temporarily named Peevey—emerged from his coma and spoke his first words since being admitted to Billowing Pines three weeks ago."

Vaguely, smiling outwardly but wincing inside, knew there was absolutely no kernel of truth in any of this.

"It goes on to say that...," Pons read from a handy copy of the document itself, "under the supervision of Dr. Paul Vaguely..."

Double wince.

"... said patient will spend the next few days undergoing readjustment therapy, learning again how to walk and accept solid foods, while also being questioned about the experiences that brought him here. According to Dr. Vaguely... well, here, you read it."

Vaguely took the sheet from Pons, found where he'd left off, and mumbled aloud: "Our staff are heartily encouraged by the patient's progress, and have every expectation that he will be sufficiently recovered to meet his well-wishers, face to face, in the days ahead."

"I've taken the liberty of calling a press conference for the end of the business day," Pons continued.

"'Phase Three'?" Vaguely inquired. "So soon?"

"No," Pons said, "the *set-up* for 'Phase Three,' if you will. 'Phase Three' will come later. After. Anyway, at which time, Dr. Paul Vaguely will recount for the benefit of all assembled reporters all the relevant details of his famous patient's miraculous and unprecedented recovery."

The thing that clicked in his mind yesterday was now in the pit of Vaguely's stomach and making him cringe.

At 5:00 that afternoon, Dr. Paul Vaguely took the stage in Billowing Pines' impressive main auditorium. Reporters were to said auditorium as sardines are to a can. As he approached the podium and its cluster of microphones, he felt himself all but X-rayed by a bombardment of flash bulbs, sparking, sizzling, popping. He understood in this moment, on an almost cellular level, why some outlying cultures believed that photography had the ability to steal one's soul. Vaguely's vision never really cleared during his brief time before the assembled press representatives, but he was conscious of Lorraine Cadbury standing somewhere up front, basking in the afterglow of her previous night's exclusive and relishing the status of sharing her quarry with the rest of the pack.

"Good afternoon, ladies and gentlemen of the Fourth Estate," Vaguely began. "I am pleased to announce," he continued, turning to the crutch of an index card, "that our patient… whose plight has us all on the edge of our seats, I think I speak for everyone here… shows every sign of recovering. It is too early yet to know how he has been affected by this . experience, and I cannot guarantee that the effects of his experience, and his… shock won't… in some way interfere with his recall…"

A gasp of suspense ripped across the audience. Vaguely held up the palm of his hand to arrest the audience's ripples and ribbits of teased disappointment.

"Up to this point," he continued, "our patient has discouraged all questioning… and—I must impress upon this gathering—has not volunteered any information. We hope to be in a position soon… to tell you more about… everything, as we learn it for ourselves."

"What's his name?" someone shouted. A moment later, it sounded like the entire world was shouting the same question through a sea of upraised hands.

"I will not be accepting questions at this time… I would now like to introduce Billowing Pines' chief administrator, Dr. Constantin Pons!"

At this, Vaguely fled the podium and rushed past a startled Dr. Pons into a backstage restroom, where he vomited for the first time in probably eighteen years.

The press conference was being simulcast on the public address system throughout Billowing Pines and so, as Vaguely steadied himself against a sink, he could clearly audit Pons' resumption of the conference.

"Ladies and gentlemen," he said, "please bear in mind that, in all the annals of recorded history, never before has Man nor Woman been able to say, 'I have seen The Only Criminal… and lived!' Yet, inside this building, we—the staff and trustees of Billowing Pines—are harboring just such an individual, under the expert supervision of Dr. Paul Vaguely. I would say, and I think you will all agree, that such a proud boast as this entitles our patient to a most singular distinction. Please understand! It would not be in the best interests of our patient's safety, nor the safety of his loved ones, for us to reveal his identity to the general public at large—which would bring neither he nor they any measure of anonymity or protection from the outreach of malicious hands. Therefore, I suggest that, when you do mention our patient—in your newspapers, in your magazines, on your newscasts, as you will… even as you speak about him discreetly among yourselves, as you certainly will—that you refer to our remarkable friend with the deferential yet anonymous cognomen of… *The Only Witness!*"

What followed this pronouncement was much more than mere plaudit; it was a sound heard perhaps once in a lifetime, when a gathering comes together to ponder the answer to a damnable, cramping conundrum, only to receive from a respected leader—without quite expecting it, without quite believing it possible—a solution of such simple elegance, a *denouement* so utterly sane-making that their relief cannot be held down, will not be suppressed, and surges heavenward in a massive, joyous, surging bolt of unanimous cheer.

Vaguely pushed himself from the sink back to the toilet and retched a second time.

A star was born.

TWO

THE ONLY WITNESS

Murder leads to lying.

—ALFRED J. HITCHCOCK

Chapter One
SEEING IS BELIEVING

The following week was a circus, particularly when it was formally announced that The Only Witness had recovered to the extent of feeling ready to meet with the press.

It was decided that this first (and, all were assured, only) public appearance of The Only Witness would be televised with the strict understanding that certain safeguards would be in place to preserve his anonymity. Questions would be permitted at that time, though no one-on-one interviews would be granted to anyone, under any circumstances. Don't think this was big news? Every network, every station, every channel around the world elected to air the program live, pre-empting the usual roster of Only Criminal news, soaps, sitcoms and dramadies in order to do so.

The anthropologist in Vaguely was fascinated by how swiftly this media creation had attained such totemic value, comparable in the public mind to that of The Only Criminal himself. Evidently, to have *seen* The Only Criminal was more valuable, at least in view of the media, than to actually *be* The Only Criminal. Of course, the great difference between the two celebrities was that news stories about The Only Criminal offered evidence (i.e., crime) of the intangible (i.e., The Only Criminal), whereas news stories about The Only Witness had the irresistible cachet of being thoroughly tangible. The viewing public was lazy by definition and, given the choice, preferred not to use their imaginations.

Dr. Constantine Pons scheduled the presentation of The Only Witness for Sunday afternoon at 1:00 p.m., a psychologically-savvy time slot ensuring that all who would be attending would be fresh from the acquiescence of church-going and still formally attired for worship.

The location he and Dr. Vaguely had chosen for this event was Billowing Pines' second auditorium—more intimate than its main one, with a more exclusive seating capacity of only 150, of which the first few rows would be roped-off. They took some heat for this decision, but they explained that the reduced size of the venue was vital to the protection of The Only Witness and his privacy. This hall was used primarily for the annual presentation of professional papers, and the occasional therapeutic play staged by the resident patients, such as the previous year's *A Funny Thing Happened on the Way to the ATM.*. Its dimensions ensured that everyone present would be appreciative of how privileged they were to attend, and less inclined to throw their journalistic weight around afterwards.

Members of the press began filling the space shortly after noon. Those present saw onstage a background of red and pleated velvet with a podium, festooned with microphones, positioned at extreme stage right, foregrounded in a pool of lamplight. At center stage was a simple desk fashioned out of cherry wood, with an array of brute arc lights positioned behind it, not yet illuminated. The desk too was swarming with live microphones.

Dr. Vaguely observed the arrivals tensely from backstage, feeling the nape of his dress shirt growing cold and sticky with perspiration. He watched reporters scurrying to their seats, giddy as teens at a general admission concert. Some of them, having missed their breakfasts, carried Styrofoam cups of hot java and hunks of fruitcake bought at the half-price shop at the nearby factory. The cameramen in attendance assembled behind a battery of cameras provided by Billowing Pines for their use at set positions below the proscenium.

Things were now shifting into second gear, from cautious consent to reckless abandon, when it would be too late to apply any brakes. This volatile moment in time was about to become television, where the way things looked became the way things were, even if limited to a single pair of eyes. This particular broadcast promised infinitely higher numbers.

Dr. Constantin Pons took the stage at exactly 1:00 p.m., the 10 pounds gained by being televised adding to his already imposing air of stout authority.

"Good afternoon, home viewers and ladies and gentlemen of the press," he greeted the assembly. "I am Dr. Constantin Pons, co-founder and chief administrator of Billowing Pines, a psychiatric hospital and sanatorium which, as you know, was the first to introduce the idea of offering asylum and rehabilitation specifically for those traumatized by direct brushes with The Only Criminal."

He paused for the applause he was sure would follow.

"I have called this assembly today," he continued, "so that you might all make the acquaintance of a man… whom many of us thought we might never meet. We know, without knowing their names, that throughout the course of human history, there must have been someone who first beheld the great oceans… or first knew fire and curbed it to his own control, so that it might yield to his requirements for comfort or self-protection. We know there must have been a first person to meet and name the animals, to discover new species, to connect the dots of our constellations. Today you will meet such a man. A man who will be remembered by history as the first man to see the face of The Only Criminal… and live to tell the tale!"

These words elicited, as they were designed to do, a tremendous outburst of applause. Dr. Pons remained in the spotlight for its duration, looking alternately meek and humbled, beaming and yet also deserving.

"Today," he said, repeating the word several times until the applause had fully died down, "today," he paused dramatically, "that tale will be told in this very room… to this exclusive assembly… *by The Only Witness!"*

The applause unleashed by these words was even more tremendous, nearly deafening. Even nationally known journalists, known nationally for their impartiality, helplessly rose to their feet, clapping like so many smelt-driven sea lions.

"But first," Pons added, cutting off their resounding applause with authoritarian calm before it fully died down, "I say, but first, ladies and gentlemen, allow me to introduce to you our other man-of-the-hour. I mean, of course, Dr. Paul Vaguely. He is a brilliant young psychologist here at Billowing Pines, the fellow who single-handedly innovated the burgeoning field of endeavor that is becoming known in our industry as *Criminology*. Dr. Vaguely has been in charge of this most unique case since the discovery of this patient, more than a month ago. Every day, *it was he* who supervised the exercise of the patient's dormant limbs to keep his muscles strong and vital. Every day, *it was he* who massaged the patient's face, striving—hope against hope—to dissolve the frightful rictus of fear that seized this poor man's face and was truly unnerving to look upon. How he struggled to establish contact with the isolated mind of this lost soul! And, just a few days ago, it was the careworn face of Dr. Paul Vaguely that swam into focus as The Only Witness stirred to consciousness and reopened his eyes, thus bringing to conclusion… a sit-u-a-tion… that might… have dragged on… in…definitely… And now…" (Theatrical pause.) "… allow me to excuse myself from these proceedings by presenting to you—with the greatest of professional pride—a member of my staff, whom some astute members of the press have taken to calling 'The Only Criminologist'… *Dr. Paul Vaguely.*"

Pons led the applause, or attempted to, but the general expectation that Pons would introduce The Only Witness next resulted in Vaguely's entrance being greeted as something of an anticlimax. Maybe half the house clapped along, but even those dear idealists—Lorraine Cadbury included—quickly shifted to majority rule, so that Vaguely's long walk to the podium was mostly accompanied by the sound of his own echoing footsteps.

This was it, The Moment, the reward of recognition at the end of years of hard work, plowing like a pioneer in the new-tilled terrain of Criminology, but now, under these circumstances… how he wished he could be anywhere else! His consciousness had been too brimming with recriminations to permit the preparation of any opening remarks, so he had no idea what he would say, now that he had reached the podium, but he knew it must be said fast, lest all those sensitive microphones pick up the irregularities of his breathing and his panicked heartbeat. Should he reiterate the case? (Why waste valuable TV time?) Should he confess? (To what? No law, only his once-spotless code of honor, had been broken and any attempt to portray himself as criminal would surely be ridiculed as a show of poor sportsmanship, the attempt of a vain shrink to upstage his own pathetic patient.) Should he reintroduce himself? (No, you idiot, just press on.)

"Ladies and g-gentlemen," he began timidly, "to humbly, um, reiterate the wise words of our chief administrator, the times are few in the pages of history when s-someone of truly unprecedented character arrives on the scene to embellish the, um, the story of ourselves. Imagine being an Israelite, living under the laws of ancient Egypt, and seeing the coming of Moses. Imagine being a Native American and seeing the coming of The Only Criminal, who, armed with some cheap paste costume jewelry, stole their entire country out from under them. But you know what? You needn't imagine anything of the sort," he closed, "because your world is about to change just as significantly. Ladies and gentlemen, members of the press, it is in all humility that I give you… *The Only Witness*."

At this, the houselights dimmed and a spotlight followed two workmen as they rolled to center stage a wide, convex scrim, which they positioned in front of the desk positioned there as an opaque barrier. Once this key prop was in place, the lights arranged behind the desk were raised by a dimmer. This left the desk area silhouetted from the audience perspective. Once these dramatic preparations had been completed, the red pleated curtains further back were seen to rustle, separating only to the extent of admitting an unseen personage onto the stage, who stepped into the field of light to take the seat behind the desk, projecting to one and all the shadow form of someone scarecrow-thin with shortish, spiky hair.

To Vaguely's surprise, the featured guest was met with even less applause than his own introduction had provoked. The gathering's response to The Only Witness was something altogether more extraordinary: an outburst not of noise, but palpable emotion. There was a sound out there in the dark, the sound of a collectively tortured people letting something go, something deep within themselves, something never before tapped. Grown men wept, women grieved, and their outpouring was blended into an alternately surging and ebbing murmur that moved through painful feelings and associations toward empathy and requital. Here and there, adult yelps of relieved anguish were heard to rip through the crowd. Confused, Vaguely peered out from the stage wing and glanced about for the only point on the compass of this audience he could read. He spotted Lorraine Cadbury in the third row on the aisle. Her mascara was in weepy ruins, her lower lip clamped trembling between her teeth; she was rocking back and forth in her seat, wringing her hands. As he looked around the audience, he saw that everyone—all those professional men and women who brought to their audiences the worst stories the world had to tell about The Only Criminal any given day—they were all using this occasion to purge themselves of their own lives' horrors and tragedies and disappointments. They were looking upon something the human race had never had before: a living symbol of survival and triumph in the face of The Only Criminal. It left them feeling unburdened and affirmed and almighty.

Had Vaguely thought to leave the theater and step outside, he would have heard a variation of the same sound suspended in the very air, coming from houses, apartments, taverns, sidewalks and storefronts—all the places around town that were tuned into the event. It was a sound that far exceeded the boundaries of Auditorium 2 and even the city of Amelia;

it was, in fact, now being summoned into being by venting people all around the world.

Vaguely was deeply, unexpectedly, physically moved by the spectacle, but he was almost alone in being moved by his particular spectacle. He looked center stage at the illusion he had prepared for the world's delectation.

The frail-looking man seated at the desk behind that scrim *wasn't* The Only Witness. It wasn't even Peevey.

In fact, the man of the moment was Jimmy Ostinato, Vaguely's actor patient, whom Pons had enticed to play The Only Witness only by stressing the complete anonymity of the role. Reluctant at first, but hungry to act before an audience once again, Jimmy was further enticed to give his greatest performance with the promise of free therapy for the rest of his days.

"You won't be billed for your treatment," Pons had promised, "nor on the marquee!"

Nevertheless, as Vaguely scrutinized the mute, tragic, strangely noble figure that Jimmy was projecting onstage, he was impressed by the actor's professional refusal to tip his hand, to break character—not even to wink at the fellow perpetrator standing at Vaguely's post of privilege.

There was undeniable magic in the air, a magic that made Vaguely's own heart yearn to break the bonds of his ribcage, to fly to unprecedented heights with all the others assembled there, to rush toward the shadow figure in sweet deliverance and thankfulness and consolation—an actor who, through some alchemy of craft, succeeded for the remainder of the event in *becoming* The Only Witness, the mythic character whose presence was so desperately needed by these people, and by everyone watching all over the world.

Vaguely stood there, his eyes smarting with stubborn male reluctance to weep in the presence of a miracle. He hadn't felt anything this huge since he had seen the film version of *Swindler's List*. He looked around for Dr. Pons and found the burly chief administrator standing offstage, his back turned to the audience, to everyone, his shoulders quaking as he sobbed under the full weight of the deception he had helped engineer.

Like all great works of fiction, this assembly was a profound lie that, despite itself, expressed thoughts and feelings that were even more profoundly true.

For the duration of this deception, Peevey—the real Only Witness—would continue his residence in Comaville in an unguarded, closet-sized room down the hall where no reporter in their right mind would poke their nose, while his previous quarters, still guarded, was set aside for those acts of Jimmy Ostinato's performance still to come.

In the hours that followed, Vaguely retained almost no recollection of the news conference, but he could read the effects of it in every face that passed him by. Television commentators, newspaper columnists, people gabbing on street corners with born-again faces—they all agreed on never having experienced anything quite so purging or fulfilling. Perhaps they hadn't, Vaguely considered; perhaps by bringing so much hope together under one roof, and by simply exposing it to the proper catalyst, a much-needed mass hallucination was triggered. Strangers who attended the event—and others who viewed it on television in the privacy of their homes, or in the communal atmosphere of dive bars (where reportedly not a drop was touched throughout that entire spellbound hour)—surprised Vaguely for days afterward by bowing to him slightly with hand over heart, then passing on, not wishing to intrude upon his civilian privacy.

The sated press now provided Vaguely a wide berth to walk about unmolested. On the sidewalks, strewn now with autumn leaves, Vaguely found himself tenderly aware of the others who passed him by, who looked at him with reverence or gratitude, who chose not to make spectacles of their appreciation. He could read it in the clenched jaws of men, in the widened gazes of women, and he received it gratefully from two or three children who ran up to him and hugged him around his legs. Closer to home, Whimsy Plunkett greeted him with his latest verse:

The Only Witness has had his say
None shall forget this historic day
This afternoon we saw unfurl'd
De healing flag of a brave, new world.

It was all a bit overwhelming, so much so that Vaguely felt the need to go directly home, skipping his nightly ritual visit to Lawson's News, where Abel would doubtless have asked him to sign some copies of this most special edition of the Sunday *Times*. The thought kicked his imagination into overdrive: Sunday. That means tomorrow would be Monday. Might his own face appear on the cover of next week's *Crime* Magazine?

Passing through the front door of the Oakley Apartments, Vaguely found Miss White standing in the antechamber, collecting her mail. She was holding a handkerchief to her nose, under eyes turned puffy, moist and stinging red, much like everyone else who had bowed to him along his homeward journey. Of all the triumphs of the spirit that had filled him that Sunday afternoon, Vaguely felt the greatest satisfaction at having finally caught this elusive and attractive woman—who had thus far made it her habit to talk through him or around him, never to him—in a state where she could no longer deny the extent to which he and his works had touched her life. She would surely acknowledge this now—and directly. He made a show of collecting his own mail, even though it was a Sunday and no mail was delivered that day; he had already collected Saturday's mail, of course. So he reached inside the empty box, waiting, waiting for Miss White to notice him, to shed a bit of her grace on him.

Vaguely's hope began to ache in its vulnerable outreach, and then his neighbor stuffed her bills into her purse, sneezed into her ready handkerchief, groaned sluggishly, and sauntered past him in saddle shoes, out the door and into the midst of flu season.

Climbing the stairs to the third floor, wondering how much of a celebrity he would need to be to have a lift installed, Vaguely thought back to the aftermath of the broadcast.

As The Only Witness thanked his audience after responding to the final question, exciting the most tumultuous and tearful applause of the day, Vaguely had rushed onstage, dashed behind the scrim, dropped a black hood of ventilated velvet over Jimmy Ostinato's head, and raced with him to an express elevator where Dr. Pons and Jim Westerfield stood waiting. Westerfield remained there, as he and Jimmy and Dr. Pons ascended directly to the penthouse floor. There, they were met by a second security guard who escorted them to what Imogen Risk's serialized newspaper story had exposed to the entire reading world as Peevey's room. The three men had locked the door behind them and stared at one another with disbelief.

The silence rang in their ears.

"I-I've never seen anything like it," Vaguely eventually managed to say.

"Nor have I," Pons intoned gravely. "Nor has anyone! That was unlike," he paused to find the words, "any performance I've ever *seen*... *heard* about... *read* about!"

Jimmy Ostinato, leaning heavily against the locked door, then reached up with both hands to drag the hood from his head. His face, his true face, looked nakedly exposed by the harsh hospital lighting—and tears, genuine tears, streamed down his cheeks, acid rivulets of astringency and joy. His back against the door, he slid to the floor, burying his face in his knees, weeping and beating at the floor with his fists with such fury that Vaguely feared that his patient might shatter every bone in his hands.

The two doctors rushed to his side and held the actor still until his fit subsided.

"What in the name of all that's decent have we done?" Vaguely demanded—not of his superior, of course, but of God. "We never should have done this! I don't know what made me suggest such a thing! This man is a patient, his mental state is far too fragile to subject it to such demands!"

At this, Jimmy Ostinato looked up at Vaguely, then at Pons, then at Vaguely again. His eyes were stone cold, his entire bearing charged with the command of an accomplished, world-class stage performer.

"FRAGILE?!" Ostinato roared, pulling himself free of their clutches and rising to his feet. "Dr. Vaguely, did you not see, did you not feel what just took place out there? I'm an actor, not a writer... You gave me little more than a desk on a stage. You gave me no lines to say, only a list of things I *mustn't* say, and I memorized them. There was nothing for me to do as I sat before the most important audience any actor has ever faced. Nothing! Nothing but to sit at that desk *and make myself available to the moment.* I inhabited that moment as I inhabited my character, body and soul; and, somehow, I managed to tap from myself everything that my character would be feeling in that situation—what all of us in that room were feeling... Somehow, the soul of that character entered into me and *I became that character. It was, without a doubt, the greatest performance I have ever given!*"

But then the actor sank tragically to his knees and shook his purpling fists with impotent anger.

"But where did it come from? How did I do it? If I live to be a hundred, I'll never feel so alive again!"

Chapter Two
HE IS MY EVERYTHING

The following Tuesday afternoon, Paul Vaguely received an urgent summons to the office of Constantin Pons. Upon arriving, he was surprised to find Jimmy Ostinato seated there, in front of Pons' desk, wagging his foot excitedly but irregularly, as if to the beat of one of The Only Criminal's bebop tunes, like "Jack the A Train" or "Affright in Tunisia." The patient was not wearing the hospital's standard issue uniform or pajamas, but rather a designer shirt, stone-washed jeans, tennis shoes, and a light leather jacket—the kind of flashy, knockabout clothes an actor on the move might wear to an audition. His hair had been dyed back, from Sunday's white, to a facsimile of his original hair color.

Vaguely took the vacant chair in the triangle, opposite Jimmy's.

"What's going on, gentlemen?" he asked, half-fearful of the answer.

"Our Mr. Ostinato has made the decision to check himself out of Billowing Pines," Pons announced.

"That's right" Jimmy said, flashing a million-dollar grin. "Broadway, here I come!"

Vaguely then noticed a suitcase at rest near the office door.

"But, Jimmy," he sputtered. "What about your therapy? Remember, our promise of complementary therapy was your compensation for yesterday's… you-know-what."

"Dr. Vaguely, I am deeply grateful, but yesterday's experience was its own therapy," Jimmy effused. "I owe you both more than I can possibly express, but I'm done with all that. I have to go with my triumph!"

He looked more composed and spoke with more confidence and self-control than Vaguely had ever seen him. He had always regarded Jimmy as one of his most neurotic patients and, judging from the archival reviews he had read of Jimmy's stage performances, he had never been that much of an actor. Jimmy pounced on Vaguely's facial expression, which he could not fully disguise, but he did so with uncommon grace:

"I know what you must be thinking," he said. "Believe me, I'm as amazed as you are, but when I awoke this morning, I knew from the instant I opened my eyes that all of my old fears were behind me! It's like the power that spoke through me on Sunday somehow reversed the negative charge of my trepidations, chasing all that bad blood out of my system. Now I'm feeling courageous and on the brink of the great adventure that is the rest of my life! All I can think of is how badly I want to get back onstage and sink my teeth into a big, juicy part!"

"Broadway?" Pons sneered, in spite of himself. "Why not Hollywood, you arrogant, unappreciative whipper-snapper?"

"Dr. Pons!" Vaguely exclaimed involuntarily.

Jimmy's beaming expression suddenly looked struck by lightning. He rose to his feet and crossed the room to the window in a nakedly theatrical manner.

"You know, Dr. Pons," he reasoned, turning slowly toward them, "you're right! On a Broadway stage, nobody's going to see me—I mean *really* see me—except for those people in the first few rows. That's okay for an actor who doesn't mind working for the good of the play, the good of the company—but for me? *I'm fed up with hiding! I want to come out! I want put my talent on the line! You know what? You're right! I want my face out there, six stories high! And my name! I want to see 'Jimmy Ostinato' in big letters a mile wide!* And by my third picture, maybe just 'Ostinato'—or 'Ostinato the Uncanny'! After the performance I gave yesterday, *anything's* possible! Right?"

"We've created a monster!" wept Pons.

"You do remember, don't you, Jimmy," Vaguely hemmed and hawed, "that you promised not to say anything about your participation in yesterday's…"

"No sweat, no worries, *no problemo!*" the actor assured them. "The way I see it, yesterday was like doing a *pro bono* infomercial. You guys got your publicity for this place, and I got my Muse back. You're happy, I'm happy. A deal's a deal."

"But what if The Only Witness is needed to make a second public appearance? Or a third?" Pons fretted out loud.

"Now wait just a minute," Jimmy objected, looking from Pons to Vaguely and back again. "I signed on for a pilot, not a series!"

"That's absolutely correct," Vaguely reassured the actor. "As far as I am concerned, Jimmy, you've fulfilled your responsibilities to the letter. Isn't that right, Dr. Pons?"

Pons, who had removed his monocle to rub his face, replaced it and turned the full force of his monocular gaze on the former neurotic he was about to unleash upon the world as a born-again narcissist.

"Of course," he said, as if deciding on the spot to wash his hands of the whole affair. "Please forgive me, Mr. Ostinato, but… well, this whole episode has been very stressful for me. You understand."

He rose to his feet and extended his hand to the actor. They shook hands and the heartiness of the motion seemed to shake all the wariness out of Jimmy's otherwise ebullient deportment.

"We wish you the best of luck—don't we, Paul?"

"Of course," Vaguely said, standing, and shaking the actor's hand in turn.

"I appreciate it," Jimmy said, flashing a professional smile. "And I want to thank you, especially, Dr. Vaguely, for everything you've done for me. None of this would have been possible, if not for you."

Vaguely didn't know how to respond to such an accolade, so his face reacted without his guidance. His cheeks rose as they did when he smiled, but his lips turned down in a frown. He looked like someone fighting back grief. Jimmy had never seen anything like it, and furtively filed it away for future reference.

"I wish you gentlemen the best of luck," he said, taking his leave. "I guess there's nothing else to say," he closed, hoisting his suitcase, "except… See you in the movies!"

Let's hope it's not a prison picture, thought Vaguely.

That afternoon, Billowing Pines had no choice but to issue a press release announcing that the man popularly known as "The Only Witness" had made the decision to leave their professional care and return to private life. The document stated that, earlier that day, at an unspecified hour, he had re-entered the world anonymously, wearing a disguise and using the facility's rear exit, wishing to avoid recognition and the demands of further accountability.

His decision had been approved by the facility's resident criminologist Dr. Paul Vaguely, who was quoted as opining that "continued therapy had little to offer this unique patient, who gradually formed a mental block against all recollection of the nightmarish encounter he described with such harrowing eloquence" during his recent television interview, "which will no doubt take its rightful place in our history books, to be memorized and recited by schoolchildren for generations to come."

Dr. Constantin Pons was similarly forthright, declaring, "We at Billowing Pines have treated him—raised him, if you will—to the point of social reintegration." He was assured in his belief that they were doing the best thing in releasing him and "making his former quarters available to one of the many other applicants so desperately in need of post-traumatic care and shelter."

The press release went on to quote Vaguely again as saying that "The legend of The Only Witness is in no way spoiled by his leave-taking from the limelight. On the contrary, his anonymous presence among us, as one of us, marks the beginning of a new legend: a redefinition of our public sector."

Wholly fictitious, of course, this issued statement confirmed most people's perceptions of The Only Witness as a noble figure, mythic in his own right, who had appeared out of nowhere to intone universal truths and act selflessly. It spoke volumes about the extent to which members of the press could be bamboozled by a preposterous hoax, that even the most tenacious of their ranks agreed to respect The Only Witness's privacy, and pursue this story of the century—if not of all time—no more.

Paul Vaguely had achieved a great deal as a result of this charade, not least of all local and international recognition for the work that he did in fact, but the most penetrating and lingering of its dividends was depression. With Jimmy Ostinato now out of the picture, he could trace the reasons for his low spirits not only to his recent abandonment of the real Only Witness, but his own recent neglect of the exploits of The Only Criminal himself, which had been his defining interest since childhood. In neglecting these, Vaguely understood that his chief neglect was to himself.

First things first: determining to get his life back onto the right foot, Dr. Vaguely went directly to Peevey's private suite on the penthouse floor, where he had already been reinstalled. His security guards, no longer necessary, had been excused from their posts. He found Nurse Carver in the act of sponge-bathing the patient. There was no change in his condition. Vaguely vowed to himself that getting at those secrets locked away in Peevey's mind would now become his first priority.

Knowing how easily his star practitioner could get lost in this case, Dr. Pons paid a visit to the suite at the end of the day and was not surprised to find Vaguely there. Pons effectively took the criminologist by the scruff of the neck and steered him out of the room, down the hall, into the elevator, and finally into a hailed taxi. He reassured him that he would be notified without delay in the event of any change, but otherwise forbade him to step foot in Billowing Pines for the next 48 hours.

His parting orders: "Physician—heal thyself!"

During the cab ride home, Vaguely felt like a crab torn from its shell. He felt like he'd been away from the outside world for a hundred years. One Hundred Years… he remembered the taxi driver with the Marquez book and looked up to see who was driving. It wasn't she. He leaned forward and looked on the driver's seat to see what he was reading. There was no book riding shotgun—not even a paperback.

He slumped back, his back bouncing as he settled once again into his seat and, as the taxi came to a halt at a stop light, Vaguely's glazed stare fell upon the headline of a newspaper being read by someone at a bus stop bench. It read THE ONLY CRIMINAL STRIKES!

Vaguely quickly estimated that he hadn't seen, read or clipped a newspaper item since… Had it really been at least three weeks? There must be so much he had missed!

Where had The Only Criminal struck? he wondered, his imagination suddenly racing. *And how hard had he stricken?*

Vaguely reminded himself that he was Abel Lawson's best customer—at least the most reliable—and, unless he missed something, he was also Abel's only *celebrity* customer, so he had every reason to expect that his habits had been looked after with customary efficiency. If this were so, it should be a simple enough matter to bring himself up-to-date regarding the events of the past weeks, and recover the precious, lifelong thread of action, violence and misadventure he had inadvertently let drop.

"Let me out here," he told the driver as Lawson's News came into view, along with the latest wisdom on the sign at St. Tim's:

GOING ON VACATION?
AREN'T YOU GLAD GOD ISN'T?

It seemed that they were now experimenting by diverging from actual scripture. Shrugging off this decline in quality, Vaguely determined that he would surprise the good Mr. Lawson today by picking up all the newspapers he was surely saving for him—and how generously he intended to reward such kind and diligent attention to his needs! Afterwards, Vaguely mused, he would indulge himself with a sinful dessert at The Hideout, then spend a quiet evening at home with the finest of creature comforts—a glass of port, a fine cigar, and a pile of newspapers published at home and abroad.

The little bell announcing his arrival at Lawson's News was comfortingly familiar, but Vaguely was alarmed by the extent to which everything else about the place had changed. The two paperback racks that formerly blocked his initial view of the wall-length magazine display were now reduced to one—and it was now positioned at the far end of the store. The magazine display was now bisected, with one half relocated between the cash register counter and the paperbacks, while the other half was superseded in view by two noisy Only Criminal pinball machines. Most of all, Vaguely was surprised to find the usually busy store without a single customer—unless you counted the two kids who were pumping quarters and periodic groans of defeat into those pinball machines. Most disturbingly, when their eyes briefly connected over the counter, Abel Lawson offered his "favorite customer" no indication of special favor. There was no effusion, no special wink of recognition, no "Where ya been, pal?"

Vaguely smiled apologetically as he approached the checkout counter. "You're a sight for sore eyes, Mr. Lawson! Long time no see!"

"I guess so," he answered unwarmly.

"I've been very busy with my duties at the hospital," Vaguely explained by way of apology. "I didn't mean to desert you, old friend—not that I ever would! This little corner of the world is important to me, and I've been away too long. What's with the machines?"

"A man's gotta get payin' customers in the door somehow."

"Business is that slow?"

"That slow? That *dead*. You might not believe this, but even my regulars stopped comin' in."

"Well, this regular is back and here to stay."

"Well, that's what we like to hear," he admitted, unconvinced. "What can I getcha?"

"I'll take the last few weeks of papers off your hands."

"Papers? What papers?"

"*My* newspapers? The newspapers I've missed? Since the last time I was in? I hoped you might be saving them for me."

"Sorry, Doc," Abel apologized, grumpily. "You should have called and asked me to hold 'em for ya. A lot of 'em sold out as soon as they came in. That Only Witness brouhaha was a pretty big deal, y'know. I might not have had 'em for you even if you *had* stopped in. Don't they send ya a free paper when they do a story on ya?"

"I guess not," Vaguely groused. "On the bright side, business can't be too bad if you're selling out of newspapers!"

"Who lives on newspaper sales? Look around, man. Nobody's buyin' books. Nobody's buyin' magazines. After what happened this week with your buddy The Only Witness, it's like people don't care about anything except what's happening *right now, with them*. And if it takes longer than a second to soak up, it ain't news anymore! Magazine news is too stale, books take too long to read. People want everything *now*, so they can forget it before tomorrow comes. Today's reality? Shee-it. Tomorrow's garbage, if you ask me."

Vaguely frowned.

"Hey, you know," Abel threw out as a malicious joke, "it's trash night. Maybe you can pick up some old newspapers along the curb."

"Maybe," Vaguely echoed, having no intention of rifling through other people's rubbish.

"Anyway," Lawson continued, "I'm gonna have a hell of a time stayin' open if I can't interest my customers in anything but pinball. Papers don't bring anybody in—you can find 'em on any street corner. Hell, there's a paper rack right outside my own store! If you're a real lazybones, now you can have 'em delivered right to your own Welcome mat. So sue me, but yeah, I brought in some pinball machines. The kids and all their noise is drivin' me nuts, but those quarters add up." Lawson turned to his compact humidor. "Hey, I got your stogie, though. *Arma del Fuego*, right?"

"Yes, Mr. Lawson." So he hadn't entirely forgotten him.

Vaguely added three sundry evening papers to his purchase: local, national, international.

"You didn't sell out of papers today, I see," he mentioned in the spirit of commiseration.

Lawson blew a discreet raspberry. "Without your guy in the headlines, the pages might as well be blank."

Vaguely took this as flattery of extravagant excess, but discovered later in the evening, upon perusing them himself, that what Abel Lawson had said was basically the truth.

Even in his greenest days of shadowing and chronicling of The Only Criminal, Paul Vaguely had noticed that reporters and would-be scholars often compared him to a blow from an unexpected direction. He was the two-car collision that took place on a corner where a joke was being told; he was the deathwatch for an elderly relative, at the end of a long and draining illness, that was suddenly upstaged by the violent death of someone young and strong and healthy; he was the divorce papers served on wedding anniversaries, the happy and wanted pregnancy that climaxed in miscarriage, the rained-out golf tournaments, the writers who died before completing their *magnum opera*.

These analogies came back to roost in Vaguely's now more seasoned thoughts as he settled down that night with his three newspapers, whose contents struck him as if from an unanticipated direction. Had he been more attentive to the newspapers of the past weeks, less involved with unresponsive Peevey and in masterminding the ruse of The Only Witness, or less impressed by the fact that he had been chased by reporters and interviewed on television, Paul Vaguely might have taken notice of the warning signs and been better prepared for the revelation now before him.

He read each article with complete absorption, an absorption so complete, he forgot that night to smoke the *Arma del Fuego* he'd bought. At first, it seemed that all coverage of The Only Criminal had been eclipsed by the continuing resonance of the news stories that had been coming out of Billowing Pines. There was a subtle distinction about this evening's papers, one that might well have been lost on anyone else casually perusing them, but which stood out to Vaguely's trained, professional taste buds like anchovies on a pizza.

Simply put, in none of the three papers was he able to find and savor an Only Criminal story; there were none whatsoever. Granted, his name was all over the pages. There were stories that mentioned him, that referred to him, that cursed him by association, but in none of the three papers was there a shred of breaking news concerning him.

When the doors of the Amelia Public Library opened the next morning, Vaguely was there as the doors were being unlocked. He spent most of that morning and afternoon reading through the newspapers published during the period of his preoccupation. Collectively, and oh-so-quietly, they seemed to confirm that, in the past few weeks, The Only Criminal had done little or nothing to maintain his epic reign of infamy.

The crimes that were reported, he noticed, were older transgressions that had only recently come to light. There were more timely crimes reported, but these, in the days following, were ultimately discredited as crimes. Of the last such instances reported—the theft of the Capstone Diamond in Antibes, a recording studio arson in Detroit, the robbery of a San Francisco bank that had long prided itself on being "The World's Safest"—these turned out not to be criminal acts at all, but rather the unfortunate results of human error: clumsy misplacement, overloaded wiring, a concurrence of incorrectly balanced checkbooks.

He flashed back to the headline he had spied from his taxi's window yesterday, on his way home: THE ONLY CRIMINAL STRIKES! It appeared on none of the recent newspapers he found on file, but what a telling headline it would have been! Because, as far as Vaguely could determine, The Only Criminal hadn't struck anywhere.

On the contrary, he seemed to be *on strike*… sitting out his life of *crime!*

Chapter Three
WITHOUT HIM

It is always interesting to see how people handle themselves in the midst of a catastrophe.

As the sun rose on a new assortment of decidedly thinner newspapers, Paul Vaguely used his time off to put them under his personal microscope. He discerned certain unmistakable patterns in the way their reporters had been instructed to cover The Only Criminal's alleged disappearance. Some papers sought to downplay the awful potential of the situation with timid, tongue-in-cheek headlines like ONLY CRIMINAL ON THE LAM. Others, more sensationalistic in their approach, grabbed readers by the lapels (ONLY CRIMINAL ON VACATION—*IN YOUR TOWN?)*, while the more ironic, level-headed *Times* declared: ONLY CRIMINAL STEALS OUR CONTENT.

Sitting in a corner booth at The Hideout, Vaguely took care after sipping his coffee to replace his cup on the java-colored halo it had left on the tabletop. He munched distractedly on a little pig, dunked in egg yolk, while reeling from one newspaper account to the next. In all his born days, he had never seen anything like this: every newspaper was its own compendium of opinions, suspicions, hunches, hypotheses, guesses and guesstimates; they argued that The Only Criminal was probably having a mad laugh at everyone's expense… that he had temporarily stepped offstage to prepare himself for a major *coup du theâtre*… or that he was not retired, not dead, but merely asleep, luxuriating in a dream of murder.

The Hideout was itself a microcosm of this journalistic controversy. It was wall-to-wall with breakfast customers, all shouting at one another in eagerness to learn as much as anyone else knew, or professed to know. Vaguely wasn't listening to them; they were all so much background noise to his own quietly panicking thoughts. But then he was recognized by one of the regulars, who called out to him: "Hey, Doc, you know about these things. What do you think is up with this disappearance deal?"

Vaguely looked up and didn't see the face of the person who asked the question, but rather a couple dozen who might have asked it.

"I wish I knew," he said, turning back to his newspaper. "Your guess is as good as mine."

"But your guess is supposed to be better than ours!" It was a woman's voice, this time.

"Yeah, Doc!" said another. "What's going on here? You trying to hide something?"

"Hide? I'm out in public, just having my breakfast…"

"C'mon, Doc, what's the deal? Do you think he might be sleeping one off?"

"Sleeping one off? One what?"

"I dunno—a murder, a heist. All that globe-hopping's bound to tire a body out, even *his*! Right?"

"It's possible," Vaguely managed. "Anything's possible."

"If anything is possible," called out a voice from farther back, "is it possible he's *dead*?"

This speculation unleashed a densely renewed rhubarb of speculation, some three dozen voices deep, some of them yammering with their mouths full.

"Please, please!" Vaguely pleaded. "Try to remember, my work is with people whose lives were damaged by The Only Criminal, not with The Only Criminal himself!"

"Dr. Vaguely," ventured a voice at a more conversational level. It came from a middle-aged, careworn woman who at with her children at the booth opposite him. "Tell us this. You had The Only Witness in your care at your hospital."

"Yes," Vaguely confirmed.

"He was present at that disaster scene on the highway. He was found inside The Only Criminal's own car."

"My good woman," Vaguely protested, "that man is—I mean, was—he was in a coma…"

A man in the booth next to hers cut in: "Yeah, I didn't even think of that! I think I know where you're comin' from, sister!"

The woman acknowledged him nervously.

The man continued his line of thought: "Anyone who can be in Paris one minute and in Peoria like"—he snapped his fingers—"*that*… can sure as beans fake a coma! Dr. Vaguely, didn't it ever occur to you that The Only Witness might have been… The Only Criminal himself?"

Vaguely's heart thundered.

Another voice from the far end of the place: "You could've had him! And you released him! You let him *walk*!"

Vaguely's heart skipped a beat. He couldn't speak. In truth, he had never considered this possibility and the sudden prospect terrified him—all the more so for the reason no one suspected: that the real Only Witness still lay comatose in that private room at Billowing Pines. Was it possible that that little fellow with the freckled face and the white hair was actually The Only Criminal himself?

"Alright now, everybody! Settle down. Doc Vaguely's our friend and neighbor."

The voice, projecting firm authority but also warmth and friendliness, belonged to Officer Phil Mead, who had overheard the disturbance while walking his beat outside the restaurant.

"You have no call to be disturbing him while he's having his breakfast. He doesn't get to take his breakfast here very often, and The Hideout could use the business. Couldn't you, Cora Lee?" He looked at the woman in the white uniform standing beside the cash register.

Cora Lee put something in her cast iron skillet and said *nada*.

"What do *you* think, Officer Mead?" another woman asked. "Do you think The Only Witness might have been a disguise for The Only Criminal?"

"Now, Mrs. Busby, where did you ever get *that* idea? Is that what this little mob scene is all about? Haven't you people seen the papers? The Only Criminal has dropped out of sight. He's just plain lying low. Don't you people know anything about The Only Criminal, for heaven's sakes? Haven't you ever known him to take us by surprise… to pause as he makes plans for his next attack? Maybe he's takin' it easy and counting his money. He could garden, for all I know! The way I heard it—and correct me if I'm wrong, Dr. Vaguely—The Only Witness was released the other day from Billowing Pines, and has now returned to private life. Mrs. Busby, if he was The Only Criminal, like you're supposing, wouldn't that mean The Only Criminal was still *at large*?"

"I didn't think of that," the woman admitted, and it was as close to an apology as Paul Vaguely got—that, and the peace and quiet in which he was finally able to finish his breakfast and pay his check. The worried townsfolk of Amelia withdrew and went back to their bacon and pancakes, and Cora Lee tried to pacify Dr. Vaguely by bringing him a coffee-to-go refill and an extra big side order of goetta, on the house.

The sidewalks of Amelia were thick with abstracted, distracted, harried faces. After leaving The Hideout, Vaguely moved among these milling forms like a ghost, neither he nor they knowing whether the day's headlines were news they should embrace or reject. Vaguely was intrigued by the societal sea change prompted by this worrisome turn of events; instead of the mood of pensive perturbation he had always known on the streets, there was now a more pervasive sense of wild expectancy—like, if this could happen, what couldn't happen? Could the very gravity that held them to the ground be suddenly cut off?

Of course, there was the very real possibility that The Only Criminal's apparent withdrawal from active duty might be the first stage of some hellish Master Plan. After all, The Only Criminal was the very core of Vaguely's profession, his innovations, his income, his interests, his hobbies, his existence, his world, himself! *He couldn't just disappear!* But what of the other possibility now raised? That The Only Criminal might be on hiatus because he was, at present, lying comatose in an unguarded room at Billowing Pines?

Vaguely saw a telephone booth and ran toward it. He shoved the appropriate coin into the pay phone and dialed Billowing Pines.

"Dr. Pons' office, please... Hello, Beatriz—this is Dr. Vaguely calling. Yes, I know... Well, might I speak with him for a moment anyway? It's urgent. That's not true, Beatriz. I do *not* think *everything's* urgent. I *have* been trying to rest, but have you seen the papers? How am I supposed to rest when The Only Criminal's gone? It's a hell of a time to expect a criminologist to be taking a rest! The sooner you put him on, the sooner I... yes... thank you."

He waited a few moments, looking through the glass panels of the walls surrounding him at the abundant, browning greenery. *This place would have been so pretty in summer, with everything green*, he thought, *but now it's all going rotten...*

Pons came on the line.

"Dr. Pons! Yes, hello. How is Peevey doing today? What do you mean you won't tell me? Just because you told me not to come in today, that doesn't mean I can't check in, does it? Everything's alright, I hope... Yes...

Yes, I see. Look, I will find it much easier to relax and make use of this time off if you would just agree to do one thing… Yes… Please make sure that Peevey's quarters remain guarded at all times. I *know* he's still comatose. I understand that, sir. But, you see, I had the most horrible realization today… I've been reading the papers and, well… The Only Criminal has been out of action for approximately the same period of time that Peevey has been in our care… so you see… he might actually *be* The… What do you mean 'preposterous'? Of course I know The Only Criminal has been around since time immemorial! Peevey has white hair, or haven't you noticed? No, sir, I'm not calling you incompetent… I'm sorry, sir… It's the pressure and the not knowing and the not being there… Couldn't I *please* come back in to work? I don't know what to do with myself out here in the world, without… No change? Hm-hm, I see… Alright… Yes, very well… But you *will* station the armed guard outside his room? Good… yes, that will bring me some peace of mind. I will… I promise… Yes, I'm going home now. Yes, I will sleep. You have my word, sir. Yes, yes, goodbye."

Vaguely wended his way back home. He spent the main part of the afternoon indoors and would have contentedly remained there; however, as he removed his stereo headphones after a tributary listen to his favorite Only Criminal album, he was drawn outside by the sound of St. Tim's clanging bells, hoots and hollers, and the sound of a motorcade.

Stepping back outdoors, he found Oakley Way stocked shoulder-to-shoulder with celebrants of all ages, ethnicities, and walks of life. Some people were filing into bars and restaurants, while others poured back out onto the streets—there being no room left inside to accommodate them—with napkins, drinks and meals on paper plates bunched between their hands. The air of festivity was literally spilling out of these places back onto the sidewalks and streets. Everywhere there was laughter, happy reflection, even dancing, though the only music at that moment came from the clanging bells at St. Tim's. They went beyond six (the hour); they went beyond 12 (the limit); they went beyond 666. They went mad with jubilation.

A chain of convertibles was parading at a slow crawl down the middle of the street, with various local businessmen waving genially to pedestrians from their back seats. The doors of the cars carried signs painted with the names of their passengers, along with advertisements for their businesses, which had been cleverly conceived to tie into The Only

Criminal's vanishing act. The owner of Wardell's Dry Cleaners, for example, waved from a car whose doors proclaimed, *"We can make any stain disappear... like What's-His-Name we used to fear!"*

Whimsy Plunkett, smiling under soft eyes that looked curiously bereft, passed between Vaguely and the storefronts, strumming a mellow tune on his 12-string. He sang:

I thought I'd never see the day
When TOC. would go away
I never thought we'd reach the year
When he would up and disappear
I thought I'd never see a time
When we would say goodbye to crime...

But, as you see, that day has come
And our cheers may bring a tear to some...

The troubadour's song faded as he receded into distance.

Across the street, Vaguely saw Abel Lawson sitting glumly on the steps outside his newsstand, openly swigging from a bottle of beer. It was not a time for reading or business, after all, but for celebrating.

"Mr. Lawson!" Vaguely called out, across the street. "Shouldn't you be in this parade with all the other local businessmen?"

Lawson waved his bottle at the spectacle dismissively. "I wouldn't be in that goddamn parade if they paid me," he sneered, taking another slug from his brown bottle.

"How long has this been going on? All day?"

"All day," Lawson brooded. "Like a sucker!"

Vaguely overheard a woman's voice fawning about how much she loved a man in a uniform. He traced the dialogue to the sidewalk outside Bemelmans' Bakery, where Officer Mead was holding court with a few ladies of marriageable age who were flirting with him. They were giggling, asking him for the badge they assumed he would now no longer need, as a memento.

"It's not my badge that you ladies are after," he said, lewdly. "What you *really* want is my nightstick!"

Vaguely winced, feeling a disgust for the man he would never have believed in his most boundless dreams.

As he turned back to face his apartment building, he saw Red Grinter holding Ringo like a baby, showing the Scottie various points of interest in the passing parade as if they were driving past for his exclusive entertainment. They both looked giddily incredulous to be part of a moment in time when the fall of night called a stalemate, when not one of the people caught outside at the 6:00 cusp of night made a move to rush indoors.

Then, over Red's shoulder, Vaguely noticed Miss White standing absently by, observing the block party with a studious expression he was hard-put to interpret. He followed her line of vision to the manager of Puddly's Toys, who was taking advantage of this public opportunity to proclaim that all Only Criminal-related toys were now 40% off—like candy past its expiration date.

Vaguely then returned his attention to her and had to acknowledge that he felt a strong yet forbidding connection to this peculiar woman, who had entered his life at the same time as Peevey. He felt a strong desire to speak to her, to speak with her, but for some reason it wasn't a strong enough desire to override his sense of propriety. Instead, he decided to imitate her way of speaking to him by addressing a third party, by speaking to Red in a voice loud enough for Miss White to overhear and intercept.

"Good evening, Mr. Grinter," he greeted. "Hello, Ringo."

"Hey, look, Ringo!" Red called out. "It's The Only Crimino-lologist!"

Vaguely glanced over and back: no reaction from Miss White.

"Say 'Hi' to Doc Vaguely, Ringo. Hey, Doc, you gonna be on TV again soon?"

Vaguely looked: no reaction to the mention of his TV appearances from Miss White. No reaction from Vaguely either.

Except: "Well, all this is quite something, isn't it?" he said, nodding at the parade.

"I'll say," Red confirmed. "Ain't this somethin'?"

"Something—*or other*," Vaguely said cryptically.

"He's got that right," Miss White said aloud, turning on her heel and going back inside, as the bells of St. Tim's rang and rang and rang.

Chapter Four
HELP ME

What can I tell you? With nothing new forthcoming to report, the newspapers and newscasts of the world began to fill—okay, let's face it, *pad*—their page counts and air-time with all manner of teasers, temptations and come-hithers, all clearly planted with one special reader in mind.

There were stories about a fabulous split meteorite with jeweled interior that was being exhibited in St. Louis for one week only at the Anitra Von Hoene Memorial Museum, whose security system just happened to be on the blink. There were also profiles of the nation's latest big lotto winners, complete with their home addresses, and human interest filler about certain upscale communities where citizens, now feeling properly secure, were no longer locking their doors and windows at night.

Though these sly enticements swelled daily in type size and estimated value, none of this bait was ever reported as taken. Months passed, and sales and ratings continued to plummet.

In a last-ditch maneuver to regain their audience, such poorly-disguised provocations as these began to be replaced with reprints and rebroadcasts of the most sensational crime stories in recorded history. Dr. Paul Vaguely disparagingly referred to this archival material as "The Only Criminal's Greatest Hits." These daily/nightly/hourly retrospectives had the opposite effect of reassuring the public with an illusion of The Only Criminal's continued presence, at least in Vaguely's opinion; to him, they played more like the litany of lifeworks which fill obituaries. He could see his acquaintances and neighbors being implicitly encouraged to accept The Only Criminal's hypothetical death by their steady, persistent exposure to these inescapable recaps of an abruptly halted career. With all stories concerning The Only Criminal now occupying the past tense, they might still be considered entertaining by some nostalgics, but they no longer flexed a serrated wing of real and omnipresent terror.

Deprived of their fear of The Only Criminal and the vicarious pleasure they had always taken from his reign, no longer able to pay him the gooseflesh that was his preferred applause, people began to turn cranky. Then, desperate for new diversion and distraction, they became self-conscious. Appalled to discover their unexplored souls in such a state of disrepair, they became nosy—the petty, squalid dramas of others being easier to address than the putting of their own houses in order. Their next step was to become reclusive, because when people cease to belong to the world in which they live, the next step is often enlistment in the inner worlds accessed through drink or prescription drugs. Vaguely could picture them all in his mind's eye, the people that filled the happy streets of Amelia not so long ago: now sitting alone at their kitchen tables, a half-empty liquor bottle beside them, with no crook to turn to, burying their faces in the crooks of their arms.

This rising sense of desperation among the populace eventually reached a point of expression within the walls of Billowing Pines.

One afternoon in a particularly cold November, many weeks after Dr. Vaguely was welcomed back to Billowing Pines, Nurse Brand—while attending the needs of the still-comatose Peevey—let loose a scream that reached Dr. Vaguely, who was in session with a patient at the other end of the hall. He excused himself and responded at once.

"Who screamed?" he demanded to know, bursting into the room.

"Doctor, look!" she shrieked through a hand clamping her mouth. "There on the window!"

Vaguely could see nothing out of order from where he stood, so he crossed the room in long strides to examine the window more closely. Written there, in the wintry condensation accrued on the window pane, was the menacing inscription: *"I'M BACK!—TOC."*

He scrutinized the warning and its signature with skepticism. His expert eye knew at once that The Only Criminal never signed anything, not even billboards, with his initials. He never had to; the author of the deeds he committed was indubitable. Even so, Vaguely held his doubts close to his vest, half-hopeful that, from the ashes of someone's commendable if inept ruse, potent life might somehow find the spark needed to regenerate.

As he stood there, carefully deciding on his own next step, Dr. Constantin Pons crashed into the room.

"What has happened here?" he demanded.

Vaguely pointed balefully at the window, like an actor in a silent film.

Pons's response to the misty inscription was met with similar ambivalence. He was at first concerned that the note, if authentic, would reflect poorly on the security staff at Billowing Pines, but he—like Vaguely—readily identified it as counterfeit. The two colleagues exchanged looks, but not a single word was necessary for them to forge their agreement. Both men noticed the self-conscious way in which Nurse Brand was holding her hands behind her back, but neither had the heart to ask to see them. As it happens, she was proven innocent within an hour, when a hysterical Nurse Mallet tearfully confessed to the forgery, which she had executed during an earlier shift, knowing that Nurse Brand (the type of woman who would scream if you whispered "boo" at the back of her head) would surely discover it.

"I don't know what made me do it," weeped the woman in white. "I guess I thought that, if even one person believed it, maybe two could believe it, and if it got reported by the papers, and enough people believed it, it could be true again..."

Behind his official wall of silence, Vaguely looked upon the deed as the valiant act of a great hero and humanitarian. As such, he didn't like seeing her reproached for what she had done, so he turned away from Pons's grilling of the poor woman, and looked past The Only Criminal's forged signature to what was happening outside the steamed window above the radiator.

It looked out upon a view of the rear grounds at Billowing Pines, where there was a walled garden, the founder's memorial fountain, and a long straight road leading somewhere else. Two orderlies, who had been approaching Billowing Pines on that road, could be seen in deep, and apparently controversial, conversation. As their two figures enlarged in nearness, it became clearer to Dr. Vaguely that their discussion was actually heated. At that point, they stopped walking.

"Dr. Pons," he spoke aloud, causing the room behind his back to fall silent. He felt the space behind him fill with the presence he had summoned. They watched the unfolding scene together.

One of the orderlies pushed the other.

Then the other pushed back.

Then the other pushed back harder, causing his companion to fall. The other quickly regained his footing, and stared back at his oppressor in anger.

The two orderlies glowered at one another in a moment wild with possibility—then stormed off in separate directions.

Dishonesty.

Forgery.

Disorderly conduct.

None of it was really serious or, needless to say, criminal; it was all, or would be, forgiven. Nevertheless, Vaguely realized that something awful was starting to happen.

Since Dr. Vaguely's return to Billowing Pines, he was ordered to focus on his patients, as there were now a great many of them—sometimes actual encounter survivors as before, but of late, a discernible increase in people in fundamental need of reassurance. He was told by Dr. Pons that his expertise was a precious resource and that it would suffice to have a shift of interns keep their eyes on their comatose patient until his hoped-for awakening. In the meantime, he sought refuge from the world's dawning madness in the worlds conjured by his patients.

On this particular day, he was meeting a new one, a young woman by the name of Angel Paget. Angel had the kind of beauty seldom encountered in reality but often described in storybooks as having the quality to attract the force of evil. Pick any illustrated fairy tale at random, and you will find her prototypes depicted in poses of love and danger, dwelling in the spires of candy-coated castles, under spells in deepest sleep, spinning flax into gold and lowering their hair. Her eyes were of a changeable, indeterminate color that kept her admirers guessing but, seen now, there was something about the black pools at their center that was more fractured than fetching.

"May I ask your age, Ms. Paget?"

"I'm 22."

"I see here that you attend college at St. Catherine's," said Dr. Vaguely, peering at a clipboard at rest on his crossed knee. "What's your major?"

"Art history."

Vaguely scribbled a note in the margin. The nib of his pen was so plush that his scribbling would have gone unheard by his patient, if not for the defensive flourish he put into it.

"Tell me what happened."

"What happened?"

He looked up from his writing: "I assume you're here for a reason?"

"Yes, I'm here because something happened… but I can't be sure I didn't bring it on myself."

"Oh?"

"I don't know where to begin," she half-sobbed, half-chuckled.

"At the beginning," Vaguely instructed. "But first of all, when did this happen?"

"Oh, about three months ago now. You've become very popular and it takes a long time to get in to see you."

"I am sorry about that, but my hectic schedule at least shows that many, many people are receiving the help they need. Please tell me your story."

"Okay then… I live by myself," she began. "I have an efficiency apartment about four blocks from the university. I had a boyfriend, a musician, who sometimes played gigs at a nearby coffee house."

"Had a boyfriend?"

"Had," she confirmed. "It's over, but it's relevant."

"Which coffee house?"

"Pascal's, near the campus. Devlin—that was his name…—Devlin and I had been going together for almost a year. He was such a sincere person… I felt I could trust him completely."

Vaguely was confused. "*He* did something to upset you?"

"No, it was the caller. Let me backtrack a little. Devlin and I, we were so much in love, my school work began to suffer. Exams were coming up, so I suggested we take a break from each other, just till I got through the worst of them. He looked so sad as I sent him away, but I kissed him—it was a very nice kiss—and told him it wouldn't be forever. It was after that, that very night, when my phone rang."

Hello?

"And a strange voice said—**Good evening! How lucky I am to find you in!**"

I'm sorry, I think you have the wrong number…

"But no… The voice repeated my correct telephone number, and asked if my name was Angel Paget."

Yes, this is she. Who is this?

"He identified himself as the friend of a friend. He wouldn't give me his name, because doing so, he said, might prevent him from speaking frankly."

Well, in that case, I'm hanging up.

"But if I hung up, he told me, I would be making the worst mistake of my life."

What do you mean? What is this?

"He asked if I knew where Devlin was at that very moment."

Yes, I do. He's at work, playing guitar at Pascal's.

"He's playing alright, but not at Pascal's."

I don't understand.

"The caller told me that he was calling me out of friendship for our mutual friend, Devlin."

You know Devlin?

"He told me how sad it was that Pascal's had fired him… how sad it was that he had been losing his inspiration as a musician… how embarrassing it had been to see him play so badly one night that his audience, all those college kids with their Heinekens, had booed him. He told me that, if I really loved Devlin, I never would have turned him away that night."

Oh, Devlin, this is you, isn't it?

"But he said, No, he wasn't. He told me that he hoped it was worth it to me, to recover my grades, because at that very moment, my boyfriend was searching for the inspiration he'd lost when I sent him away. In the bed of another woman."

What other woman?

"He asked if it really mattered what her name was."

If you expect me to believe you, then yes, it does!

"And then he told me that, if I really must know, Devlin was in bed with . his wife."

"What?"

"Not *his* wife—not Devlin's wife—but the *caller's* wife. He told me that I had no choice but to believe him, because he was as compromised by this information as I was. Moreso, actually."

What makes you think he's sleeping with your wife?

"He chuckled at my naïveté, chiding me by saying that, while they were in bed, they certainly weren't sleeping. He proceeded to tell me the whole story. He explained that, one night, while he was hanging up his wife's coat, a folded piece of paper fell from her pocket. On that folded piece of paper he found Devlin's name and two telephone numbers. He read them to me. One of them was definitely his."

And the other?

"The other was mine. The one he had just dialed."

"And why would the caller's wife be in possession of your number?" Vaguely questioned.

"Because sometimes Devlin stays over, of course," she said in a tone of worldly experience, belying her air of storybook innocence.

"He told me that next to my telephone number, in his wife's handwriting, were the words 'Say Wrong Number.' And I remembered that I *had* been receiving some wrong numbers recently… more than usual… It was always the same woman's voice, apologizing."

I haven't had any wrong numbers, lately.

"I was lying, of course. He told me not to waste my breath lying for two selfish lovers who were conspiring, at that very moment, to break my heart as well as his."

Look, even if what you say is true, it's not a crime to have an affair, is it?

"That, he said, **depends entirely on the laws to which one subscribes—the laws of man, or the more ancient laws."**

Look, I don't know anything about your wife, but I do know Devlin. And I know that he loves me. I know he does. He wouldn't do something like this.

"And the caller stressed that he wasn't blaming anyone, not at all. What his wife had to offer… **Well**, he said, **few mortal men could resist such an invitation."**

It's your fault that your wife does this! Can't you keep her happy?

"The caller then confessed that, in all honesty, he and his wife had been having marital problems. He hadn't been capable of responding to her in the way a husband should for some time. So she had started looking at the men about town, in the various places she frequented. Places like Pascal's. "

If all that's true, why do you stay married to a woman who betrays you?

"The caller reminded me that I was a young woman, old enough perhaps to have known love, but too young to understand what love becomes with the passage of time. He told me that marriage was a country unto itself, with its own history, its own language. The heartbreaks one experienced in a marriage were like the wars that ravage and redefine countries. He said they made you wiser. They had both invested too much in their marriage to simply throw it all away. **Of course,** he went on, **there have been times when I would have dearly loved to empty a firearm into her mouth…"**

Vaguely's recording pen froze on the page. He insisted on confirming this point: "He actually said that to you?"

"If he didn't say it, it would be me saying it. Which would you rather believe?" asked Angel Paget.

"Proceed."

"He said that he would have dearly loved to fire a gun into her open mouth, to keep pulling the trigger until her head had more bullets in it than a gumball machine has gumballs… but of course, he then laughed, he was no criminal, so that was unlikely to happen."

Alright, I'm going to hang up now. You're filling MY head with poisonous lies! You want to destroy the happiness I've found with Devlin—with the most hideous lies!

"But you must believe me, he said. **How can I convince you of my sincerity?"**

You don't know anything about me! About ANYBODY!

"But then he proceeded to tell me things that assured me he did. He knew where Devlin and I had met… the things we had discussed… the things we had promised to one another… the things I did for him… "

Vaguely recrossed his legs.

"He knew every secret I had ever whispered into Devlin's ear."

How do you know that? How do you know these things?

"Don't you see? he asked. **Your man and my woman… when they are one flesh, there are no secrets between them. No secret is more sacred than their own carnal appetites. My wife is very, very dry, he told me. The only thing that excites her—is betrayal!"**

What?!

"Yes, he told me. **She feeds on it. She thrives on it. And your randy boyfriend—sheltered little guitar boy that he is, he sneered—didn't have much currency to bargain with. He gave her all your cheap secrets for a suck!"**

You're lying! I don't believe you!

"And then he told me something that only God and the two of us could possibly know. He whispered to me, hissing like a snake, about the time…"

"You needn't tell me, Ms. Paget," Vaguely said comfortingly. "Did the caller ever get to the point of what he wanted?"

"Yes, very shortly after that. He told me that I sounded upset. He asked if I needed a friend, someone to come over and… hold my hand."

You've got a nerve!

"But Angel, dear! Wouldn't it be the most natural thing in the world for you and I to *avenge* ourselves?"

Avenge ourselves?

"You know what I mean… *Tit for tat?*"

Angel Paget winced at the memory.

"I couldn't take any more," she confided. "I just told him he'd have to tat his own tits and slammed the phone down.

"And then what?"

"I tried to call Devlin right away, but there was no answer. "

"You were upset," Vaguely pointed out, "and with good reason. Even so, you probably shouldn't have said what you… You say there was no answer. Are you certain that you dialed the correct number?"

"I got his recording," admitted Angel, her head hung low. "He might have been out playing."

"Exactly."

"Or he might have been in… 'playing.'"

"Ms. Paget," Dr. Vaguely said, now that the story of his patient's close brush with The Only Criminal was told, "you are aware of the most likely identity of the person to whom you were speaking?"

"I am aware of the possibility."

"Well, let me tell you this. If it was The Only Criminal who called you that night, I can promise you this: The Only Criminal never, ever, *ever* speaks the truth."

She averted her face and replied, "Yes, I know that."

"I'm afraid our time is about up."

Vaguely added some finishing touches to the pages on the clipboard on his lap. He had written only a few lines in shorthand, but he had drawn a rather elaborate, disturbing cartoon of a black telephone with two peering crescent eyes.

"Dr. Vaguely, tell me something," she interrupted as she stood. "Is it true what I've been hearing?"

"I don't know. What have you been hearing?"

"That The Only Criminal… you know… might be dead."

"Where did you hear that?" he asked with some alarm, because this was information that should, under no circumstances, be allowed inside the hospital where it could contaminate the residents.

"Around."

"Around," he echoed, satirizing the patient. "Ms. Paget, if you look around, you're very likely to see garbage, disorder, riff-raff. I, on the other hand, have something on my side, something called authority. I've devoted my entire life to the study of The Only Criminal. You might say I know my way around the subject. Yet your opinion, on whatever you base it, runs contrary to mine?"

"It's just that people are saying he hasn't made an appearance in weeks. I would imagine that… "

"People are saying, people are saying, people are saying! Well, as long as people are saying, imagine all the time I might have saved! Imagine the childhood I might have enjoyed outside the library, *where I sat all day long reading books about The Only Criminal!* ! Imagine the girlfriends I might have had in high school and college *had I ever considered taking my nose out of a textbook about The Only Criminal!* Imagine the lampshades I might have worn on my head! The parties I might have thrown!"

"What?"

"Because I made the foolish assumption that reliable information was the basis of all intelligence, that education was based on learning! But no! All one really needs to have—according to Professor Angel Paget—is *imaginings* about a subject! Well, for your information, *Professor*, as the most informed man on the subject of The Only Criminal you're likely to meet… as the professional consultant to whom you thought to bring your silly romantic problems… I must tell you that it is my considered opinion that The Only Criminal is *not* dead!"

"You really believe that?"

"Damn belief, child. It's my faith."

Chapter Five
AN EVENING PRAYER

Vaguely felt as though he'd spent his entire life up to this point as the romantic protagonist in some imaginary novel about The Only Criminal, only to turn the last page and find himself no more than a supporting character in some other, vaster, more ruthless narrative. There was only one thing to do about it: to "lose" himself right away in the many tomes and scrapbooks of his personal reference library.

In his personal residence of Apartment 5, he quickly got out of his work clothes and into his sweats and sneakers. He then prepared a tray of his favorite comfort foods and carried this humble repast across the hall to Apartment 6, where he proceeded to pull down from his shelves dozens of old books, stacking them within easy reach of the place he had carved out for himself on the floor. For musical accompaniment to his studies, he put on The Only Criminal's *Crime Scene 61 Revisited* album—and turned it up loud, loud enough to rub out as much of the outside world as was erasable.

It had been years since he'd consulted some of these dusty tomes, most of which he'd acquired during his years at university. As the world's foremost (nay, only) authority on The Only Criminal, Vaguely had become cocky enough to think he knew it all, but now his only wisdom seemed to reside in the absent-minded, acquisitive nature that had prevented him from throwing out these treasures long ago. So many of these volumes were now out-of-print, replaced in book stores by fresher works that always seemed to fudge on the facts, as if the publishing world was deliberately obscuring The Only Criminal's tracks with year after year, layer upon layer, of misinformation. Disappearing into these volumes once again, smiling at the dog ears he had folded into them untold years before, Vaguely realized anew that each page worked on his consciousness like a key, unlatching forgotten memories of the rooms at home and at university where he'd squirreled himself away to consume them for the first time in great gulps of curiosity and appetite. But such memories, he found, were essentially empty because, even then, he had lived for these books, inside these books. It was these books that defined those rooms in which he lived, *were* the rooms in which he lived, for as long as he could remember. He had rarely looked up to take note of the life that lay beyond them.

He had started out, like all children, with the picture books, the Little Golden Books, and the charmingly illustrated stories of The Only Criminal's reigns of terror in Oz—not an invented place, but an actual continent on the map. Vaguely still owned most of his originals, his own name unsteadily inscribed in each of them below the words "This Book Belongs To…" Then there were the shelves of serialized Young Adult mysteries he had read as a pre-teen; stories detailing The Only Criminal's capers at the House on the Cliff, the Shore Road, the Old Mill, and other fanciful locations. Vaguely had collected all of these, as well, including some variants published over the decades in which exclamations of "Jolly good!" were changed to "Far out!" or, more recently, "Awesome sauce!" (Vaguely sometimes wondered if editions, earlier than his earliest, had eluded him, in which the young protagonists exclaimed "Hark!", "Lo!" or "Forsooth!" He would have to look into this; anyone claiming the title of The Only Criminologist should be acquainted with such details.) He came next to the classic works of literature—*Kidnapped, The Pickpocket Papers, Criminal Farm* and so forth—first, through the Classics Illustrated comics adaptations and eventually through the Modern Library editions.

But all of these had been prelude to Paul Vaguely's great love, the True Crime books. It was in the arms of their truth that he found his true calling.

Having retraced in detail his life's hoarding of fiction and fantasy, while sipping a simple wine, munching on cheese and crackers and popping the occasional olive, Vaguely next turned to his old scrapbooks, the books he had compiled himself, pulling entire rows of them onto the floor from the low shelf below his television set. These were far more selective than the general histories of The Only Criminal published in book form, which, despite their frequently valuable information, sometimes failed to differentiate between authentic crimes and accidents that could be deconstructed to demonstrably non-malevolent explanations. Sometimes, even Vaguely now had to admit, a house burned to the ground for no more insidious reason than bad wiring; it didn't mean, as too many reporters had been quick to propose, that The Only Criminal had disguised himself in electrician's overalls, visited a home picked at random, and turned it into a firetrap.

When he came across a gap in the scrapbooks, discernible from a full absent year in the dates of his clippings, Vaguely recalled with a chill a period of superstition in his education. It was during that time when he became convinced that, by ruminating so intently on the subject of The Only Criminal, he might be involuntarily transmitting a vibration that a criminally-attuned mind might interpret in the manner of an invitation. Fortunately, it was around that same time that pharmaceutical companies recognized a need and began to manufacture various anti-anxiety medications—Panicaine, Scarium, Assassinax, Terropin, etc.—which he found sufficiently helpful to resume his hobby and guide it toward his eventual profession.

KNOCK-KNOCKA-KNOCK-knock. Knock knock.

Would that he had remembered to take his medications today! Vaguely jerked in alarm toward the door of his apartment, where he'd heard the most unwelcome sound in the world: a knock after dark.

It was not quite 10:00 p.m., but Paul Vaguely had never been one to receive surprise callers—and he was three flights up. Of course, he was only one flight up from the floor downstairs... Might it be that peculiar Miss White knocking at his door, in search of a neighborly cup of flour or sugar? Normally, his thoughts would have raced to the possibility of The Only Criminal's own raven-gloved knuckles rapping at his chamber door, paying a late call on perhaps the only individual who still believed in him, but now... these days, even so far-fetched a candidate as Miss White seemed a more likely visitor.

Rising slowly, and a bit guardedly, Vaguely crossed the book-strewn floor, held his right hand to his heart—*be still!*—and latched the door before accepting the dare to pull it completely open.

In the dimly-lit outer corridor stood two strangers in dark suits, both of them bulky but one much bigger up and across than the other. They stood there looking as lumpy and uneven as old furniture. Vaguely did not know either of these men, but their unbidden presence somehow disturbed him. Their squinting, somewhat porcine expressions were too earnest, too collegial, for their visit to have been prompted by mere pleasantry.

"Good evening," he said, over the chain. "How can I help you?"

"Actually, neighbor, it is we who have come to help you," said the larger Suit on the left.

"Yes?"

"Eh, eh, might we… come in, neighbor?" inquired the bifocaled Suit on the right. "Our mission is a proud one, but best served in, uh, in friendly privacy."

Vaguely ran his fingers through his dark hair, then unchained and opened the door more widely to admit them.

"I don't see why not," he smiled. "Strangers aren't necessarily to be trusted but, after all, there are *two* of you. That's comforting."

Vaguely took a step back into the room, toppling a stack of books on the floor, which had risen a bit higher than his knee a moment earlier.

"My apologies for the disorder," he said, lifting his tray of snacks and wine things and moving it out of sight. "I was working, and I don't usually receive guests."

The two Suits sidled past him and stood awkwardly in the middle of the musty room, smelling of old smoke, casting curious and slightly repulsed looks at the gnostic trappings of Vaguely's quarters—the maps, the flags, the Sweet Vanilla Crook butts in the ashtrays, the obsessive focus of the reading matter.

"I'm sorry, sir," said the ratchety little man in the Suit. "I seem to have, uh, uh, stepped on one of your uh, uh, comic books."

It had been a valuable one, too. Vaguely concealed his inner cringe behind common courtesy.

"I'm Dr. Paul Vaguely, and you gentlemen are—?"

"I am Brother Baer," said the larger one with a warm voice like griddle cakes and country butter, "and this," he said of his shorter companion, "this is Brother Helton."

The two Suits took turns sliding their dry, pink, impersonal hands into his. "Dr. Vaguely," they each said, in turn.

"May I offer either of you some refreshment?"

"We don't require any, but you go right ahead," said Brother Baer.

Somehow, Vaguely took his "but you go right ahead" as a dare to his mortal weakness.

"Make yourselves at home, won't you?" Vaguely invited. There were not too many places where they might accomplish this, but the two Suits—finding themselves near a long and conveniently unobstructed lowboy—lowered themselves onto this.

Vaguely apologized: "I'm sorry I can't offer you a better chair… Unless you wouldn't mind crossing the hall to my living quarters? This apartment serves as my study, you see."

Brother Helton looked askance at the room, plainly suspicious of whatever "studies" might take place there.

"We're perfectly comfortable here, Doctor," said Brother Baer. "You can't beat strong wood for comfort. Our Lord was a carpenter, you know."

This first Suit, evidently the spokesman of the duo, engaged Vaguely eye-to-eye. He had the unimpeachable manner of a policeman, though none of the valor; the stern regard of an authoritarian, with none of the authority; the self-satisfaction of pride, with none of the self. He and his associate huddled side-by-side, their hands cupping the knees of their well-ironed trousers.

Vaguely took the wing chair. "What can I do for you gentlemen?"

"Could we have that turned off?" asked Brother Baer, nodding to Vaguely's phonograph.

"Of course," he said, the perfect host. As he pressed a button on his remote control, the needle lifted from *Crime Scene 61 Revisited*, halfway through the especially long closing track, "Prosecution, No."

"Dr. eh Vaguely," Brother Helton began, excitedly, "there are some friendly questions that we would… like to put to you, if we may?"

Vaguely could tell that these Suits representing *something,* and something other than the daily press.

"Of course, friend," he allowed.

"Doctor, you *are* familiar with St. Timothy's Church?"

At that precise moment, the bells of St. Tim's began their hourly ringing across the street. They were impossible to ignore.

Vaguely gestured to the ringing filling the air with an ironic smile: "What do you think?"

"Doctor," Brother Baer cut in without humor, "we represent the parishioners of St. Timothy's. We may look unfamiliar to you, yet we are your neighbors. Our entire congregation is made up solely of your neighbors—men and women and children who come together under a common roof, in a common family, to fend off common doubt and reaffirm common faith. We understand you've been a resident in this building for quite some time and, frankly, some of us were wondering why you have never favored us with a visit."

"I see," Vaguely nearly stammered.

As the bells stopped ringing, the two Suits leaned forward as if hanging on the hope of an explanation to come.

"Well, you see, I work at Billowing Pines. I'm a psychologist… a 'criminologist,' actually… specializing in cases associated with…" Vaguely didn't say the words, but gestured toward a stack of unshelved books, the spines of which all had the same three words in common.

The Suits nodded, observing.

"… and it's a very demanding job, very time-intensive."

The Suits nodded, observing.

"Even under the best circumstances," Vaguely continued, "my duties allow me very little free time to call my own, but lately… I mean, ever since… the disappearance, shall we say… my duties have been multiplied a hundredfold."

The Suits nodded, forming an opinion.

"My patients, you see, are in great need of my attention, my complete attention. In fact, my focus on work is so complete, that I often lose track of time."

The Suits nodded, silently passing judgment.

"If I'm not counseling a patient, I'm tied up in professional meetings, being interviewed by the press, researching a medical paper, catching up on the evening news—"

"But the news changes from day to day, Doctor," intoned Brother Baer, suddenly fixing Vaguely with a double-barreled stare. "A man who bases his existence in the ephemera of transient events does nothing to fortify the through-line of his own life. He performs a disservice to his soul. Not to mention those who honor him with the offers of fraternity and guidance."

As he said this, Brother Helton allowed his tiny, bifocaled eyes freedom to roam the curious effects of the room, prompting occasional flinches in his pinched expression of excruciated piety.

"A-Amen," he resounded, rejoining the conversation. "The eh, the daily newspaper is as, uh, changeable as the voice… that would deceive us."

"Have either of you seen the newspapers lately—*any* newspaper?" Vaguely countered politely. "Every day, the headline is pretty much the same."

Brother Baer waved this counter-statement away, a feather of non-existence. "Of course, of course, deception comes in many guises," he proudly allowed. "It cannot be predicted. The swipe of Evil cannot be predicted. It is random and merciless. Goodness, however, is predictable.

Goodness can be depended upon. Goodness can be trusted to be there, to catch you when you fall. To be there so you won't."

"A-Amen," he was seconded.

"But—" Vaguely attempted.

"Doctor, St. Timothy's has stood across the street from this very building for the last 112 years. It has not changed. Its message, which harkens back to Man's earliest communications, has not changed. Its message was here to cure the world's seething mind before any of us in this room was born. I repeat: It has not changed. And neither has the basic need of mortal man to bend his knee before a higher power."

"If you'll forgive my asking," Vaguely objected, "how would either of you gentlemen know whether I bend my knee to a higher power, or not?"

"Oh, it is fairly obvious to us that you do, Doctor," Brother Helton interjected. "You see, we at St. Tim's focus our attention on one book, and one book only. The Good Book. I'm afraid that this apartment tells us everything we need to know about the Lord you worship. That's why we have come to save you, our brother. So many books here, and not one capable of saving you. Your obsession with evil, Doctor… Can you not see that it's overwhelming you? Defiling you?"

"You misunderstand," Vaguely told them. "I have a highly articulated sense of Right and Wrong."

The ratchety one spoke up: "You see yourself as The Only Criminal's ad-adversary?"

"As would any decent man."

"Only… moreso?" added Brother Helton.

"If only by virtue of my authority on the subject… Yes, moreso."

Brother Helton twinkled with beaming aggression. "But if you see yourself as The Only Criminal's adversary," he asked, "why choose to become a doctor? Why not a policeman? Or a lawyer?"

"Put The Good Book down long enough to read a newspaper," Vaguely responded sharply. "The police and the attorneys have never seemed to make much of a difference, have they? They never seem to get close enough to make a difference."

"Ah-ha! So is that what you want, Doctor?" Brother Helton presumed to joust. "Not to *oppose* The Only Criminal, b-b-but to be *close* to him?"

"Only in the endeavor to better understand him," Vaguely explained.

"That I might learn how to better help those whose lives he has disrupted, injured, even destroyed."

Brother Baer smirked. "You don't really believe that, do you, Doctor? Surely you're not so deluded as to believe for one moment that you're helping anyone but yourself?"

"The better one understands fear, the less one feels it oneself," Vaguely threw out in an insolence he regretted, now openly offended.

Brother Helton tossed a knowing glance at the array of locks on Vaguely's front door, and Vaguely understood what he was looking at. "Of course, of course," the bifocaled guest pontificated. "Know thy enemy. But don't you find the diversity of opinion in all these books obscuring? Have any of these books ever yielded a single truth that you could accept with absolute certainty? My questions are, of course, heh, rhetorical."

"As would my response to you," Vaguely promised. "Look, these volumes represent everything that is known about The Only Criminal. This is my reference library, perhaps the greatest single such archive in the country. Possibly, in the entire world."

"Is it, Doctor? Or is it your suit of armor, a skin with which you surround yourself to keep the outside world at bay?"

"I need these books for my work."

Brother Baer blithered this argument away, a floating fleck of effluvium. "You need these books for your work," he repeated, as if repeating those words in a different voice was all that was required to deflate his argument of its value. "Even a simple layman like myself knows that diseased words cannot speak of health to the sick of mind."

Vaguely promptly corrected the Suit: "The first ingredient of any effective vaccine is the germ of the disease being treated."

Brother Baer blew this comeback away likewise, a bubble of conjecture. "So you counsel your patients by contaminating them with your own fears? Full-strength, Doctor—or diluted with your own delusions? You see, we've heard about you, Dr. Vaguely. A friend described you to us as… a soul adrift."

"A friend?"

"Yes. Think of your soul as a lifeboat, Doctor. How can a drifting soul be of service to needy refugees—like your patients?"

"Better to be adrift than anchored and unable to budge," Vaguely countered.

Brother Helton cut in with amusement: "He has an answer for everything, doesn't he, Brother Baer? The Evil One has taught his advocate well!"

"Who cannot budge, Doctor? We, after all, climbed these steps to your door. Here, take my hand, while there is still time!" With sudden drama and aggression, Brother Baer shot out a stiff pink hand, his wrist thrusting from its cuff. "Are you prepared to give me your hand—here! tonight!—in the bond of brotherhood?"

"Cast away this evil, Brother Vaguely!" rejoined the other, gesturing to the books abounding on shelves, in stacks. "And join us in prayer—here! tonight!—that your soul may be washed and saved in the love of our Almighty Lord!"

The two Suits leaned forward, hands outstretched, their heads bowed and groomed, their eyes clenched in prayer, their manners intensifying with fervor. Brother Baer bellowed, summoning forces from deep within his barrel chest: "Are you-ah prepareDAH to give us your wordDAH—here! tonight!—that you will join us at St. Timothy's Church on Sunday morning? Take my hand now, Doctor!"

"HesitationHAH is doubTAH!," grunted Brother Helton, lacing his platitudes with punchy, nay lustfully, rhythmic persuasion. "And doubTAH is uh-innnnnvocationHAH!"

"Amen! Join hands with us now, Doctor!" Brother Baer rumbled, his livery lips and glutinous mouth then easing into some other, more liquid and rhythmic tongue, some other language, his heavy padded shoulders swaying to the externalized rhythm. His entire bulk—save for his obdurate, outstretched hand—was swaying to the raw tempi of his intonations, his heft squeaking the lowboy.

"Join hands, DoctorHAH!" yelped Brother Helton, as if encouraging him to hop aboard a hayride.

Brother Baer continued speaking in tongues.

"Hesitation is Doubt, Doctor! And Doubt is Invocation! Join hands with us—*here! tonight!*—against the darkness!"

The Suits were eventually persuaded to take their leave of Vaguely's den of iniquity. Vaguely pretended to accept their Lord as his personal savior just to get them the hell out, but something of these intruders remained on Vaguely's lowboy in spirit for a long time after they had physically gone. Vaguely sat in hawk-eyed vigilance, seething, waiting for the aftermath of their intrusion to stop wounding the very air of his sanctuary.

He had always loved the bells of St. Tim's, but now they meant something else. When they sounded again, and from that point onward, he could take no comfort in their joy. He could hear only arrogance, condescension, bullying.

Chapter Six
HE KNOWS JUST WHAT I NEED

"Paul! It's over!"

That explained it. It was the End of the World. The only possible explanation for the sound of wind howling down the streets, for its rattling at his fragile windows.

"Don't you hear me, man? It's broken!"

Vaguely had been rudely awakened by his telephone, had answered it while still more than half-asleep. As this Cassandra-like tiding of apocalypse came into fuller focus, he realized that he wasn't hearing anything more exceptional than the sound of the pipes carrying heat to his apartment, and a subcutaneous thudding in the vicinity of his temples.

"What's broken? The pipes? The windows?"

"The coma!"

Of course: the coma was over. He was awake, wasn't he? Or at least getting there. What time was it?

And then it clicked.

"My God, *the coma!* Who is this?"

"Pons, you idiot! Snap out of it! Get here ASAP!"

The smeary fingerpaints of utterance were now coalescing into language, resuming sense and sensibility, but alphabetical symbols were still too complex to penetrate the pervasive fog at Oakley Square.

"A recipe?" he queried. "You want me to bring a recipe?"

"ASAP! Get back here as soon as possible!"

"Yes, sir! Wait a minute: Is Peevey speaking? Is he—? I mean, tell me what happened!"

"Nurse Garotte noticed him stirring just before 4:00 this morning. He opened his eyes at 4:06. I happened to be here and was summoned. I have introduced myself and informed the patient of where he is, but I've not questioned him as yet. I was reserving that privilege for you. How soon can you get here?"

"In the wink of a moon," Vaguely promised, still without quite understanding what he meant.

Once again, standing outside the Oakley Apartments building, strumming his 12-string, was Whimsy Plunkett. He nodded at Vaguely, who skipped down the front steps and broached the curb with an air of watchful urgency.

I thought I'd never see a dawn
When all unease had been and gone
I thought I'd never get o'er the fright
Of singin' songs outside at night
I thought a day would never pass
Without the sound of shattered glass
But now such times are here, my friend,
Yesterday
Won't come this way again.

"Can't you play something else?" Vaguely snapped irritably. "Like a *real* song?"

The troubadour shrugged his shoulders and obliged by playing a familiar melody—"The Sound of Sirens"—but when he began to sing, the lyrics had changed. To Vaguely's bewilderment, he found that he knew these new lyrics as well as the others he remembered.

It was a cold morning, which made Vaguely all the more impatient for a taxi. He looked up at the old tattered billboard above Lawson's News. He patted down his pockets to find his snapper case of Sweet Vanilla Crooks but found it empty. He shot a sideways look of contempt at St. Tim's. He heard in the distance the bell above the door at Lawson's News, which meant it was open. He looked at the billboard again. It tempted him with that packet of Consolations. The Only Criminal smoked them; his house smelled like them. Perhaps he should try them. Just then, a Yellow Cab puttered into view. The smokes would have to wait.

Vaguely hailed the taxi, and it was still just dark enough in the morning light for the driver to reply by blinking the headlights. Whimsy Plunkett abruptly shifted from the cover version he was playing to another original, played over a brisk skiffle beat. Vaguely was able to hear the entire first stanza and chorus before the taxi pulled away with him:

A Yellow Cab is on the way
And once that taxi's taken
Two sleeping men will meet today
And only one awaken.

But I rejoice
But I rejoice
But I rejoice
But I rejoice
The void, at last, has found a voice
The void has found a voice!

Indeed it had. After arriving once again at Billowing Pines, Vaguely took the elevator to the penthouse suite. He had spent the entire taxi ride in silence, imagining all the different ways this historic meeting might play out; however, the way things finally did play out indicated that his story was being written by an altogether different hand.

Dr. Pons and Jim Westerfield had laid on extra security and, after passing a few necessary tests of identification, Vaguely was given the go-ahead to step inside the patient's quarters. Behind the door, he saw Dr. Constantin Pons, facing him, seated authoritatively in one of his midnight blue pin-striped suits, one eye glowering through his monocle at a man seated in a wheelchair, whose scrawny back was turned to Vaguely. He knew from the man's spikes of white hair that he must be Peevey.

"Good morning, Dr. Pons, I got here as fast as I—," Vaguely began, but he momentarily lost the power to speak as the patient—wearing standard-issue pajamas, robe and slippers, with a quilt folded over his lap—slowly turned his wheelchair to face him.

Vaguely gulped. *Could this man actually be The Only Criminal? Or had he merely touched and been badly singed by the hem of his horrid garment?*

"This is Dr. Paul Vaguely," Dr. Pons explained. "He's quite the expert on you... *Perry*."

Peevey regarded Vaguely as if from a very great height. He pivoted his chair back to face Dr. Pons and barked, "Not if he's been telling you my name is Perry, he's not."

"I never said—" Vaguely blurted aloud.

Pons cut him off with a curt karate chop against the moment. "Now that you're here, Paul," he interrupted, "I'll leave you and *Percy* to get better acquainted."

"Do I really look like a Percy to you?"

"Then, for the last time, man… What *is* your name?" Pons yelled.

Peevey leaned forward like a master provocateur.

"My name is… irrelevant!"

Pons rose in exasperation, beaten down. "Whatever you say .. *Patrick*!"

"Nor am I Patrick, Preston, Pasquale or Pablo!"

"May I have a word with you in private, Dr. Vaguely?"

"He doesn't want me to hear anything," chided the patient, "but he expects me to tell all!"

Vaguely followed his superior into the bedroom of the suite. Pons closed the door behind him.

"Look, Paul," Pons said, "I haven't slept in close to 48 hours. It's time you took over."

"Certainly, sir. I only wish you had phoned me sooner."

"First impressions?"

"He seems awfully feisty for a man who's just arisen from a two-month coma. What was the height on his chart?"

"Five feet, five inches."

"But he seems so much…"

"Yes, I noticed that. He has a powerful aura. He has enormous presence."

"That much is a given," Vaguely agreed. "The question is, is it something he acquired, or does he come by it naturally?"

"See what you can squeeze out of him, but don't let on that you're squeezing. I made that mistake. He may act like he's holding all the cards, but if you ask me, it's a carefully constructed artifice, meant to conceal… oh, whatever the hell he's concealing."

"Does he remember anything?"

"How would I know that? I'm stuck at proper introductions! Don't keep at him too long; we don't want to overtax him. Try to win his confidence. Stay with him till he asks for rest. I won't be leaving the building; I'll grab some winks in my office. If you need me, call the office. Beatriz will be screening my calls. Yours are the only ones I'll be taking. Assuming you don't need me, I'll be back on my feet to rejoin you around 3:00."

Pons patted Vaguely's arm encouragingly, then took his leave. The young doctor then carefully walked back into Peevey's presence with a list of questions trailing behind him, nearly as long as the days of his life.

Vaguely was on the point of taking the chair Pons had used, but then felt Peevey's eyes on him, like the eyes of an opponent in a game of chess. He paused and considered the placement of the chair, which had proved disadvantageous to Pons. He considered its distance, its, position, its specific opposition to Peevey's wheelchair. There was nothing favorable about it. Should he surprise him by taking a seat on the floor in front of him? No, that would place him at a lower, inferior position. He didn't demand superiority, but equality at least would be advantageous. He did think sitting closer than Dr. Pons had done might accomplish more, so he grabbed a lightweight chair from elsewhere in the room, plopped it down and sat close.

Peevey viewed Vaguely's every movement with keen suspicion.

"First of all," Vaguely began, "I should tell you—that I've been looking forward to meeting you for some time. You've been my foremost concern in life now for months. I can't tell you how many nights I've spent, watching you sleep, wondering what you might be dreaming."

"You're mistaken if you think it gives you any rights."

The patient's controlled sarcasm made Vaguely ache to vault past the civilities and demand answers to all the imponderable questions dominating his own existence, but he knew that such gnostic secrets lay, if at all, on the far side of a psychological mine field. So he took another approach.

In an attempt to match Peevey's self-control, Dr. Vaguely casually crossed his legs (something which the patient was not yet able to remaster), interlaced his fingers, and projected an air of cool professionalism.

"I suppose that one way to begin," he began, "might be to find out whether *you* have any questions that you'd like to ask *me*."

This drew no response.

"Presumably, Dr. Pons told you where you are… how long you've been with us… and under what circumstances you were found. Yes?"

Nor did this.

"I want you to know that I am here to serve you," Vaguely found himself saying. For some reason, the remembered image of the two Suits leaped into mind, then leaped away. "Is there anything I can tell you?"

"There is one thing."

"What is that?"

"Am I under arrest?"

"Why on earth would you ask that?"

Peevey directed Vaguely's attention, with a single flash of his eyes that implied "over there," to the suite's barred windows. Then he lifted the folded quilt from his lap, exposing a manacle that held him firmly to the wheelchair.

"Not at all," Vaguely answered. "On what possible charge?"

Peevey said nothing.

"It's true that all the windows on this floor have iron bars," Vaguely noted. "Like that manacle, they're a security measure. To protect *you.*"

"I don't need your filthy protection."

"Not to interrogate you," Vaguely smiled apologetically, "but would you mind explaining that? You don't need our protection because… there *is* no source of danger? Or because there never was?"

"I don't *want* your protection."

"But that isn't what you said," Vaguely said, pouncing on details. "You said that you didn't *need* our filthy protection. I find myself wondering why your first question would concern the possibility of your arrest. You do remember, don't you, that arrest is a rather outlandish measure reserved for… well, for only a… special case?"

Vaguely had chosen his words carefully, and watched the man's face closely for a flinch or some other sign of unspoken disclosure. He made a mental note of an involuntary twinge in the upper corner of Peevey's mouth when the word "only" was spoken.

"Well, as I say, I'm not here to *make* you talk," Vaguely continued in a smooth, soothing voice. "Of course, there are some things, obviously, that we would like to know. That would be *helpful* for us, and good for you, to know."

Peevey stared back.

"Things that might make you feel better, were you to get them off your chest. Things that, if you were to tell me… I can assure you… would go no further than this room. You can trust me."

Peevey smiled at Vaguely, but not in a kindly way. "Naïve twat, aren't you?" he said.

"Now, Mr. Vincent, whatever do you mean by that?"

"Must we play these boring games?"

"My apologies," Vaguely apologized. "Dr. Pons made me promise to try. And now that I have… Let's just forget about it, shall we?"

"If I'm *allowed* to."

"What would you *like* me to call you?"

"A taxi, thank you very much."

"Is there a reason why you don't want us to know your real name?"

"Next boring question."

"It's my specialty to help people like you."

"People like me? Are there lots like me walking about? If so, well then, go ask *them* your lunatic questions," Peevey suggested with horrible, exacting authority. "I gather from the morning I've had that there *are* no other people like me. Isn't that why you and I are sitting here on this pleasant morning… having this little talk… behind barred windows?"

Vaguely leaned forward and addressed the patient *sotto voce*: "If you have loved ones you wish to protect, we can help with that. But, in the meantime, surely you'll want them to know you're safe—that you're alive?"

"I have nobody, and I don't need anybody." Peevey leaned forward in his wheelchair, adding *sotto voce*: "You least of all."

In that moment, Vaguely lost it. "Then tell me! Tell me what happened! You saw him, didn't you?" He all but fell to his knees before his patient.

There was an abysmal pause.

"That," Vaguely pressed further, "or…"

He stopped himself—or was stopped by what he saw in Peevey's eyes.

"I haven't got the slightest idea what you're talking about," the patient said. "And neither do you."

Vaguely, to his embarrassment, was on the point of weeping. *"Tell me what you saw, Peevey!"*

"Why do all of you insist on calling me that insipid name?"

At last, the patient dealt him some ammunition in this battle of wills. Vaguely reached into his coat pocket and unfurled the torn silk pajama pocket he had held since the moment of their first meeting, embroidered with the initials they had in common. He handed it over to Peevey with the air of a man holding a trump card.

Peevey looked indifferently at the swatch. "This is this supposed to mean something to me?"

"It's your pajama pocket," Vaguely told him. "That's your monogram."

"No, it's not."

"Yes, it is."

"Is not."

"Is."

"I tell you, it's not."

Vaguely pointed to the first, then to the second, letters of the monogram: "Pee, Vee!" he explained loudly.

"Piss. Off. Not mine."

"Then whose is it?"

"It could be yours, for all I know! Paul Vaguely, right? You look like the type who might wear poofy, monogrammed pee-jays, pee-vees and what-have-you."

Vaguely, insulted, grabbed the swatch back.

"Have it with my compliments," Peevey said, unconcerned. "I wipe my bottom with it. Now, if you're finished boring me, I'd like some clothes and a Get Out of Jail Free card. I want to see the back of this looney bin."

Chapter Seven
IF WE NEVER MEET AGAIN

"And that's when he rang for Nurse Hooks, who came along and took him into his bedroom to rest," Dr. Vaguely concluded. He had laid the silken PV pocket swatch over the crest of his knee, where he stroked it like a talisman for the duration of his account.

The pudgy, swarthy hands of Constantin Pons carefully arranged a mug of black coffee and a cube of carrot cake near the edge of his desk, in front of his protégé. Pons's nurturing side had been provoked by noticing that a certain decrepitude was beginning to manifest in his young mentee's personal appearance, traces of a lack of attention to self. Vaguely was clean enough, cleanliness was never his problem, but his eyes were wild, his hair was looking unkempt, and his nails showed the unevenness of chewing. His clothes sagged baggily on his thinning frame, and one of his bent legs seemed to be forever pumping air into the bellows of an invisible harmonium.

"Get this into you," Pons ordered, pointing a stubby finger at his offering, while lowering himself heavily into the swivel chair behind his desk, built to support up to 500 pounds. "It's not exactly health food, I'll grant you, but it's what's available until the kitchen serves dinner." He watched Vaguely take an absent-minded bite of the cake, a sip of the coffee, another deeper sip, and then sit them both back down.

"All of it," Pons commanded. "Doctor's orders."

Vaguely then consumed the cake in a series of three C-shaped reductions of its iced and orange mass. He did not drink all the coffee at once, as it was piping hot, but after an additional sip, he appeased Pons to the extent of holding the mug in his hand.

"There was something about his defiance," Vaguely shivered. "I didn't expect it to be so…"

"Wicked?"

Vaguely nodded, appalled.

The two doctors shared a few minutes of silence.

"He has every right to leave, as you know," Pons reminded his fraying associate. "Unless you can think of some valid reason for us to detain him. I'm afraid I'm at a loss to think of any."

"But, sir! Think of the danger!"

"I have, and I do," Pons admitted, "and to be perfectly honest, Paul, what frightens me most is how terrified you seem to be, in regard to the prospect of his release."

"I know the very idea sounds preposterous," Vaguely apologized, "but what if he *is* The Only Criminal? If we set the genie free, we'll never get him back into the lamp."

"Oh, come now! He's intimidating, I'll grant you, but he's a shrimp!"

"If The Only Criminal can commit crimes in Paris, France and... I don't know... *Bardstown, Kentucky* in the blink of an eye... then who is to say that shape-shifting can't also be part of his repertoire! He's our responsibility, Dr. Pons. He's in our custody. Think of what we might be releasing back out into the world!"

"Yes. Newspaper stories, television programming, motion picture fodder, restored equilibrium for the general public—and, let us not forget, something for you to base a career upon," Pons responded, neatly. "Don't look at me that way, you've said it yourself! He's either the real thing, or he's been somehow contaminated by the contact. Look around, Paul. The signs are everywhere that this planet of ours is teetering on the cusp of a mass nervous breakdown! Given the possibilities, there is a better than 50/50 chance that releasing Peevey into the world might be just the medicine we're all craving."

"You mean... if we let him *become* The Only Criminal?"

"I mean, just let him be. See what happens."

"I had so looked forward to getting closer, to getting to know him, to hearing his stories..."

"I gave you a private audience, Paul," Pons observed. "Okay, it wasn't the encounter you hoped for, nothing you imagined came of it, but at least you've had that. Who else has?"

"You may be right," Vaguely allowed, forcing himself to look on the bright side, the dark side, or whichever side it was..

Good shrink that he was, Vaguely observed in his mentor's

demeanor that something else, as yet unexpressed, was hovering between them, like an invisible shoe needing to be dropped.

"What is it, Dr. Pons? There's something more. I can tell."

"I don't know how to break this to you, Paul," Pons continued delicately, "but our star patient is not the only patient who has decided to leave us."

"Oh?"

"Go on, drink the rest of that down. Good man. Yes, I'm afraid that this news of The Only Criminal going on hiatus has inspired rather a large number of our other patients to leave Billowing Pines."

"Our patients? Sir, I think you mean *my* patients."

"Well. I had hoped to spare you some of the pain."

"Who, in particular?"

"You want particulars? Here, have some particulars!"

Dr. Pons passed two sheets of paper over to Dr. Vaguely, stapled in the upper left corner, printed on Billowing Pines stationery. His eyes scanned down the list of nearly 25 patients, their surnames arranged in alphabetical order. All but a few of the familiar names and cases had already been discharged. One of them, the very last on the list, was "Wakening, Ruta"—a name which had never before held for Vaguely the ironic value that it held for him now.

"They were all safe here," he muttered in shock. "And we've released them back into a world where the danger they could not bear may soon again run rampant?"

"Peevey hasn't been released yet, Paul. Give me a reason to hold onto him!"

Another name that Dr. Vaguely saw on the list was that of Jasper Ruddle. Jasper was a jittery man of roughly Vaguely's own age, with a compulsive habit of wringing his hands, as if trying to scrub them clean of some irreducible filthiness. In one of their recent therapy sessions, he had mentioned to Vaguely that his parents had managed a hotel…

"My earliest memory of, of, of, of him"—he confided—"was probably something that my parents said to me. Like any other boy, I was taught that it wasn't right to touch a hot stove, to pinch little girls, or annoy the guests. My parents managed a hotel, you see. To warn me against doing such things, my parents told me that The On—The On—"

"Some of my patients find it helpful to use the acronym TOC," Vaguely had mentioned helpfully.

Ruddle smiled with faint embarrassment and proceeded gamely.

"My parents told me that… TOC… there! That was easy! That he might not understand, if he ever heard that I had done bad things. They explained to me that TOC might think that some of his evil had somehow rubbed off on me, and come after me, wanting it back. N-Naturally, I didn't want this to happen, so whenever I felt the urge to, like, misbehave…"

"As normal children will," Vaguely assured him.

"I started wondering where these feelings came from, how they were getting inside me. And I think I figured it out. After school, you see"—he continued—"I used to go to this little penny candy store, and one of the things I liked to buy there were the O-On-O… the TOC Licorice Footprints. Do you remember those?"

"Oh my!" Vaguely chuckled, sinking back into his seat. "I haven't thought of them in years! They were footprints made of licorice that you could arrange on the floor and make it look like The Only Criminal had been there, right?"

"Exactly! The same company also made those TOC Crime Scene Taffy Banners, but the TOC Licorice Footprints! Gosh, I loved those things! I was chewing on one of them, one day… one of the black ones, though I preferred the red ones…"

"Oh, right," Vaguely interjected. "The *bloody* footprints!"

"… and it dawned on me that I was eating little pieces of TOC when I ate those footprints. I know it's nonsense now, Dr. Vaguely, but to a six- or seven-year-old kid, those footprints are the real thing!"

"Don't I know it!" the professional exclaimed.

"So I stopped buying them."

"What did you do with your spending money then?"

"I *saved* it. I mean, what else was I gonna do? Well, one day, my mother found all my unspent allowance money in the back of my sock drawer, and let me tell you, all Hell broke loose."

"I don't understand," Vaguely broke in. "Didn't your parents encourage you to save your money for a rainy day."

"I grew up in Palm Springs, Dr. Vaguely," Ruddle explained. "It never rains there. So when Mom saw all the money I had saved, she went to my Pop and told him about it. Then they came to my room together and they explained that having so much money around might lure, you know… TOC to our home, that he might rob and even kill us."

"Some parents are now calling this 'Tough Love,'" Vaguely noted.

"The government tells us that it's our responsibility—to everyone's common safety—to spend our money rather than save it."

"Don't get me wrong, Dr. Vaguely. I'm not here to blame my folks. They raised me with a strong sense of tradition and family values, values I hope to pass on to my own kids someday. I c-could see the sense of what they were saying, and I swore to them that I didn't mean to do any such thing. But they cautioned me that if I didn't spend that money soon, I would see soon enough what would happen. And boy, wasn't that the truth!"

"What happened?"

"Well, I d-didn't spend the money right away. I didn't know what to spend it on. Everything in toy and candy stores was an Only Criminal product."

"Naturally," Vaguely reasoned.

"Well, after a couple of days had passed, I came back home from school and found my room completely wrecked!"

"Every little boy's room is a wreck," Vaguely smiled, fondly remembering his own.

"Not as wrecked as this! It wasn't just messy… it had been ransacked! Do you know what I found?"

"Tell me."

"A trail of TOC Licorice Footprints spread across the floor, leading from the door of my room directly to my sock drawer. All my money was gone… except for one quarter."

"A quarter?"

"The exact price of one Only Criminal Licorice Footprint."

So many empty rooms now at Billowing Pines… Vaguely had to convince himself of this latest turn of events by making the rounds and confirming with his own two eyes that most of his patients' quarters had been vacated.

He had never visited their rooms before, having relied entirely on private interview sessions in his own office for insights into their problems. From the moment he crossed the threshold of the first sanctuary, he understood at once, profoundly so, the fundamental arrogance and stupidity of his past approach to therapy. Just by seeing how his patients kept their rooms would have given him more insight to each of their cases. Angel Paget, for example, had painted the walls of her quarters in the image of a 360° fresco, *à la* Arthur Rackham. It depicted a forest of very thin birch trees, like those found in Germany's Black Forest, where a beautiful princess—with Angel's own face—was fleeing a shadow like that of The Only Criminal on the edge of those woods. The entire fresco was mostly colorless, except for a single blob of red that she had painted on the breast of The Only Criminal, where he had been impaled by a spear, presumably hurled to target by a handsome prince awaiting her just outside the composition. He knew the bloodshed was a recent addition to the panorama because the paint was still wet to his touch.

After visiting five or six such rooms, Vaguely turned a corner which led him to the corridor where Jasper Ruddle's quarters had been. As soon as he turned the corner, he felt that slow, malignant turn of the air, the knife-twist of time and space that all of his patients commented upon, at one time or another, when they had felt the source of true evil nearby. That was mere milliseconds before he first saw them, running almost the entire length of the corridor, one after another—a series of Only Criminal Licorice Footprints. They were of the black licorice variety until they crossed the threshold of Jasper's room, where they abruptly changed from Original Black to Bloody Cherry.

Jasper's quarters leading me to his quarters, Vaguely thought. He could not help but follow them.

He took a deep breath before stepping inside the vacated room. It was absolutely austere and orderly, aside from an open dresser drawer. Vaguely silently reprimanded himself that he and his patient would now never get to the bottom of Jasper's secret candy binges—but, if his patient was ready to abandon the matter, he was obliged to let it go too.

Vaguely crossed the room and looked inside the open yawn of the dresser. Inside, a single quarter shone.

Despite himself, Vaguely gasped.

As he turned away from this horror, he found himself facing Peevey, framed in the doorway, in his wheelchair. There was no nurse present to push or attend him. The mad patient leaned forward, his hands perched on both his wheels, openly leering at the self-styled criminologist.

"What are you doing here, Peevey?" Vaguely demanded, asserting his authority with somewhat more volume than resolve.

"I thought I might take a little evening exercise before turning in," Peevey replied in measured tones. "Imagine me having to tell you!" he added.

"What do you mean?"

"I mean, aren't you the one who is supposed to hold all the answers about a certain subject?"

"Those candy footprints scattered all over the corridor. Is that your doing?"

"I don't know. Is it a crime?"

Peevey let the question hang in the air as he reached inside the breast pocket of his standard issue pajamas and produced an Only Criminal Licorice Footprint, a black one. He bit the corner of its cellophane wrapper and tore the candy footprint free, wiggling it lewdly for Vaguely's edification before biting into a stretchy, gummy mouthful. "I could eat soles all day."

"Where did you get that?"

"This? Don't you know? They sell them right here, in your own commissary."

Vaguely had not known this. For as long as he could remember, he passed through the halls at Billowing Pines so absorbed in his work as to be no more than an automaton. He couldn't tell you what the commissary served, who worked there, or what color its walls were painted.

Then, as if infiltrating the realm of his own thoughts, he heard Peevey's voice, deep within his own skull, said "**See you in the funny papers!**"

At once, he snapped back into the present, looked at the wheelchair and saw that Peevey was gone! The wheelchair remained, yet Peevey was gone!

There was no explanation for what had just happened. Accepting this, Vaguely meekly turned off the light in the room and wheeled the empty chair down the now-unlittered corridor, back to the penthouse suite before going home.

The Only Criminologist left Billowing Pines that night brimming with equal parts terror and insecurity. Staring out the window of the #27 as it wove its way back to his unchanging neighborhood, Vaguely's eye was drawn to a neon light standing out against the darkening sky.

BAR
BAR
BAR 2000.
BAR
BAR
BAR 2000.

Vaguely was neither a teetotaler nor prone to excessive imbibition. Self-obliteration through total absorption in his work had always been his favorite *modus elabi*. Even so, as far back as he could remember, as he rode through the streets of his childhood in the backseat of his mother's car, he had been attracted to the reassuring, predictable repetitions of neon signs. He remembered a bowling alley called the Rock 'Em Bowl whose sign showed a stationary neon bowler rolling a neon ball that scored the same strike over and over and over. He had found its predictability, its reliability, comforting and he needed comfort tonight. He told his driver to drop him off outside the Bar 2000.

He soon discovered there was far more awaiting him behind that sign than a simple scotch or a beer. The Bar 2000's cocktail menu was at least a dozen white-knuckled thrills to a page, and Vaguely resolved to experience their wares in all their vast variety. In the first hour, in his secluded booth, he tried—in alphabetical order—a Blackjack, a Culpritini and a Desperado, before deciding the alphabet was murder and preventing him from trying some of the equally tempting flavors nearer to Z, such as a Slaughter on 10th Avenue or a Tequila Bloodshed.

As he discovered, on the other side of these decisions, to break away from alphabetic law brought not only freedom but also confusion. He would hold up an ever-floppier hand to signal the waitress but, as the room began to tilt, as the checkered linoleum floor started playing hopscotch with itself, his arm would drop in a dither; he lost his way, unsure of whether to sample a Hit & Run, a Red-Handed, a Fallen Angel, an Electric Chair, a Slippery Eel, a Peccadillo, or if he should perhaps backtrack to a Blackjack. In the final analysis, they were all Hit & Runs.

People in bars are nostalgics at heart and tend to be fond of old songs. Someone hazy in Vaguely's fuzzy orbit kept pumping coins into the jukebox, summoning up the same old number, one of the most popular ever recorded by The Only Criminal:

Alabama wants me
Lord, I can't go back there
Mississippi wants me
Lord, I can't go back there
California wants me
Lord, I can't go back there
Cincinnati wants me
Lord, I can't go back there

... and so on and so on, until every four-syllable city and state had been scratched off the singer's remaining list of welcome ports. Vaguely could easily imagine The Only Criminal in such a true-life situation that very night. *Might this be the explanation for his leave-taking? Could he cross no more rivers because every last one of his bridges had been burned?*

In time, Vaguely settled his tavern bill by laying all of his money, paper and coins, on the bar for the cashier's choosing. Once she had taken her honest due, he scooped the rest back into his pockets, like so much sand—and staggered back to his apartment building under the light of what looked to him, in his cockeyed state, like a single moon.

Vaguely did a double take. *A single moon?* Perhaps the other had temporarily passed behind a cloud, but yes, it was true. There now appeared to be only one moon in the night sky, as though The Only Criminal himself were winking down at him in crafty complicity!

Once back within the comforting known geometry of the newsstand, the bakery, the laundromat and the spires of St. Tim's, the besotted Dr. Vaguely marveled at how compact, how sufficient, how like a dream the tiny little world of Amelia was—so adorably and perfectly simple—it all seemed to begin and end, to Genesize and Revelate, to be wholly encompassed in a neat little package of all of what anyone might possibly want. His little niche in this world was so perfectly drawn that could almost pass for a simple Hollywood-style *façade*. He began to wonder what would happen, were he to wander down Oakley Way to the corner down there, which he had never walked—much less looked—around.

Is that what happened? it occurred to him.

Had The Only Criminal, loitering ominously outside Vaguely's apartment one night—perhaps stepping gigantically down from that Consolations billboard above Lawson's—had he decided to stroll around that corner and fell off the edge of the world? Perhaps he should take a look…

The two-dimensional vista beckoned invitingly. The street seemed to reach an end with the locksmith, yet cars drove farther down that street and around that corner all the time, did they not? Vaguely almost mustered the courage to brave the edge of its proscenium by peeking around the corner… but he was reeled back from ever knowing what lay around the bend by the suddenly greater thrall of the Consolations billboard. Since the start of this story, it had aged into a state of disrepair, a loose sheet hanging down and flapping in the wind.

Vaguely's neck craned back as he gazed up at it, while walking into the middle of the street. "I smoke them!" he shouted out, though it was well after midnight, his projected voice bouncing off the fronts of familiar dwellings and businesses. "My house smells like them!"

But he knew, in his heart of hearts, that it didn't. Even his apartment didn't. When he wanted a smoke, he wanted his *Arma del Fuegos* and those Sweet Vanilla Crooks. Had he let The Only Criminal down? Why didn't he ask Peevey for a smoke when he had a chance?

Vaguely staggered the rest of the way across the street to Lawson's, having somehow staggered across the street to Lawson's, and stood squinting through the picture window—past the barrier of his own reflection—at the Consolations display on the counter. It was a likeness of The Only Criminal, based on the billboard design, with two rows—five or six packs deep—of Consolations Filters, Regular and Menthol, arranged in a rack in the form of his suavely extended cardboard hand. In Vaguely's condition, he saw each individual packet as a symbolic lung of The Only Criminal; they were proof of his existence; they were, if you will, his life's breath. As long as there were Consolations cigarettes in the world, The Only Criminal could not be far away, because cigarettes were addicting. He designed them that way.

Vaguely *had* to have a pack. His house—such as it was; it was an apartment but still, you know what he meant—*had* to smell like them or his life, his very existence, would be meaningless!

He was seized by a powerful desire to smash the window—to do away with the ridiculous 9 to 5 barrier separating him from 'round-the-clock nicotine-and-tar ecstasy! He couldn't wait till opening time to press those cellophane-encased packets to his nose, to inhale and engorge his needy senses with their nurturing criminal aroma! He would gladly pay for the privilege of breaking the window, he would gladly leave the cost of the cigarettes he took and all the shattered glass, he would gladly leave a courteous note explaining and apologizing for what had happened—beyond his control! But he knew that, no matter how well he compensated Mr. Lawson and his property, to effect such vandalism would be mathematically, geometrically, metaphysically, philosophically and existentially impossible—*would it not?*

Go ahead. You know you want to.

He did. He really did.

There's a rock right over there that would do the trick. You

know you won't want them in the morning. Now is the only time that lighting one up and tasting that toasted taste would make a difference. You know it's true, because you're hearing it from the horse's mouth. This is a one-time offer, Paul. Break that window, take one of those little packs of Heaven, light one up—and maybe then I'll come back. You'll be astonished how fast I'll come back. Take some matches too. Better yet, grab one of those fancy flip-top lighters. Stainless steel. No one will ever know.

"No," Vaguely said aloud, steeling himself. "It's an impossibility. A perversity."

This is the only chance you'll get tonight to enjoy the superior flavor of a Consolations cigarette. I smoke them. My house smells like them. Pass this up, and I won't be responsible for what happens. And neither will you.

"I'm going home."

Vaguely resolutely turned away from the window, feeling beaten yet also triumphant. Then a peculiar smell reached his nostrils. It was not a readily familiar odor, but it was strangely arresting and comforting. It was a musty sort of aroma—like roasted nuts, the sort of dust that settles on old books, and strong black tea all played a role in its combination, which produced the hearty hogo of an inviting, pungent acridity. He looked right and left before crossing the street at the crosswalk; it was midway through his crossing that he saw the source of this sorcery: Miss White sitting solitarily on the front stoop of the Oakley Apartments, bundled up against the night's winter air, smoking a cigarette. Undoubtedly a Consolations cigarette. As if she had just reached up to the billboard and taken it from his own hand.

Before he could halt or reprimand it, the alcohol in him pressed forward through his crowding inhibitions and was heard to say: "Pardon me, pretty neighbor, but I would kill for a cigarette."

She laughed through her nose, able to tell at once that he'd tied one on, and fished one out of her pocket. "Now you don't have to," she said, handing it over.

From his hand into hers, from her hand into his. It was a Consolations.

Somehow she was in a mood to chat, perhaps because there was no third person present to enable her usual oblique approach. "I know it must look weird to see someone smoking outside their own apartment, especially in this weather, but if I smoke inside, the smell clings to everything—the walls, my furniture, my clothes," she explained. "I may smoke 'em, but no matter what the billboards say, I don't want my place to smell like 'em."

This opportunity—what to say of this opportunity? Had Vaguely lingered, had he stayed, how long might the two of them have talked there into the wee hours upon that sacred stoop? Might the passing minutes have led to the sharing of secrets, exchanges of confidence, reminiscences of rapture—things that would have led them to recognize all that they unwittingly had in common? But Paul Vaguely, in his alcoholically diminished state, was simply too in awe of her troubling perfection to remain.

"With your leave, fair lady, I shall take this cherished gift indoors," Vaguely said, bowing slightly, not wishing to tarry, as he continued to string sentences together which, lost in a kind of tizzy, sounded absurdly Lizzy, which is to say Elizabethan, and he with not so much as a hat to doff in tribute to the generous maiden. "My place is already a lost cause. I have this on the highest authority."

"Enjoy," she said, turning back to her view of the local set design. "And watch the stairs."

Vaguely watched each and every one of the 48 steps of the zig-zagging staircase inside, but they did nothing unusual. Once safely back in his personal quarters, Vaguely settled into his green wing chair and smoked his treasure. As he did this, some pieces fell into place.

1) He was more of a cigar man.
2) He should have remained outside on the stoop with Miss White.
3) He remembered where he had first smelled Consolations cigarettes. His mother had smoked them. Their house had smelled like them, and so did her clothes.

Chapter Eight
I BELIEVE

By morning it was official: at some point during the night, Peevey had somehow managed to leave Billowing Pines without an official discharge. Dr. Pons was vexed with curiosity about how he had accomplished this without having recovered the full use of his limbs, but Vaguely kept quiet regarding his own insights about this matter; after all, he had not actually seen Peevey walk away from his wheelchair. There were certain billings which had piled up but—without a forwarding address and with their inability to obtain fingerprints from his badly burned hands—there wasn't much that could be done about it.

Vaguely still had a straggling patient or two left at Billowing Pines, but he could sense their restlessness and knew it was only a matter of time before they too found the courage to check out. He was already reduced to half-day schedules and understood that it was only a matter of time before Dr. Pons saw the wisdom of turning him loose, too.

In his now-abundant free time, Vaguely continued to follow the newspapers and telecasts from his office desk. He did this with interest and trepidation, knowing that Peevey—whoever or whatever he might be—now roamed the earth freely. With him marauding about, there was every possibility that The Only Criminal might start making headlines again… but it soon became evident to Vaguely that, if this was indeed Peevey's plan—or even within the realm of his power—he was in no great hurry. Vaguely took this very personally, knowing that Peevey was having more diabolic fun at his expense by doing absolutely nothing than he would have carrying out his ump-millionth heist. Vaguely's professional responsibility had always been exclusively directed toward his patients at Billowing Pines, but as those patients were now mostly on the outside, his allegiances began to shift from private practice to the larger canvas of the outside world.

He determined that he must use his position at Billowing Pines—precarious as it was, while it still lasted—to convince the press of the mistaken change of direction they had taken with their reportage. For the sake of the public mental health, he must somehow persuade those journalists and publishers within his reach that they should not be glossing over The Only Criminal's inactivity—whatever its ultimate purpose—with stale replays and demoralizing reprints. After all, audiences would not stand for it if movie theaters fed them a steady diet of remakes, would they? Instead, the press should be perpetuating The Only Criminal's primacy over the daily lives of their readerships by actively reporting what was really going on—which was, in his professional opinion, a mind game of unprecedented scope, unquestionably Criminal in origin.

Plan A in this campaign involved re-establishing contact with Lorraine Cadbury. After his usual spartan breakfast, Vaguely telephoned the WTOC-TV newsroom, only to learn that the station's call letters had been changed. Already! This was not a good sign. The receptionist patched him through to Ms. Cadbury's office, where his call was taken by a male secretary named Monty.

"May I ask who's calling?"

"Dr. Paul Vaguely."

"Will she know what this call is in reference to?"

"I'm calling about The Only Criminal."

"I think you want the morgue."

"I beg your—"

"Our archival department. One moment, I'll connect you."

Of course, Vaguely didn't want the archival department, much less the morgue, so he disconnected and placed the call again.

"Lorraine Cadbury's office."

"Monty, this is Dr. Paul Vaguely calling back, for Ms. Cadbury. She's expecting my call."

"I'm sorry, Doctor. One moment, I'll see if she's in."

After a minute or two, Lorraine Cadbury herself appeared on the line, greeting her caller with her most provocative voice: "Dr. Vaguely, my secret admirer! I thought you'd forgotten all about me."

"Forgetfulness seems to be running rampant these days, Ms. Cadbury," Vaguely said, skipping the niceties. "I'm calling because you're the only person I personally know who might be able to answer this question..."

"Alrighty, good-lookin'."

"Why isn't the press reporting what's *really* going on in the world today?"

"I'm sure I don't know what you're talking about."

"I'm talking about the way everyone continually obfuscates the truth of what's happening today with all of these… retrospectives! You're turning the news into—into *an entertainment program!*"

"It always *was* an entertainment program, Dr. Vaguely!" she laughed. "Are you telling me this is… *news* to you?"

"I'm trying to tell you that you're acting as an accomplice in the worst crime against humanity ever conceived!"

"Oh, come now."

"Ms. Cadbury—Lorraine—I urge you: Don't feed your audience a steady diet of Only Criminal reruns! It's your responsibility to show people that he's still among us, by showing them the calculated damage that is being done to their daily lives by this… this ruse! This is the biggest story of the century and you're overlooking it!"

"As a commercial station, we have to give our viewers what they want."

"But what they want isn't *good* for them!"

"It never was. Did you just wake up, or something?"

"I have a proposition for you, Ms. Cadbury," Vaguely declared.

"Well. You certainly took your time."

"What if I were to consent to another interview, with absolutely no prior restrictions? You could ask me anything! Or, better yet, what if I could arrange to let you bring a camera crew past security, into Billowing Pines itself—where I could tell you *the true story* of the last man ever to see The Only Criminal?"

"The Only Witness? But that's old news, Doctor. He left Billowing Pines weeks ago, don't you remember?"

Vaguely caught himself. He had not meant to reveal this much, but as they say, confession is good for the soul, and he knew that it would feel very good indeed to lift this burden off his chest. So, without clearing anything with his place of employ, he took the plunge: "That's one of the things we need to discuss, Ms. Cadbury," he confessed. "The Only Witness, the man released from Billowing Pines last month, the one you remember, was an imposter. He was a hired actor. The real Only Witness was just released. Or let loose. His name was Peevey."

"Peevey?" The anchorwoman blew a raspberry. "'The Only

Witness' sounded a whole lot better, Doc. 'Peevey' sounds kind of… I don't know, kinda shrimpy."

"He was kind of shrimpy, Dr. Pons used that very word, but he seemed much bigger than he was. He was still in a coma at the time of the deception, Ms. Cadbury, but now he's awake! Working in concert with the police, you could cast a statewide net. What a story this would make! He can't have gone very far! I could give you an exclusive interview, offer you a description! Your staff could create an exact portrait of the last man to see The Only Criminal! You have an artist on staff, don't you?"

"We've had to let all of them go, I'm afraid."

"No matter, he might turn up. Do you understand what I'm telling you? *This is what's happening now!*"

"Nice try, Dr. Vaguely, but no dice."

"Why not?"

"Let me put my cards on the table, Dr. Vaguely. You're cute and funny with your fetish and everything, but I know the score. I've heard rumors about what's been happening out there at Billowing Pines. I mean, that you've been having trouble holding onto your patients since The Only Criminal's disappearance. Boy howdy, can I sympathize! I do. Times are tough for everybody. I'm having to add to my own paycheck by doing stupid voiceovers for Alpine Laundromat commercials! I've scratched some pretty pimply backs in my day, but I can't let you use my newscast to drum up publicity for…"

"I am *not* trying to drum up publicity!" Vaguely protested.

"Okay," she allowed, "I'll give you the benefit of the doubt. Let's say, for the sake of argument, that The Only Witness *was* an actor. Aside from making you and the hospital appear fraudulent, how does a report about this help anybody? How does that help Billowing Pines? The world thinks it's *already* heard from The Only Witness. People's hearts were touched by the words he spoke that historic afternoon. I consider it a privilege to have been there, as part of that audience. I'll be telling my grandchildren about it someday, if I can just stop giving men what they want on the first date."

"But it was all a lie!"

"Well, you know, sometimes it takes a placebo to cure a cancer, Doctor. Whether that event was real or staged—'it don't matter none,' as they say in my home state. It served its purpose. We can't pretend that afternoon didn't happen. Even if we were to put you on the air and let you tell your story, do you really think anyone would tune in? If you had this Poovey…"

"Peevey!"

"Whatever. If he was the real Only Witness like you say, do you really think he could out-perform the fake one? I don't, and believe me, Handsome, it's my business to know."

"But you're missing the point! I—"

"Look, my other line is beeping me," Lorraine interrupted. "I'd better run. Just between you and me and the ol' fire hydrant," she added in a lower voice, "I've been sending my tapes out to other markets, 'cause this gig here ain't gonna last much longer."

That *ain't* stung Vaguely's ear. "What do you expect to cover?"

"I dunno… Politics? Movie stars? This station needs an anchorwoman like the moon needs swimmin' pools. Gotta run, Doc. Don't forget me."

And with that, only the tone of her absence lodged in his ear. That and the question "Did she say 'moon'?"

Vaguely advanced straightaway to Plan B.

He arranged for a meeting and set out for the Amelia branch office of *The Crimes*, the newspaper which had been covering The Only Criminal's reign of terror for more than two turns of the century—long before Paul Vaguely began using plastic scissors to clip out his favorite stories for his scrapbooks. He had booked a meeting with its current editor-in-chief, Thaddeus S. Kasch IV, saying that he wished to meet with him about a matter of the gravest importance.

Remarkably, it was Vaguely's first time inside the venerable Crimes Building's hallowed halls. He entered by dialing his way through a revolving door, which he did with an appropriately awed, devout mien. However, after making it past the usual office flak, as Vaguely was introduced to Mr. Kasch, he felt his thrill collapse like a house of cards. He had envisioned a man behind an impressive oak desk, a man whose face would be imbued with sagacity and worldly experience, not unlike those stamped on the national currency. Instead, Mr. Kasch turned out to be a preppy-looking whippersnapper whose personal dynamic suggested a lucky inheritance rather than a position earned through dogged endeavor.

"Call me Thad, Doc," he said over a damp handshake, presuming to already be on informal terms.

When they took their seats, Vaguely noticed that this young man had not quite mastered the gentlemanly art of sitting up straight; he either reclined with the heels of his shoes against the edge of his desk, rocking back-and-forth or slouched like someone poured spinelessly into his chair; or leaned forward, using his desk as a crutch. Nowhere in the room did Vaguely see the tools of the journalist's trade; there was no writing machine, no telephone, no calendar, only an intercom and a bowl of red Jonathan apples.

"So," he opened, crunching into one, "you wanted to see me about something concerning The Only Criminal?"

"Yes," Vaguely confirmed. "This is vitally important. I'm concerned about The Only Criminal's disappearance and was hoping to convey some of that concern to you and your newspaper."

"Convey away," he invited. "Care for an apple?"

"No, thank you."

"And you represent…?"

"I represent no one," Vaguely said, surprised. "That is, no one in particular. No no, scratch that, Mr. Kasch, I represent *everybody.* That is, I'm acting as a concerned citizen."

"Oh! And 'Thad', please."

"I want to know: what does *The Amelia Crimes* and its sister papers in the larger cities intend to do about this?"

"Well, you know, we keep pretty busy around here," he said through his chewing noises. "There's answering the telephone… meeting with concerned citizens like yourself… and there's always a lot of filing to do." He called out, over Vaguely's shoulder, to the receptionist in the outer office, who had shown Vaguely in. "Isn't that right, Trace?"

"That's right," said Tracy, filing her nails in the adjoining room.

Vaguely was nonplussed, but charged ahead. "Perhaps I'm not as aware of how you do things here as I thought, but…"

"Yes?"

"I have been a faithful reader of your newspaper from the time I was a child and, well," Vaguely hesitated, "it was always my impression that *The Amelia Crimes* enjoyed the benefit of, how would you say… a direct link-of-sorts to The Only Criminal?"

Thad stopped enjoying his apple and tossed it into a nearby wastepaper basket with a somewhat less amused demeanor.

"Dr. Vaguely, now, when I agreed to see you, I didn't anticipate that my lawyer should perhaps also be present. But you heard what he asked me, didn't you, Trace?"

"Yep," Tracy's voice confirmed, adding a *voila* flourish to a now-perfect cuticle.

"Please don't misunderstand me... Thaddeus," Vaguely said. "It's just that, on every Sunday, for as long as I can remember, *The Amelia Crimes* has carried a column signed by The Only Criminal himself—describing his past week from the avowed criminal point of view. For the past couple of months, you have taken to reprinting these. For example, you ran one last Sunday called 'What I Did With Hoffa.' Now, to obtain these columns, and keep them coming, someone here must be in touch... and that is what I would like to be. In touch. "

Thad leaned forward and squinted at his visitor. Interlacing and flexing his fingers, as he rocked back and forth, he spoke slowly and carefully, as if tip-toeing with each sentence through a minefield of legal loopholes.

"Yes... in a matter of speaking... I guess you *could* say—in an off-the-record sort of way—that *The Times* had... an arrangement... of sorts... with The Only Criminal... or someone representing themselves to be... whatever. We used to have this... special safe here in the office. It wasn't... used for anything, except to hold The Only Criminal's... salary for the column, you understand. Every Friday, the kid from the mailroom who delivers the paychecks would place... a couple grand in the safe—in cash—spin the dial, and go home. Sometime during the night... someone would... break in, crack the safe and make off with the two grand... leaving the next column in a manila envelope in its place."

"I don't understand. Do you mean to tell me that The Only Criminal had to steal his own salary?"

"Yes and no," the publisher clarified. "I just called it his salary so you would understand our arrangement. It was the only way they were able to set this up, back when it started. There *was* no salary, *per se*. The Only Criminal wasn't interested in getting paid... any more than he was interested in writing a newspaper column. All this happened before my time, you understand... I'm just telling you what my father and grandfather told me when I was in short pants. Okay, okay, here's *exactly* what they told me...

"Back around the turn of the century," he continued, "or the last century rather, the founders of this newspaper which subsequently spread to Los Angeles and New York, printed an Open Letter to The Only Criminal, full page, inviting him to write a column for the paper."

"I have in my collection a facsimile of that document," Vaguely boasted.

"Well, I don't know if you know this, but the cat didn't bite. My grandfather—Thaddeus Kasch Jr, who was the founder…"

"A great, great man," Vaguely averred.

"Uh, thanks… he decided to use a little reverse psychology. He had the idea to publish another Open Letter, in which their invitation was, shall we say, curtly withdrawn. It said that the publishers of *The Amelia Crimes* had realized that no one would be interested in reading about current events from the Criminal perspective, that the very notion of inflicting such a column on the general public would not only be improper, but obscene. Not long after that issue hit the streets, that rock"—he pointed to a large but common rock on a plinth inside an acrylic display box across the room—"came sailing through that very window." (Thad nodded at a large picture window to Dr. Vaguely's left.) "A note was attached, written in letters clipped from ads published in this very newspaper. It told my grandfather, in no uncertain terms, that he, The Only Criminal, was going to write a weekly column for *The Crimes* whether my grandfather liked it or not. He was told that he would *have* to publish it, or run the risk of having this building blown up at any time. So Granddad, smart old goat that he was, got what he wanted."

"Brilliant. Absolutely brilliant."

"But that's not all," Thad explained. "You see, in order to copyright the columns, *The Crimes* had to pay for the work. They didn't know how to go about that, but Granddad had another brainstorm. He told TOC—in another Open Letter—that, as long as he was intent on foisting this column upon the public at large, he could leave it in the office safe on Friday nights when the newsroom was empty, right? That way, he wouldn't be seen. And he mentioned, in a way that sounded like a reluctant confession, that this was the same safe where *The Crimes* stored its weekly contribution to the Crippled Children's Fund. He told The Only Criminal that, when he opened the safe to submit his articles against Granddad's will, he would find $2,000 inside. He begged him to *please, please* leave it alone, because it was 'for the children.' Naturally, every Saturday morning, a new column appeared, and every last greenback had been Hoovered up. Like ol' Granddad used to say: 'You just have to know how to *deal* with some people.'"

Thaddeus Kasch IV, grinning slyly, swiped a second apple from the bowl, and sank his teeth into it with a wink.

Vaguely was incredulous. "So the way things are now, it's like he's stopped coming and you've stopped paying."

"From a business point of view, with the reprints, it's like he never left." The businessman sighed, leaning back in his chair like one whose fortune was made. "He's just stopped taking money out of our safe."

"What about your family's tradition? The tradition of this newspaper?"

"The reprints *are* that tradition. Literally."

Vaguely could hardly speak, but he managed. "Even if the disappearance of The Only Criminal from our daily lives doesn't concern you, Mr. Kasch…"

"Thad."

"… the disappearance of your main source of revenue certainly should!"

"Oh, there's no loss of revenue here, believe you me. There's less news, to be sure, but advertisers have been coming in to fill the breach. Flooding in, actually, and the old columns and stories don't cost us anything to reprint. In time, and sooner than you might think, it will all be new stuff to the majority of our readers, as the new ones come up and the old ones die off. So, from our perspective, business is better than ever. To be perfectly honest, it's almost like having a license to print money!"

Vaguely's conversations with Lorraine Cadbury and Thaddeus Kasch taught him that, to a television station or a daily newspaper, The Only Criminal had been much more than a source of daily, global entertainment and oppression. He had been a kind of cash cow, milked and bilked of the black and oozing petrol that kept vast industrial machinery up and running. As it turned out, he no longer needed to be present to be profitable or effective.

It was a lesson that businesses and organizations, both big and small, appeared to understand almost innately. Even the President of the United States announced that The Only Criminal's birthday on April 15 (how this information was found was anybody's guess!) would continue to be observed in his absence, and that everyone's tributes of 25-33% of their annual earnings (depending on their level of income) would be held until his return by a special new government department that was being set up specifically for that purpose.

Vaguely's Plan C came about by serendipity.

While waiting outside the Crimes Building for a taxi, and reflecting back on the moment of his encounter with Miss White over the previous evening's proffered cigarette, it occurred to him that his job was not the only one threatened by a possible eternity of no-shows by The Only Criminal. Should he try to book a meeting with the head of Consolations, who must be smarting without a spokesperson? But then it occurred to him that Consolations was a business too, likely to be towing a similar line to Thaddeus Kasch at *The Amelia Crimes*, so he ransacked his brain in search of others who would literally be feeling the devastation of his loss as much, if not more, than he was. Then it came to him: With The Only Criminal seemingly dead or retired, why would there be any further need for a police force?

Of course, he reasoned, kittens would always need rescuing from trees and old ladies would always need help crossing the street. Taking the law of averages and the natural rates of birth and death into account, The Only Criminal, even at his best, had never victimized a majority of society; therefore—in the eyes of that majority—the men and women in blue were making good on their oath to serve and protect. But the fact remained that, as long as there had been a police force in this country, there had never, ever, *ever* been a single arrest. Now Vaguely was not what you would call a naïve individual; he understood how cannily, how coolly premeditated those words "serve and protect" had been in their selection. The police did serve and were here to protect, should the need arise. They might arrive too late to be useful, because a crime had to be committed before they could be summoned, but nowhere did they claim that their role was "to arrest and imprison."

During Vaguely's college years, when his personal nature was at its most idealistic and questioning, he had often pondered the extent to which the police might soft-pedal their investigations, not wishing to rock the boat, not really being all that keen to slap the cuffs on someone who was, after all, their *raison d'etre*. However, even then, he was never so radical a thinker as to suspect them of being in cahoots, simply observant of the value of a system kept in balance. But in the wake of his eye-opening talks with Lorraine Cadbury and Thaddeus Kasch, Vaguely found himself wondering if there might not be something more to it—if there hadn't *always* been something more to it.

He hailed the first taxi to come along and asked to be taken to Police

Headquarters. He had no intention of dilly-dallying; he had every intention of taking his pleas for pro-activity to the very top.

Upon arriving at the station's front desk, Vaguely introduced himself and supplied his credentials to the desk sergeant, requesting to speak to no less than the officer in charge. A name was proposed to him, but Vaguely pooh-poohed this suggestion; no siree, he insisted on seeing the man in charge. He insisted on speaking to the policeman whose reputation was legend, whose morals were above question.

He wanted to speak to Inspector Brick Haymaker.

"Lt. Hammacher?" the desk sergeant corrected him.

"Is that how it's pronounced?" Vaguely asked.

"Yes, sir. Is this an official matter?"

"That should be clear enough!"

"And your name?"

"Dr. Paul Vaguely."

The desk sergeant signaled for Dr. Vaguely to stay put, and ambled down the hall and around a corner. He returned a few minutes later and waved to Vaguely in the way he would have asked an automobile to inch forward. The good doctor was then escorted down the hall and around the corner to an office that belonged—according to the name painted on the beveled glass of the door—to a Lt. Rick Hammacher. Vaguely peered at the door with a superior air; even the names painted on the office doors at Billowing Pines had been done with a good deal more professional pride.

Inside the office, Vaguely found a man who was somewhat less than the wavy-haired wall of chin and muscle that he had always imagined The Only Criminal's arch-adversary to be. The reality of Brick Haymaker, he discovered, was that he had brown hair lined with gray and a double chin with a few white hairs around the furrows of his mouth that his razor had failed to catch; that his shirt was poorly ironed and that his tie was outmoded; that he did not wear a shoulder holster while sitting behind his desk. He would have pegged him as an imposter if not for the professional deference he showed to Vaguely as he entered his cramped office.

"Doctor," he greeted his visitor, standing, "won't you come in?"

"You're Inspector Haymaker?"

"Hammacher," the lieutenant corrected him. "Won't you have a seat and tell me how I can help you?"

"Thank you! Well, Inspector…"

"Lieutenant."

"My apologies, sir," he apologized again, *sotto voce*. "I expect you have reasons for keeping up these appearances. Anyway, yes, as I said, my name is Paul Vaguely, Dr. Paul Vaguely. I'm a psychologist—a criminologist, to be exact—at Billowing Pines, specializing in trauma cases associated with The Only Criminal."

"Out by the fruitcake factory," Hammacher noted. "That must be very interesting work."

"It is, it is indeed. It's also work in which I have a vested interest, Inspector. It's my life, just as I know your work is yours. I've come here today to bring to your attention a disturbing change I've begun to notice in the very fabric in society since the disappearance and possible death of The Only Criminal."

Lt. Hammacher tensed and leaned forward. "Death? Who died?"

"Indeed, you may well ask! I couldn't agree more, my good man. It's my considered opinion that The Only Criminal is not dead at all! It's my professional belief, as a lifelong student and present expert in such matters, that he is more than likely standing just offstage, waiting for the expectations of the unsuspecting city to be lowered like the mantle of night; that he is plotting something heinous and terrible, something that requires him to be, first and above all, conspicuous in his absence."

"Now, that's an intriguing speculation, Doctor. I'm sorry—your name again?"

"Vaguely. Paul Vaguely."

"What, in your professional opinion, Dr. Vaguely, do you assume the ultimate goal of this disappearing act to be?"

"Nothing less than the systematic ridicule, defamation, and obliteration of the man best poised to unmask him—that is to say, myself: Dr. Paul Vaguely!"

"Aha. And what would you see as the role of the police in this particular matter?"

"No offense, Inspector," Vaguely prefaced himself, "but despite the best efforts of your department, The Only Criminal was never restrained for more than a heartbeat by the police, despite the valiant efforts of yourself. I hope you will forgive my candor in saying so."

"Oh, of course, of course," Lt. Hammacher said.

The world-weary lawman rose and crossed the length of his tight quarters to a water cooler that stood to the side of a heavily marked calendar illustrated with vintage cheesecake photography. He gulped the cold contents of his paper cup, squinting slightly as he sized-up Vaguely from this vantage point.

"Don't get me wrong," Vaguely added with some urgency. "Regardless of however many times you were foiled by his brilliance and alacrity, I regard you as a real hero. Most people who come into physical contact with The Only Criminal are so shattered by the experience that they come to me for consultations. Yet you never have. And I see there is very little gray in your hair; there is some, so I assume you don't color it… Most remarkable."

Hammacher reseated himself behind his desk. "I've enjoyed getting acquainted with you, Dr. Vaguely, but what's say we get down to brass tacks. The desk sergeant said this was a professional matter. You've got something to report?"

"Indeed I do."

"Now we're getting somewhere," Hammacher said, flipping open a handy note pad and grabbing a pencil from a nearby coffee mug. "When did this crime occur?"

"It's happening now," Vaguely said, almost proudly. "You see, Inspector, I've devoted my entire life to the study of The Only Criminal. In fact, it was I who took the first steps toward the definition of a new branch of human psychology, what is known today as Criminology. You might say that I am The Only Criminologist."

"Interesting," the lawman muttered while scribbling, "very interesting."

"Interesting or not, it is the truth," Vaguely confirmed. "In my estimation, The Only Criminal is an ancient superstition, who found himself on the verge of becoming a science. His only option for survival was his greatest crime of all."

"Which was?"

"Why, his disappearance, of course!"

Hammacher stopped writing in his pad and slapped it shut for dramatic effect. "Dr. Vaguely," he said, his patience finally caving in, "why me? Surely there are any number of police stations and police officers you could have run up the flagpole. Why pick mine?"

Vaguely's back stiffened. "You are a self-sworn opponent of his evil, are you not? And I presumed that you might appreciate a visit from a citizen of this district who just happens to be the leading authority in this field of endeavor that concerns you, who cared enough to bring to your attention, and to the attention of your department, the fact that you can expect more problems than you can handle, unless The Only Criminal can be tempted back out of hiding very soon."

The lieutenant's expression assumed a dawning light. "Wait a minute," he said. "You're from Billowing Pines, did you say?"

"Yes, Inspector."

"Do they know you're out?"

"No, this is not an official call. However, it is on the basis of that professional association that I wish to impress upon you that it's *essential* that The Only Criminal come out of hiding."

"Well, I don't see what I can—"

"You can tell me this: How does a policeman get promoted to the lofty position of Inspector, Inspector? I'm sorry... Lieutenant, Lieutenant. Don't tell me it's by solving crimes. Don't tell me it's by catching the bad guy. No no no no no. I assume it's by... some other means."

"Such as?" asked the seething lawman.

"I don't know. Keeping secrets, perhaps? Keep one, and maybe they make you a Sergeant who sits at the front desk. How many secrets must you keep to be made a Lieutenant?"

"It's a secret," Hammacher sneered sarcastically. "Dr. Vaguely," the lieutenant continued, "would you be so very kind as to tell me what I might do to get you out of my face?"

"Put me in touch with The Only Criminal. *Now!*"

"What do I look like, his *keeper?*"

"No," Vaguely guffawed. "Because to be his keeper, that little jail cell would have to be *occupied*. No, Inspector. Listen, I can be a help to you... or I can be a hindrance."

"I believe about half of that."

"All I am asking is one thing and one thing... only. I want you to share your secret with me."

"My secret."

"His address. If not his address, then the address next door."

"The address next door."

"You know what I mean: an address where I might find a lead. You can sit here behind your desk all day, drinking water and doodling in that notepad of yours, but I, sir, am a man of action! I, for one, am determined to get to the bottom of this problem before it's too late! I would like some help!"

"You do seem like a man who needs help," Lt. Hammacher allowed, "and I would like to see you get it."

He took one of his own business cards from a desktop dispenser and jotted a name and address on the back. He then stood up, Vaguely understanding that this was also his cue to go, and he proffered the card to his visitor. Vaguely reached out to take the card, but the lawman held onto it tightly, not yet ready to let it go.

"This is privileged information," he said. "You promise to keep this information to yourself?"

"You have my word, and my word is my honor."

"Good enough for me," Hammacher said, releasing the card into Vaguely's care.

Vaguely looked at what the Inspector had written on the card. "I never would have guessed," he almost spluttered.

"Now, Dr. Vaguely, if you'll excuse me?"

"Busy man?" Vaguely smiled.

Inspector Haymaker winked. "One must keep up appearances."

The inscription on the back of Lt. Richard Hammacher's business card led Vaguely to a flat in a decrepit, brownstone apartment building, located within walking distance of the center of town. Viewed from the outside, the building appeared to have been pulled down—in the spiritual sense—by whatever its mysterious tenant knew about The Only Criminal. Vaguely had witnessed this diseased look of poverty before, on other homes and houses visited by The Only Criminal's malice, but it was never anything that couldn't be set right by simple cosmetic repairs, like a fresh paint job. In this instance, the information harbored by this person and place seemed to infect the surrounding structures as well, like a bad tooth.

The inner door was locked, so Vaguely pressed the appropriate doorbell, which was missing half of its rubber nub. He was buzzed through. On the other side of the door was a dark foyer. Gliding under his hand as he mounted the dusty stairs, the moldy banister felt like a stale, powdered donut. If the world's most sensitive secrets had to be sequestered somewhere, Vaguely supposed, this dump was probably secure as any.

Vaguely's very first knock on the door was pre-empted by its opening. He was greeted by an aged face—only abstractly female—covered in wrinkles that resembled a network of interlocking jigsaw fissures. The harridan's cologne of choice seemed to be roach spray. She extended a turkey-like claw decorated with glass baubles and warts. Vaguely passed her the card he'd been given, keeping his hand to himself.

"Today I went to this gentleman with some important questions," Vaguely explained, showing her the card name-side up. "The answer he gave me was this," he added, turning it over to the hand-written inscription: MADAME ZENA'S TEMPLE OF PROPHECY, the address scribbled beneath.

Madame Zena raised her eyebrows delightedly. "You have come to the right place," she intoned.

"You weren't easy to find."

"If the truth were easy to find, only fools would seek it," she explained, ushering Vaguely into a room cluttered with musty antiques, dusty must, broken dolls, upended empty picture frames, a stuffed owl, and ashen pyramids of spent incense. The shadows in one or two of the room's corners were alive with cats showing and washing themselves. At the center of the room was a table. At the center of the table was a crystal ball. At the center of the crystal ball was Vaguely himself, upside down, walking toward it.

"Please be seated," his hostess invited.

The crone took Vaguely's hands, one on either side of the refracting orb, and stared deeply into him. Not into his eyes, but into him.

"I have many things to ask…" he began.

"Ask me nothing," she wheezed, cutting him off. "If you already knew what you needed, I could be of no use to you. Therefore, trust in me to tell you what you need to know."

"Very well."

Madame Zena squeezed her eyes shut, their lids wrinkling like peach stones. Her mouth appeared to be chewing something, over and over, and then it smiled: peek-a-boo to a gold tooth.

"You are a man in love," she saw.

"I am a man *obsessed*," Vaguely clarified.

"Is the same, foolish man, is the same," she chanted, squeezing his hands. "And love… this love is returned. Not love from the head. Real love… come from mystery. From the heart."

"I don't understand. You're saying that he's obsessed with me, too? The Only Criminal is obsessed with me, too?"

"The only crime... is two people afraid, refusing their future, denying their destiny, finding reasons... not to talk."

"Afraid?"

"That way lies madness. The future is written. Until you face the real issues of your life, the void you feel will remain."

Vaguely frowned.

"The spirits tell me now," Madame Zena continued, "and I am very sorry to say, that your worst fear will be confirmed."

"My worst fear!" Vaguely exclaimed.

He tore through his feelings. What *did* he fear most? Learning that The Only Criminal was really dead? That he was indeed among the living, faking his own death to drive the world insane, to bump Vaguely out of the only work for which he was suitably equipped? Or that he literally had him once behind bars at Billowing Pines and, through his own incompetence at the only job he knew, had to let him go?

"Is not my place to decide this for you," said Madame Zena, anticipating him. "It must be wrenched by your own hands from your secret place."

In truth, Vaguely did not know which eventuality he feared most, or that he had a secret place, but he could see the wisdom, given this opportunity, of choosing one fear over the others. Having already been assured that his worst fear would be confirmed, he used this opportunity to ensure that his dearest dream would come true.

"My greatest fear," Vaguely announced and not completely honestly, "is that The Only Criminal will return."

The oracle intoned: "The darkness you know is nothing compared to the darkness you have yet to inhabit."

"In other words, the truth is out there somewhere, in the dark? The Only Criminal might still be among us?"

"Ouchamagoucha!" cried Madame Zena in frustration, dropping her customer's hands. "One who receives the truth and continues to seek other answers can be told nothing. *Except...*"

"Yes?"

"That will be $25."

Chapter Nine
HIS HAND IN MINE

What now? Vaguely left Madame Zena's Temple of Prophecy feeling adrift. He sauntered aimlessly for the better part of an hour, the sage advice of the baubled seer reverberating through the gallery of his thoughts as wintry dusk metastasized around him. Feeling a bit underdressed to meet the chill of evening, he took temporary shelter in Harbinger's department store in downtown Amelia, where there was a diner where he could count on a cup of hot coffee and a warm sandwich. Upon reaching this portion of the business district, he was taken by surprise to find all the downtown stores decorated for the coming Xmas season. He had been so absorbed in the matter of The Only Criminal's disappearance, that he'd lost all track of where things stood on the yearly calendar.

Xmas, as if we need reminding, is that holiday when families all over the globe prepare for that most foreboding of all nights, when one house in every neighborhood is marked for visitation by The Only Criminal, who leaves after painting a large X on their rooftops. Operating on the possibility that he might visit, everyone went out and spent their hard-earned money on expensive appeasements—usually things they need or covet themselves, in case they are overlooked, which they arrange beneath their Xmas trees in a ritual enactment of fear and obeisance. The law of averages dictate that most houses will never experience the trespass of the malign intruder (whose traditional method of access was the chimney). Whatever remained of the appeasements the next morning were considered gifts to be shared with family and friends, or more freely distributed in the spirit of charity. Yet the awful possibility of his intrusion always existed for one and all, exciting the imaginations of small children in their beds, as well as the concerns of adults who took care to leave out a cold glass of milk and a plate of cookies in a pathetic gesture of appeasement. Such tokens were widely believed to sometimes soften the alleged heart of The Only Criminal, to the extent of withdrawing with his sweet tooth satisfied and finding some other place to plunder.

Vaguely wondered how, now and in the future, the Xmas holiday might be redefined. Might The Only Criminal—if he still survived as himself or as one contaminated by the touch of his evil—choose this auspicious occasion to return, even to stage a "grand slam"—or would everyone awaken on Xmas morning to find all their gifts and safeguards exactly as they had left them?

Newspapers, as was usual for this time of year, began to print daily polls in which people were asked if they were looking forward to "a certain someone" (believe it or not, there was now a reluctance in the press to actually mention someone as *passé* as The Only Criminal by name!) emerging from their chimneys this year like a black cloud of squid's ink. This year, the responses were generally negative and this fact had a curious effect. Assuming he might not come, all of the goods people purchased would remain theirs, to have and to hoard. Consequently, people were spending more, and more on finer things, because the odds of retaining them were newly stacked in their favor.

For his own part, Vaguely resolved to not spend a single dime on Xmas. Let The Only Criminal come and get him, if he could! The more he looked around at the holiday decorations and the novelty of new products, Vaguely found his thinking perverted to the extent that he conceived of a way that he might celebrate Xmas in a manner that would insult The Only Criminal to the same degree to which he felt himself slighted by his abandonment. He had the brazen idea of, for the first time, using his allotted funds in flagrant denial of The Only Criminal—by purchasing presents only for those nearest and dearest to him. After all, they had not abandoned him—they should be gifted for their loyalty! This is what he resolved to do, there and then.

Alas, they were all hard people to shop for; indeed, he had spent so much of the past year (year? So much of his past *life!)* immersed in books and newspapers and such that he was forced to admit to himself that he knew little about the people who were the brightest ornaments to his shadowy, academic existence.

However, it was in this perverse spirit that Vaguely—after having that fortifying bite to eat in Harbinger's diner—took the elevator upstairs to the Men's department and purchased a suitably somber woolen scarf for Dr. Pons, a box of premium cigars for Abel Lawson, a six-pack of award-winning international beers for Red Grinter. Downstairs, where things were displayed that had no proper department, he selected a fruitcake from the factory near Billowing Pines for his fearful, kale-and-cabbage-loving neighbors also on the ground floor. After having done all of this, Vaguely then found himself painted into an unexpected corner—the corner of what to get, if anything, for the maddeningly unreadable Miss White.

What did women want? What did women need? This, of course, had never been the subject of Vaguely's studies. In the Ladies' department at Harbinger's, he was like a fish out of gravy. He lingered with bachelor discomfort near perfume counters where there were arrayed any number of scents in petite bottles branded with unhelpful names like Peril, Feral, Poison, Ransom, Ruthless, Truthless, Damage, Faithless, Spectacular, Oracular, Dracula, Opium, Delirium, Goading, Exploding, Foreboding. This was a decision to be left for another day.

As he was felt himself torn in multiple directions by these and other perfume labels, Vaguely happened to overhear a conversation between a mother and a son of perhaps only six years. They were sitting together near the perfume display on a bench provided by the store for customers needing a place to rest and put their shopping bags down.

"You're a big boy now, Teddy," said the mother. "I think you're old enough to understand this. There's no such thing as The Only Criminal."

Naturally, the boy's gut response was to cry.

"Teddy, don't cry!"

"I don't believe you!" the child jerked, rejecting the comfort of the hand she tried to perch on his shoulder.

"Well, I'm afraid it's true."

"Then the Only Criminal would be a lie, and grown-ups ain't supposed to tell lies!"

"We're not supposed to, but I'm afraid we do, Teddy—just about that, of course, but that's enough. It's been going on for far too long."

"If he's not real, why'd you tell me he was in the first place?"

"To bring a sense of magic into your life?" the woman floundered. "To give you a childhood? You'll understand better when you've got kids of your own. I guess the real reason is, it's what people have always done. It's what your grandmother did with me, and her mother before her. But look at the facts, Teddy. Every toy we've ever had under our tree has gone to you, you know that. What would The Only Criminal want with children's toys?"

"He always ate the cookies we left out!"

Eavesdropping from the next aisle, Vaguely grinned and punched the air as if the child Teddy had scored one for their team.

"I'm sorry to break this to you, Teddy, but it was your father. He always ate the damn cookies and drank the damn milk. And now that he's no longer with us… well, this year, you'll see. If we put out milk and cookies, they'll still be there the next morning. I'm lactose intolerant."

"Mama," reasoned the boy in desperation, "if the milk and cookies are still there in the morning… *I'll* be gone! You gotta make the kind of cookies The Only Criminal likes! You gotta make sure the milk is still cold when he gets there! If you do something he doesn't like, he'll take me… and you'll never see me again!"

"Teddy," his mother said, patiently. "We can't afford a lot of appeasements this year, now that your father's run off with that woman. You're acting like a selfish little brat who wants me to spend my last dollar to put as many appeasements under the tree for you as I can, because you know that there's no Only Criminal and you know you'll end up getting them all anyway! Teddy, look at me. Look at me now. I'm *sorry* your father left us. I am sorry that he found another mommy he liked better than he likes me. I could put all the appeasements in the world under our tree and it wouldn't bring your father back. It wouldn't fill the emptiness that you feel inside. Teddy, you have to believe me. Read, my lips. *The Only Criminal—there is no such thing!*"

Vaguely had repositioned himself as the woman spoke so that the boy could catch his eye and receive his silent signs of encouragement. His mother happened to notice and, grabbing her son by the wrist and her shopping bag in her spare hand, dragged him away from Vaguely as though he were some hovering species of undesirable.

Vaguely looked around to get his bearings. He noticed that he was standing near a rummage bin piled high with winter gloves, all tagged with the same bargain price. His hands were still cold from being outdoors and he thought how fortuitous it was to find himself ideally placed to do something about this. An appeasement for himself! Why not?

There were so many styles to choose from! Wanting to be surprised,

Vaguely closed his eyes and plunged his hands into the warmth of the bin's bounty, sorting through the gloves not by sight but by touch. His sensitive palms and fingertips probed their ways through the various unseen colors below the jumbled surface. With eyes closed, he fancied that he could tell the reds from the greens by touch alone, along with all the other colors so evocative of winter fashion. Then, suddenly, his hands came into contact with a pair buried deep, the seductive feel of which called an end to his searching. Up from the depths he retrieved, opening his eyes now, a pair of black gloves—apparently the only such pair in the bin. They were remarkably like the gloves he had seen since childhood on every billboard, in every movie, on every dustjacket, in every storybook illustration. As he extracted them from the rummage heap, the right hand glove fell into position across Vaguely's own right hand, like it was meant to be.

Like a handshake.

Like an agreement.

Like a contract.

His brow furrowed as he touched them and squeezed them and passed them from hand to hand, once, twice, three times, just to get the feel of them. Then he unfastened the elastic clap that bound them at the wrist in order to try them on for size.

Voila!

They were exactly right. They weren't very thick; on the contrary, they were as tissue-thin as a second skin. They didn't seem quite substantial enough to keep his hands warm, yet there was something about them that made his hands feel as warm and toasty as if they were held to an open flame.

Vaguely upheld his hands and gazed at their new reconfiguration in flexing, black alacrity.

But of course.

And he thought to himself: "But of course!"

He was wearing them as he left the store, tightly gripping his various purchases, the price tag torn off.

Now feeling quite full of the season, he saw and joined a gathering of people outside Harbinger's famous holiday window displays at the corner of Main and Central. Vaguely remembered his grandparents bringing him here as a child to revel in their animatronic ingenuity.

At first, Vaguely found this year's windows unusually mundane, at least the ones on Main Street. The first showed a wintery forest, with a cabin nestled into its snowy valley with a smoking chimney and a snowman built outside. The second was a holiday kitchen scene, as a suburban dad, dressed as The Only Criminal, lifted his wife off the checkered linoleum floor repeatedly to kiss her under the mistletoe.

However, as Vaguely moved with the crowd toward the front corner of the store, where Main met Central Avenue, he came to a display that invoked his pleasure. Anyone seeing this display for the first time would have thought they had bungled into a crime scene. The glass of the window was broken, or appeared to be, as though shattered by a thrown fist or some other blunt object. Inside the display was a double bed and bedside table, framed by a matching cedar armoire and mirrored dressing table or vanity, respectively positioned against the rear and left walls of the window frame. On a papered wall a large, jagged X appeared to bleed like fresh, wet paint. A cheap but acceptable Tiffany-style lamp swung back and forth over the room's depicted disarray, as though set in motion by an act of violence. Beneath the inviting, disheveled comforter adorning the bed, the figure of a female mannequin in delectably sheer negligée could be seen sitting half-upright, on the verge of a scream, while—reflected in the vanity mirror—was the shadowy form of an intruder gripping a dagger, glittering with the varicolored reflections from the swinging light overhead.

Vaguely then moved around the corner to the next and final display, where Harbinger's traditionally placed their annual Xmas masterpiece.

Here a wall safe had been blasted open, its metal door dangling, barely hanging onto its hinge. Vaguely's cold pupils misted with delight as he saw, just before the violated keep, two black-gloved hands held in the large round beam of a powerful flashlight of no discernible source, their 10 fingers interlaced with a cat's cradle of magnificent, plundered pearls. The burglar was like no representation of The Only Criminal Vaguely had ever seen: she was a tall, exquisitely slender mannequin, her long-spilling auburn hair and startled expression offset by a purple bandit's mask. Green eyes blazed from the mask holes—outraged, apprehensive, caught. She stood svelte in a dark purple turtleneck leotard, a black belt equipped with stun-gun holster, a grappling hook with rope, and thigh-high leather boots of a more moderately violet color.

Vaguely felt thunderstruck by a violently new, revolutionary idea. He lingered for several minutes in untempered admiration of this clever display, whose evident purpose was to promote the glittering wares available for purchase or layaway in Harbinger's jewelry department. For most of those minutes, Vaguely was more physically than mentally aroused by what was arranged before him but, inevitably, his mind took over from his body to analyze his response. The image was primarily shocking because he had never heard it suggested by anyone that the fair sex might be capable of criminal behavior. Traditionally, depictions of The Only Criminal had been, without exception, masculine in nature.

It was unthinkable… but now it had been thought.

"Magnificent!" Vaguely gasped aloud, helplessly, to no one in particular.

And yet… "Thanks," said a voice near to him.

He turned to see who was taking credit for envisioning this.

Do you really need to be told who it was?

That's right. It was she.

Chapter Ten
ARE YOU WASHED IN THE BLOOD

They not only lived in the same neighborhood, on the same street, in the same building, and seemed bound to one another in some strange way; they also had in common a strange destabilization of composure in each other's presence. We don't know what the cause of this might have been in the case of Miss White; however, in Paul Vaguely's case, his unsettled feelings in his neighbor's presence seemed rooted in an unfortunate confusion of the Criminal unknown and the Female unknown. Whatever stars held them in their sway, the criminologist and the window display designer at Harbinger's department store sat apart and said nothing further as they shared the next 30 minutes on the same bus to their shared destination.

As they stepped off the bus—the gentleman allowing the lady to step off ahead of him—Vaguely was already worrying about how he was going to say goodnight to this comely peculiarity, this strangely intimate stranger. Whether or not they said another word to each other, it was a certainty that he would be accompanying her to her door, because he had to pass it to reach his own apartments.

They stood together near Lawson's News, waiting for the crosswalk traffic light to change, not talking but each plainly waiting for the other to do or say or attempt something engaging. Vaguely had not yet given up hope of saying something else before the night was through. He wanted badly to offer her an excuse not to go in right away, but could not find the right route to such a proposal. The Hideout was still open and should have been self-evident, but coffee was somehow too provocative a suggestion, and tea a tad too polite. By the time he thought of hot chocolate, which might have been just the thing for a cold winter's night, it was too late: the red light had switched to green and Miss White, bolding the winter breeze, was halfway across the street before Vaguely noticed.

Vaguely dashed after her, his dark overcoat flapping about him like a cape. He reached the front steps of the Oakley Apartments at almost the same moment she did, whereupon the two of them bumped into their landlord. His face was unkempt with stubble and looked more pale, haggard, careworn than usual.

"Hey Doc, have you seen Ringo?" He asked this as though he hadn't noticed their actual collision.

"No, Mr. Grinter, I haven't," Vaguely answered. "We just got off the bus," he added, nodding in Miss White's hovering direction.

"Ain't like him," he fretted, rubbing the side of his face, and continuing the sweep over his bald head. "Ain't like him to run off."

Vaguely's features darkened. "I suppose…" he began.

Miss White cut him off with a glance of discouragement, then touched Grinter's arm with solicitous empathy.

"Where did you last see him, Mr. Grinter?" she asked.

"In the park," he said with an air of disorientation, his emotion cutting his sentences either very short or very long. "It was still before six. I took him to the park for walkies. He's always good about coming back when I let him run around without his leash. I mean, it's not like he's gonna bite anybody and he knows better than to run out under some car or somethin'. I was sittin' on a bench. I watched him run around. He was havin' the time of his life. Sometimes I couldn't see where he'd run to, but I'd hear some kid behind me sayin' 'lookit the doggie lookit the doggie' and I'd turn around and there'd be Ringo, makin' a new friend. I let him run, I let him play. And then a long time went by without me seein' him, so I got up and I went lookin' for him, but he wasn't around nowheres I could see. So I thought, Well, maybe he went back to the bench and found me gone and went home by himself, so I came home too. But he wasn't here either. And now what I keep thinkin', and what I'm trying not to be thinkin', is that the only reason he might not come home is because he can't."

"What about his squeaky toy?" Miss White asked. "He always comes running when he hears that, doesn't he?"

"Oh yeah, that's an idea!" Grinter reached into the pocket of his winter coat and pulled out a rubber rolled-up newspaper that squeaked when it was squeezed. Its headline, Vaguely noticed, read *Only Criminal Frees Dogs from Pound.*

The three of them waited. Squeaked and waited. "I don't know," Red muttered, close to tears. "I don't see him comin'."

"Patience, Mr. Grinter," Vaguely offered encouragingly. "Ringo has a collar. Whoever finds him will read his tags and bring him back to you."

Red Grinter wasn't about to wait for that. He was already wandering away from Vaguely before he finished his sentence, already standing near the corner bakery, holding and squeaking the rubber newspaper like the Statue of Liberty's torch and bellowing his dog's name into the approaching dark.

"Riiiiiiiiiin-goooooo!" *Squeakysqueakysqueaky.* The squeaks echoed off the huddled fronts of Amelia's apartments and businesses and billboard, a violation of silent night that could only be forgiven as the act of genuine love it was.

"Would you like us to help you look for him, Mr. Grinter?" Miss White called after him.

"No, thanks," Grinter said with a crumbling voice. "I know it's late."

"You're sure? We don't mind."

Vaguely looked at his neighbor, feeling their weird complicity deepen as she felt free to recruit him for such an operation without discussion.

"No, you two better get inside; it's late. Hey, Riiiiiiiiingoooooooooo! Hey, Ringo!"

Squeakysqueakysqueaky.

Vaguely and Miss White stood and watched for a short while as Red Grinter proceeded to hobble south on Oakley Way.

"Poor man," Miss White said, looking after him. "That dog means the world to him."

"Why did you cut me off earlier," Vaguely asked, as the two of them were climbing the stairs, "when I was about to tell him…"

"… that Ringo might have been dog-napped? Why make him lose hope?"

"*That* would make him *lose* hope?"

Miss White looked at Vaguely a little sadly, but also as if she understood where he was coming from for the first time, and Vaguely reached out to sweep aside a gleaming curtain of ash-blonde hair that covered her ear when he was jolted from his slumbers by a soul-rending cry, arising from the heart of his apartment complex.

In slippered feet, he cracked his door and keened his hearing deep into the outer area, down the stairwell, past the second floor to the first, hoping that the sound was something overheard from an old Only Criminal movie on late night television. For half a minute, there was nothing, but then the cry sounded again, stopping just sort of becoming a scream of horror. Vaguely had never heard anything quite so wrenching. Though sudden screams in the dead of night tend to encourage the opposite reaction, Vaguely stepped out onto the third floor landing and peered down over the bannister.

He was coming down to the second floor landing as Miss White also stepped into the hall. The two of them exchanged fuzzy glances: she looked funny in a nice way as she knotted the belt of her white terrycloth robe. Vaguely surreptitiously checked his reflection in the hanging mirror and smoothed a cowlick. The man from Apartment 4 tottered morosely into the scene, a sleeping mask clutched in his right hand. Seeing his immediate neighbors alert to the situation, he shook his head and went back inside, to bed. All heart.

Vaguely and Miss White wordlessly decided to venture downstairs. The door across the hall from Red Grinter opened slightly. The old apple-muffin-faced couple peered at them through the protection of a chain lock, then finally dared to emerge from Apartment 2, padding slowly toward them in their nightshirts and slippers, the wife in curlers, her husband in an old-fashioned nightcap.

"Somevon is cryink?" he asked. Vaguely shushed him with a gesture and listened closely.

The next sob they heard was close enough to be visible. The next thing Vaguely heard was Miss White, who made an involuntary sound of tenderness. Instinctively, Vaguely placed his hand on her shoulder and felt the warmth of body and bone beneath her terrycloth.

He followed her line of vision to Apartment 1, whose front door was half open. Inside, they saw Red Grinter kneeling on his living room carpet, violently sobbing as large men do, over the inert body of little Ringo. The four neighbors stepped inside, the two youngest ones lowering themselves to their knees in the most dreadful sympathy.

Vaguely silently asked to examine the dead dog, making it known to Red, intuitively, that he had cared for the animal. Ringo's eyes were glazed and empty, the merriment in them gone, their soul gone, the once-curious tilt of his head now forever slack. His fur looked matted and artificial. His mouth was open, tongue trailing out, and there was some blood.

"Ringo, my poor baby," the strong man whimpered, never taking his eyes away from his only companion.

"Tell us what happened, Mr. Grinter," said Miss White.

"I was… I was watching the late movie," the landlord explained through his tears, "and I heard a noise out there"—he gestured to the open ground floor area between its two apartments—"like the front door slamming. I knew all of you were in for the night," he said, looking up at the other tenants, "so I figgered, have a look-see. He was lyin' out here… like this!" Grinter looked at Vaguely with childlike innocence. "Anything you can do for him, Doc?"

"I'm sorry, Mr. Grinter," Vaguely managed. "I'm not that kind of a doctor. No one is."

Continuing his inspection of the lifeless animal, Vaguely found some minute hard crystals in his bloody drool. He saw Miss White notice this; they somehow mutely exchanged the intelligence that this discovery was better left unmentioned.

"I'm not a vet, but poor Ringo looks like he was probably hit by a car or something, Mr. Grinter," Vaguely lied. "An accident, probably, the way things are. Perhaps the driver read his tags and just brought him home. I can understand why they might not wish to stay."

"So this is how… his story ends," his owner grieved, struggling to put his pain in perspective.

"Mr. Grinter," Vaguely suggested, "if you would allow me, I'll look after Ringo for you."

"Thanks, Doc," he said, touching the animal with a hand with only four fingers, fondly, unbelievingly. "Ringo always liked you."

"Perhaps Mr. and Mrs…?" Vaguely looked at the elderly Lithuanian couple from Apartment 2.

"Westerkamm," the wife said.

"… Westerkamm will be kind enough to stay with you for awhile, maybe make you some tea?"

"Uff course," they said in unison. "Poor man."

Mr. and Mrs. Westerkamm led Mr. Grinter into his kitchen, leaving Paul Vaguely and Miss White alone with the dog. Very soon after entering that next room, they heard Red buckle as he came within view of Ringo's bowls of water and food, and a corner where he liked to make Ringo bark by playing "Peek-A-Boo."

Miss White, moving from her knees to a seated posture, leaned in closer to Vaguely. "What was that you found?" she asked.

"Miss… This is silly, but I don't know your name," Vaguely found himself admitting.

"Melanie," she said. "Melanie White."

"*Felony?*"

"*Melanie.*"

Vaguely swallowed hard and showed her the granules on his bloody fingertips. "See this?"

"What is it? Sand?"

"Glass," Vaguely corrected her. "Ground glass. Ringo was fed something which had been salted with ground glass."

"Oh, no! Who would ever do such a thing?"

Vaguely looked into her disbelieving eyes and admitted that—for the first time in his life—he didn't know.

"I should try to find Officer Mead," he said.

"That's a good idea. Shall I stay here or come with you?"

"Stay here with Ringo," Vaguely suggested. "I won't be long."

With that, he rose to his full height. However, as he passed through Red's front door into the main hall, he happened to look up, high into the arrangement of stairwells and mezzanines that reached up to the doors of his own apartments. And there, poised on the bannister rail between his two doors, he glimpsed a dark hand—the hand of an eavesdropper, the hand of someone apparently standing in wait, encased in a black glove.

"Melanie," he said, snapping his fingers—and something about this gesture and his first use of her given name caused Miss White to leave Ringo and stand beside him. Vaguely instinctively moved her back, closer to Red's door, which would be outside the range of visibility from that higher vantage, and held his index finger to his lips. He then used the same finger to point upstairs to what he saw. When he heard her sharply draw breath back into her throat, he knew he was not dreaming.

Everything about the character of the hand, even the macabre way the overhead lighting fell upon it, served to emphasize the malice of its character and portent. The sight of it triggered in Vaguely a sense of recoil, as people feel when they turn on a kitchen light and see a cockroach skittering out of sight. It was a sight that light was never meant to touch. There was something about its position that suggested that it knew it had been seen, detected, and that it was cornered—it and whoever might be wearing it, still concealed in the midnight shadows.

Vaguely wondered: Might it be Peevey, coming back into his life, or perhaps…? He felt himself at an awful disadvantage, yet also raised by the responsibility he felt toward this young woman who trusted him with her protection. Had this situation occurred the day before, he might have recognized that the moment he'd always wished for was suddenly (and literally) at hand—that he was standing on the threshold of experiencing for himself everything that he had ever sought to learn from his patients; but now that he and Miss White had shared a life and death experience together, now that he had been entrusted with her given name, it did not occur to him that he and she could simply run away until the halls were clear. He glanced around the hall area for some form of weapon that he might carry as he braved the stairs. He settled on a sharp-pointed umbrella, which he grabbed from a barrel stand at the foot of the stairwell.

Melanie clutched his arm: "You're not going up there!"

"It may be nothing," he admitted, "but then again, it might be everything. Stay down here."

With that needless advisory, Vaguely began his silent, stealthy ascent up the six flights to the third floor, not for a moment taking his eyes off the malignant gloved hand. As he turned the first corner and continued up to the second floor, a second short scream exploded from the woman below.

"What happened?"

"It moved," she called up to him. "Oh, Paul, I'm *sure* it moved! It knows you're coming!"

Well, it does now, Vaguely thought, gulping. Still, it was the first time she had called him by his first name; the first time anyone had spoken his first name out of genuine caring and concern for as long as he could remember. This emboldened our hero. Tightening his grip on the umbrella, he now advanced on the inevitable two steps at a time. Having reached the second floor, he peered up through the spiral of the bannister and saw the gloved hand, much closer now, at rest there in pride of place like a tarantula.

He advanced to the next flight and, involuntarily, yelped as he passed his unexpected reflection in the hanging mirror. This bit of childishness embarrassed and angered Vaguely, so much so that he girded himself for the final confrontation by giving full vent to his fear-constricted voice, roaring as he hammered up the final flights, in robe and pajamas, lashing out at the corridor walls with the spike of the borrowed umbrella as he completed the distance.

Then, somewhat winded, for Vaguely was something less than a man of action, he found himself inhabiting that disturbing band of twilight wherein the things that do and do not exist mingle. Here, he found himself standing face-to-fingers with the black hand. Here, he could more plainly see that it was not really one gloved hand, but two—the left hand caressed the bannister, while the right hand lay caressingly over its mate in a pose of macabre affectation.

It had been so easy for Vaguely to believe that someone was standing there, almost within reach, smirking in his direction with deadly, deliberate, singularly criminal condescension, that he began to feel a premonitory tingling spreading over the map of his scalp—the sort of sensation that he imagined, if unchecked, might actually bleach a man's hair white with pure terror.

Vaguely brought the umbrella up over his head, and swung it down upon the pair of hands with all his might. The umbrella broke, the pieces falling over the bannister to the tiled floor three levels below.

Upon impact, the gloves tumbled off the bannister to the carpet beneath his feet—and lay there, palms up, looking for all the world like a pair of cooked crabs… or, more to the point, like a pair of empty gloves. Like the pair of empty gloves they were… like the pair of empty gloves he had placed on the bannister for safekeeping as he came home earlier from his Xmas shopping and last entered his apartment… like the pair of empty gloves he had evidently left there after futzing with his packages and repocketing his door key.

No sale.

Miss White heard the loud whack six flights up, saw the pieces of the umbrella fall on the other side of the hall, and finally the slamming of a door somewhere up there. She looked up to the bannister and saw that the gloved hands were now gone. Out of concern, she bravely climbed the stairs to Dr. Vaguely's pair of apartments. She didn't see him. He was gone. The gloves too were gone.

She walked from one door to the other. She was certain that she could hear excited breathing on the other side of the door numbered 6 but she sensed it would be wrong to disturb him, to press for an explanation of what had just happened.

On his side of the door, Vaguely was fairly certain that he could hear Miss White listening in, but he could not possibly open the door and admit to what had happened… the fact that he had found these gloves in a rummage bin at Harbinger's, that he had tried them on, and that he then walked out of the store—in front of God and the whole world—without paying for them.

THREE

THE ONLY CRIMINAL

"Le Criminal Seul… c'est moi!"

—GUSTAVE FLAUBERT

Chapter One
THE LONGER I SERVE HIM

The facts surrounding Ringo's death never came to light. The killing was not regarded as a criminal case because the victim was canine; as far as the law was concerned, animals were nothing more than a piece of property. In the days that followed, Paul Vaguely happened to overhear Officer Mead as he told Red Grinter that, in the unlikely event the cause could be traced to an individual, his innocence and the accidental nature of the death would surely be certified by legal precedent. The most he might legally expect by way of apology would be financial restitution. Red, however, was not interested in estimating Ringo's equivalent in cold cash.

As Xmas loomed, Mr. Grinter's once boisterously outgoing personality curdled into a darker distortion of itself. No longer was he the greeter inside the front door at the Oakley Apartments, but the greeted. His voice, once hearty and raspy, turned ashen; no longer was he friendly, but sullen and withdrawn, looking at everyone in the complex, on his street, in his town with beady, accusative, beer-reddened eyes. Until he knew for certain who was responsible for Ringo's death, *everybody* was.

Doggone world, doggone town
Won't somebody tell me what's going down?
Everything's changin', I'm gonna flip
Can't get a grip, can't get a grip
That's why I wear this doggone frown
In this doggone world
Doggone town.

Doggone world, doggone town
No answers to my questions have I found
I keep on lookin', can't find a clue

Can't feel happy for feelin' blue
I'm startin' to hate every sight and sound
In this doggone world
Doggone town.

Whimsy Plunkett, wearing woolen gloves with the fingers snipped off, strummed this song into being while sitting in an almost fetal upright slouch on the stoop of the Oakley Apartments one crisp, mid-December morning. It was the first thing Paul Vaguely heard as he emerged from the building. He had been summoned back to Billowing Pines that morning, where he was more than half expecting for the axe to finally fall. He felt no excitement, only trepidation. The cold outside bit into his extremities, but he refused to don again those gloves, not legally his own; he also refused to let them out of his sight, lest someone else find and put them on, so he kept them stuffed into his overcoat pockets.

He paced at the bus stop, as Plunkett plunked, thinking how ironic it was that his pending termination should coincide with his dawning awareness that there were more imperative reasons to have a job than to indulge one's own obsessions; namely, the desire to establish security and share it with someone else… a partner—no, *an accomplice*—in life.

When he stepped off the bus, perhaps 20 minutes later, Billowing Pines appeared to Paul Vaguely as a ghost town. There was no security, indeed no apparent activity whatsoever on the ground floor. As he pushed at the front entrance, he nearly expected from the abandoned look of things to find it locked; and yet, when the elevator doors opened on the executive office level, Vaguely was startled to discover the place positively humming and bustling with industry.

Dr. Pons was taking a private call and Vaguely could not be admitted to his office right away, so he cooled his heels in reception. Pons' receptionist Beatriz expressed some concern to Vaguely about his weight loss; he wasn't the sort of man who had much weight to spare, but it wasn't at all deliberate; it was due more to excessive smoking, crying jags and lack of hunger than to active dieting. Vaguely glanced over the magazines spread over a low table of blonde wood. He settled on a copy of the former *Crime* magazine, whose publishers were now experimenting by calling it *Time.* Its totally black cover page asked the rather impertinent question (he felt), "Is The Only Criminal Dead?"

Vaguely read the cover story with disdain, looking in vain for mentions of himself and quotations ascribed to his name. Didn't the writer know that he was the only expert on this topic? It was a couple of minutes after he flung the rag aside in disgust, feeling that this important and widely-seen article had disavowed his own existence as much as that of The Only Criminal, that Vaguely was finally admitted to see Dr. Pons.

He found his superior seated behind his large desk, monocle pinched between brow and cheek, signing paychecks to be distributed among Billowing Pines staffers on the following day. The drab winter light in the office dipped intermittently as the rising sun hovered behind passing clouds, interrupting the sweep of his handwriting from time to time.

"Good morning, Dr. Pons," Vaguely announced himself. "You asked to see me?"

"Yes, Paul," said Pons, looking up brightly and gesturing fussily. "Take a seat, I'll be right with you."

Vaguely sat.

Pons scratched his signature, ever more briskly and sloppily, across five more checks, and capped his fountain pen with showy deliberation, before turning his sights to Vaguely. "Now then… I imagine you're wondering why I've summoned you," he preambled.

"I imagine you've called me in to hand me my walking papers," Vaguely said with glum candor.

Pons upraised brow caused his monocle to drop to the full length of its chain. "Dr. Vaguely, you astonish me! Now whatever makes you think that?"

"May I speak frankly, sir?"

"Always," Pons insisted.

"One," Vaguely began, "The Only Criminal is gone. Two, my once unique field of specialty would no longer seem to be unique or particularly viable, seeing as most of my former patients have quit me. The few remaining stragglers are probably faking anyway. Ergo, walking papers."

Pons laughed just once, like a braying animal. "I have no intention of letting you go, Paul."

"You don't?"

"Absolutely not. In fact—in view that Xmas is just around the corner—allow me to seize this opportunity to present you with your next week's pay… with an additional holiday bonus tucked in."

Pons, while remaining seated, reached across his desk to a small stack of envelopes on its green felt blotter. He found one inscribed with Paul Vaguely's name and handed it over.

Vaguely examined the contents of the envelope with as much astonishment as he would have regarded the only known photograph of The Only Criminal.

"I'm speechless, Dr. Pons," Vaguely said, eyeing the envelope gladly but also warily. "I'm more appreciative than you know. And, I must admit, more than a bit bewildered."

"It's true," Pons admitted, "that we've had more than our share of growing pains these past few months—one might even call it 'shrinkage'—but I have good reason to believe that things will soon be set right. Indeed, better than right. Between you and me, one or two heads may still need to roll, just to help ease us through this transitional episode... but you needn't worry about yours being one of them. We've been through a lot together, you and I. I consider you to be a valued and trusted advisor... and confidant. *If* we understand each other."

"Of course," said Vaguely, though he didn't really.

Pons rose to adjust the room's Venetian blinds, reducing the amount of sunlight striping Vaguely's face like so much *film noir*.

Newly cloaked in semi-darkness, Pons turned to Vaguely with an air of purpose. "I assume," he said in lowered, intimate tones, "that you've heard... Our old friend Mr. Ostinato has been cast in the lead of a new production being made in Hollywood?"

Vaguely's features tightened with incredulity. "No, sir, I had not."

"Hmm," Pons hummed affirmatively. "It's in all the papers."

"I'm not reading the newspapers much, these days," Vaguely groused. "They don't seem to describe anyplace or anyone I know."

"Exactly!" Pons underscored a dramatic thrust of his finger. "I've noticed this too. People are lost! People everywhere are looking for something, some solid rock, to hold onto. And I believe you'll agree with me when I aver that Billowing Pines should be that solid rock."

"I don't understand."

"I can only forgive myself for not realizing this sooner because what our world is experiencing at this moment is epochal, totemic—wholly new to human experience," Pons said, excitedly pacing about. "But I was having dinner the other night some with some fellow businessmen and women, some of whom are on our board of directors, as well as some others involved with the Chamber of Commerce. We were all bemoaning our fates when this bright young chap at the table—who happens to be the publisher of our city paper—gave us the most extraordinary pep talk. He helped me to see that, just because the germ is gone, this is no reason to proclaim the disease as cured. Have I intrigued you?"

"Yes, sir."

"Good man. Anyway, according to this young fellow—Thaddeus Kasch is his name—his newspaper is actually more lucrative now that every page of it is now 3/4s or more of advertising. It seems to me that we might apply this same principle to our own situation."

"I don't follow you, sir."

"Think of it this way, Paul. Given the way things are now, we, as psychiatrists and psychologists, aren't really dealing in mental illness anymore. We're dealing in something else entirely. What we are dealing with is nothing more, nor less, than…" He theatrically looked from side to side, as if for eavesdroppers, before completing his thought in *sotto voce*. "… human *vanity.* People aren't pining for peace or protection or security anymore. What they want, what they need, what they desire, is… *glamour.*"

"Glamour, sir?"

"Take your former patients," he began to clarify. "They weren't merely traumatized by their supposed close encounters with The Only Criminal…"

"Supposed?"

"… they were *elevated* by them! These were not brushes with disaster, but with… celebrity! The Only Criminal brought more than terror into their lives; he also brought *glamour.* And who better to cater to their need for that sense of exclusivity and privilege than Billowing Pines? At the going rate, needless to say. Which, incidentally, is up, up, and up."

Vaguely's look of befuddlement persisted.

Pons burrowed deeper. "I know what you're thinking, Paul: 'Billowing Pines? Glamour?' Let me explain. Effective immediately, Billowing Pines is raising its standard fees—both sanctuary and out-patient—by 300%."

"Three-hundred percent?!" Vaguely choked.

"My advisors assure me that we can demand 300%and get it. In fact, and I tell you this confidentially, *we must…* in order to survive. Remember, Paul, we're not in the service of treating sick minds, we're in the *business* of treating sick minds. That is a *most* important distinction!

People may borrow money from their children's piggy banks and never pay it back, they may keep four out of the five dollars they have set aside for the collection plate on Sundays, but rarely will they skimp when it comes to lollygagging in their own neuroses."

"But surely it's our job to cure those neuroses, not to encourage our patients to… luxuriate in them!"

"A noble thought," Pons judged, "but seriously flawed. Look at it this way: if we cured our patients' neuroses, wouldn't this just free them up to cultivate new ones? If we dare to cure our patients' neuroses, to rob them of that rich scenario which most preoccupies and interests them, we should not be surprised if they simply pack up their troubles and dreams… and find some other doctor, some other facility, *willing* to indulge them. And the facility that will be most attractive to them will be Billowing Pines—the most expensive, the most exclusive, and the most legitimate—and that's where you come in, my boy!"

"Dr. Pons, you know as well as I do… I'm not a real criminologist. It's just a word I made up in a theoretical paper! What legitimacy?"

"You started it all, idiot! Wittingly or unwittingly, you blazed the trail! Do you imagine for a moment that Sigmund Freud left his practice dangling while he dashed off back to school to pursue a diploma in psychiatry? Any accredited criminologist from now to forever will owe the professional path they walk to you! That's right, we must welcome more young men and women into this trail you've blazed—and I fully intend to see that we profit from it! We have one or two gentlemen on our Board of Directors who are affiliated with the University of Amelia, and—congratulations are in order, my boy—because I have arranged for you to be presented sometime in the New Year with the first Honorary Doctorate in Criminology! I'll be hiring the best publicists in the country to attend the honors being bestowed upon you, to attend all of the inspirational speeches you are going to give at every university I can book you into. By the time you're done with your first tour, there won't be anyone in this country, highest nabob to lowest neanderthal, who hasn't heard of you—*and* Billowing Pines."

Vaguely rubbed his face, chuckling nervously. In a way, the scenario Pons had described was everything he had ever wanted; but now that it was presented to him as something on the verge of really happening, he realized that what had been lifelong fantasy might not make such a perfect fit in reality.

"I don't know how I feel about this, sir," he hedged.

"Try to understand, Paul," Pons impressed upon his star employee. "The world is different now. Things are different now. It's not so easy to assign blame anymore, not as definitively as people could when people had this... phantom to believe in. It's not so easy anymore to distinguish sickness from health, when so many people's *status quo* runs counter to all our old concepts of well-being. We're coming out of the darkness into the light... but no one wants to be told that, least of all by a doctor! They want to stay in the womb, to *pretend* a while longer. Because coming out of the womb means certain death. They want their neuroses to be excited, teased—hell, as you well know, *made tangible, if possible!* They want to hold onto the magic, even if it's as ephemeral as an old newspaper reprint. Now, you know and I know, man to man, that the magic is dead. We don't expect miracles, do we? You and I, we're *realists!*"

Vaguely said nothing.

"Every ace fisherman needs a hook and I believe I have the hook we need. Now. Let me tell you about 'Discrimination Complex.'"

"Discrimi...?"

"Discrimination is a term of my own invention for the deep-rooted feeling of inadequacy now being suffered by millions of people—and why? Because The Only Criminal, during his infamous reign of terror, never once darkened their doorsteps. *Why*, these pitiful masses must ask themselves, were they considered so inconsequential? Did they not matter? Why had their lives, their loved ones, been so far beneath The Only Criminal's notice? Once this stigma is articulated, once it's promoted, made known, the majority of people will recognize it as a facet of their own existence! And because Billowing Pines will be associated with the complaint, they will then seek us out to treat it!"

At last, Vaguely could see how Thaddeus Kasch had influenced his superior's train of thought. Dr. Pons had seen, through the corrupt example of *The Amelia Crimes*, that the *absence* of The Only Criminal might become an even richer cash cow than his *presence*.

Pons concluded: "Our current projections show that Billowing Pines should be able to claim as much as 40% occupancy by next spring, based on the signs of interest—and a few actual commitments—we have already received. You *are* with me, aren't you, my boy?"

"I have nowhere else to go," Vaguely answered.

"If you don't mind, I'll just take that as a hearty *Yes!*" Pons laughed, coming out from behind his desk to shake Dr. Vaguely's dishrag hand vigorously. "There's enough in that envelope to tide you over until you're needed back here. I don't imagine we'll have all the promotional cannon loaded until sometime next February."

"Yes, sir."

"Silly ass! Isn't it high time you started calling me Connie? After all, you and I—we're thick as thieves."

It was the first time Vaguely had ever heard this expression. A few minutes later, as he was leaving the meeting, he was cheerfully invited by Connie to help himself from the bowl of apples tabled next to the door.

Chapter Two
I'VE JUST COME FROM THE PLACE OF PRAYER

Dr. Paul Vaguely had entered Billowing Pines with sunken spirit and low hopes, but emerged from it later that morning with his feelings further conflicted by the provision of a paid Xmas/New Years holiday and the promise of a substantial raise in salary upon his return to full hours, sometime in mid-February.

Vaguely had always considered Xmastime the most beautiful time of year and, at the moment, he found Amelia radiant with it. The cold winter air brought out the best in what remained of its storefronts and the faces of its women. Telephone poles were festooned with tinsel-ruffled leis and the peak of each streetlight was crowned with the plastic facsimile of a gas-lit lantern, giving its avenues the nostalgic aspect of a scene out of a holiday story by Dickens, like *The Crook at the Hearth,* or perhaps *An Xmas Peril.*

The only cognitive dissonance that Vaguely noted was that more and more shoppers were showing shortness of temper as they were out making their last-minute rounds. People in general were less hesitant to behave rudely or disagreeably. He saw others pushing ahead of their neighbors in shopping queues, cutting people off to take their parking spots; he saw mothers grabbing toys out of the hands of other mothers shopping for their children. Once or twice, he even overheard some cursing.

Vaguely decided to make use of his raise by returning to Harbinger's to find the ideal present for Miss White, something that might help her to overlook and forgive his abrupt departure on the night of Ringo's death, something that might also embody the endearing mystery of their interaction. He found what he considered to be the perfect gift.

For some reason, there was something about this Xmas that

encouraged him to behave, shall we say, sneakily. When he boarded the bus for home and found Miss White also aboard, he had the bag from Harbinger's right there in his hand but he found himself lying about it. She too was carrying a Harbinger's bag and divulged no secrets. They did, however, speak.

"Season's greetings, neighbor," she said, offering him the vacant seat beside her. "It looks like you and I had the same idea."

"Thank you, Melanie," he accepted. "How do you know that?"

"We've both been Xmas shopping, obviously."

"Oh, this," he said, looking at the bag. "Not really. I had to pick up a few necessities. Things I could have picked up anywhere, like, oh, you know…"

"Shaving goods, toiletries, cigarettes…"

"Exactly. Well no, not the cigarettes… But, you know, a man likes to look right for the holidays. I've been cooped up lately and thought it would do me some good to be out among the holiday crowds, people full of the holiday spirit, you know? Other believers. But you've been doing some last-minute Xmas shopping, have you?"

"No, not exactly," she smiled, clutching her bag more tightly to her chest. Xmas was making her sneakier too. "Just toiletries and what-not."

They rode on for another minute or so in silence, watching the scenery pass. Then Miss White turned her face to him. "Dr. Vaguely, I…"

"I thought we were on to Paul," he said, looking wounded.

"Oh yes, of course we are," she apologized. "I don't know if I should ask this, but… What happened to you that night? You just disappeared. You had me worried."

"Yes, I remember. I was…" He looked deep inside himself for the correct word. "Embarrassed" turned out to be the prize of that search.

"You were embarrassed?" she repeated, as if asking for an explanation.

"By the time I made it up to the third floor, I was terrified of what I might find, what I might confront, up there. I was so agitated, I struck a blow and then I found out that—after all I'd put myself through, to conquer my fears, to conquer *myself* ultimately, in an effort to go up there, all to protect *you*—that it was all over nothing more than a pair of empty gloves. I had left them resting on the bannister earlier that evening as I was letting myself in."

"They were yours?" she asked.

Vaguely auditioned a number of answers before answering. "Who else's would they be?" he finally said.

"Well, brave knight, you slew the gloves and the princess is grateful," Melanie smiled. He could tell from the look on her face that she spoke not with sarcasm but with ameliorating humor. She went on: "I found Officer Mead and he took care of Ringo, got him to the vet to be cremated. He brought the ashes back to Mr. Grinter in a little urn with a little silver terrier on top. Poor man."

Vaguely sighed. "I know from my line of work," he told her, "that, when something like this has the misfortune to befall a person at holiday time, it comes back to haunt them on every holiday thereafter."

On Xmas Eve, Vaguely put into action the plan of his most recent daydreams. He unlaced and removed his shoes, replacing them with the softest, most whispery slippers in his possession; he then turned the knob of his apartment door ever so quietly, virtually in slow motion so that it made almost no sound, not even to the termites possibly sleeping in its wood; then he sneaked out the door and all the way down the stairs to the ground floor. He managed this without being detected by a single living soul. Then, moving from apartment to apartment, he worked his way just as stealthily back upstairs, leaving little ribboned tokens of his thoughtfulness outside each of his neighbors' doors. Even those neighbors to whom he seldom spoke received, at the very least, a card of holiday sentiment. Inside these cards, he wrote "To So-and-So, Enjoy this—I stole it from someone else, Signed, The Only Criminal," but only as a gesture of whimsy and not as an act of forgery, fraud or identity theft.

On the second floor, he came to a halt outside the last door to be visited, having saved the best for last. In his hands, he held the most thoughtful, the most precious, the most momentous of his gifts. The package (as he imagined Jack Webb narrating the scene) was rectangular in dimension, wrapped in blue and criss-crossed in purple ribbon.

Dare he leave it? Dare he declare his intentions so boldly?

He weighed these questions for some moments and then—sensing her standing alertly on the other side of the door, aware of him, or at least someone hovering without—he hurriedly left the gift on the mat outside her door, and dashed up the remaining flights of stairs, not breathing again till he was once again safely behind his own bolts and chains.

Vaguely thrilled to the idea that his little holiday mission had been successful, that he had not been caught; but, as the minutes ticked closer to 12, the idea began to sit less comfortably with him that he had gifted Miss White (whom he had really not known for very long, and was still Miss White to him, much more than she was Melanie) with a pair of handcuffs.

What had possessed him? Did he not realize that such an accessory carried serious connotations? No, he had not; he had found and bought them with innocence, as the sort of memento that someone expert in the field of criminology might bestow on a friend with similar interests. Nevertheless, as the seconds ticked closer to midnight, he began to admit they might also be misread as an invitation to intimate games, even mistaken for a proposal of marriage.

Morose with misgivings, Vaguely sprang back to his door, then to the outer stairwell, and cat-footed his way back down to the second floor. Halfway down the stairs, he stopped—as did his heart. For a moment, he froze in his tracks as he thought he heard a door closing. He leaned over the bannister to peer at the spot where he had left the present.

The area outside Miss White's door had been swept clean.

It was too late. She had taken it in. He would now have his say, whether he liked it or not.

It was nearly midnight. If The Only Criminal was going to strike at all this hallowed night, he must do so soon.

Vaguely prided himself on having done all that he possibly could to tempt The Only Criminal back to active duty. At a time when those he loved had ceased to believe, had stopped putting out festive offerings representing their annual sacrifice, Vaguely had stepped in and provided for them, out of his own substantial fund of affection and fear. As long as this night passed on his watch, they would always be protected.

But with this responsibility came a new, higher tier of fear. He did not feel pride in what he had done, but rather a redefining intensity of exposure. As the only person in the entire world to have done this for his fellow men and women, he felt pierced by a thousand knives of abject terror, each of them a second thought.

In that moment, he never believed in The Only Criminal more.

He then experienced regret of its own special singularity. How devoutly did he wish that he might retract the brazen, presumptuous steps he had taken, inviting a backlash of presumption that would lash out not only at he, but against them all! Whatever could have possessed him? Did he harbor secret doubts, secret even to himself? Had he not been warned that doubt was invocation?

Extreme danger calls for extreme measures.

In an outburst of apologetic terror, Vaguely bolted back upstairs Apartment 6. There, he went to his library shelves and took every Only Criminal scrapbook he'd ever compiled, every diary he'd ever written, and he stacked them all on the floor until their piles took the form of a four-walled fortress surrounding his vulnerable person. Vaguely knelt inside the barrier formed by these most important tomes of his life as midnight lowered its boom, scrunching his eyes shut. He curled into the pose of an embryo and sent pathetic animal sounds into the ear of the listening void. Were they translated, they might have said:

"I have been such a fool! You finally convinced me that you would never return, but only a fool trusts a criminal or takes him at his word and deed! Nevertheless, take me at mine! If you can hear my voice, my model, my hero, my master, this I swear: take these books as my appeasement! Here they are—take them! Touch them! Wither them! Disintegrate and obliterate them! Burn my books—ahhhh, Only Criminallll.....!"

As the sun rose on Xmas morning, newspapers around the world reported that the holiday eve had indeed come and gone without The Only Criminal clambering down anyone's chimney. It was also reported that some people, determined to give their little ones a proper holiday, had vandalized their own homes (no crime in this, of course); there was also editorial speculation that, in future years, some people might go into business offering holiday vandalism services for hire. It was all about the children.

As for Paul Vaguely, he unfolded himself from his embryonic crunch and found himself at the site of an Xmas miracle—explicable only as The Only Criminal's last. His fortress of scrapbooks had vanished into nothingness, as had all of the other professional papers he had assembled and hoarded in Apartment 6 for so many years. Other than his physical self, nothing more of him existed there.

All that remained was suitable only for letting someone else in.

Chapter Three
THE UPPER ROOM

The days following Xmas in Vaguely's world passed without incident, without ripple. In regard to the be-ribboned appeasements which Paul Vaguely had left outside his neighbors' abodes, there came no acknowledgment, no response.

This precarious, worrisome silence could have meant a couple of things. Possibly the gifts and the protection they represented meant nothing to their recipients, but Vaguely preferred the alternative explanation: that The Only Criminal had indeed manifest on that dread night and taken to his bosom each and every one of them. There were no newspaper stories from Amelia nor anywhere else in the world to confirm such a hypothesis, but Vaguely felt something new in himself that might have been a tacit confirmation of this second explanation. He was experiencing for the first time a feeling of humility.

Even so, Vaguely was also disconcerted about what had become of the special gift he had purchased for his favorite neighbor, which he felt sure had disappeared from where he'd left it after his hearing the closing of Miss White's door. Either she saw it and took it into her apartment, or in the short space of time between his leaving it and his attempt to take it back, it had been carried away by other hands, never to be seen by her. His worry was compounded by the fact that he did not see her again in the days that led up to the New Year. He assumed that she was alright because, throughout this period of her disappearance, he could hear the sounds of work being done in her apartment below, initially minor but later at times quite loud. He was on the point of thinking that she might have accidentally handcuffed herself to a radiator or something else, something outside the reach of their key and her telephone; but surely if this were the case, she would have screamed or called out for assistance. But no word? No thank you? What was he to infer from her silence, from her noise? Perhaps, had all the books in his library been written on the subject of Melanie White, he would have known the answer.

It was one evening late in the year, late enough to dangle from it like a vestigial appendage, that Vaguely heard another unexpected rap on his chamber door as he was untying his shoelaces in preparation for bed. It was late enough to be the next day, the last of the year, and so the knocking sent a jolt through him that made him feel exposed and vulnerable. After all, in order for a visitor to reach his door and knock upon it, they must first get through the front entrance of the Oakley Apartments complex; then they must traverse the antechamber with the mailboxes and make their dogged pilgrimage up the respective stair flights to the second, then the third floors; once there, they would be faced with two apartments and must choose one door over the other. Somehow, someone had surmounted all of these obstacles to find him, and at an hour on the wrong side for receiving visitors. He briskly retied his shoelace and hesitated near his door.

He could have asked who it was, but why bother? The Only Criminal would have chosen a less direct and lawless method of gaining access. He unlocked the various chains and deadbolts and, opening the door, saw she whom the Angels had named Melanie standing there, a small box in hand, returning his wary look with one just as unsure.

"Hello," Vaguely managed.

"I was just sitting downstairs," she began, "and feeling like doing anything but what I should be doing, which is coming up with designs for the store's Harbinger's Valentine's Day window displays. And I…"

"And you knew from my footsteps on your ceiling that I was still up."

"Guilty," she smiled. "Anyway, I come bearing cookies."

Vaguely invited her in, with a smooth "entré" of his hand. As she stepped inside, he felt a little something inside him die—and it was bloody well time it did.

She handed over the box. "Not homemade. They're from the corner bakery. Bumblebee's?"

"Bemelmans," he gently corrected her, accepting them.

"I asked them what you liked. They seemed to know. I took one of them. Okay, two."

"Thank you—*and* you're welcome!"

Vaguely hugged the box of cookies to his chest while watching his magical, unexpected guest walk in and poke around. It was she who had dared to visit him in his native habitat, yet it was he who looked at her as if she were the zoo critter, looking at this and that and forgiving the dust and trying to make sense of a world she never made, and perhaps wondering where she might fit into it all.

"Your place has the same basic floor plan as mine," she observed, while examining a little knick-knack that Vaguely remembered choosing for its very neutrality, intending to keep Apartment 5 as normal a hideaway as possible. "I was wondering if it did. Even so, your place looks completely different to mine."

Vaguely countered: "So you do your design work at home rather than in an office?"

"I do my final work from an office at Harbinger's," she explained, while continuing to look around. "But all of my preliminary work—the sketches, the mistakes, the balled-up wads of paper—that all happens in my studio downstairs."

"So you have a studio down there," Vaguely marveled.

"It's home too. Just a corner of it's my studio, where I have a drafting table and my other necessities." Using the width of her reach and the length of her stride, she estimated in Vaguely's own space the area occupied by her studio downstairs. "It's basically from here… to here. I only go into my office downtown to execute the final drawings, to present them to my boss (who sometimes sends me back to the drafting board), and to supervise a new window as it's going up, or when an old one is being taken down. They save the pieces in storage."

"Don't look at me like that," Vaguely suddenly blurted.

"Why not?" asked the little minx,.

Thanks to the author of that particular evening, Vaguely's telephone chose that unlikely moment to ring.

He looked at the device with its inverted horns with dread and suspicion. "No one ever calls at this hour, unless it's an emergency," he reasoned.

"Then you'd better answer it," his guest suggested.

"Hello? Yes, this is Paul Vaguely… No… No, I'm not interested… No… And please don't call me again. Thank you."

He hung up.

"Who was it?"

"It was one of those—oh, what do they call them? Oh, yes. A telemarketer."

Miss White's nose wrinkled with companionable dislike, and then she continued to poke around, long after it was painfully obvious that she had seen everything the place had to offer.

"What is it?" Vaguely inquired. "Or isn't."

"Oh, it's nothing… It's just that I expected to find something here that, well… isn't here."

"Like the Hope Diamond?" he joked.

"No," she began, wondering how to phrase it. "More like… *you.*"

"Me?"

"Yes," she explained. "This sofa, these chairs and tables, these knick-knacks… They could belong to anybody."

"Indeed they could," he admitted. "When I moved in, this apartment was furnished," he explained. "Since then, I've added a meaningless knick-knack or two, but I've always made a point of keeping my professional life elsewhere."

"That's right! You keep another apartment across the hall!"

Vaguely nodded. "Follow me."

With Miss White tagging along, he exited the apartment, crossed the hall to Apartment 6, and searched his trouser pocket for the appropriate key. He found it, fitted it, turned the lock.

The door swung open on darkness.

"Here I am," he said. "This is me."

He reached inside ahead of her and flicked on the overhead lighting. Miss White stepped inside and found herself in the inverted mirror image of the rooms across the hall. It was almost completely empty, save for one or two places to sit and the marks on the walls and floor, which testified to the fact that it had once, not so long ago, been overflowing with stuff. She could see where books and shelves had been, how high they had risen up the walls. She could see where maps and various relevant images had hung, from the tiny pinholes left behind.

Miss White sneezed.

"Bless you," said Vaguely.

"Thank you," she said, plucking a dusty tissue from a dusty desktop dispenser and wiping her nose.

"So what happened here?" she asked.

"It may take a lifetime to find out… or forget. I called it my *pièd-a-terror.*"

"Is it safe to be here?"

"I think so," he reassured her. "Some gentlemen from the church across the street came by, not too long ago, and exorcised the place."

"I knew that The Only Criminal was your big subject," she admitted. "The books that were here… on the shelves that were here… you read all of them?"

"Some more than once. One or two I also wrote," he confessed.

"Really?" she asked, impressed. "Which ones?"

"It doesn't really matter now. They were mostly in manuscript. I hadn't really published anything—except for my doctoral thesis. It was anthologized in various professional journals, and in the book that was shelved right about here," he illustrated, pointing to a spot on the wall. "It was called *The Only Criminal—Blueprints in Contemporary Psychology.*"

"Where are they now?"

Vaguely, Vaguely gestured toward his sternum. "In here, I suppose." An awkward silence followed, first broken by him. "It was always my dream, you know, that… Oh, never mind."

"No," she said, coming closer and resting her hand briefly on his crossed arms. "Tell me."

"Well, that someday my expertise in this field would be recog-nized…"

"But it was!" she protested. "I saw you on television and in the newspapers!"

"I mean… *by him*," Vaguely clarified. "I hoped that someday he might acknowledge me in some way, the way I had consecrated my entire life to the study of him, to my belief in him. Isn't there some master in your own line of work whose approval you seek?"

"Yes, but they're…" She stopped at that.

"They're what?"

"They're not important," she insisted, "because what's really important is how *we* feel about the work we do. Tell me this. How do you know when you've done a really good job, when you've really knocked one straight out of the park?"

Vaguely looked deep inside himself and chuckled warmly. "I have a feeling, deep inside, that… that I've wrapped the gift I've addressed to him… and he's taken it."

She simply nodded in reply. When she next broke the silence, it was after they had returned to Apartment 5. That's when she mentioned, "You know, Paul, there's one pretty significant difference between you and me."

"Oh?"

"I would have offered me a cookie by now."

Chapter Four
CRYING IN THE CHAPEL

In the first days of the new year, Dr. Constantine Pons embarked on his long-stewing media campaign, making the first of his conspicuous appearances on television and radio. Sometimes he was interviewed as the (self-styled) "foremost authority" on Discrimination Complex, while at other times he appeared in round table discussions in the company of leading authorities on related maladies such as Restless Leg Syndrome. His name was always mentioned in connection with that of Billowing Pines and, at some point during each interview, he made a point of invoking the name of Dr. Paul Vaguely as well, always with the greatest respect and stressing his long and esteemed professional proximity to what he called "all things Only Criminal"—which struck Vaguely as an incongruity, if not an oxymoron.

The surgical precision of Pons' media campaign had the desired effect: the switchboard at Billowing Pines began to be besieged by calls applying for appointments and inquiring into residency from casual viewers who had recognized themselves in the symptoms Pons had compiled under the heading of his recently defined malady. To his surprise, as well as Vaguely's, these callers included a number of Billowing Pines' former resident patients (with the notable exceptions of Jimmy Ostinato, Angel Paget, and of course Peevey). Pons's initial projection of 40% restored residency by April proved to be short-sighted as every available room was claimed before the end of the new year's first month. Such was the campaign's success that, before anyone was actually admitted, it was decided that an entire floor of the sanatorium's living spaces would be divided into two, allowing the revenues of this new venture to be doubled..

Dr. Paul Vaguely returned to work full-time in February, beginning with a couple of settling-in days. As he met with his first patients, it didn't take him long to realize that Pons was onto something with his new, post-Criminal approach to psychology. Witness this excerpt from a one such session:

"How long have you been feeling this way?"

"Ever since The Only Criminal disappeared."

"Can you describe your feelings?"

"I'll do better than that. I'll describe my day. I wake up in the morning with absolutely no energy, no sense of anticipation. I know how each and every day is going to go, from beginning to end, because I've already lived it. I lived it yesterday, and I'll be living it tomorrow. That is, if I can make it through this one. I tell myself, if I can just make it to the shower without putting my head in the oven, I'll be alright. It's a struggle to get dressed; I don't really care anymore how I look. I don't apply myself to my work because I no longer have the drive to succeed. No matter how successful I become, my wealth will be insignificant because I know he's not out there coveting it. I'll never feel the chill of those imagined eyes on the back of my neck, as I go to the ATM to make a deposit. Food has lost its taste for me. I can't stand coffee. I smoke like a trout. I used to love watching television; I can no longer tolerate it. Like those elections last November; I knew that none of the candidates would be assassinated, so why watch? To see the better man win? The candidates are both good, fine, upstanding men, after all—where's the interest in *that?* So I turn off the TV, turn down the sheets, and lie there, awake for hours and hours of boredom, of nullity, of nihilism, till I wake up the next morning, again with absolutely no energy, no sense of anticipation. And I ask myself, 'Wasn't I just here? Am I back to Square One already?'"

"Why, Doctor!" his patients would exclaim after listening. "That's exactly how *I* feel!"

Of course, Vaguely wasn't being entirely truthful in this dour assessment of his average day, but Dr. Pons had adjudged that this form of early confession on the part of the criminologist was the ideal way to bait the hook of a long-lasting and lucrative therapy.

And so—exactly as had happened with the newspapers and their reprints, with television and its reruns, and with motion picture theaters and blockbuster remakes—the great wheel of criminology continued to turn… *without* the actual participation of The Only Criminal.

The world that formed the backdrop to these activities, and the single ray of hope that was Vaguely's dawning relationship with Melanie, was indeed suffering more palpably from the entropy that resulted from not having The Only Criminal to kick around anymore. The signs were everywhere, and sometimes they took the form of actual signs. For example, on another February evening, as Vaguely stepped off the #27, he saw a new motto adorning the illuminated sign outside St. Tim's. It read: WHAT'S MISSING FROM CH_RCH? U ARE!

But this was not the worst of it.

Staggered by the steep contrast between the sign's former philosophy and the cornpone humor that was passing for wisdom today, Vaguely craned his face skyward to take in the reassurance of the Consolations billboard above Lawson's News, only to find it papered over with a new advertisement. There was nothing dark, unhealthy, or nocturnal about the new ad, yet it changed the complexion of Vaguely's neighborhood totally with the image of the phantasmal, cigarette-loving Only Criminal no longer there to lord over its rooftops. In his place was a summery beach scene. The subject was a handsome, fit, solitary man in black swimwear and wraparound shades, walking along a sandy shore beside low, tumbling waters of glassy green. The skies behind him were of a rich blue hue, with traces of crimson barely limning the horizon, as if all the world's former bloodshed was now behind him in this haven of bliss. The sign read "Working Your Life Away Is A Crime." It was an advertisement for Getaway Airlines.

Nor was this the worst of it.

Vaguely was pained by this crass revamping of all he held sacred. Lowering his eyes from the billboard to the shop below, Vaguely was taken doubly aback by a sign hung inside the front door of Lawson's News. It read CLOSED. Indeed, the store was not only closed but visibly padlocked. Vaguely felt stunned; it had been open just that morning, when he had arrived at the stop just in time to board his bus, which was running slightly ahead of schedule and thus stole his opportunity to say hello to Abel Lawson and buy his morning papers for the ride into work. Vaguely had assuaged his fears by picturing Mr. Lawson on some faraway beach, in the manner of the vacationer on the advertisement above his store, and telling himself that he would be back. However, in the weeks that followed, there was a noticeable, gradual diminishment of inventory visible through the store's windows, which were finally opaqued with whorls of white soap.

As the crosswalk light turned green, Vaguely staggered across the street and into Bemelmans' Bakery, knowing that on this particular day in February, everything on display would be pink or heart-shaped or covered in chubby cherubim.

"Hi, Doc," smiled Juanita, the uniformed salesgirl in her seventies. "What can I gitcha?"

"I don't see what I'm looking for, Nita. "You do still carry those little candy hearts with the cute sayings on them?"

"Let me look," she said, briefly disappearing behind the scenes. When she returned, she was carrying a full display box of the boxed candy hearts, which she situated atop the display case. She took one out and handed it to her customer. "You just need the one?" she asked.

"Only one for the Only One," Vaguely quipped, smiling with nostalgia at the slogans peeking through the box's heart-shaped cellophane window: BE GOOD NOW, BAD GIRL, PAT ME DOWN, YOU'RE UNDER ARREST. Rattling the box brought different sayings to the surface: STICK EM UP, ROUGH STUFF, PUNISH ME. He couldn't resist reading a few of these aloud for Juanita's amusement, but unexpectedly, they precipitated quite a different response than expected: "Oh, how did that get in there? I'm so sorry, Doc—that's old stock, sitting around in the back room since a year ago! Those will all be stale!" She disappeared into the back room for a moment and then came back with another display box. "Here! This is a fresh box—with the new sayings!"

New sayings? Vaguely couldn't wait to see what they said.

What he now saw of the pastel hearts through the box's cellophane window was of an entirely different, insipid character: BE MINE, KISS ME, TAKE CHARGE, CUTIE PIE.

Vaguely recoiled, telling Juanita that he didn't want these; he wanted the old box.

"Like I said, they're old and stale. I can't sell 'em to you, but… oh, here—just take 'em!"

After all, candy is only candy; it's the thought that counts. The string which held all these destabilizing events together had yet to run out.

As Vaguely later pushed through the front door of the Oakley Apartments building, after checking his mailbox and finding nothing but a few bills, he exited the antechamber and saw in the entrance hall that the door of Red Grinter's apartment was slightly ajar. In recent weeks, Red had been increasingly distracted and absent-minded, so this was not so surprising, yet he was vigilant about the old fellow's safety. He rapped at the door, causing it to swing open more fully. Beyond the welcome mat, he saw a more orderly, better-kept apartment than he expected his gruff but good-hearted old landlord to maintain.

"Mr. Grinter?" he called out, stepping inside to be better heard. "It's Dr. Vaguely. Your door was half-open, I wanted to make sure you knew about it."

There was no answer. Given pride of place atop Red's television set were the urn with the little silver terrier on top and two cheaply processed color photos in a hinged, dime store picture frame. One of the photos, of indeterminate age, was of Ringo; the other, somewhat more determinate, showed a sunburned, young woman in a white blouse, khaki shorts and white knee socks, laughing on the lap of a man with a Hawaiian shirt, a roundish nose and thinning red hair.

Maybe he's downstairs, doing his laundry, Vaguely thought.

Vaguely pondered whether or not he should close the door behind him, but, for the time being, opted to leave it as he found it, in case Mr. Grinter wasn't carrying his keys.

He walked to the far end of the entrance hall, where the door to the basement was positioned behind the main stairwell. He clambered down the slatted wooden steps, the roar of the building's immense boiler growing louder with his descent. There was a smell of mild mildew and mustiness. It was mostly dark down there, so he followed the available light to the storage area, beyond which were the laundry facilities—usually kept illuminated but presently in total darkness. He stepped into the pitch to flick the On switch, being reasonably familiar with the layout of the place, and felt something brush against his face—something heavy, swaying and draped in loose cloth.

With the coming of light, Vaguely recoiled. He squeezed the rattling box of candy in his hand, expulsing a stream of stale hearts and sentiments across the cement floor. The illuminated bulb, suspended from the ceiling, swung to and fro, casting leapy shadows and, higher up, exposing a pair of black shoes and dress trousers, upheld high where they didn't belong.

Someone's legs and feet were still in them.Vaguely recovered his breath and courage and angled the dangling light upwards until it met an empurpled, blackening face above a white bowtie.

And that, dear reader, was quite the worst of it.

Vaguely was so slammed with shock that, the next thing he knew, he was halfway up the stairs to Miss White's apartment, where he stammered out the news, and used her telephone to summon the police. In their joint presence, the body of Red Grinter—already, conveniently, dressed for burial—was cut down and carried away on a stretcher.

As he had watched one of the policemen encircle Red's waist with both arms to accept the burden of his weight, while another sawed at the rope with an unfolded blade, Paul felt Melanie's hand flutter into his own. He began to contradict the officers' hasty description of Red's death as a suicide, but a gentle, guiding squeeze from Melanie's hand persuaded him to back down.

He and she remained present to answer questions as Red's apartment was searched and locked, pending notification of any close relatives. Later, when there was nothing left to do but climb those stairs again, Melanie told Paul, "I don't want you up there, alone with your ideas" and took him inside her apartment.

This was the first time. He had longed to see it, to explore it as she had previously explored his two domiciles, but now that he was here, he was too emotionally benumbed, his head too pounding, and he was altogether too self-involved to admit any details other than that Mr. Grinter was dead.

Melanie guided him to her sofa, closed and locked the door behind them, then took her place beside him. She patted her lap. "Lay down here," she invited. "Rest your head. Let me show you an old trick."

He followed her suggestion. With his head in her lap, her fingers spread and sank into his dark hair and followed the map of his veins to those places where her sensitive touch located the physiological evidence of his anxiety. There, she systematically applied and relieved pressure until, many minutes later, Vaguely confirmed that he was feeling better. He did this not by saying so, but by saying other things, by relieving his mind of all that had been crowding it.

Melanie listened with infinite patience to his account of how he had discovered the body, which he repeated from a variety of angles until he found one that began to allow him to accept the tragedy as fact.

After he had related, deconstructed and reassembled all this information for some time, Vaguely turned over onto his side to let this gentle woman's fingers extend the range of their grace. Finding relaxed to a deeper level within himself than he usually occupied, he noticed that the tips of her fingernails, softly raking his head and shoulders were doing so in specific patterns. They were forming letters, sequential letters. Those letters formed his given name.

"You're writing on me!" he murmured.

"That's 'Pencils'," she whispered.

"Pencils?"

"Mm-hm. When I was little, my sister and I slept in the same room. Mom and Dad didn't like us talking after the lights went out, so we started writing messages to each other on our arms and legs. It let us communicate, but it was also soothing. It calmed us down and made us want to go to sleep. So this," she repeated, using her fingernail once again, "is 'Pencils.'"

She wrote something simple.

"TOC.," Vaguely smiled, perceiving what she had written. "The Only Criminal!"

"M-hm—and this," she said, moving her fingers over what she had penciled, lightly brushing his skin in a sensual manner with her fingertips, "is 'Erasers.'"

Vaguely grunted; it was ecstasy. There were no words written in "Erasers"; they were all about oblivion, sweet oblivion.

"I envy you your family," he finally said.

"Don't you have a family?"

"They're all gone now, so now they feel more like a story that was told to me than a real family."

"You can tell me that story, if you want to."

"There's not much to tell. I was the only child of a single mother. My earliest memories are of living with my grandparents but, when I was about seven years old, my mother came back from wherever she had been and took me back into her life. We moved around a great deal—but never outside Amelia. We moved from North Amelia to West Amelia, East Amelia to South Amelia. I don't think my mother meant to be nomadic, but she wasn't able to stay in the same place for very long. I couldn't make sense of it at the time, of course, but as time went on, I realized that what I had always seen in her character as eccentricity was a more serious, chronic inability to tell the truth. Mother was a compulsive gossiper and liar. She lied to people, left and right, about anything at all, including our neighbors. After I grew up and acquired some perspective, I realized that our neighbors must have somehow found her out for what she was, learned something about her that she couldn't bear to have known, and this was not something she could live with, so it would goad her into uprooting us once again, so that she could start over again in a place where she could pass for some other kind of person, and be liked. But it was never for long. I was always saying goodbye to friends as I was moved into new school districts, so I eventually stopped making friends altogether."

"You became a solitary person."

"There was a counselor at my junior high school, a nice woman whom I saw a great deal. She was aware of my problems, sensitive to them, even though there was nothing she could really do about them. But she gave me an outlet, and some advice I never forgot."

"What did she tell you?"

"She said, 'Paul, if the ground is unsteady beneath your feet, make your home in the sky.' I never gave this idea much thought until… I met a girl at one of my schools, someone I felt strongly about…"

"Your first love?"

"She might have been. But, just as I worked up the nerve to approach her, my mother told me that we would be moving again. This time, I put my foot down. I really fought her on this, tried to change her mind. But she was so stubborn, so autocratic—she never gave a damn how my life was being affected by her afflictions. I was so angry, I thought for a moment that I might actually strike her…"

"You'd never do that."

"No," Vaguely admitted. "Instead, I ran out of our apartment—I've never lived in a house—and I ran and ran and ran until I remembered what my counselor had said to me. I looked up into the sky and saw the moons in the sky, very large and full… and I felt all my problems shrink… because I knew The Only Criminal was looking down on me."

Miss White started to say something, but bit her lip and continued listening.

"I felt a great calm come over me—like I feel now, with your Pencils and Erasers."

"What's your earliest memory of The Only Criminal?"

Vaguely thought back, back to those primal scenes before which there was nothing else to articulate.

"Storybook time," he said. "The storybooks my grandmother read to me at bedtime."

"And after that? What place did he occupy in your life before he became this sort of comforting presence?"

"My mother would tell me about him."

"In what way?"

"I guess, if there was something I wanted to do that she didn't want me to do, she would tell me a story—perhaps a story that she had been told by her own mother, my grandmother—something about The Only Criminal that would scare me straight."

"Maybe this isn't the best time to ask, but didn't it ever strike you as odd that you would find your path in life, the road to your eventual profession, in the form of something that you first knew as fairy tales, and which were further impressed upon you by someone you've described to me as a chronic liar?"

Vaguely sat up abruptly, shocked. "Now wait a minute…" he began—shocked that Miss White would say this, and shaken to realize that this was true. He could not argue the point.

Melanie pressed on. "So, when you went back to your apartment after your encounter with the man in the sky, what happened between you and your mother?"

"She was gone," he answered. "In the time I was gone, she had packed all her things and… disappeared. I never saw her again. I waited a day or two, expecting her to come back, then I notified my grandparents and they came to get me. They saw that I finished my education, my hard work won me scholarships, my accomplishments won me national recognition… What am I saying? That's not true."

"No?" Miss White was confused. "Then what is the truth?"

"The truth is… I never went back. It was I who abandoned her. I slept on the floors of friends, one after another, till all their hospitality was used up. I found a cheap place and paid the rent with Social Security checks from my father…"

"From your father?"

"My dead father—that my grandmother forwarded to me, from my mother. It was enough to cover the rent and cans of soup. When I got tired of soup, there was a pizza place in my neighborhood that had a special offer. They promised that your pizza would be absolutely free if they failed to deliver it within one hour. I could afford maybe one pizza a week, but then I discovered it was hard for their delivery people to find my street. My street sign was obscured by a tree or something, so I began to gamble. Very often, they had to hand the pizza or the spaghetti or the lasagna or whatever it was over for free. If they delivered on time, if I didn't have the money, I just wouldn't answer the door. It wasn't illegal, but it wasn't honest, either. I hope you won't think too badly of me. Anyway, they soon suspended the offer. There were times when I thought I might starve. There were times when I thought I might have to… but never mind that. I became something else."

Melanie began smoothing his hair slowly with the palm of her hand.

"You reinvented yourself," she summarized. "You survived. No crime in that."

Vaguely turned on her lap and looked up, in the direction of her voice—into the kindness of her own two eyes.

"I'm sorry I said 'damn,'" he told her.

For the next few days, the talk of the town told and retold in whispers the tragic story of how Red Grinter, the landlord of the Oakley Apartments, had cleaned his apartment from top to bottom, left it spotless, then dressed himself in a rented tuxedo, went down to his basement's laundry room and hung himself from a strong pipe—on what was later discovered to be the anniversary of Ringo's day of adoption.

The body of Harold "Red" Grinter was laid to rest in St. Timothy's Cemetery, entombed with the ashes of his beloved Ringo in a plot beside his wife Yvonne, whose gravestone marked her passing eleven years earlier. He had few living relatives, but he had been a life-long Amelian and was always highly visible in the community, so his memorial service in St. Tim's adjoining chapel was well attended. Paul Vaguely and Melanie White sat together in a second row pew with the Westerkamms (to whom Red had bequeathed ownership of the Oakley Apartments) and also town troubadour Whimsy Plunkett, who was credited in the program of the service with his given name of Raleigh.

"This here is a song for Red," the balladeer explained awkwardly into a microphone, after tuning his guitar at the altar. Most of the people in town had never heard Whimsy speak. "I based it on something he once said to me, after little Ringo passed on. He kept saying it over and over. It kinda stuck with me, though I didn't really understand it. Then, when I heard that Red was gone too, well, I sorta got to understanding what all he meant. So this one's for you, old buddy."

Vaguely knew from the first few notes that this song was like no other Whimsy had ever performed about town. Deep, resonant strums across all 12 strings of the sunburst-finished guitar lashed out at the walls of the chapel and stung the smarting eyes of the mourners. When the words came, Whimsy sang them low, with the wrenching pain of loss, reverence and an air of dust-blown devastation. The song was a spiritual.

Sometimes a phrase will cross my mind
When friends I have just chanced to find
Join the ranks of long-lost friends:
"So this is how their story ends."

Sometimes the sound of it is sweet,
When fairy tales are made complete,
But, in this case—how it offends!
"So this is how his story ends."

The chorus never came; instead, each stanza restated its inevitable rhythm, the rhythm of a sobbing chest. At this point in the performance, Whimsy turned his gaze to the mourners in the foremost pew, and seemed to focus on Paul Vaguely in particular.

What once was six is down to five
Poor souls who want to stay alive
And one who hopes to take a bride.
One last chance to turn the tide.

Vaguely felt the words penetrate, and he crossed his legs in the other direction in an effort to regain his comfort.

We yearn to turn back to Page One
With Life's adventure just begun
But the rules of Time will not bend...
For this is how all stories end.

Paul Vaguely didn't hear this last stanza. His ears were still ringing with the line that transcended his feelings of loss and mourning and issued a challenge which he knew had been aimed squarely at him, a challenge that seemed to offer the whole mad world its only hope:

One last chance to turn the tide.

Chapter Five
WORKING ON THE BUILDING

With each passing month that The Only Criminal did not return, the world that Paul and Melanie shared seemed to mutate into something else of its own accord. Perhaps that accord had something to do with Paul beginning to see things through eyes he believed he could gaze into forever.

One evening, as the two of them were gentling together in her apartment, at what she had carefully judged to be the appropriate moment, Melanie broached a delicate subject.

"Now that things are settling down," she began, "now that you've begun to face some things about yourself and about your past and the ground has become a bit firmer beneath your feet, don't you think you might begin to admit to yourself… the possibility, anyway… that The Only Criminal is really gone?"

Vaguely was thunderstruck. He jumped to his feet, unable to continue sharing the same sofa with this blasphemer.

"Gone?!"

"I believe he's gone. Most people believe he's gone, nowadays. Gone means it doesn't exist. And reality is whatever the majority of people agree upon."

Vaguely couldn't believe what he was hearing.

"How can you not believe in The Only Criminal? Just because he's not there any longer to be…"

"Seen and touched?" she countered. "Did you ever see him? Touch him?"

"Have you never read a newspaper? Or seen the evening news on television?"

"Of course. And I know full well that the media specializes in promulgating shameful simplifications of the truth and controlling the people of the world—yes, even through terror."

Vaguely spluttered. "B-but how can you call devoting the entire contents of a daily newspaper to a single subject a 'simplification'?"

"Because there's a lot more to daily life than a single subject," she stated.

"Need I remind you that I majored in The Only Criminal in college?"

"I went to college too, and while you were pursuing your degree in psychology and theoretical abstractions, I was studying stage decoration and art history. You can't study art history without also learning something of real history."

"So?"

"So I know something about the world as it existed *before* The Only Criminal. I know something about other things *besides* The Only Criminal. The Only Criminal is something, a phenomenon, that grew out of people's collective inabilities to deal with complex issues, with the vast gray area that exists between black and white. People couldn't accept the idea of living in a world where neighbors weren't to be trusted, where the police were sometimes corrupt, where priests were sometimes pedophiles, where governments prized self-interest above the common good, and where the true extent of such problems could not even begin to be grasped, much less solved. People had to simplify their world views to cope with the world on a day-to-day basis. First they protected themselves by limiting the information they let in; they listened only to those radio stations and watched only those television shows and read only those books that they could trust not to challenge their points of view. Anything other than their own viewpoints became simplified, polarized, *demonized... That's* the primordial ooze from which The Only Criminal arose!"

"We're not just talking about me. I deal every day with patients who have been traumatized by actual encounters with The Only Criminal. People whose lives were shattered because they once stood too near his dark presence."

"We all stand in that dark presence," she refuted, holding her ground. "We're all born into a world of crime and sin and vice…"

"On that we are certainly agreed!" Vaguely affirmed.

"But most people can't own up to the fact that they enable this evil to perpetuate itself, so they give it a separate shape and identity and a far greater power than they have to combat it. Perhaps the patients you deal with have subconsciously realized this for themselves and, as a result, have retreated deeper into their psychoses, to a place nearer the literal presence of The Only Criminal."

Vaguely could say nothing in response to this.

Melanie looked into his eyes—spiraling, lost and overwhelmed—hoping she had not taken this line of communication too far. The two of them had yet to reach that place of sweet accord where two people can begin to admit their love for one other, so she backpedalled slightly:

"All I ask is that you try to acknowledge that there may be other ways of looking at the world."

The weather warmed and the time came when more and more people took to the streets of Amelia after dark. Paul and Melanie were among them, embarking on a new and shared habit of taking after-dinner walks around the neighborhood, talking about their days' events under canopies of starlight. Soon enough, they started noticing more teenagers out and about, and there was something about them, and their tendency to cluster together in idle groups, and later gangs, that inspired them to cross to the other side the street whenever they saw them approaching in numbers of more than two.

These teens were never found engaged in intellectual discussion, excited by the ideas and possibilities presented to them by the world and its open opportunities; rather, they stood or sat about, brooding and sullen and without point, and resentful of anyone who didn't visibly share their common burden. . They looked as though they had been ordered out-of-doors by parents unable to suffer another moment of their useless indolence indoors. Amelia used to be such a happy place, full of neighborly spirit, but Paul and Melanie could sometimes hear these youngsters sneering the names of their elders for the miserable lot in life they had inherited from them, belly-aching about how tiresome it was to always be told how much they had missed by not being around during the time of The Only Criminal. Their inheritance of a lesser world seemed to roast their restlessness, insolence and resentment over an open spit. Teenagers had once been polite, respectful and articulate, but now they spoke among themselves in loud, rude, indecipherable slang, lowering their voices whenever adults like Paul and Melanie happened to pass by, and then snickering over rude, indecipherable remarks they made about them after they had passed out of earshot. Officer Phil Mead, whose presence once helped to moderate and modulate the nocturnal activities of the neighborhood, was now nowhere to be seen. Rumors abounded that he had been laid off—something about budget cuts.

Similar budget cuts resulted in the closings of some schools, the first of which were first announced in late May and early June. It all made Vaguely feel ill at ease, as though unfamiliar, invisible hands were interfering with his world. Young people, eager to learn, had every right to be incensed about so many paths to a brighter future being closed to them after the vacation months, but it was their manner of dealing with these heated, unmanageable emotions that worried him. Initially, they flocked to meeting places where there was lots of light—storefronts and street corners—but, as they grew more and more bored and frustrated with all the empty time on their hands, not to mention the emptiness of each other's company, they withdrew into pockets of shadow and wondered in conspiratorial whispers how they might squeeze some cheap sensation out of an otherwise unpromising evening. From this point on, the sweet, natural *nachtmusik* of Amelia—the nightbirds, the balladeering of Whimsy Plunkett—gave way to the harsher sounds of youthful shouting, gunned automobile motors, and the raucous cussing and thudding of portable radios stationed all over town.

One night, as Paul and Melanie were returning home from a walk to the local library, there was a heart-stopping crash very near to where they were passing—as an empty bottle was hurled out of darkness in their general direction, onto the street.

Occasionally Vaguely saw such young people being interviewed on television, telling Lorraine Cadbury (who had by this time worked her way up to a New York station) and other interviewers that they saw no point in continuing with their educations. Why should they spend another four to eight years of their youth in study, reading a lot of books that everyone knew to be meaningless and irrelevant, just to learn a trade that might have its bottom drop out from under it before they were ready to retire? As one thoughtful young girl put it: "What do we got to look forward to, after graduation? Working in some factory that makes Betty Crocker cake mix, Aunt Jemima syrup, or Ben & Jerry's ice cream? I mean, what's to stop Betty Crocker, Aunt Jemima, and Ben & Jerry from suddenly disappearing?"

Then came the day when the renamed *Amelia Times* took the historic step of reporting the misbehavior of teenagers, and even the occasional adult. Said incidents ranged from the mischievous to—incredible as it may seem—the near-criminal. Some writers editorialized that the worst of these miscreants should be held accountable for their actions, taken off the streets altogether and herded into prison. Law enforcement officials shrugged their shoulders. The jails, they said, simply weren't big enough.

Of course they're not big enough, Vaguely ruminated. *They were built to hold one person!*

Newspaper sales, in the dumps for so long as to threaten the very future of print, began to climb steadily with the introduction of these harrowing local and national stories. As Monkey did what Monkey saw, television news soon followed suit, broadcasting the names and photos of deadbeat teens who opened fire hydrant valves to cool off, got into friendly fights, or painted nihilistic slogans on the sides of buses and abandoned buildings. Starved for attention and soon overfed, none of the teens' antisocial actions were discouraged by being pegged as "trouble-making" by the media; indeed, there were multiple repeat offenders. Evidently, to be noticed was to be encouraged.

Sometimes, as Vaguely watched the evening news in Apartment 5, his phone would ring and he would smile indulgently as Melanie gave him an earful of her editorializing. She was disgusted that teenagers were being blamed for everything that was wrong with the world, when it was really the elders who were up to no good and using these stories—much as they had once used The Only Criminal—to cleverly divert attention from their own misdeeds. The next group to be incriminated ("You just watch!" she said) would be *the foreigners*. And sure enough…

Vaguely's daily newspapers—which now had to be picked up from the corner racks outside Bemelmans' Bakery—were soon emblazoned with uncommon words in their headlines: BEIRUT, ISTANBUL, IRAQ, KYIV, GAZA, GOMA… These stories were bred only for continuation, never seemed to be resolved, bleeding serially from one day into the next like some unstoppable rupture of the brotherhood of Man. And, in Vaguely's personally held view, it had all been precipitated by the aneurysm of The Only Criminal's disappearance, and the international disagreements over its particulars.

Of course, The Only Criminal wasn't entirely gone. He continued to survive in movies and on television. Hollywood never had any use for new ideas; they continued to churn out new remakes of old Only Criminal storylines, sometimes without mentioning The Only Criminal in so many words. When the word "remake" became a disparagement after a parade of unsuccessful ones, movie company publicists put new spins on the film industry's lack of imagination by describing their pre-chewed cud with new, unapologetic, hipster terms like "reimagining" and "re-do." One of these reimaginings, a remake of *The Only Criminal at Bay* entitled *Crime Immemorial*, marked the big screen debut of Jimmy Ostinato—yes, Vaguely's former patient and the former "Only Witness." Vaguely attended its local premiere with Melanie, though he kept the secret of this earlier acquaintance from her. During one of the brighter moments in the picture, Vaguely spied his boss, Constantine Pons, seated a few rows closer to the screen, in the company of his secretary Beatriz. They were looking awfully chummy. Though not quite the equal of his Only Witness impersonation, Jimmy Ostinato's performance in *Crime Immemorial* was impressive and had lasting, worldwide repercussions. The producers of the film had intuited that the audience for what they called "nostalgic fantasy thrillers" was dwindling, and so had proceeded to make a more "reality-based" picture. Here—for the first time in Vaguely's experience—the bad guy was no longer portrayed as a silhouette in a smart black fedora and cloak, with ogling lunar eyes peeled for peril as he strode gigantically from one worldly hemisphere to another.

With his earthy and visceral style of acting, Jimmy Ostinato became the battering ram of what was soon recognized as a history-making cinematic trend—one which told the uncanny (and frankly hard-to-believe) stories of everyday people who were pressed, by bad luck and other circumstances, into the commission of crime. It was a revolutionary idea, to Vaguely's mind, and also a dangerous one. Some politicians and pundits agreed and brought attention to themselves by anticipating some trouble if such genies were let out of the bottle, but Hollywood argued back that fiction was fiction, so anything was fair game. There was no reason, they contested, why everyday individuals should not be portrayed onscreen as criminal in a work of make-believe. This broke no laws, dramatic or otherwise… and besides, the film business needed new gimmicks to survive.

Successful as he became, Jimmy Ostinato couldn't star in every movie that was being made, so other, lesser talents began to star in imitative melodramas with increasingly blunt, decreasingly syllabic titles minted in keeping with the public taste: *Bigamist, Hooker, Hatchet,*

Addict, Rapist, Axe, Knife, Cut—ad absurdum. Made for Television movies also followed suit, some of them taking the audacious step of falsely asserting that their dramas were "Based on a True Story", "Based on Real Events", or "Inspired by Real Events." More often than not, the real events to which such hyperbole referred were the box office successes of similar scenarios.

In the midst of this mounting mess, as the daily newspapers grew fat once again, Vaguely's heart was gladdened by a single indication that his world might yet return to normal. As the return of Autumn coincided with the reopening of some area schools, a new sign was hung on the door of the place once known as Lawson's News.

It said OPENING SOON.

In time, the soap swirls obscuring the property's windows were wiped away and replaced with drawn shades to conceal the renovation that was taking place inside. One Saturday afternoon, Vaguely happened to meet one of the workmen as he stepped outside for a cup of coffee. He tried stealing a peek at the new interior before the door slammed shut, but didn't see much more than one to two inches of gluteal cleft protruding from the blue jeans of a workman bending over to saw lumber.

"So, when's the big day?" Vaguely asked him.

"Soon," the worker told him.

"I can't wait," Vaguely enthused.

The workman eyed him strangely. "What's your hurry?"

"This neighborhood's going to Hell in a handbasket."

"I hear a lot of that."

"Yes, sir," Vaguely continued, "when this store reopens, you'll see a big change around here. Teenagers will go back to their old, respectful ways, and adults will go back to feeling more secure, better respected. A store like this gives a community its *backbone*."

"I know what you mean," said the worker, as he drained his paper cup and tossed it at the corner's trash receptacle, which it missed. After the man returned to work, Vaguely retrieved it and returned it to its proper place.

When the store finally reopened about two weeks later, it was no longer called Lawson's News. It didn't appear to be called anything. But there was a large, black-lettered sign in the window that told passersby everything they needed to know about this place of business.

It said GUNS.

Chapter Six
PUT YOUR HAND IN THE HAND

The newly hung sign froze the blood in Paul Vaguely's veins. It was a change too far, a note that soared beyond the bitter into the sour, and one that he took as a personal threat.

That night, as he stretched out on the sofa in his only apartment, he had the unnerving sensation that something viral and insidious had come along to subvert and devalue everything he had ever known to be unassailable and true. With his apartment complex now facing the promise of a gun store, he felt the time would soon come when this was no longer his neighborhood—but only if he allowed it.

It was a summer night, so Paul took to the streets as he was, without a coat or sweater. He ran for a few blocks, sometimes not even waiting for the stop lights at intersections and crosswalks to turn green, if there was no one there to see him. In about 10 minutes, he reached what he felt was his last hope: Amelia's Public Library. It stood out against the night sky like an imposing bank vault—not of money, but of knowledge. He ran up the front steps and pushed his way inside.

He rushed to the front desk, where the pretty librarian was quick to tell him that the library would be closing soon. Knowing this, Paul rushed over her words, apologetically: "I'm sorry, but I must know: do you have any books about The Only Criminal?"

"About the what?" she asked.

"Not you too," Paul winced. "The Only Criminal. I know he's not much of a current subject, but surely you don't throw out old books. You're a library!"

"Sir, I'm afraid we do thin out our collection periodically. We have an annual sale, for example. It's the only way we can continue to accommodate what's new."

"Is there someone else here that...," he began, but before his question was entirely voiced, an older library worker appeared and joined the conversation.

"May I help?" she volunteered.

"Ma'am," Paul said, "do you have any books about The Only Criminal?"

"I know what this gentleman is asking about," she told her younger co-worker, excusing her. Then she spoke directly to Paul in a quieter voice: "I know what you're looking for, sir. We took all of those books off our shelves sometime last year because our records showed that no one was still taking them out, so I believe they were consigned to our reference department. That means, they can be read on the premises, but they can't be taken out."

"Please, lead me to them," he wheedled. "Time is of the essence."

"Yes," she agreed. "We'll be closing in about 20 minutes. Follow me."

Vaguely followed her upstairs. Together they climbed four flights of stairs, exactly as many as Paul Vaguely had to ascend in order to reach his own apartment from his building's main hall. When they reached the third floor, the older librarian took him across a curiously familiar floor to a curiously familiar door, which led into a curiously familiar room which held hundreds of curiously familiar books. It was as if everything he had owned and sacrificed the previous Xmas eve had been supernaturally transported here. He knew exactly where to find what he needed.

"I'll leave you to your research, but I will return to show you out in fifteen minutes."

The moment she was gone, Paul instinctively reached out to the place where he had kept his own copy of *The Only Criminal Through History*, and there it was, in his hand, as though waiting for him—an oversized coffee-table tome that traced The Only Criminal's reign of terror from ancient cave paintings to the most discussed thefts, arsons and murders making headlines at the time of the book's publication. Vaguely found this book particularly confirming of his beliefs in that it was profusely illustrated with photographs rather than artist's renderings, each of them inarguable in their certainty. As his eyes roamed over vintage images of stolen cars, blasted vaults, detonated bridges, derailed trains, bullet-riddled white-haired bodies, collapsed buildings, invaded homes, nuclear meltdown sites and blood-and-hair-splashed walls, he felt something restored to his being that was essential rather than voluntary—a belief in something bigger than himself.

For the next 15 minutes, he absorbed all the old, familiar lore that his new world now denied, and felt infused by it. As the librarian came back to collect him, he asked if there was a washroom he might use, and she took him downstairs to where there was a door marked MEN. He could tell from the markings left on the door by a recent removal of letters that the door had once read GENTLEMEN. He went inside—not to urinate but to splash some water on his face. As he rose from the sink, he noticed something new in his reflection. He didn't see this in his own dimly-lit apartment, but there—in the bright men's room of the library—he could see some new traces of gray threading through his dark hair.

When he returned to his apartment block, on foot and experiencing a strong rush of gratitude, he found Melanie sitting on the stoop outside, hugging her knees. He knew at once that wasn't merely getting some fresh air but specifically waiting for him.

"I was worried about you," you confessed, looking up. "I heard you rush out of the building so fast that it scared me. I wasn't dressed, and by the time I was, you were gone."

What she didn't mention was that she heard the door of his apartment slam and his heavy footfalls down the stairwell and looked out her front door in time to see him racing toward some mysterious destiny. She had stepped out of her apartment and looked over the bannister all the way down to the entrance hall, where she saw his figure dash out the front door like a man possessed. In that moment, there was something alien about him, about his tone, about his stance that saturated her with the worry that she might lose him, either gradually or, just as possibly, all at once. She wondered what it might take to hold him and keep him, to preserve him as the man she knew, the man she was beginning to love, if it was not already too late.

"Is everything alright?" she asked gently.

"I'm not sure, to be truthful."

"Why don't you come upstairs and I'll make us some tea?"

"Not tonight," Paul said, as kindly as possible. "I'm going to stay out for while."

"I could stay with you," she offered.

"You should go in," he answered, in a tone that left her no choice.

When Melanie had done what was in keeping with his wishes, Paul Vaguely turned to the sign that said GUNS and heard:

One last chance to turn the tide.

Was that his own inner voice, or was it Peevey's voice? No matter: judging by all outward signs and facts, Peevey must have forsaken his own profane responsibility, but his doctor—a man who had always stood outside (if not above) his own kind, who had yet to experience the physical intimacy of women—had at times touched him intimately… to change his dressings, to insert his catheter, to bathe him and monitor the contents of his bedpan. Peevey was likely only one degree of separation from The Only Criminal himself; therefore, if Peevey truly radiated evil, Dr. Paul Vaguely had surely been contaminated.

He was aflame with something he had once written in his doctoral thesis: If there was no Only Criminal, it would be necessary to invent him. And now that there was no Only Criminal, there was nothing left to do but prove himself right.

Moving with alacrity, Vaguely reached inside his trouser pockets and removed the black winter gloves he still had in his possession—yes, the ones for which he hadn't paid. In all the months which had passed, he had never dared put the dreaded things on again, knowing that if he did, he would claim those stolen goods and be forever in their possession. Come what may, he now slipped his hands inside them. Again, they seemed to fit him more like coats of lacquer than leather; they sucked him in, up to the wrist. With that, he turned and marched with purpose toward the former site of Lawson's News, where he seized a public trash container with both hands, raised it above his head, and hurled it at the window that promised the coming of GUNS.

Then, without stopping to admire his handiwork, he began to walk and continued walking till he turned the corner and embarked on a collision course with the question mark of the night—determined to find where it was most dark and to claim that place as his due.

Three blocks further on, his fate began to make itself known. He ignored the easy temptations of trespassing where NO TRESPASSING signs were posted, and parked cars with keys left agleam in their ignitions. Vaguely found no calling high enough to break his purposeful stride until an abrupt, violent sound of gunfire erupted from a second floor window. The voice inside him said **Wherever there is crime, there I should be** and, though he was normally someone who avoided heights, things would be different now.

Raising his gloved hands, their palms facing him, Vaguely marveled as they moved, seemingly of their own will, with the elegance of a master magician, as if to say **But of course!** He pressed them to the edge of the two-storey brick building from which the sounds of gunfire had broken out. Without hesitation, they latched onto the spaced and alternated projections lining the corner of the building and he used these to climb, his shoes likewise making use of them as footholds. In this way, he effortlessly scaled the full height of the apartment building, evidently under attack from intentions not yet his own.

Peering through the window where the sounds of gunplay had originated, Vaguely saw a middle-aged couple on a loveseat, watching an old Only Criminal movie on television. The man, lumpy as four 50-pound bags of cat litter, was sound asleep. The woman beside him, too dry of skin and substance for the nightie she was wearing, sighed and reached for the remote control—which replace the violent programming her mate had chosen with something silly.

Disappointed, Vaguely retraced his steps to terra firma where, almost at once, from the depths of the night, the sounds of other kind of danger reached his ears. This time, it was hooligan laughter, followed by a woman's scream; there was no question this time that they were real. He ran towards the sounds until he found their source.

A taxi driver was trapped at a stop light by a band of ruffians out for fun. Two were standing in front of her cab, preventing it from moving forward; another was clambering in a simian fashion onto the hood; and the fourth was forcing himself inside the driver's window, pestering her—shall we say, romantically?

Vaguely saw no need to calculate what had to be done. He upheld his gloved hands to frame the scene of disturbance in the manner of a film director. Once again, they went through a refined series of thaumaturgical motions culminating in the one that seemed to say, **But of course!**

Without thinking about it, Vaguely stepped into the fray, his arms poised powerfully at either side as he channeled all of his emotion—his determination, his anger at the world's degeneration—until he could believe that an intense lunar light was shining from his eyes and face. It worked: the four troublemakers did not require the newcomer to be announce himself by name or reputation. At the same moment, they saw how very bizarre and potentially dangerous he was, and backed away as though so compelled by a hive mind. Their leader—the one who'd been making advances to the cabbie—led their retreat, and Vaguely could not resist sending him the additional shiver of an upraised fist and an index finger extended in foreboding. He continued his march toward them—a living beacon, he imagined, of sheer Evil—as the four of them ran like the children they were to the safety of their homes. The safety of their homes, *they hoped!*

His back was turned to the taxi, but he knew only too well what he would see once he turned to face the driver. Through the gloves of a retiring Only Criminal that had found themselves on the hands of a worthy successor, Paul Vaguely had been deconstructed and recomposed—not as a mere man, but as a totemic manifestation of malice! Thus, the driver would be curled in her driver's seat in a fetal cringe, her eyes wide and shadowed with violet, her bare legs askew, her bosom heaving with excitement. Then, a strap from her undergarments would suddenly snap—simply because he willed it! Vaguely turned slowly, relishing the weight of the dark legacy laid on his shoulders, the better to relish the moment before ripping away its goose-pimpled rind, the better to squeeze from its shuddering pulp every last drop and gobbet of its juicy fear.

Now. Now to turn your hair white…

"My hero!" cried the cabbie, as she flung herself gratefully into his arms. In the warm shock of her embrace, Vaguely was incredulous. He didn't do what he had done to be a hero; he had asserted his primacy of Evil Incarnate in the face of amateurs. His towering terror had sent them all away. The woman looked into his face with relief: "I've been stuck at this light for five minutes. I didn't want to run those guys down… I was worried I might have to do them some serious favors just to get outta here! Say, don't I know you?"

I am… I am…

"You're the guy who works out by the fruit cake factory! Hey, can I give you a lift back to your place? It's the least I could do! On the house!"

"No, thank you," Vaguely managed, extricating himself and moving on as brusquely as possible. "I mean 'no—*not* 'No, thank you'. I don't say 'thank you' to anyone! I'm not polite—I'm a bad man—not a hero!"

He stomped away, clenching and unclenching his gloved hands as a dark cloud formed (only figuratively) above his incensed head. It occurred to him that his costume was perhaps not complete enough to exact his full inheritance. He walked on, block after block, knowing the right opportunity would come his way—as indeed it did, when he caught sight of his reflection moving across the glass surface of a clothing store's picture window, where mannequins of both sexes modeled different outfits. As Fate would have it, Vaguely's reflection matched perfectly the body of a male mannequin sporting a high collared black trenchcoat and a matching black fedora. He flexed his magic hands and, needless of key, entered the closed shop, where his flashing black hands brazenly availed themselves of the costume at hand. Like the gloves, the coat and hat seemed to be supernaturally provided for him; they embraced him as a strong wind embraces a sea-faring sail bound for high adventure. How he laughed, how he roared at the thrill of taking these goods that did not rightfully belong to him, too self-involved to notice in his wake the dimmed overhanging sign of the Amelia Free Store.

What now? he thought.

The world is your plundered oyster, my son! Buy me a drink; we'll talk.

Vaguely decided that it might not be a bad idea to stop for a moment and collect his thoughts, so he walked into the nearest bar, taking care to look at anyone who tossed a regard in his direction with the double-barreled, pitted eyes of the two moons.

Inside the bar, he was greeted by a woman in her early thirties. She had curly red hair and wore too much makeup; she was gussied-up in something skimpy topped off with a white frilly dickie, a black bowtie, and a red vest.

Monkey suit.

"Good evening, sir," she greeted him, like someone who thought this dive was as good as it got. "Welcome to Desperado's. My name is Bethany; I'll be your hostess this evening. Will you be joining us at the bar or at a table?"

Upscale joint. Piano. At least a couple grand in the till on a night like this.

"Is there a booth available?" Vaguely stammered, his gloved hands thrust inside his pockets.

"I think I can arrange one," she smiled. **Her eyeteeth are caps.** "Follow me."

She led him to exactly what he requested: a booth against the far wall, rendered invisible to the other customers by the backlighting of the piano, which was situated in the middle of an intimately proportioned dance floor.

"This is **ideal**," he said, seating himself.

"What can I get for you?" she asked, poising her pen over a tablet of checks.

One Fuzzy Nipple, straight up. Make it two.

"I'll have an Old Fashioned," Vaguely ordered, taking a seat.

As Bethany went to fetch his drink, the voice continued to bully him.

A secluded booth, it sneered disdainfully. **As if you fear being seen wearing your new gloves! We can't have this, Paulie. No, you hopeless prat—this won't do. A man with your powers should be sitting in the place of honor. Go on—sit at the piano.**

I don't play the piano.

I said, Go sit at the piano.

But I don't play the piano.

But we do!

"You do?" Bethany exclaimed, returning with his drink. "By all means, sir, yes! Feel free." **Yes, free. Free!** She placed his order on a Desperado's coaster atop the piano. "It's Open Mike night."

Go on, Paulie. Play a little piano, and then we'll find Mike, whoever he is, and cut him Open.

Vaguely fretted.

"Don't be shy," Bethany pressed.

Do it now. Or I'll make sure you soil your nice, new gloves with this bitch before we leave.

Vaguely gulped his Old Fashioned straight down. Standing, he squinted as he penetrated the spotlight shining on the piano, his gloved hands sunk in his pockets. It wasn't literally true that he had never played the piano, but neither had he ever made music with one.

I don't know what I'm going to do, he said to himself as he lowered himself to the bench. His voice was picked up by the microphone above the keyboard, and broadcast throughout the room.

You're going to take your hands out of your pockets, for starters.

Vaguely obeyed, slowly, reluctantly.

His eye was drawn to the door, where he saw someone who might have been Abel Lawson stumbling out.

"Play 'Piano Man'," someone yelled, laughing.

Atta boy, Paulie. Now you're going to put your right hand... here, and your left hand... there, and you're gonna close your eyes, see, so I can show you just a few of the things you can look forward to. And as I show you these horrors beyond description, I want your fingers—your oh-so-sensitive fingers—to interpret every last detail through these black and white keys. Do you understand?

If you say so.

Are you ready?

Vaguely looked at Bethany, his eyes wan with sorrow and self-sacrifice.

Yes...

Vaguely's gloved hands pounced on the keys, bounced off the keys; they made the high notes glitter, the low notes thunder—and, while the astonishing performance given at Desperado's that night was well above the heads of nearly every troubles-smothering lush who was privy to it, it was recognized and appreciated by Bethany as a note-perfect rendition of the Only Criminal standard "Rhapsody Turned Blue," from his classic blues album *Misbehavin'*. Admiringly, too awed to shut her mouth, she seated herself at a ringside table and watched the performance play itself out. Looking at her customer's hands, she could almost believe that she was watching the very hands that performed on the album in question—one of her parents' favorites, and therefore one of the treasures of her childhood. But, as she looked up into the pianist's face, her heart went out to him. He appeared to be suffering, tearing the music from his innermost being, weeping freely from his closed eyes, his face flinching from the fierce pyrotechnics of his own make.

When Vaguely finished the piece by raising his foot from the sustain pedal, clipping the resonance of the final chord, there was more uninterrupted conversation to be heard than applause, though Bethany—who was most won over by it—was stunned to silence. Vaguely raised his gloved hands from the keys and stared at them fiercely, incredulously.

"I don't understand," he marveled Vaguely aloud. "How? Why?"

Then, independently of any command from his brain, Vaguely's left gloved hand dropped down to the bass keys and doodled a small musical passage of seven notes that spoke to him with horrible eloquence:

D D D C D C D.

One last chance to turn the tide.

One last chance—how would he use it?

You enjoyed it, didn't you, playing the piano?

I must admit I did.

Look at the way that girl is looking at you. You're a bold one, Bethany. Imagining how those hands of yours might play over her body.

When will it go away?

When will WHAT go away?

This trepidation.

It's not trepidation that you're feeling, Paulie. It's delectation. Excitement. You're having fun.

Fun has always been for other people. Not me.

That's their fun. Your fun is different.

How long before it all kicks in?

Such as?

Being able to travel from one earthly hemisphere to another in a single stride?

Where do you think you are now?

Somewhere in Amelia, seven or eight blocks northwest of my apartment.

Think again. Look out the window there, at the skyline.

Vaguely did as he was told. On the other side of the glass window, where the name Desperado's was written backwards, he could see the skyline of New York City in the distance. He must be somewhere in New Jersey!

Think of where you would like to be, and you will be there. It's your privilege now. It's your right.

Vaguely looked down at his gloved hands, still criminally poised upon the ivory keys of the piano. He began to play "*La Vie en Rose*," allowing his thoughts to migrate toward Paris, France. He looked over to Bethany, now in black fishnet stockings and a beret, her eyes sparkling back to him—*avec admiration.* She quickly rose and approached him to meet the question he was holding back.

"*Quelque chose pour boire, Monsieur?*" she asked.

His cold eyes scanned the smoky room from his pianist's vantage: Gitanes, warm water being poured over cubes of sugar on absinthe spoons, today's edition of *Libération.*

This cannot be happening.

One way to find out.

I could shatter this illusion by merely reaching out with my hand.

"*Monsieur? Etes-vous malade?*"

Go ahead. Reach out. Grab her by the throat. Strangle the life out of the *chienne.* No demerits.

"*M'amener un autre Old Fashioned,*" he told Bethany, whose name tag now read Bethanée.

"*Certainement, m'sieur.*"

I won't pay for it.

It's a step.

It's nothing of the kind. I won't pay for it because I cannot really be here.

Now you're catching on. Why is all this possible?

Because none of it is real.

***Exactement, mon cher.* Therefore, *everything* is possible. And everything is permitted.**

When Bethanée returned with Vaguely's Old Fashioned, he drained the glass at once, looked at her with his best impression of Parisian insolence, and left Chez Desperado without paying a sou. Because Vaguely was, in his heart of hearts, a fundamentally good man, he took no pleasure in performing this dark liberty. He realized that even his impulse to assume the burden of being The Only Criminal had been based in selflessness, not selfishness. His dissatisfaction only grew darker as he exited the bar onto the streets of Amelia, when it became more apparent to him—because a man who can wish himself to Paris must also have the power to peer into any pocket of happenstance—that Bethanée was so impressed by his impromptu piano performance and the magic it brought into her everyday existence that she had no intention of charging him for his drink. It's true that he had also breezed out the front door without thanking her, but she had been around artists for much of her life and understood that they could be moody. *Ce n'était pas un crime.*

Vaguely had to admit that he was very poorly cast as The Only Criminal. He was ready to opt out of this hopeless charade but his gloved hands began to itch with inactivity. They became literally insufferable with itchiness, so eager, so desperate were they to do wrongs of ever higher and higher caliber. He struggled to remove the gloves, tugging at their fingers, yanking at their cuffs, but they seemed no more likely to give way than his own flesh could have slipped off his bones. That's right, his gloves were stuck, as if bonded to his hands by the sincerity of his invocation. It was like trying to peel night away from day, but he persevered. **No!** He stood and threw his hat to the winds, removed his overcoat and allowed it too to tumble over the horizon. Only after great effort, cursing and exertion did he finally manage to peel the gloves away, little by little, until, crackling like snakeskin, they were completely shed… only to reveal *another, identical pair underneath!*

No! He tossed the first pair into the street, repelled… then the second… then the third pair found under the second… followed by yet another pair under the third! He pulled off so many pairs of black gloves that it crossed his mind that he might never see his own hands again—might never recover his own fingerprints, the very proof of the man he once was! He winced and nearly wept with despair, having flung hundreds (it seemed) of gloves into the street, which were all carried away by the winds, or skittered away on their fingers, in as many different directions.

Now you've done it.

Vaguely looked down at his bare hands.

Yes, I did it! I'm rid of them now!

No, Paulie. You'll never be rid of them now.

Chapter Seven
AMAZING GRACE

Rain began to fall on Amelia as Paul Vaguely stepped off the #27. He dashed and splashed across the street to the Oakley Apartments, against the traffic lights, hoping to outrun anything oncoming, hoping to outrun Mother Nature herself as her tears streaked the asphalt roads with rich, impressionistic colors.

He pushed his way inside and raced up the winding staircase with hammering feet, stopping and knocking loudly—for his sanity, for his life—on the door of the last place on earth where he felt truly safe.

The door soon opened and there stood Melanie White, in her white terrycloth robe. She hooked her ash-blonde hair around her ear and peered into the dim hall of the apartment building, where the man who had become her closest friend stood trembling, beaded with rain and pale with panic.

"I was so worried," she told him. "Where have you been?"

"Paris, France."

"And you didn't invite me to come along? Shame on you."

"Yes," he affirmed solemnly. "That's it, exactly. *Shame on me*. Melanie, I've done something terrible. Will the world ever forgive me?"

"Come inside."

Once they were alone together, behind her closed door, Melanie asked Paul, in a way that he found most pleasing, "You—have done something terrible? How is that possible?"

It was a question that seemed to belong to another world, a world of innocence and naïveté that Vaguely had outgrown.

"I held the very seeds of evil in my hands, Melanie… dozens, hundreds… and I scattered them to the winds."

"In Paris, France? Honeychile, they'll never notice!"

The joke was lost on Vaguely, who stood there staring at his bare hands, left and right, one wringing the other.

"What are you doing?" Melanie demanded to know, grabbing, arresting his two hands in both of hers. "Why all this fidgeting? Tell me what happened."

He said nothing, lost in the deflated myth of himself, perhaps the deflated myth of all his kind.

"Tell me what happened tonight," she insisted.

This caught his attention. He followed her inside, took a seat beside her on her sofa, and related with deep shame the events of his evening—more or less in the way they have been conveyed to you. As he related the tale, he felt all the more acutely aware of what a feeble Only Criminal he had made, of how no real opportunities for crime had really come his way. Even when given all the metaphysical requirements of the job by his retiring master, he could do nothing more flamboyant than running out on an unpaid bar tab. "I don't think I have the *imagination* to be The Only Criminal," he concluded.

"There's nothing wrong with your imagination. You never wanted to be The Only Criminal. You only wanted to believe in him. I took that away from you, didn't I? We all need something to believe in."

Vaguely found the courage to look fully into Melanie's face, deeply into her brown eyes, and say, "I believe in you."

"I'm just a woman," she said.

"All the better," he told her.

She took his damp hand and placed it on the side of her face. Her eyes lowered as she turned her mouth to his palm and kissed him there, then his fingertips—and then she dared to do as he had done, to look at him plainly and directly and with no avoidance of her feelings. Then their lips met for the first time, in such a spontaneous way that neither of them would ever know if they had initiated that fortuitous moment, or if it had been governed by someone standing just outside them and looking in.

"Give me a couple of minutes," she said, disappearing into her bedroom.

Vaguely had never found himself in a situation like this before. He felt much as he had felt at the beginning of the evening, when the GUNS sign in the store window seemed to darken the blood in his vitals and forced his hand into a more sinister glove. The air in the apartment seemed to sparkle with portent. *There is her drafting table*, he told himself. *There are the cigarettes she smokes. Those are her books. These are the things that mean home to her. Here I am, among them. I have been trusted among them. Perhaps I am one of them.*

He listened to the rain hissing now and again against her windows. In the distance, through the weather, he could hear a choir of police sirens, heading out, spreading out in response to numerous emergency calls. Closer still, outside and below the window that faced the street, he could hear the raucous profanity and heavy footfalls of passing teenagers up to no good. It was well past the curfew hour—if he opened the window and reminded them of this fact, what would happen? Would they curse him too? Fire a bullet into his face? The thought crossed his mind that he might reach over and turn on the television to drown out those outdoor noises, but with what would he be drowning them—the evening news with the evening's new stories of war and torture and corruption?

Then he heard Melanie scream, her piercing shriek closely followed by a sound of shattering glass.

Paul sprang to his feet and ran to her assistance in urgent, selfless strides. There was a deadweight that lay against the door, causing all manner of horrors to flood his imagination. He shouldered the door repeatedly until he gained full entrance. He knocked over the deadweight; it was a tall wicker basket filled with clothes ready for laundering. They all appeared to be underthings—delicate, remarkable underthings. The bedroom beyond was a shambles; an overturned lamp cast cockeyed shadows onto the walls, a jewelry box on a vanity table lay overturned, empty.

Vaguely glanced at the bed. There, spread over the disheveled comforter, was Melanie's terrycloth robe, empty of her as though it had been ripped from her nude body and cast aside. He felt his heart pound as he intuited another presence in the room.

The figure advanced toward him from staggered shadows; he first saw it reflected in the webbed glass of the vanity mirror. High-booted and auburn-tressed, the lone figure stepped, its curves concealed by a Danskin of dark purple. The costume was garnished at mid-waist by a leather belt arrayed with all the tools of the cat burglar's trade. Two hands, gloved in black to mid-forearm, were upheld, their long and tapering fingers interlaced with a cat's cradle of plundered pearls. The brown eyes behind the mask flashed with menace.

Finally! thought Vaguely. *A White Level encounter!*

Casting away the baubles as though they were worthless, the

intruder grabbed a handful of his dark hair and pulled it back till his chin pointed skyward.

"Arrest me," she commanded.

He saw his Xmas gift to her displayed on a bedside table.

"I can't."

"Oh, yes you can, my love. Only you."

And so Melanie White made known to the man she loved that she could be, for him—and only for him—everything that he had ever lost or hoped to find. Through the warm conduits of her flesh and blood, her creativity, and whatever accouterments she might borrow tonight or in future from her window displays, she had the power to summon The Only Criminal into Paul Vaguely's presence whenever he needed to simplify his complex perception of the world to a more manageable equation of fantasy.

"What's my name?" she demanded.

"Felony," he said, swooning—and he fell, for good—out of his world and into theirs.

"I like the sound of that," she said, accepting her pet name. They kissed again and then, rising from his lips, she admitted, "I'm a little scared."

To which Paul added, "I'm glad I'm not the only one." Then—for the first of countless times in what would be a happy life together—Paul Vaguely pulled Felony's auburn wig away from a tumbling cascade of ash-blonde hair and surrendered to the embrace of a strongly beating heart and a tingling of Godhead covered in a paradise of spandex. June rhymed with spoon, spoon rhymed with moon (yes, a singular moon), and the bells of St. Tim's rejoiced.

Then went the devils out of the man and entered into the swine: and the herd ran violently down a steep place into a lake, and were choked.

FIN

AFTERWORD

The story behind the story of *The Only Criminal* is a long one. For my own information, as much as for your own, I decided to chart its unusually lengthy gestation and some of its offbeat sources of inspiration.

It's the closest to my heart of all my novels, as I've lived every day of my life with it for the past 47 years. Friends and acquaintances to whom I've confessed this saga of servitude usually express surprise, astonishment, or even doubt, especially those already aware that my 2007 critical biography *Mario Bava—All the Colors of the Dark* was the product of 32 years of research. Yes, it's true: the annual distance between those two works is itself old enough to shave.

While I want to leave the matter of what this novel "means" to its readers, I think the long history of its development is worth charting and sharing. The concept of The Only Criminal first appears in entries from a journal I kept during my early years as a writer. I beg you to kindly overlook my younger tendency to wax florid and pretentious; I was 20 years old when this notion first took hold of me, when I was still familiarizing myself with classics from centuries past, and had yet to write anything of my own that was more than strange or pretty. Had I not been pretentious enough to keep a journal, this idea might have been lost to me—and we would not have the book we finally have.

The Only Criminal first appears in entries from a journal I kept during my early years as a writer. Kindly overlook my younger self's tendency to wax florid and pretentious; I was 20 years old when this lightning bolt first struck, still familiarizing myself with the classics, and had yet to write anything of my own that was more than strange or pretty. Had I not been pretentious enough to keep a journal, this idea would have been lost to me—and we might not have the book we finally have.

Here are his earliest recorded footprints:

15 February 1977:

Nature of a possible novel: *The Only Criminal.*

Who knows where such notions really come from? The idea of a criminal in a really pure, vice-free world is terribly romantic. The possibilities grow limitless.

26 March 1977:

Began writing the fable *The Only Criminal* (subtitled "A Book to Be Read in Times of Leisure")… [which] I envision as a booklet in a white jacket, in the hands of someone relaxing in a backyard recliner. It shall be no longer than 40 typed pages… I should dedicate this work to Georges Franju.

I will interrupt myself here to mention that the French film director Georges Franju (1912-1987) was certainly a seminal influence on me and the idea behind this book. As a child, I had seen Franju's delicate yet searing horror film *Les yeux sans visage* ("Eyes without a Face," 1960) and was fascinated by stills and articles about his later film *Judex* (1963)—a remake of Louis Feuillade's 1916-17 silent film serial of the same name—of which I first learned sometime in 1966. I wouldn't have an opportunity to actually see *Judex* until it became available on videocassette sometime in the 1980s, but I was sufficiently haunted by my early exposure to Franju's work to notice a copy of Raymond Durgnat's book *Franju* (1968) on a shelf in the Greater Cincinnati Public Library. I absorbed it like a sponge, just in time to catch Franju's last feature film *Nuits rouges* (1974) under the title *Shadowman* during its local theatrical release in early March 1976. My late wife Donna was with me and could tell just by sitting next to me that I needed to see it a second time. She indulged me, even though it meant sitting through the co-feature, Sergio Garrone's not-so-winning *The Stranger's Gundown* (aka *Django the Bastard*, 1969).

Shadowman—which is at least equally the achievement of its author and star, Jacques Champreux[i]—is hardly Franju's best work, but it was as close as I was able to come to *Judex* at that time. Even so, I became infatuated with it due to a lengthy rooftop sequence in which the police pursue a sleek masked cat-burglar played by Gayle Hunnicutt. It's not a fast-paced action sequence but rather a slow, oneiric dance of seminal Eurocrime tropes, set to a spooky, elegantly romantic library track melismatically sung by the incomparable Edda Dell'Orso.[ii]

When I finally caught up with *Judex*, I found Franju's true masterpiece. Feuillade made the original serial in response to public outcries against his earlier adaptation of Pierre Souvestre & Marcel Allain's *Fantômas* (1913), which, on the eve of the first World War, was criticized for glorifying crime. Judex (conceived by author Arthur Bernédé) was a self-appointed judge who used his wealth to fund a one-man war on crime and political corruption. Using such accouterments as a flowing cape and slouch hat, a subterranean headquarters, a squad of masked facilitators, and a tricked-out limousine, Judex was essentially the progenitor of both The Shadow and Batman. Nevertheless, the film is most enjoyable for its delicious depictions of the criminal element, which are graced by the evil ringleader Diana Monti, played by the cult movie siren Musidora (b. Jeanne Rocques, 1889-1957).

This goes double for the Franju film, with bests its inspiration with a beautifully sustained air of enchantment and a magnificently curated cast including the American-born magician Channing Pollack as Judex, Edith Scob (the masked monster-heroine of *Les yeux sans visage*), and the remarkable Francine Bergé as the ruthless Diana Monti. In the film's final moments, there is a breath-taking clash of leotards as Diana (in black) has a rooftop grapple with Daisy (Sylva Koscina), a traveling, wall-scaling carnival trapeze artiste (in white) who, as in dreams and fairy tales, just happens to be passing by.

Aside from the example of Franju, whose work I could mostly only imagine from still photographs, *The Only Criminal* had other important sources of inspiration, including Alfred Hitchcock's *Shadow of a Doubt* (1943), whose script originated with Thornton Wilder. It would take away too much of the fun to explain how it was inspiring; I'll leave that to you to sort out.

Also to the point were my childhood memories of seeing television shows like *The Adventures of Superman*, *Batman* and *The Green Hornet*, all of which seemed to suggest that their protagonists were unique and that their locations were just as imaginary, cities with names like Metropolis, Gotham City and Central City, all of them small enough to encompass all the world's Good and Evil, at least in my nascent perceptions. Part of me has always regretted that the cancer of realism has infected each new generation's versions of those heroes, taking away the treat of accepting everything they do at face-value. I'm reminded that, while writing of *Judex,* Raymond Durgnat memorably noted that the film evoked "a world which seems tenderly aware of its own unreality."[iii] From the moment I first read those words, I have lived with at least one foot planted in that world, and I wanted to—somewhere—wholly engage with this tender awareness and naïveté.

I must also add that I had in mind the idea of someday writing a novel in which the protagonist gradually becomes aware of the reality that they are no more than a character in someone's book. To some extent, my earlier *Translucent Skin* had also toyed with this idea as its heroine, the fragile Julia Lofting, ultimately disappears from her own story, becoming the novella we are reading.

4 April 1977:

I tell people of *The Only Criminal* and all of them remark, "Oh yes, it'll be wonderful… if you can sustain it!" At least they aren't saying, "Such a fine idea… if only you could write it!"

14 April 1977:

I would like to write *The Only Criminal* in Toronto, on the train to Toronto—on the train while drinking bourbon in the club car.

Who knows where the above came from, but I would in fact spend some valuable time in Toronto, beginning in 1981 when I was covering the making of David Cronenberg's *Videodrome* (1983) for *Cinefantastique*. I would also spend valuable time drinking bourbon.

29 April - 9 May 1977:

Decided to incorporate *The Only Criminal* into a book of fables to be titled *Saturday Reading*, a collection to be "hosted" by a character named The Man in the Black Clothes. Other fables considered for collection were *The Sailor of Martinique* (co-written with Robert Uth, never begun), *The Devil's Good Looks* (written as abortive novel), *A Witness In Blood* (barely started, abandoned) and *The Man Who Blew Up* (frivolous novelette, completed 13 June).

26 May 1978:

Completed *TOC* today at 5:03 pm. A birthday gift to myself! Strange as it sounds, the very minute I laid down my pen, there was a car collision in front of my apartment. I had to call the police. In one car, a blue Ford, was a black man in a Baltimore Orioles baseball

cap; my landlord was in the other. The road is streaked with the dregs of a crushed water tank.

29 May 1978:

Last entry at [age] 21… *The Only Criminal*—finished, revised, read by a satisfied reader. Donna got up this Memorial Day morning and read it. Thinks it superior to *The Man Who Blew Up* but inferior to *Translucent Skin*.[iv] Manuscript length: 67 pages.[v]

14 August 1978:

***TOC* rejected by *The Paris Review*.**

25 November 1978:

Public reading of chapter from *The Only Criminal* at the University of Cincinnati. About 40 people in audience. Wore blue trousers, white shirt, colorful tie, black leather jacket and a beard. Also reading: Chris Parks and Arthur Solway.

At this point in time, I used the name Timothy R. Lucas as my fiction byline. I remember this evening well. I introduced myself to the audience—a mix of academics and students—as "a comic novelist," which attracted some positive conversations during the intermission. They responded very well to the chapter I read, with warm chuckles and the occasional audible wince. The latter was invited by a character in this early version, inspired by André Gide's self-abusive Lafcadio in *Le caves du Vatican* (1914, US: *The Vatican Cellars/Lafcadio's Adventures*), who in private moments used a pin to probe his own urethra. One of several blind alleys I explored in search of a story worthy of my main idea.

In the meantime, I moved on to other ideas, but the bulk of my time in 1981 through 1983 was spent writing my book about *Videodrome* (finally published in 2008) and other film criticism.

6 May 1982:

Yesterday read through my 1978 tale *The Only Criminal*, making adjustments and edits as I read. Today made a few additional corrections and began typing a new draft on [Donna's] typewriter. My idea was to prepare a publishable version for *Twilight Zone* magazine, but it soon became obvious that the piece

was too long, even with the edits. I'm too far along to stop now and damned if I'm going to cop-out on another piece of prose. I'll give it to one of the literary magazines if I have to. But at least it'll be out of my hair.

At 1:15 a.m., I had to summon the police because a fellow across the way went berserk. The window of my office looks straight into his bedroom. I was sitting in my office reading Updike's *Assorted Prose* when the noise from his apartment became extreme. There had been booming FM rock coming from there all night, along with the usual cries of "Rock and Rollll!" I turned in my seat and saw [out the window] two men punching each other, both in blue jeans and bare-chested. The taller one lifted the other, bumped him against a chest of drawers, dropped him to the floor and began kicking him violently three or four times, in the head or stomach, I couldn't tell. Throughout the attack, the kicker made horrible, half-human roars. There were teenage girls over there, too, and he [triumphantly] grabbed one and steered her onto a bed, [still] roaring. She got away and shouted, "Y'almost broke my fuckin' bra!" Three police cars answered calls placed by myself and other neighbors. I watched… as a pot-bellied cop watched the loud one dress, after which he handcuffed him.

What a neighborhood. What a world.

7 May 1982:

The landlord tells me that the two rowdies arrested last night had just finished moving into that apartment and were celebrating. Their "celebration" got them evicted.

Looking back, I think there is no question that the dangers in the neighborhood where Donna and I were living had a lot to do with the direction *The Only Criminal* subsequently took.

We lived in one of three matching apartment buildings composed of four single-bedroom apartments. Our floors were thin and we were forever hearing too much of our downstairs neighbors' business, just as they were forever complaining about me stomping around and typing at all hours. Things finally reached an intolerable pitch when a young couple with a baby moved in downstairs. The husband was a meek fellow who became Mr. Hyde when he snorted coke, cranking up his stereo to play Led Zeppelin and Bad Company ("Feelin' kinda dirty / Feelin' kinda mean…") at whatever hour, whenever he felt like assaulting his wife—or their baby. Donna had an office job at this time and had to be up at 6:00am when this jerk had a tendency to feel his oats at 4:00. It was not uncommon for everyone in our apartment unit to be shocked awake by sudden, intrusive volume. When we heard his sobbing wife scream, "Get off my baby!" one night, I called the cops. When they left, I heard him climb the stairs and knock at our door. He told me (as if *I* had done the wrong thing) that his family had enough problems without me adding to them, and I told him that if he insisted on broadcasting his problems, he was involving other people as well. On another night, he silently crept up the stairs and screamed as loud as he could outside my door, as I was watching a late movie. And on another occasion, one of the downstairs arguments ended with him putting a fist through his bedroom window. This was directly below our bed, and I can remember Donna and I holding each other, literally trembling with fear.

They were evicted soon after, and by then we had finally saved enough to put a down payment on our house in 1983, where Donna and I would live the rest of our years together. Our early years of apartment living were genuinely traumatizing; the lives we were forced to eavesdrop on were in such violent contrast to the old-fashioned neighborhood settings where we resided. It was another 10 years before I could listen to Led Zeppelin with any pleasure, and I still can't stand Bad Company.

I have lived in this same house now for more than 40 years, and my neighborhood has gone through its ups and downs. The novel's Gloating Car episode was inspired by a loud, thudding car that passed our house almost every night, terrorizing the street with its volume, much as our previous neighbor had done. The car's headlights always seemed to sweep across our bedroom walls, slicing through the venetian blinds, then drove on to the far end of our street, where the houses were not so well looked after; it parked and went quiet. I once heard the hideous, inarticulate voice of the driver as he stumbled home and described it to the best of my ability.

On another occasion, one night as I was preparing for bed, I heard a voice outside and looked through the venetian blinds. There was a man standing directly under the streetlamp gazing at the asphalt beneath his feet. He had an aura of unspeakable evil. I stepped away. I later looked again and found him looking up, directly at me. Some years later, I read an interview with the film director Wes Craven, who recalled a similar experience and said it had inspired him to create his *A Nightmare on Elm Street* (1984) villain, Freddy Krueger.

* * *

I wish I had kept closer tabs on the full gestation of the project from that point on. The storyline of the original 67-page novelette was quite different to the novel it finally became. In that first version, Miss White was named Elvira (whom, for some forgotten reason, I made verbally dyslexic) and disguised herself as a nun outfitted with a switchblade crucifix stashed in her garter belt. That initial draft was also set in a more fairy tale-like, European location where I was completely out of my depth. The simple truth of the matter is, I had not yet lived enough to write this book. I did not yet have the skill nor the life experience.

I shelved *The Only Criminal* and moved on to other projects, including another novel called *TV Heaven* for which I had great hopes. After working on it for three years, I submitted my manuscript to a prominent New York publishing house. After a month or so, I received a marvelous response from an editor there (who went on to become a published author in her own right) who compared my writing to Thomas Pynchon while at the same time stressing that the book's lack of causality kept it from being publishable. She encouraged me to look at the book's weaknesses and try again. I then spent the next two years revising the book, but after sending it off to the same editor (still in their employ, I verified), it came back to me almost as fast as it could be slipped back into the return postage-paid envelope I'd provided, with a rejection form letter attached. It broke my heart and I turned my back on the idea of ever becoming a novelist.

Occasionally, during this interim, I would see films that suggested my abandoned ideas had migrated elsewhere and taken a different form. David Lynch's *Blue Velvet* (1986) certainly emanates from the same inspirational place as *The Only Criminal*, as does Gary Ross's *Pleasantville* (1998).

Then, in 1985, I was fortunate enough to become acquainted with comics artist Stephen R. Bissette, who remains one of my dearest friends. In 1987, he and *Swamp Thing* associate John Totleben conceived the idea of a no-holds-barred horror comics anthology that Steve intended to self-publish, called *Taboo*—and he invited me to write something for it. In

1988, when *The Comics Journal* reviewed the debut issue, somehow my contribution—"Throat Sprockets," illustrated by Mike Hoffman—was singled-out as its highlight, in a book that also featured the superb work of Alan Moore, Clive Barker, Charles Burns, Dave Sim, S. Clay Wilson, Eddie Campbell and many others, including Steve himself.

It was the surprise success of this casual endeavor that tricked me back into writing fiction.

* * *

It was in 1992 that my agent Lori Perkins sold my first published novel *Throat Sprockets* to Dell—initially for their Abyss horror line but eventually, after a two year wait, for their new "literary horror" imprint Cutting Edge. When the book was sold for a nice advance and then published in 1994 to an enthusiastic response, I submitted *The Only Criminal* to Lori as a follow-up. I'm happy to say that she recognized its importance right away but, for whatever reason, the zeitgeist seemed to be working against it. My enthusiastic editor had stepped down from her position at Dell, and her replacement was not at all interested in what I was doing or trying to do.

As Lori was shopping the manuscript around, I remember her telling me of her meeting with an editor at a publishing house notable for publishing horror in paperback. As she told me, the manuscript was handed back to her with the judgment "I would love to publish *anything* by Tim Lucas… *but not this!*"

In hindsight, the book's resounding rejection was a blessing because that version—while much closer to the version you've just read—was still not fully baked. I'm honestly glad it was rejected at that time because, as I now know, the draft read by that editor still wasn't what it needed to be.

In the period following those rejections, which extended to my overseas agent and publisher, I continued to tinker with the book whenever my demanding schedule at *Video Watchdog* allowed. In the early 1990s, cable television was a new diversion and I remember one night watching an hour-long news-oriented talk show that grouped together four or five young women whose sexual experiences had turned them against men. As I watched this program, I felt a particular sympathy for the anonymous interviewee with blonde shoulder-length hair and brown eyes. She became my model for Miss White. Once I decided this, her character started gaining dimension and coming to life.

In September 1994, my mother was widowed and stayed with us until Donna found a nearby apartment for her. Her neighborhood—which happened to be the St. Lawrence district of Cincinnati's Price Hill—became the model for Paul Vaguely's Amelia and the Oakley Apartments. My mother also has a cameo in the book as one of the bakery workers, as she did indeed work in a bakery that is now no more. With her apartment, the church across the street, and all those quaint neighborhood shops firm in my mind, the novel took another quantum leap forward.

It was just before (or just after) this that I had the preposterous idea of The Only Criminal acting as a pitchman for Consolations cigarettes, a product I'd playfully introduced in *Throat Sprockets*. Today, it's become almost a cliché to link one's creative work to multiverses, but it was less common in the 1990s. That said, I may well have drawn inspiration from Michael Moorcock, William Burroughs, J.G. Ballard, or another of my literary heroes when I decided to invite Lorraine Cadbury—the heroine of my aborted *TV Heaven*—to play an important supporting role in *The Only Criminal*.

During this period, I once found myself wondering what kind of a teenage street gang would exist in a world without crime. In response to this question, I came up with a roving pack of wild youth whose black leather jackets identified them as The Choreographers. They appeared after nightfall, brooding around Amelia in their black leather jackets and jeans, snapping their fingers and striking ridiculous Bob Fosse postures, but doing nothing more confrontational than insisting that passers-by be entertained by them.

I lived with this idea for years, and even toyed with an episode in which Paul Vaguely met and tagged along with them on a long night's journey toward the dawn. As I began writing this piece, I had no recollection of ever committing the Choreographers idea to paper but, in looking through a 13-page file of "deleted scenes" from *The Only Criminal* (dated 2006), I was tickled to discover this sole remnant of an alternative idea:

... a sound of snapping fingers—just two at first, then twice as many as the snapper used both hands, and then several more as his companions joined in. Vaguely spun about and saw a pack of slender shadows leaning in his direction.

For as long as there were teenagers, there were teenage gangs—sullen youngsters who found respite from parental misunderstanding and peer pressure by roving in numbers under the canopy of starlight. Some gangs took to the streets to express themselves through spontaneous outbursts of choreography; others acted as neighborhood patrols, unofficially assisting locally posted police officers.

As the approaching shades drew nearer to the grace note of a streetlamp, Vaguely recognized them as Cudby, Canby, Wilby and Isby—collectively known as the Consolations. Of all the local gangs known to Vaguely, the Consolations were the most literary. It was their particular mission to confront unsuspecting pedestrians with the shock of art, slipping postcard reproductions of great paintings into unsuspecting people's pockets, pummeling them with spontaneous outbursts of poetry, and occasionally commandeering neighborhood landmarks to stage public readings. They wore T-shirts and dungarees with poetry books and packets of Consolations cigarettes in their back pockets, and marauded in leather jackets bearing their names above their breast pockets and a shared club motto sewn on the back: "We Played at Love and Death But Our Hearts Were Pure."

Whereas some gangs attracted members who were handsome or athletic, The Consolations were composed of faces that, however pimply or uneven of tooth or knob-nosed, had the huzzah of great character.

"Dr. Vaguely!" exclaimed Cudby, the visionary of the gang.

"Yesh?" answered the good doctor, feigning sobriety.

"We didn't expect to see you," said Canby, the assertive one. "We were all down at the park, discussing Barthes' theory of reversible narrative, when we saw a shadow lurking about down here and decided to take action."

"A shadow?" Vaguely jerked with alarm. "Where?"

"Yours," offered Wilby, with something like reverence.

"We thought for a moment that it might belong to..." Isby began, falling short of completing his thought.

"No no," Vaguely dithered. "But how do you fellowth know my name?"

"How do we know Dr. Paul Vaguely?" Cudby laughed. "The Only Criminologist? Amelia's only literary figure?"

"You're our hero, Dr. Vaguely!" Canby beamed.

"I'll say!" Wilby piped in, returning front and center from a single orbit of Vaguely, during which time he had imperceptibly slipped a

reproduction postcard of Duchamp's 'The Only Criminal Descending a Staircase, No. 2' into his coat pocket, undetected. "You wouldn't know this, Doc, but many is the time we've seen you out walking at night and followed at a polite distance, just to see you safely home."

"Really!" Vaguely marveled, his intuition at last explained. "Whatever on earth for?"

"In the words of Voltaire, 'Where it is a duty to worship the sun, it is sure to be a crime to examine the laws of heat,'" replied Isby, solemnly. "That is, sir, knowing you as the scholar you are, we feared for your safety."

"How very shweet of you fellows," Vaguely managed.

"'Heroic' is the way we prefer to look at it," Isby insisted.

"He who should write heroic poems should make his whole life a heroic poem," agreed Cudby. "Thomas Carlyle."

"Though the pen is mightier than the sword," Isby hastened. "Edward Bulwer-Lytton."

"So is this what you fellowzh tend to do of an evening?" Vaguely inquired. "Stand around outside and, er, quote at each other?"

The five figures, as a group, resumed their movement, though slowly and prolongingly, in the direction of Vaguely's apartment building.

"The night is our bowman," Canby said, gesturing dramatically toward the sky, "and we are as arrows aimed at the heart of mystery. We live for random encounters with poetry, myth and literature. Whatever inspired the first stories, the first crimes, it happened out here—in the dark—and we're hot on its trail."

"We're looking for adventure," Wilby paraphrased, "and whatever comes our way."

"But not one of you looks old enough to raise a whisker," Vaguely observed. "Don't your parents worry about you?"

"Not so much anymore," Wilby noted. "There doesn't seem to be anything out here to worry about."

"I know," Vaguely agreed, suppressing a shudder. "That's what worries me."

Cudby spat on the end of a spent cigarette, pinched it, and deposited the butt safely in a curbside waste container. He said: "My old man gets so fed up with me trying to engage him in debate—about whether or not the novel is dead, or if the works of André Gide can themselves be considered Gidean—I think he's relieved when he sees me putting my jacket on," he added, popping a Chiclet. "He doesn't like me smoking, though. I am thinking of quitting. Just to please him."

"Fortunately, there's no law against it," Isby observed.

"Except in restaurants," Canby footnoted.

Cudby suddenly cartwheeled to a triumphant halt in the middle of the vacant street. "Questing without limit," he shouted with arms outstretched, like an actor center stage, "aimless though inspired... fueled by dream... guilty only of what Samuel Johnson called 'the atrocious crime of being a young man'!"

Looking at these stillborn pages now, I realize I should have called them The Quotations. Grand as they are, and I do love them, this wonderful bunch of boys simply didn't make the cut—or, rather, they took another form, ultimately assuming the ambling shape of Whimsy Plunkett, combination balladeer and town crier.

A surviving draft of the novel from 2007 features the subtitle "A Novel in the First Degree." It's 346 pages and 95,521 words long. As best I can tell, this was the first draft to include chapter titles, all taken from traditional gospel songs—in fact, gospel songs recorded by Elvis Presley, which to my mind made them doubly sacred. I remember the day I assigned appropriate titles to all the chapters and called Lori to boast of this feat. Not one of them was deliberated or forced; it was like each of Elvis' gospel numbers had a preordained place in the narrative.

For the longest share of its history, the novel had a different ending. Earlier versions ended with an Epilogue that I finally decided was too harsh. It was like welcoming real, earthly evil into a book that had vigilantly addressed itself to keeping it out. But these were its closing words:

Angel Paget curled up in a living room chair, alone, chain-smoking Consolations, as the fading of another day was given a last burst of definition by the 11:00 News.

She could remember a time when the world was much simpler, when all the evil in the world seemed to originate from the same long-cast shadow. But as Angel grew up, it seemed there were actually more criminal than law-abiding citizens in the world; it wasn't true, but night after night, the Media read her bedtime stories of other people like herself—people disappointed by the real world they had inherited after graduating from a shelter of dreams, people who mistakenly believed that they could turn the whole mess around, at least for themselves, by embracing a life of violent crime. The Media adored its serial killers and kidnappers and brainwashed fanatics and the arsonists and the suburban cannibals and the mothers who left their babies in dumpsters and every last drug-running, machine-gunning crackhead; they were the very trees that made their desks and chairs and their pencils and pads and the cabinets for people's television tubes. They never told the stories of people who were lucky enough to find a little piece of Heaven in the world to sustain them through its Hell; the only success stories they ever told were about the scum who succeeded in twisting the world's unjust nature to their advantage—like the man recently found innocent of murdering a bus driver in a garage in Amelia, whose televised trial resulted in his being signed to endorse a brand of men's gloves on billboards all over the country—including one which overlooked the decedent's former route in Amelia.

Angel had given up painting after giving birth. There was no place in this forsaken world for art, no place for primeval forests or fairytale castles, and Princesses were only good for how far and how deep they could be dragged through the mud. But no matter how much she drank to deaden the sound, there were times when Angel could almost hear the hooves of the black unicorn, galloping here and there, through all her painted canvasses that never happened.

Sometimes, when she felt its horned presence most acutely, her telephone would ring... but she never answered it. Not because it might be him, but because she couldn't bear further proof that the possibility no longer existed. The cuffs of reality bit into her wrists.

Fantasy was under arrest, and The Only Criminal had the right to remain silent.

* * *

On 6 October 2012, Lori Perkins resumed contact with me to ask if *The Only Criminal* was still available. She was about to launch Riverdale Avenue Books and was interested in publishing it. I was flattered that she even remembered it, that she was interested in making it a foundation block in her new business, but for many reasons, the timing was not right for me. I was up to my neck in Video Watchdog business and it had been years since I'd looked at it. Those early rejections still stung. I didn't feel capable of giving the book the attention it needed before it could become the book it had to be.

Odd as it may sound, what finally slapped this stubborn book into shape was—of all things—a online competition, announced in 2014, seeking new works of Catholic Fiction in the tradition of Graham Greene. The publisher behind the contest was offering both publication and an additional cash prize for the chosen Best Novel. Now, I am not a Catholic in the least, but having extensively read certain authors who were—like Greene, Evelyn Waugh, and Anthony Burgess, all of whom still managed to write dark, adventurous, even perverse novels—I have always seen a pronounced religious, arguably Catholic, dimension in *The Only Criminal*; it has many possible interpretations, by design, but one of them is that it may depict a man's struggle toward the understanding and acceptance of his own God. I'm one of those writers who works best under pressure and the contest's deadline inspired me to look at all I had written on this theme with greater understanding and a merciless scalpel. It was a long shot, I knew, but the contest was the excuse I needed to do the necessary work.

As I hardly need tell you, *The Only Criminal* did not place (nor even show) when the winners were announced in 2015. Even so, I had the satisfaction of making the manuscript as good as it was ever going to get and, at the same time, to make its submission a kind of harmless revolutionary act against those who sat in its judgment, whom I don't think knew as much about Graham Greene as they thought they did.

Anyway, after losing another round, *The Only Criminal* went back into its proverbial drawer until the day in March 2020 when—in the midst of working on something else—one thought bumped into another and I was suddenly reminded of Lori's abiding loyalty to it. That very day, roughly 10 years from the time of her previous inquiry, I offered it to Riverdale Avenue Books.

I have two versions dating from 2020, one dated 5 March and another dated 22 June, which are indicative of extra care being shown before I finally cut the umbilical cord. For various unavoidable reasons, it has taken some additional time to get here. In that time, I lost my *dédicace*, but in all other ways, the time went only to the book's good. It became even better as I went over the text with a fine-toothed comb one last time before we went to press.

And now, as with The Only Criminal and the entire world, we hold it in our hands.

Put End notes here

ABOUT THE AUTHOR

TIM LUCAS is the author of four well-received novels: *Throat Sprockets* (1994), *The Book of Renfield: A Gospel of Dracula* (2005, revised 2023), *The Secret Life of Love Songs* (2021) and *The Man with Kaleidoscope Eyes* (2022). *Throat Sprockets*, which is included in Jones & Newman's *Horror: Another 100 Best Books* and was selected by *Rue Morgue* as one of 50 essential alternative horror novels, is set to be published in an expanded 30th anniversary edition by Valancourt Books. The revised edition of *The Book of Renfield*, published by Riverdale Avenue Books, won the 2023 Rondo Hatton Classic Horror Award for Best Classic Monster Fiction.

Tim is now in the fifth decade of his career as a film critic, essayist and journalist specializing in horror/fantasy cinema, which began when his first publication appeared in *Cinefantastique* magazine at the age of 15. He and his wife Donna (who passed away in 2022) published the much honored and influential *Video Watchdog* magazine from 1990 to 2018. His writings on film have appeared in other publications around the world, including *Sight & Sound* (where his "NoZone" column ran for almost ten years), *Film Comment*, *American Cinematographer*, *Cahiers du Cinéma*, *Starfix*, *Metro*, *Little Shoppe of Horrors*, *Eyeball* and *Fear*, as well as his long-running blog *Video WatchBlog*.

He has also written two movie monographs, *Videodrome* (2008) and *Spirits of the Dead* (2018). A third monograph, focused on Franco's film *Succubus* (aka *Necronomicon*), is awaiting publication. He is also the author of *Mario Bava – All the Colors of the Dark* (2007), a monolithic critical biography on the life and works of the Italian filmmaker heralded as the "Maestro of the Macabre".

Well-known as a prolific audio commentator, Tim has produced more than 150 lecture tracks released on DVD, Blu-ray and 4K Blu-ray discs all over the world.

His work has been honored with two Saturn Awards (for *Mario Bava – All the Colors of the Dark* and his commentary for Kino Lorber's Blu-ray release of Alfred Hitchcock's *Lifeboat*), the Independent Publishers Bronze Medal Award and the International Horror Guild Award. He additionally holds a record 22 Rondo Hatton Classic Horror Film Awards, including their Legacy Award; in 2011, he and Donna were inducted into their Monster Kid Hall of Fame.

Tim is presently working on a number of new book projects, including an intensive study of the Adults Only films of Joe Sarno.

ALSO BY TIM LUCAS

FICTION

Throat Sprockets 1994
The Book of Renfield: A Gospel of Dracula 2005
The Secret Life of Love Songs 2021
The Man with Kaleidoscope Eyes 2022
The Book of Renfield: A Gospel of Dracula (revised edition) 2022
The Only Criminal 2024
Throat Sprockets (30th Anniversary Expanded Edition) 2025

NON-FICTION

Your Movie Guide to Movie Classics Video Tapes and Discs 1985
Your Movie Guide to Horror Video Tapes and Discs 1985
Your Movie Guide to Science Fiction & Fantasy Video Tapes and Discs 1985
Your Guide to Mystery & Suspense Video Tapes and Discs 1985
The Video Watchdog Book 1992
Mario Bava—All the Colors of the Dark 2007
Nozone: Reviews of Art, Cult and Genre Cinema 2024
Pause. Rewind. Obsess. One Man's One Year Escape Into Cinema 2024

MONOGRAPHS

Videodrome: Studies in the Horror Film 2008
Spirits of the Dead (Histoires Extraordinaires) 2018
Succubus (Necronomicon) 2024

If You Like This Title, You Might Also Like

The Book of Renfield: A Gospel of Dracula
By Tim Lucas

Untrustworthy
By JR Gershen-Seigel

Sixers
By John Patrick Kavanagh

ENDNOTES

---

[i] Jacques Champreux (1930-2020) was literally born to play this role, being the grandson of Louis Feuillade and the son of Marcel Champreux, who directed the now-difficult-to-see first remake of Judex, Judex 34 (1934).
[ii] Though *Nuits Rouges* credits its library track score to the director (who selected the various cues), this piece of music by Peppino De Luca and Carlos Pes was first heard as the end credits theme for Massimo Dallamano's *Dorian Gray* (1970).
[iii] Durgnat, Raymond. *Franju* (University of California Press, 1968), p. 123.
[iv] *Translucent Skin* (1976) was my third attempt at writing a novel, much liked by the people close to me. I've never published it because it's a novella at best, and also something of a prose poem, showing the influence of Raymond Radiguet and Anaïs Nin. To make it presentable, it would probably need a ruthless edit, if not a complete rewrite—and honestly, I love it too much to take a knife to what it is, to who I was. Sample sentence: "Her humanization was cause for celebration; she smiled to eat her cake."
[v] This original draft was dedicated to Georges Franju, still alive at the time.

www.ingramcontent.com/pod-product-compliance
Lightning Source LLC
Chambersburg PA
CBHW030641030726
47497CB00006B/1896
9781626016927